Suddenly
In Love

A **LAKE HAVEN** NOVEL

Suddenly In Love

JULIA LONDON

Montlake
Romance

Published by Montlake Romance, Seattle

www.apub.com

Amazon, the Amazon logo, and Montlake Romance are trademarks of Amazon.com, Inc., or its affiliates.

ISBN-13: 9781503953284
ISBN-10: 1503953289

Cover design by Eileen Carey

Printed in the United States of America

For Jameson, Jaylynn, Sage, and Savannah.
What I wouldn't give to muster as much enthusiasm for
anything as you have for Minecraft.

Prologue

March

The ghostly light of cell phones being held aloft looked like thousands of tiny beacons, beckoning him. *Come here, come closer.* Teasing him, daring him to walk off the stage and into the sea of them and disappear. He was tempted.

Everett Alden, the lead singer in the alternative rock band Tuesday's End, felt slightly stoned and completely numb as the last of the band's pyrotechnics ignited, showering the stage in shards of colored light. It was the big climax of their two-hour show, culminating with the performance of their biggest hit to date, "Dream Makers." He'd done this more times than he could count, had stared out into a darkened sea of moving cell phone lights and sung to the point of exhaustion.

The shrieks of the seventeen thousand fans were so deafening that he could hardly hear himself. There were girls down front—little girls, really, barely old enough to be out on their own—dressed provocatively and screaming up at him, their arms outstretched. They all wanted him to look at them, anoint them with sex, with money, with fame.

Tonight's performance was at Madison Square Garden, the last gig of one hundred and fifty cities on the best and biggest tour yet in the twenty years Tuesday's End had been together. They'd been met by crowds just like this around the world, little girls everywhere, their arms reaching, their hands grasping, their cell phones aimed at him.

Everett sang, but there was no heart in him tonight. He'd lost it along the road somewhere, left it battered and bruised and flattened in some hotel room. Not that any of the cell phones knew—he was a professional. He knew how to deliver a performance even when he was somewhere else. Even when he couldn't hear himself. Even when he was singing bubblegum confection with no heft in the music or lyrics. He could fake it with the best of them.

But he was done. He didn't want this anymore, even when he tried to want it for the sake of his band. He couldn't *feel* it anymore. He couldn't feel anything but bone-deep weariness. His life had become a nebulous, undefined question, the same question Trey had asked in the hours before he'd died. *Is this all there is?*

That's what Trey had wanted to know. In his last days on this earth, he'd wanted to know if this was all there was.

Everett didn't know the answer to that. He couldn't feel anything but the tear rolling down his cheek.

One

March

This was one big ship of hope—otherwise known as the 6 train—bobbing along on a sea of lollipop dreams. Otherwise known as the bowels of Manhattan. But even the stale air and the snores of the man next to her couldn't keep Mia Lassiter from believing that things were turning around for her, that the cosmos had at last opened and shined its glorious light on her.

It wasn't every day a perfect opportunity fell in her lap. Lately, it had been just the opposite. She'd recently lost her job (not the greatest, but at least something in her field), and her boyfriend (not the greatest, but at least she'd gotten some average sex out of it), and was on the verge of losing her apartment (yes, it was a pit—but a pit in a great location). So to have something so unexpected and so clearly meant for her fall into her lap filled Mia with optimism, and she was practically sailing uptown with the wind at her back and her portfolio tucked up under her arm.

When at last she emerged from the Big Hope Ship onto Lexington Avenue, she began striding purposefully across the street. *Move out of my way, people!*

Sure, she noticed some looks in her direction from well-heeled women with small children and dogs in designer carriers. Because Mia was wearing a dress she'd made from white muslin and had stained with Earl Grey tea, a vest she had knitted from thrift store sweatshirts, a pair of ankle boots, graphic tights, and a cloche hat she'd made from a piece of felt she'd found at a sidewalk sale. Her father accused her of living in an episode of *Project Runway*, and he most certainly would have advised her against this outfit for a job interview. He generally advised her against this sort of outfit, period.

But this was different. Mia's father didn't know August Brockway.

August Brockway was one of America's most important artists and he was hiring an intern. When one of Mia's former instructors from Pratt Institute had called her out of the blue to tell her about it, Mia had shrieked with excitement into the phone. She'd studied his legendary work. She loved the ethereal quality of his landscapes, the use of light and shadows in his still-life paintings. He was the artist she wanted to be.

It was a dream come true to have an opportunity to intern for him. It was the sort of opportunity Mia had assumed she'd get after she graduated from college.

She had *not* dreamed of being a textile designer, but that's what she'd been the last few years.

The perfect jobs she'd assumed would come her way after graduation hadn't materialized. She'd been unable to find a job in a gallery with her fresh, never-used fine arts degree. So she'd taken the textile design job, creating fabrics for furniture. At the very least, it was creative. And it was definitely a way to pay rent until she could establish herself as an artist.

Which was *now*! At last, at long last, she was getting the break she needed, the chance to follow her dreams.

She arrived at the address where her interview would be conducted. The building had a doorman. A *doorman*! It would be weird and exciting to come here to work every day. Mia would make friends with the doorman, she decided. She'd bring him a muffin from the corner bakery near her apartment. He would tell her what the weather was going to do that day and she would suggest a tie or shirt he could wear for a weekend party.

This was going to happen. Mia had a sixth sense about these things, and could feel it tingling in her bones. She was confident that August Brockway would see her work, would see that it was obviously inspired by his, and he would be bowled over by it. He would give her the job, and she would clean his paintbrushes and change out his drop cloths and listen to every word he said as he taught her everything he knew. It was fate.

She checked her vintage watch; she was ten minutes early. She took the opportunity to put down the heavy portfolio and straighten the dress she'd made. She loved this dress. Obviously, designing textiles wasn't her first career choice, but Mia had turned out to be pretty darn good at it, if she did say so herself. She was so good, in fact, that when her boss had invited her out to lunch a few weeks ago, Mia had been sure she was finally getting the raise he'd been promising her for over a year.

Don was an overweight, lumbering man with oily black hair and wire-rimmed glasses that never sat straight on his face. He took her to lunch at a fast-food chain. That should have been her first clue, but ever hopeful, like a too-stupid-to-live princess in a fairy tale, Mia hadn't caught on. And then, between big bites of burger, punctuated by the shoveling of fries, Don said, "We're closing shop."

"What?" Mia had cried, loud enough that the ladies next to them had turned to look at her. "I thought I was getting a raise!"

"A raise!" Don had chuckled as he stuffed another fry into his mouth. "We're barely paying the rent." He dragged a paper napkin across his thick lips. "So look, we lost that contract in North Carolina. Something about the percentage of natural fibers in our fabrics wasn't meeting their standard—well, whatever, that's way over your head," he said with a wave of his meaty fist, ignoring her look of indignation. "It was a big contract, obviously, so corporate is going to have to consolidate some things and this shop is sitting in the most expensive real estate, so . . ." He'd shrugged and munched on another fry. "We're shutting down."

"But . . . but what happens to everyone?"

"Well, *I'm* moving to Scranton. And the rest of you will have to find new jobs."

He'd said it so matter-of-factly, as if it were nothing for the little group of misfits who designed couch fabrics to find new jobs. Mia thought of Charles with his brown bag lunches and e-reader. And Maureen, the obese diabetic who baked cookies every weekend and brought them to the shop on Mondays. Maureen designed the most intricate, beautiful patterns. And what about David and Jean and Asmara? Where would they go? The injustice had left Mia speechless.

"Look on the bright side," Don had said, pausing to stifle a belch. "You're getting two weeks' severance."

"You're kidding. Considering my paltry hourly wage, that's not a bright side, *Don.*"

He'd shrugged. "Take it or leave it."

Yeah, well, Mia had had no choice but to take it. And then she'd spent every day searching for a job that was even remotely artistic. She'd applied to teach a weaving class, to be a gallery receptionist, a graphic designer, and even a bookbinder . . . but no one wanted her. No one cared about her art portfolio. Employers cared only about her experience answering phones or designing websites.

Well, Mia didn't have that sort of experience. She didn't have any experience other than art school and textile design. No, wait, that wasn't fair—she was pretty good at busing tables. Her brother Derek had pointed that out. "You can wait tables for Mom and Dad at the bistro. You know how to do that."

As Mia had spent all her teenage years doing exactly that, it was absolutely the last thing she wanted to do.

It had all looked very hopeless until the day the cosmic powers of life had delivered this interview to her. What was that saying, that a person had to be completely torn down to be built up again? Mia liked the idea that her life had been deconstructed, and that after today, she would get the chance to construct it in a way she'd wanted for a very long time.

"Okay!" she said to herself. "Here goes nothing." She clutched her hat and jogged confidently across the street.

She was directed to the tenth floor, Apartment B. The elevator opened up to a long hallway. Overhead, two small gold chandeliers illuminated the path to the door of the apartment. Mia's boots were absolutely silent on the thick hallway carpet as she walked down to the end and knocked lightly with the little brass door knocker.

The door swung open and bright sunlight spilled out into the hall, blinding her for a moment. A young man with doe eyes and plump lips, tight pants, and a lock of gold hair over his brow stood before her. He smiled. "Mia Lassiter?"

"Yes." She juggled her portfolio and clumsily extended her hand. Lord she had to outweigh this Ken doll by thirty pounds.

"I'm Vincent," he said, taking her hand in his. His grip was as limp as linguini, his skin as smooth as a baby seal. "Please come in."

Mia stepped across the threshold and was instantly assailed by the smell of oil paints. *Heaven.* She followed him inside, taking notes. The floors were hand-scraped wood, the walls painted a pristine white. The crown molding was painted a slightly grayer shade of white, just enough to give it a slight contrast and draw the eye upward.

"Oh wow," Mia murmured. The apartment looked like pictures she'd seen in the pages of glossy architectural magazines. "This is *amazing.*"

"Original floors and moldings," Vincent said. "Reworked, of course."

"Of course," she echoed dreamily. There was a fireplace at one end, the mantle distressed raw wood. The windows facing the street were at least ten feet tall and marked with cornices carved to resemble leafy vines. But the most spectacular thing about that room was the paintings and drawings in various stages of completion. They were hanging on the walls, stacked on the floor, and graced two opposing easels. It was truly a treasure trove of August Brockway artwork, and her heart began to flutter with joy.

Between the two easels was a stool, and Mia pictured August sitting there and swiveling between his works in progress as his mood dictated. Drop cloths, spotted with paints, covered a big swath of floor. Next to the stool was a small table with bowls and pitchers crowded onto it. Near the windows, a bistro table, on top of which was a plate with a half-eaten sandwich and some chips.

Mia slowly turned around, taking it all in. She could picture herself in this studio, assisting a master. This was exactly what she wanted: a real art studio. A peaceful, beautiful place with nothing but a blank canvas and her creativity.

The click of heels against the wood drew her attention to an arched door that led into a kitchen. Mr. Brockway emerged, wiping his hands on a towel, which he handed to Vincent. He was a slight man, barely taller than Vincent, with neatly combed silver-gray hair. Mia, with her average height and curves, felt very roly-poly in comparison to the two of them.

Mr. Brockway was wearing jeans that had been splashed with drops of paint, loafers without socks, and a salmon collared shirt with cuffs rolled to the elbows.

"Mr. Brockway," Mia said, trying to keep the nerves from her voice. "It's *such* a great honor to meet you." She thrust her hand forward.

"Yes, I'm sure," he said absently, and took her fingers and gave them a little shake before letting go. His gaze skipped over Mia's body and settled on the portfolio she held. "Is that your work?"

"Yes." She'd brought six of her best pieces, carefully selected with an eye toward color and spatial relevance, qualities she'd learned were important to Mr. Brockway.

Vincent took the portfolio from her and laid it on the floor. He unzipped it as Mr. Brockway knelt down on one knee to have a look.

Mia was uncertain what she was to do, but she felt awkward standing above him. She managed to negotiate her way down onto her knees in a manner that didn't require props and rested her fists against her thighs as he examined her work.

Mr. Brockway held up the first painting, an abstract, and squinted at it.

"I call that *Breathe*," Mia said nervously. "It's supposed to symbolize the first breath. Like a new experience."

He said nothing, but shifted the painting to catch more of the natural light coming in from the windows, and then the other way, where the painting was in the shadows. He wordlessly put it aside and picked up the next.

"That one is—"

"It shouldn't be necessary to explain your work," he said without looking at her. "The art should speak for itself."

Yes, yes, art should speak for itself!

Even so, Mia was desperate to tell him what had inspired her, and she had to bite her lip to keep from blurting out what she was thinking. Her knees ached as he studied the paintings and her nerves were a jangly mess. She wanted his approval so badly she felt slightly nauseated by it.

When Mr. Brockway had finished reviewing her work, he put the paintings back in the portfolio and gestured at Vincent to zip it back up. He stood up. So did Mia, coming to her feet about as gracefully as a toddler. "No, thank you," he said. "Vincent, you can show Miss Lassiter out."

Stunned, Mia looked at Vincent, then at Mr. Brockway. That was it? No questions about her goals or experience? No critique, no comment whatsoever? As Vincent tried to usher Mia out, she ducked around him. "Mr. Brockway!" she called, before the artist could disappear through the arch and into the kitchen.

He paused and looked back at her with one brow lifted imperiously above the other. "Yes?"

"Why not me?" She hadn't meant to ask it precisely that way, but yes—why not her?

He shrugged. "You don't have the talent."

She gasped softly. An old wound, deep but tender, began to open. It wasn't the first time she'd heard it. More than one instructor had advised her to consider a career in something other than canvas work because she didn't have the talent necessary to make it. But Mia had worked so damn hard for it, and she knew she'd improved.

"You should come with me," Vincent said, his fingers lightly on her arm.

"What do you mean?" Mia asked August Brockway as she brushed Vincent off.

Mr. Brockway turned full around and planted his hands on his waist, considering her. "Would you *really* like to know what I think of your portfolio, Miss Lassiter?"

No! No, no don't ask! "Of course I would," Mia said. *Oh God, this was going to hurt.* "You're a renowned artist," she continued with far more confidence than she was suddenly feeling. "I'm just starting out. I would work really hard for you, Mr. Brockway, and I *know* I would learn so much. So yes, I would like to know what you think."

"I've no doubt that you would work hard, Miss Lassiter. You seem very . . . earnest," he said, his gaze flicking dismissively over her dress. "But I disagree that you would learn much. Your work lacks vision and depth. *Breath?*" he said, gesturing to her portfolio. "That's the name of your piece? It's such a fundamentally bad concept that I can't even begin to critique it."

"But I can learn. I—"

"Your work looks as if you took all your instruction to heart. But you don't have raw talent or a unique vision that I can see in your work, and I can't teach that. Either you have it, or you don't. If *you* don't know what your vision is, Miss Lassiter, your work will always appear to the world as it did to me—sophomoric."

Well there was a dagger right through the center of her heart, plunged so deeply that it was a miracle Mia didn't sprawl right there onto his drop cloths in a pool of tears and snot and blood.

"But I will say this—your use of color is very good," he said. And with that, he turned and walked out of the room.

♦ ♦ ♦

Mia had no idea how she got out of there. Had Vincent thrown her out, or had she crawled out? She remembered being on the train, staring at the ad across from her of a handsome man with shaving cream all over his face. She remembered slowly realizing that Mr. Brockway was right. His delivery sucked, but he was *right*. He'd hit the nail on the head, had zeroed in on the thing that had nagged at Mia for a very long time, but she hadn't been able to name. Her work had no clear vision, no real point of view. It was what her professors called "needs improvement" and "let's work on what message you're trying to convey." She tried one idea after the next, never finding that common thread in her body of work. Her subjects were run of the mill.

He was right—she didn't have what it took to be a working, viable artist. It was so unfair! Her love of art was what ran through her veins. She couldn't keep the desire out of her. She couldn't *not* create.

Mia was so shaken that she didn't notice her landlady until she almost collided with her. Mrs. Chalupnik was standing in the entry hall with one thick arm across her body, holding her threadbare bathrobe closed.

"Oh, hi, Mrs. Chalupnik." She put her head down and tried to scoot past. She was on the verge of a meltdown and didn't have time to chat.

"The check, it's no good," Mrs. Chalupnik said, waving a paper at Mia with her free hand.

Mia's step slowed. "What?"

"Your rent check is no good!" Mrs. Chalupnik said, only louder. "It comes back with *insufficient funds!*"

Mia felt a horrible twist of impending doom. "That's impossible!" she cried, and took the paper, staring at it. How was that possible?

"Now you owe me two hundred dollars on top of rent," Mrs. Chalupnik said. "You have until Friday."

"But I can't get it by Friday," Mia said. Her head was reeling. "There has to be some mistake. I'm very careful about this—it's impossible I bounced a rent check."

"My eyes do not lie," Mrs. Chalupnik said, jabbing a finger dangerously near her eye for emphasis. She snatched the paper from Mia's hands. "Your bank, it doesn't tell you this?"

Her bank. The truth was that Mia hadn't collected her mail in several days. And she had turned off notices on her phone to keep the battery from draining.

"You find the money," Mrs. Chalupnik said. She turned around and opened the door to her apartment. The smell of sauerkraut wafted out and hit Mia squarely in the face before Mrs. Chalupnik slammed the door shut.

Mia whirled around, hurried to her mailbox, and opened it. Several things fell out, and among them, two notices from her bank. She fell back against the wall and slid down to her haunches in her stupid tea-stained dress and with a rash where her portfolio had rubbed against her leg as she'd trudged home.

So this, apparently, was how a life was completely deconstructed.

Two

May

On a scale of one to ten, ten being everything-is-awesome, and one being someone-stole-my-puppy, coming home to East Beach in the early spring was a solid three. And only that high because Mia loved her family.

She did *not* love East Beach, especially this time of year, when life around the lake was dead. It was too early for the summer people to come up from the city and occupy their stunning vacation homes that dotted the hills around Lake Haven. Winter would, without warning, drag its claws through the season once more, striating cold and gray misery across the emerging vivid greens and blues and colors of spring.

It was too nippy for the full-time residents of the village, or the year-rounders as they called themselves, to take advantage of the empty beach, save those rare, sundrenched days. Mostly, they spent the early spring cleaning their gardens, hosing down their lawn furniture, and waiting for the summer people to arrive.

This spring, there was a lot of gossip circulating around the lake along with the baby strollers. Everyone was talking about the inaugural Lake Haven Music Festival, to be held over Memorial Day weekend. That was new and different. The festival had been designed to kick off the summer rush and promote better tourism economy around the lake. Competition with the Hamptons and the Berkshires had ratcheted up in recent years, and the Lake Haven Chamber of Commerce was determined to take back their fair share of tourist dollars.

There was also quite a lot of sniggering about Mia's uncle, Larry Painter, who'd shown up at the Chamber of Commerce brunch with ditzy Britney Johnson on his arm. The same ditzy Britney Johnson who had graduated high school with Larry's daughter, Emily. Mia knew her cousin was a bit bothered by her father's choice of dates because she'd complained, "If he's going to rob the cradle, couldn't he at least have robbed a smart one?"

Aunt Amy, who was the sister of Mia's mother and also the ex-wife of Larry, laughed when she heard the news. "I hope he's kept up his Viagra prescription."

In the local coffee shop, tongues wagged. *Who did Britney think she was? Who did Larry think he was?* Mia knew this, because she waited in line for lattes every morning. Not just one latte, mind you, but three. Lattes were part of her new career duties working at Uncle John and Aunt Beverly's home interiors shop as head gopher.

Obviously, Mia should have taken the sage advice of her high school guidance counselor, Mr. Braeburn, and developed some of those desperately needed backup skills. Alas, she had not taken his advice, and, in truth, had been a world-class champ for not taking advice in high school. As a result, Mia had no plan B. She had nothing but the same dream she'd had most of her life—and a growing anger with her idol, August Brockway.

So here she was, back in East Beach with two choices: suit up and perform hostess duties at her parents' bistro, or work on this massive renovation project of the historic Ross house Aunt Bev was trying to land.

The former meant Mia's well-meaning mother would be in her business 24/7 instead of the current 18/7, which she was able to achieve because Mia had also ended up in her childhood bedroom. In her old twin bed. Beneath some of her early attempts at painting and the dried-up corsage she'd pinned to the wall after the sophomore dance.

The latter meant she was more or less out of the town's eye, because the Ross house was up on a hill at the edge of town overlooking the lake. Someone had bought the historic landmark and wanted to redo it completely, from attic to basement. "I'm going to need someone up there every day to keep an eye on the workers and to accept deliveries," Aunt Bev had said, confident that she'd get the gig.

That didn't sound very appealing to the artist in Mia, but it was work, and honestly, the fewer people around town who saw her, the fewer who would suspect her return to East Beach was not a triumphant one and, really, an Olympic-caliber dive into failure.

Worse was that Mia was beginning to believe she'd never be anything but a failure. The interview with August Brockway had done a crippling number on her head and had filled her with self-doubt that was continuing to morph into something much larger and more sinister.

Anyway, Mia had taken the job with Aunt Bev, and so far, she'd spent two days at the Ross house measuring rooms and taking pictures so they could firm up the bid.

This morning, Mia was waiting for Aunt Bev to pick her up, because in addition to coming home without her mojo, Mia had also come home without a car. She was standing just outside Lakeshore Coffee with her tray of lattes when the John Beverly Home Interiors and Landscape Design shop van came rumbling down the road. Mia stepped off the curb to dart across the street. Thank God she glanced over her shoulder, because out of nowhere, a black roadster came screaming around the corner. With a shriek, Mia jumped back up on the curb. "*Hey!*" she shouted as the car pulled up outside the coffee shop. Mia stood a moment to catch her breath, to make sure she was all there and hadn't spilled the lattes.

The door of the black car swung open, and one long leg in tight jeans and Dingo boots appeared, followed by another one. A man jackknifed himself out of the car, pulled his ballcap low over his eyes, hidden behind dark shades, and started striding for the coffee shop.

"*Hey!*" Mia shouted again. "Hey *you!*"

The man paused. He slowly turned toward the sound of her voice . . . so slowly that Mia had the idea he was high. He was tall, and his hair, tucked behind his ears, almost reached his shoulders. Mia started toward him, and he swayed backwards with a groan before bellowing, *"What?"* as he threw his arms wide.

Whoa. As if *she'd* done something wrong. "You almost hit me!" Mia said, her breath still short from fright. She pointed at his car with the tray of lattes.

He looked at his car. Then at her. "But I didn't hit you."

"You *almost* hit me!"

"Fine, I *almost* hit you. Anything else almost happen?"

"Are you kidding? You should be more careful!"

"Baby, I should be a lot of things. But maybe you should stay out of the street." With that, he turned around and strolled into the coffee shop.

Mia was still gaping after him in disbelief when the blare of a horn startled her badly.

It was Aunt Bev, who had pulled up across the street. "Get in, get in!" Aunt Bev shouted out the window, as if she were pregnant and about to give birth.

"Oh my God, is that *necessary?*" With her free hand pressed against her heart, Mia crossed the street and got into the van. She hadn't even shut the door before Aunt Bev was taking off.

Mia squealed when the door got away from her and swung out wide, then braced herself against the dash and caught it as it swung back in, pulling it firmly shut. "Aunt Bev, you're going to hurt someone! Did you see that black car almost run me down? Slow down, we have plenty of time."

But Aunt Bev's blue eyes were gleaming. "*Do* we? I don't think so, Mia—my goodness, *what* are you wearing?"

Mia looked down. She was wearing the skirt she'd made from fabric she'd designed, her paisley tights and combat boots, and a cropped T-shirt beneath a denim jacket. "I thought this was pretty sedate," Mia said. "I mean, compared to the rest of my closet."

"Were you drunk when you put it on and thought it was sedate?" snorted Aunt Bev. "Never mind. We have a crisis. Do you know who is up at the Ross house right now? Diva Interiors from Black Springs."

"Who is Diva Interiors from Black Springs?" Mia asked, bracing herself against the dashboard as Aunt Bev took a sharp right.

"Tess McDaniel, my chief competition, that's who. But let me tell you—this is a *million dollar job*," Aunt Bev said, stabbing the air with two chubby manicured fingers that supported several sparkly rings. "I'm not going to let it go without a fight. She's been encroaching on my territory for a year now. We have to finish our bid and get it in before she does. The owner, Nancy Yates, has to see how I could turn that house from the ugly pile of shit that it is to something really spectacular." Aunt Bev punctuated that by braking so hard that Mia almost went flying through the windshield.

"What the *hell*?" Mia cried.

Just as quickly, Aunt Bev accelerated onto Juneberry Road.

For the three miles up to the Ross house, Aunt Bev laid out what Mia should do today. "Finish measuring the rooms. Snap some pictures—you know, fixtures, outlets, windows. I need to see each room as if I'm there to finish this up. I have an appointment on the other end of the lake or I'd come with you, but maybe it's better that I don't, because I would really like to punch Tess in the *kisser*," she said, and made a swinging motion with her fist.

"Yep. Maybe it's better if you don't," Mia agreed.

They reached a narrow gate in a stone fence. There was a small plaque on the fence around the property that read simply, *Ross House*. Aunt Bev slowed considerably as she pulled into the property. "For Chrissakes," she said as they rounded a curve and saw the drive was filled with trucks. "Okay, get to work, Mia. Wallace will be here to pick you up at three."

Mia picked up her bag with her sketchbook and camera and opened the door. "See you later." She'd hardly stepped out of the van before Aunt Bev was off again.

She waved away the dust the van left in its wake as it disappeared around the corner, then remembered her latte, still in the van. "Damn it," she muttered under her breath. She adjusted her bag onto her shoulder and paused a moment to take in the gloriously warm and bright morning. The sun cast a golden light on the house, making it look much more cheerful than it had under the leaden skies of the last two days. Even the windows on the second floor had been cranked open to allow in the fresh air.

"Hi, Mia."

She looked around and smiled at Drago Kemper. He was the security here, and wore a uniformed shirt that seemed a size too small for him. His arms were massive, his chest even broader. Drago spent a lot of time at the gym.

Mia knew Drago from way back. They were the same age, had been in the same class through middle school and high school. They were a lot alike back then, both of them on the fringe of the popular circles. Mia, because she was different than the other girls and preferred to make her clothes and color her hair and paint strange, angsty portraits. Drago, because of his learning disabilities.

"Hey, Drago, how are you?"

"Good," he said, nodding. "Hey, did you check out the spin class I told you about?"

"Ah . . . no," she said, nodding. "But I'm going to. Probably today." She gave a swing of her arm in a go-get-'em manner. "What's going on around here today?" she asked, glancing back at the trucks.

"She's redoing the terrace. Anyways, you can't go in."

"Huh? Why not?"

"Because Mrs. Yates isn't here. She had to go somewhere and she locked it. I don't think she wanted those guys getting in."

"Great." Mia glanced at her watch. "I've only got a couple of hours. You can let me in, can't you?"

"Nope," he said with a shake of his shaved head. "Not supposed to let anyone in. Sorry."

Mia suspected that order didn't extend to her, but she didn't want to agitate Drago. "Do you know when she'll be back?"

"No. Sorry," he said again.

Mia remembered the latest issue of *Us Weekly* was in her bag. "I guess I'll hang out," she said with a shrug. "I don't have a ride until later anyway. I'll just go down to the lake. Is that okay?"

Drago hesitated, squinting at her. "I guess so," he said uncertainly. "But they're working back there."

"I'll stay out of their way," Mia assured him. "I'll be back in a bit to see if Mrs. Yates has come home." She gave Drago a wave of her fingers and walked down the side of the house, past blooming hydrangeas and bougainvillea to the manicured lawn and the path that led down to a low bluff above Lake Haven.

For three centuries, Ross house had sat majestically above East Beach, where one was treated to a stunning view of the lake that was impossible to buy now. When Mia and her brothers were young, they would crawl up the hill, through the thicket from her grandparents' property below, to a promontory with a bench that looked out over the lake. They called it Lookout Point. They would jump into the lake from there, climb up, and do it again. It would be a great place to read a magazine, catch a few rays, and pass the time until Nancy came home.

Mia quickly discovered the grounds near the bluff had been overtaken by the thicket in the years since she was a girl. It took her several minutes to make out the vague outline of the old footpath. But it was there, and now she was determined to see the bluff. She strapped her bag across her body and pushed back the overgrowth.

Halfway in, she questioned her judgment. Weedy limbs with thorns grabbed at her skirt and tights. Vines grew so thick that she caught her foot once, and in one particularly bad patch, the thicket had completely reclaimed the path. But she emerged victoriously on the other side of the promontory with a few scratches and some sticky plant things stuck to her tights. As she cleaned herself up, she noticed that a new, wider, and more direct path to the house and down the bluff to the lake below had been cut through the thicket. "Well that would have been nice to know," she muttered.

As she pulled something sticky from her hair, she walked to the edge of the bluff and looked down at the lake. It was chilly today; only one sailboat was gliding across. A flash of color caught her eye, and she leaned to her left to peer down. There, in the boat slip parking lot, was the black car that had almost run her over in town. *Ass clown.*

Mia walked back up the bluff to the old bench. It was still standing, but it was badly weathered and missing a slat in the middle. She dropped her bag next to the bench and sat down on it nonetheless, stretching her legs in front of her and tilting her face up to the sun.

Okay, as far as menial jobs went, this wasn't half bad, really. Where else would she be paid to sit around and wait in such a beautiful—

What was *that*?

Mia sat up with a jerk, cocking her head to one side, straining to hear. She could have sworn she heard someone talking. But when she looked around, she saw no one. It must have been voices from the house carried on the wind. Except the wind was blowing in the wrong direction for that. Maybe it was someone on the lake. She settled back in and closed her eyes—

There it was again.

This time, Mia stood up and turned around, just in time to see the jerk from the coffee shop come stalking up the path, a coffee in one hand, a cell phone in the other. He'd ditched the sunglasses and hat he'd worn earlier and looked completely disheveled. He was speaking into the phone, his speech low and rapid, as if he were arguing.

She eyed him as he marched toward the edge of the cliff. He clearly hadn't noticed her, which came as no surprise. He struck Mia as entirely self-absorbed. She ought to know—she tended to date that type. Who *was* this guy, anyway? He seemed annoyed, judging by the way he stood gripping the coffee and squinting into the distance, his jaw clenched as he listened. He said something. And then, quite suddenly, he let out a roar and hurled the coffee. It sort of plopped over the edge of the bluff. And then, just as abruptly, he roared again and threw his phone toward the lake. It flew out of his hand, arced high, then plummeted into the water.

Mia gasped and surged forward a few feet with an unthinking instinct to save the phone. She stopped at the edge of the bluff and gaped at the glittering surface of the water below her. Who did something like that? She slowly turned her head and looked at the man.

He'd definitely noticed her now. He was staring hard at her, his expression almost accusatory. He was muscular, his hair wavy and unkempt. He had a scruffy beard she hadn't noticed earlier, and he wore an expensive pair of jeans worn to a grimy sheen, and a battered, inside-out T-shirt with a long drip of a stain that looked like mustard.

"You . . . you just threw your phone into the lake!" she shouted, pointing at the lake.

"Really? I just threw my phone in the lake?"

"Yes!"

"I know!" he bellowed.

Mia suddenly had the thought that perhaps she should be less concerned about the phone and more concerned about her safety. Especially when the man began to saunter toward her, reminding her of a beast who was now overly curious about a puny bit of prey. Being that puny bit of prey, Mia shifted backward so that she could make a run for it if necessary. Unfortunately, her escape options were not good. One was to jump in the lake and swim to her grandmother's house, which she could totally do. But not without a healthy dose of hesitation, she feared, because the water was still very cold. Not to mention, she hadn't jumped in fifteen years. She'd been a lot more fearless as a teen.

The other option was to dive into the thicket and run. She winced imagining the nicks and scratches that was going to earn her, but it was the lesser of two evils.

The third option was to blow back at this guy and hope that he was easily intimidated. He didn't look easily intimidated. He looked like he was always the one to do the intimidating.

He suddenly shifted his gaze to the lake as if just remembering that he'd chucked his phone into it. Then he turned to her. His gaze meandered down her body and back up to her eyes. "Is there anyone else with you?"

What? "Yes," she said instantly. Why was he asking? What was he going to do? Jesus, what was someone like him capable of? Come on, this wasn't Brooklyn, this was East Beach! Most of the people in these parts were fairly decent. *Most.*

"Who?"

"You don't know him."

He sighed. "I know I don't know him. I don't know *you*. Where is he?"

He was a little snippy, demanding answers. "At the Ross house." She lifted her chin. "And it's not just one guy. It's like . . . four."

He blinked. And then he snorted. "Four guys."

"Yep."

"All waiting for you?"

"Not waiting, exactly."

"Not waiting at all," he said. "Do you have a phone on you?"

"A *phone*?" If he thought she was going to produce a phone that he could hurl into the lake, he was wrong.

"Yeah, a phone. You call people on it? Text them? Download apps?"

Snippy, sarcastic, and a big fat crazy-driving jerk. But he did have a pair of stunningly dark blue eyes. How ironic that twin windows into crazytown would be so striking. One would think they'd be all googly and bloodshot.

"I need to make a phone call." He stuck out his hand, palm up. When Mia didn't instantly produce a phone, he impatiently gestured for it.

"You are unbelievable," she said. "Do you really think I'm going to hand over a phone after you just threw one in the lake?"

He sighed. "Yeah, I probably shouldn't have done that," he said, and inexplicably sounded almost thoughtful as he ran a hand over his head. He studied her a moment. "What are you doing here?"

He was asking *her*? "I happen to work at the Ross house," she said stiffly.

"More good news," he said, and moved to the bench, sitting heavily, splaying his legs wide as men on benches were wont to do. Her bag was beside the bench with her phone tucked just inside.

"I'm going to go back to work," she said. "I would suggest you go back down to the public area before the owners find out you're here."

He didn't say anything. He didn't even look at her. His gaze was locked on the water and now he seemed lost in thought.

Your honor, the jury has reached a verdict: batshit crazy as charged.

Well, Mia wasn't stupid. She was going to get out of here before he ramped up again. She moved cautiously toward her bag, intending to grab it and disappear before crazy noticed. But the moment she squatted down, her arm outstretched, his gaze jerked around to her again. He sighed and rolled his navy-blue eyes. "Jesus, are you still here? I thought you'd run off with your phone clutched to your breast."

Mia gasped. "The better question is, why are *you* still here? Who are you, anyway?"

He snorted and shook his head. "Don't play dumb. I hate that."

Crazier and crazier. Mia snatched up her bag and backed away from him. "I'm not kidding. If you don't want any trouble, you better get out of here. She has security."

That seemed to interest him. "*Who* has security?"

"Mrs. Yates. She owns Ross house now, and she has security, pal," she said, pointing at him for emphasis.

For whatever reason, the man laughed. He tipped his head back and laughed. "Yeah, she's got such great security that *you* managed to get all the way up here without being seen." He flicked his wrist at her. "Go back to your *job*."

"Oh, I'm leaving," she said. "I'm going back up there and alerting her security that a strange man is wandering around down here hurling phones into the lake."

"You do that." He wiggled his fingers as if he were dismissing her.

He was unbelievably infuriating. "I am going to do that right now," she said, and whirled about, meaning to march up the path. But her canvas bag caught a nail on the bench and snagged. She tugged. Her bag did not come free.

"Just yank it free," he said irritably.

"I don't want to tear it!"

"For God's sake," he said, and stood up, crowding in beside her, his arm brushing against her side as he leaned over and worked the bag off the nail. "There. Now go on and leave me alone."

Mia tucked her bag under her arm and backed away from him. "I mean it, I'm going to report you, so if you don't want to be arrested for trespassing, you better go back to the hot dog stand you came from."

"Great," he said, nodding. "Thanks for the advice."

She strode toward the path, her bag bouncing against her leg.

"Hey!" he shouted at her.

Mia reluctantly turned around.

"Let me use your phone before you go."

"No!" she shouted, and marched on.

Crazy-ass summer people.

Three

Drago was making his rounds when Mia made her way back to the house, breathless with rage and practically sprinting. She pointed toward the bluff. "There is an insane person down there, a bum who doesn't belong on this property," she said. "He came up from the beach."

"Oh yeah?" Drago said and squinted toward the lake. "I'll take care of him. You scratched yourself."

"What?" Mia glanced down to where he pointed. There was a thin red scratch across her bare abdomen. "Oh."

"Mrs. Yates is home now. But she's leaving again, so hurry if you want in. That terrace guy's truck broke down. I'm going to take him into town to get a part."

"Yeah, well, don't go before you run the bum off. He threw his cell phone into the lake!"

"That's littering," Drago said gravely.

Mia hesitated. "Yep. It's littering all right."

"I'll handle it," Drago said, and began walking toward the bluffs. He was so big Mia had no doubt that the man at Lookout Point would scramble down the path to the lake and his death-star car and get the hell out of here. What was it about summer people that made them think they owned the world around them?

Mia moved on to the house, but just as she reached the front door, it suddenly swung open, and two white balls of fluff that could easily be mistaken for house shoes rushed out, yapping and trying to bite her feet. Behind them came Nancy Yates wearing turquoise-blue silk palazzo pants with big, showy white flowers printed on them. Her voluminous white silk top hung to her thighs and was trimmed in fringe. She wore her graying blonde hair in a ponytail down her back, and a gold chain from which a Tao symbol dangled around her neck.

Behind Nancy were two women, but Mia scarcely had a moment to register them because Nancy suddenly grabbed her in a big bear hug. "Hello!" she said cheerfully.

The gesture startled Mia—they were not on a hugging basis, seeing as how they scarcely knew each other—and she stood stiff armed, uncertain if she ought to hug her back or not. "Ah . . . hello," Mia said into her shoulder.

Nancy suddenly let her go and stutter-stepped backward to have a look at Mia.

Mia self-consciously adjusted her bag on her shoulder.

"Now *that's* an interesting look," Nancy said, not unkindly. "I can always count on you to be creatively attired. Oh! *Where* are my manners?" she asked, apparently unconcerned that the dogs were still growling at Mia and she was pushing the one with the blue bow off her leg. "Do you know Tess McDaniel?" she asked, and waved grandly at the two women behind her.

One of them, who Mia had to assume was Tess McDaniel, smiled thinly as her gaze flicked dismissively over Mia's clothes. "Hi," Mia said.

"Tess owns Diva Interiors in Black Springs," Nancy said, and to the two women, she added, "Mia is Beverly McCauley's niece. She's an artist."

"Oh no," Mia said quickly. Heat flooded her cheeks—she could only claim to be a failed artist. "No, I'm . . . I mean, not really. I'm working for Aunt Bev right now."

"Well," Tess said, presenting her hand in a manner one could possibly interpret to mean she wanted it kissed. "How nice to meet you."

Mia took her tiny hand and, uncertain what to do with the delicate thing, gave it a bit of a shake.

"We're off, sweetie! We're going to have tea at a delicious little place in Black Springs," Nancy said. She leaned over, picked up each dog, one by one, kissed its nose, tossed it inside, and did the same to the other dog. "Magda's already left for the day, so be sure and lock up when you go. There's just so much to fix up around this old place, isn't there?" She didn't wait for Mia's answer, but hurried off with Tess and the other woman, who apparently didn't merit an introduction.

Mia watched them go. Nancy Yates was the antithesis of the person Mia would have expected to buy this house. This house was steeped in American history. Nancy Yates looked as if she were steeped in Malibu.

The thing about the Ross house was that it was the oldest and grandest historic estate around Lake Haven. Every day Mia came to work, she noticed another interesting architectural detail, like the forward-facing peacocks carved into the gables above. The central part of the house was fairly plain and flat, but the wings that stretched out from either side had balustrades on the roofs, verandas along the front, and each ended in big round rooms, sort of like castle turrets.

Lake Haven hadn't become a fashionable summer getaway for the East Coast elite until somewhere around the fifties, about the time Grandma and Grandpa had opened the East Beach Lake Cottages. The houses built on the lake since then had big windows and rooms set at angles designed to capture the best views. But Ross house had its own unique charm. Once you entered through the stone gate, you knew you were entering an area of wealth and refined taste. You'd expect to find the woman of the house in Ralph Lauren, perhaps on her way to a golf game. You would not expect to find Nancy Yates.

Not until you walked inside.

Mia opened the front door a small crack. As she expected, the two little fluffy white dogs with coordinated fashion collars burst into frantic yapping, apparently having forgotten meeting her only moments ago. "Okay, all right," she said, sticking her boot through the door first. "Come on, guys, you *know* me now," she said, and inched her way in, nudging the little beasts away.

When she'd squeezed herself inside, the dogs backed up, still yapping, but then suddenly, as if they'd assured themselves she was who she said she was, they turned and trotted like a pair of soldiers off to the big farmer's kitchen and their bed.

"Little beasts," she murmured. She glanced around her. It always took her a moment to adjust to the interior—inside is where the early American style turned completely and utterly deranged.

Quite honestly, the interior of this grand house looked as if a merry band of clowns with disparate tastes had come through and partied. Mia had never seen a more curious mix of styles and colors, and she'd gone to art school.

The house had the soaring ceilings and elaborate crown moldings one would expect, as well as tall windows with views of the woods and the lake. The floors were marble and, in many rooms, the original wood. One would assume a house of this stature had been properly put together, that some historical buff or East Coast designer would have made it a showpiece.

Nothing could be further from the truth.

The conflict of styles and colors exploded in your brain after one walk through. In the dining room, bright blue wallpaper with enormous black palm leaves in velvet relief clashed with a small faux-oak table and massive crystal chandelier overhead. In the living area, oriental accents stood beside art deco and antique finishings. Vintage wallpapers competed with clear plastic shelving and modern mirrors. Rooms that hadn't been papered had jarring color palettes.

"This house needs a lot of work, but the bones are good," Nancy Yates had said the first day they'd met. "I learned that on HGTV—you have to have good bones. Then you renovate. But if you don't have good bones, renovations will get very expensive."

"This renovation is going to be expensive no matter how good the bones," Aunt Bev had whispered into Mia's ear as Nancy had shown them around.

"It was built by an industrialist, you know," Nancy airily continued like a museum docent, gesturing to the ceiling in the dining room, the wainscoting, the window casings.

"Malcolm Ross," Aunt Bev had said. She took pride in her knowledge of local history. She'd pulled her standard Chico's-issue jacket around her generous frame. "He built it for his wife, who wanted their ten kids to have plenty of places to run and play. The village of East Beach grew up around this house, did you know that? There are Rosses everywhere now—Ross Hardware, Ross Elementary, Ross Insurance, Ross Medical Group—"

"Well, anyway," Nancy had said, interrupting Aunt Bev, "this place needs a *complete* overhaul. Just look at this kitchen!" she'd complained as they'd moved into that room. "It's so *old*. I had a state-of-the-art kitchen in the house where I lived before this. It practically cooked for you."

Another weird thing about the house was that it was sparsely furnished. Mia's boots echoed on the marble tiles as she walked through a foyer devoid of any furnishing or accessory except a single mirror in a gilded frame that looked permanently attached to the wall. Not even a rug to warm up the cold floor.

The kitchen had the most furnishings of any rooms, but not the sort one would expect. The kitchen table and cane-back chairs looked as if Nancy had purchased them off Craigslist. The surface of the table was strewn with papers and envelopes, and a laptop stood open, a coffee mug next to it.

Mia put her bag down on one of the chairs and looked around at the dated kitchen with the faint smell of fish lingering in the wallpaper and the drapes. For two days now, she'd been rattling around this enormous and strangely decorated house like a nurse on night watch, poking her head in this room and that. It was hard to imagine that only two months ago, she'd had visions of being New York's celebrated new artist.

Boy, when some dreams died, it was like letting the dogs go in for the kill.

She was still shaky from her encounter with the crazy ass, and decided she'd have a cup of coffee and calm down a little before working. She walked to the Keurig coffeemaker and powered it up as Nancy had invited her to do on her first day.

She wanted cream with her coffee. She glanced around, bending backward to see down the hallway to the front door. No one here but her, so Mia opened the fridge.

Whoa.

The fridge was stuffed completely full. There wasn't even a tiny bit of space left. Leaves of raw vegetables stuck out between dishes. Fruit was piled up in a drawer. Beer, wine, milk, and coconut water were crammed into the door caddies. In the event of a major catastrophe, Nancy could feed half of East Beach.

It was a wonder Mia was able to spot the cream at all, given the competition for her focus. She made her coffee, added the cream, then returned it to the fridge. Wedging it back in the door took a bit of effort, and in the course of doing so, Mia spotted a plate of cookies.

It would be wrong to take a cookie from Nancy's fridge.

Good thing Mia had never claimed to be perfect, and hooray, there were so many cookies that Nancy would never notice one missing—she didn't strike Mia as the cookie counting type. She held the fridge open with her elbow, and worked the corner of the plastic wrap up off the plate, slipped a cookie off of the pile, held it between her teeth while she returned the plastic wrap to its full upright and locked position, and shut the door.

And then promptly dropped her cookie with a shriek of fright.

The man from the bluff was standing on the other side of the door in his bare feet. His hands were on his waist and he was glaring at her. "What the *fuck*?"

Her heart began to race painfully, making it difficult to catch her breath. Mia liked to think she was fairly street smart. That if she was ever confronted by a criminal, a terrorist, or a guy like this, she'd think quickly and act smartly. She did neither of those things.

If she'd thought a moment before she reacted, she might have questioned just how dangerous a barefoot man with a glassy look could truly be. But in that moment, Mia knew only that she was alone in Nancy Yates's house, and *she* hadn't let him in.

She whirled around and grabbed the first thing she could lay her hands on—a frying pan. She swung it out in his general direction but didn't come remotely close to him, but somehow managed to hit one of the pendant lights hanging over the kitchen island.

"*Hey!*" the man said. He lunged forward, grabbed the frying pan from her in one easy yank, and set it down on the counter. "Be careful with that thing before you break something."

"Okay, who *are* you?" Mia demanded hotly.

"I think the better question is, who are *you*?" he asked irritably as he stepped around her to the coffee brewer. He pulled open the drawer beneath it where Nancy kept the coffee pods. "What'd you do, climb the fence? Is that how you got in? Because I don't believe you walked up from the parking lot—I would have seen you."

Fence? *What* fence? She'd told Drago a crazy man was down on the bluffs—how could Drago miss him? She was going to kill him when she saw him, assuming this guy didn't kill her first. After he made his coffee, which, inexplicably, he was now doing.

The dogs. Why weren't they helping her?

She whirled around to the pillows before the hearth. The bedazzled little yappers attacked her feet every time she walked through the door, even if only a few minutes had passed, and yet they hadn't moved one inch since this guy had come in. Only one had even bothered to lift its head. What the hell was *happening*?

The man pushed hair from his face, held up the coffee pod, and said, "Totally bad for the environment," then shoved it into the portal. He turned the brewer on and looked at Mia.

In the kitchen, under the lights, Mia noticed the dark circles under his eyes. His feet were dirty, his jeans unwashed—he looked even more like a bum in the soft light of the kitchen. But there was something about his eyes that seemed wrong with this look. They were so *arresting*.

Something was off, something was wrong. Mia suddenly had that weird, parallel universe feeling, much like the time she arrived at Karen Elliot's Oscar-viewing party with her seven-layer dip that was actually only three layers, and had walked in like she always did to find two strange men sitting on a strange couch playing video games. Several stunned, heart-pounding moments later, Mia remembered that Karen had moved the previous month.

But *this* wasn't the result of her being overstressed and preoccupied, which was definitely the biggest contributing factor in the Karen incident. *This* time, Mia was in the right house, and she had to act. "I don't know what is going on here, but I'm calling the police," she said firmly, and stepped over the pieces of cookie, as if a home invasion would be made worse if she ground cookie into the tile.

"Be my guest," he said easily. "And when they get here, you can explain what you're doing in my mother's house. Just out of curiosity, I'm going to try this again. *What* are you doing here? Other than trying to brain someone with a frying pan?"

It took a moment for those words to sink completely into Mia's brain. This guy with the glassy gorgeous blue eyes was Nancy Yates's *son*?

Nancy had a son? Nancy, in her palazzo pants and the gray-streaked hair in a ponytail had a son who looked like a bum?

No, that couldn't be. First, Nancy would have mentioned him. *By the way, my son is visiting. By the way, he's a street bum.*

The bum waited for an answer as his coffee brewed. He seemed not the least bit self-conscious about his appearance. Mia was self-conscious for him. So much so, in fact, she couldn't look away.

He noticed her looking at him and his expression changed from mildly annoyed to definitely pissed. "Ah, I get it," he said sharply, and shifted toward her. Mia instinctively leaned back, ready to employ rusty karate moves learned at the age of eight. "Yeah, go ahead," he said, gesturing to himself. "You want to touch this? *Do* it."

There was a coldness in his navy-blue eyes, a strange look of resignation that was so weird, and so out of place. "The last thing I want to do is *touch* you."

He looked skeptical, the pompous prick. Maybe, Mia thought wildly, he didn't know how bad he looked. He moved again, and Mia bumped up against the kitchen island. But Nancy's son was already there, and he planted his hands against the island on either side of her, his body dwarfing hers. He stared down at her with those incongruently gorgeous eyes and said, "What do you want, baby? If you want to play, go ahead. I'm game."

"You cannot be *serious*," she said, her voice full of amazement. Maybe he was handsome beneath this outer layer of hobo, and maybe he didn't always smell like a sock forgotten in the bottom of a gym bag, but he had to be kidding. She leaned away from him. As far back as she could. "This may come as a shock to your seriously fat ego, but you are absolutely the *last* person I'd want to *play* with." She put her hand up between them to stop him from leaning any closer.

He smirked a little, and his gaze settled on her mouth. "You sure about that?"

Mia snorted. "I've never been more sure of anything in my life. Now would you please step back?" she asked, gesturing for him to move. He didn't move immediately, and Mia couldn't help wrinkling her nose and turning her head. Her gaze fell to his arm; he had the dark stain of a tattoo that went around his pronounced bicep. It looked like Sanskrit.

Nancy's son chuckled low at her obvious disgust, and Mia could feel it reverberate in her. But he pushed away from her and turned back to his coffee. "How'd you get in here, anyway?"

"*How?* The door!" she said, wondering now if he was slow.

"Just walked right through it, huh?"

"No, I cartwheeled through it, I was so happy to be here."

He glanced up, looking almost as if he believed it. *Oh, for the love of Pete.* "Look," Mia said, "there's obviously been some misunderstanding here."

"Fantastic," he said, and opened up a sugar bowl and turned it practically upside down into his coffee, adding enough to trigger an instant diabetic coma. "Go ahead, clue me in."

"I'm *supposed* to be here. I'm working for your mom." She grabbed up a brochure from John Beverly Home Interiors and Landscape Design on the kitchen counter and held it up to him.

Something changed in his expression. He closed his eyes. "*Shit,*" he said. "The *decorator.*"

He might as well have said *the grim reaper.* A bit of heat rose up in Mia's cheeks. He made no move to take the brochure she was holding out, so she laid it back on the counter. "I'm not the designer. My Aunt Bev is."

His gaze flicked over her again, assessing her, lingering a little on her tights and boots. "Okay."

"O-*kay,*" she shot back. *Okay, okay*—what did *okay* mean?

"So what are you if you're not the designer?"

"Her . . . her helper," Mia said with a shrug.

"Ah, so *you're* the decorator's helper. Well then," he said, and swept his arm toward the rest of the house. "Knock yourself out." He picked up his coffee and slurped loudly.

"Are you high?" she demanded.

"Nope. But I've had a couple of drinks." He paused and squinted at the window a moment. "More than a couple if we're going to add them up."

Well that certainly explained it. It was hardly past noon. *Summer people.*

He put the coffee down, and opened the fridge. "Are the cookies any good?"

Mia's face flushed with embarrassment. She abruptly moved around the kitchen island and reached for her messenger bag, preparing to make a quick exit, maybe even walk down the road with the hope of meeting Wallace when he came to pick her up. Go anywhere but here with this weird guy with the blue eyes.

He was still studying the contents of the fridge. Now that she knew who he was, she was revising her assessment of him. She could see that he actually looked unsettlingly hip in a very dirty way. His clothes were expensive. But he looked like he'd stepped off the plane from the West Coast and then gotten roughed up in a dark alley. Maybe that was where he'd had his few drinks. She wondered what kind of girl he went for. Stripper?

"What happened, Chatty Cathy, cat got your tongue now?" he asked, and looked over his shoulder at her. "I asked about the cookies."

Mia snapped out of her rumination. "I don't know."

"Then you should have one," he said, sounding magnanimous. The smartass practically tossed the plate of cookies onto the kitchen island. He then tossed sandwich rolls, cold cuts, cheese, and mustard onto the island, too. "So what's your name, Aunt Bev's helper?"

"Mia." She folded her arms. "What's yours?"

He arched a brow and gave her the slightest hint of a wry smile. "Like you don't know."

The *ego* on this guy! "How would I know? Your mother didn't tell me you were here. I didn't even know she *had* a son. Believe me, if I'd known you were here, I would have . . ."

"What would you have done, Aunt Bev's helper?" he asked, sounding bored.

"I would have waited outside."

He grunted his opinion of that. "Brennan."

"Sorry?"

"My name. It's Brennan."

That was a summer person name if Mia had ever heard one. Whatever happened to Tom and Harry?

He turned back to the fridge and opened it, holding it open with his foot as he put the sandwich rolls inside. "Now that formal introductions have been made, are you going to just hang around? Maybe you want me to make you a sandwich." He picked up the package of cold cuts and opened it.

"No thanks—"

"Yeah, that wasn't really an offer." He let the fridge door close. "I don't know what arrangement you have with my mom, but I'm guessing it's not standing around watching me make sandwiches or swinging pans at people's heads."

Mia had never wanted to take a swing at someone as badly as she did right now. She swiped up her bag. "I'm just going to do what I need to do here and get out," she said tightly.

"That is a *great* idea," he said.

Unbelievable. Mia rolled her eyes and marched out of the kitchen before she said something that would lose Aunt Bev the job.

Four

Brennan was in a foul mood, especially once he realized who the woman was with the honey eyes and the auburn hair and the smell of spring around her. Because he didn't need a woman banging around the house. He needed—*really* needed—peace and quiet. Solitude. *Silence.* He didn't need any more colors than those that were already splashed haphazardly around the interior of this goddamn house. He especially didn't need colors wrapped around the very delectable curves of a woman's body. He needed time to think and ponder. He did *not* need smiles or bright eyes, goddammit.

This was exactly why he'd sworn off women . . . Well. That resolution was beginning to wear a little thin. He wanted sex. He *needed* sex. But he didn't need or want women. Needing or wanting anyone was a waste of time, and women especially were too complicated, too needy. And sometimes, too fucking vindictive if things didn't go their way.

Brennan had also sworn off booze, but he'd had to reconsider that out of necessity because of his resolution to swear off women. He had to do something to dull the lust.

Yeah, well, obviously he was going to have to redouble his resolve.

Brennan had no idea how many beers he'd had by the time his mother returned home, but when she finally pulled into the drive, he was drunk enough to be irritated with the world in general and her in particular.

She seemed very pleased with herself when she swept in and care-lessly dropped several shopping bags on the kitchen table. "Do my eyes deceive me?" she asked jubilantly. "My son is *alive!*" She threw her arms around Brennan, rising up on her toes to kiss his cheek before she dropped her arms and swanned past him.

"You went into the city?" Brennan asked, looking at the bags.

"Yes, I did!" She walked to the wine cooler and bent over to have a look at the bottles inside. "Such a beautiful day for it, too. How was *your* day, sweetie?"

"Not as good as yours, apparently." Brennan moved her shopping bags around, all of them emblazoned with logos likes Barneys and Bergdorf Goodman. His mother could spend money, and she espe-cially liked to spend it when she was trying to get his attention. Brennan wouldn't be surprised if there was ten thousand dollars' worth of mer-chandise in those bags.

"At least you're out of bed," she said. "And while the sun is still up! We're making progress!"

Jesus, he hadn't lived with his mother in seventeen years and had forgotten how annoying she could be. "Mom," he said wearily. "I work late. I sleep late. You *know* that. So I'd appreciate it if you didn't send Magda up at the crack of dawn with her industrial vacuum cleaner."

His mother laughed as if he were trying to be funny. He was not.

"Magda does like to get an early start on some days," she said breez-ily as she selected a bottle of wine. "Now, don't look at me like that, Brennan. Am I supposed to tell her to come back at three o'clock in the afternoon when you've managed to drag yourself out of bed?"

He didn't sleep until three, but he wasn't going to argue with her. He was an experienced hand on that front—it led to nowhere.

She opened a drawer and rummaged around for a corkscrew.

The beers weren't doing Brennan any favors on the patience front, and he halfheartedly attempted to tamp down his irritation. But was it really asking too much to let him decompress here, in his mother's new home, away from the world? In the house that he'd bought for her? This had been a rough year for him, a rough awakening, and he didn't need his mother's judgments or her timetables for when he should pick himself up and dive back into the world.

He sat on one of the kitchen table chairs, his weight causing it to sway a little. "So what's with the girl?" he asked curtly.

"What girl?" His mother gave him a feigned smile of innocence as she put the corkscrew to the wine bottle.

"Mom."

"*Ooh,*" she said, as if a light had just dawned. "You mean the one from John Beverly Home Interiors."

"Yeah, that one. I thought she was a damn groupie. I thought she'd climbed the fence."

"A *groupie!*" She laughed roundly. "Brennan, for heaven's sake. Not every girl you meet is a *groupie.*"

Easy for her to say. His mother had not had the pleasure of finding an inebriated woman sitting on the toilet like he had at his home in LA. Or women hanging around the door of his hotel room. Or women appearing like magic on his tour bus offering to do things to his body.

"She's really different than the rest of the East Beach crowd, I think. Not so resort-y, like the rest of them," his mother said. "She has a strange sense of fashion, but I *like* that, don't you? It's refreshing. You wouldn't believe how many girls are wandering around New York in those desperately short shorts and cropped tops. Like that's a look. But Mia? She's unique and she's *adorable.*"

Brennan didn't know if he would ever use the word *adorable* to describe anything. But he could agree, at a distance, that the woman was appealing in a very unconventional way. He couldn't quite put his finger on how, exactly. She wasn't beautiful. She wasn't a sex kitten or a ball-busting model. And while Brennan knew absolutely nothing about women's fashion, she had been dressed in a very strange combination of prints and colors. He honestly didn't know what she was, besides argumentative. That was all beside the point, anyway. "Why was she even here? She had the run of the house while you were gone. She could have taken something or broken into your computer."

"She would never!" His mother laughed, as if the notion of a stranger stealing was absurd. "I know people, and she's not like that. She was here because we are going to renovate this musty old house, remember?"

There was the liberal use of the pronoun *we* again.

"Oh, I remember," he said drily. Brennan had paid three million for this house, and had agreed to pay another million for the renovation. And that was on top of his mother's impulsive shopping sprees. Sometimes he wondered if his mother understood how hard it was to come by the sums of money he routinely paid out on her behalf. Brennan was generous with his mother, and he didn't begrudge her a cent of it. She'd provided for him when there was no support from an absent father, managing to keep a roof over their head and food on the table while working two jobs, then adding a third job to pay for his guitar and music theory lessons when he'd developed an interest as a boy. So yeah, he was happy to do his part for her now. He just wished she had a healthier respect for the money she blew through.

"And besides, *you* were here, sweetie. You would have kept her from making off with the awful fixtures in this house, right?"

Don't engage. "I'm not the best babysitter of workers. And didn't we agree you wouldn't start that project until the end of summer? You agreed to give me time and space for a few weeks, Mom."

"Well," she said, her voice lilting. "*You* agreed. I didn't. Not really."

"What are you talking about? You said—"

"I can't live in a house that looks like this. I mean, my God, there's a Buddha in the sunroom that has *plaid wallpaper!* Who *does* that? The interior of this house is a train wreck, and I can't live like this."

Brennan groaned. He ran his hands over his face and scrubbed his forehead with his fingers. His skin felt gritty to him. "I get it, Mom, the house needs to be redone. I'm all for it—but I need a break. I need a *break*," he said again, and abruptly slammed his fist down on the kitchen table, startling his mother and himself. "From you, from work, from music, from renovations, from strange women in the kitchen when all I want is a cup of coffee! So just . . . just lay off of it for now, will you? Will you do that for me?"

His mother looked slightly wounded. "Here's the thing, Bren," she said, speaking coolly, formally. "You've *had* your break. You've been here a month and all you've done is buy yourself a new car and sleep and drink. Am I supposed to tiptoe around you forever? Am I supposed to pretend your manager isn't calling every other day? What made you lose your way? Is it Jenna?"

"Jenna?" Brennan struggled to keep from exploding. He wanted to put his fist through a wall, rip the fridge out of its cubby and hurl it across the room. His anger—undefined, always simmering-below-the-surface anger—was mixing toxically with the beer. "I'm not asking you to pretend or to tiptoe or to psychoanalyze me, I'm asking you not to renovate right *now*."

"It's not going to bother you," she insisted.

She was trying to manipulate him, but she was no match for the many people in his life who had sought to manipulate him. Managers, producers, bandmates. "Do you want me to leave? Is that what you want? Because I will."

"Don't be so touchy," she said. "Why would I want you to leave? You're my son, I love you, I love having you near me, and God knows that I haven't seen much of you in years. And you obviously need your mother now more than ever. I don't like how you sleep all day and go on benders," she said, gesturing at the empty beer bottles on the kitchen bar. "I don't like how you ignore phone calls that must be important, and I don't like the way you are hiding from the world. That's not you, Brennan. You're the strongest, most determined, smartest, most gifted person I have ever known. But look at you!"

"I *am* hiding!" he shouted. "I am hiding from managers and bands and paparazzi and everything else. Jesus, I'm thirty-three years old—do I really need to explain myself to you?"

"*Hey!*" she said hotly. "Watch how you speak to me. I am your mother and I am worried about you. I earned that right when I gave birth to you."

Brennan sighed. It was like talking to a rock. "Yeah, well the only thing wrong with me today is that I'm starving."

His mother pressed her lips together and walked stiffly to the table. "I was going to wait for a better time to do this, but . . ." She reached in her purse and withdrew a brochure and handed it to him. Brennan glanced at it. Valley Vista Recovery and Rehabilitation Center. He didn't understand it at first, didn't get the hint. But when he did, he sagged back in his chair, away from it. "What the hell is that?"

"Exactly what you think it is."

He stared at her. "Are you kidding, Mom? You think after what happened to Trey that I could possibly be into drugs?"

"No, of course not!" she said, sounding slightly wounded. "I know you better than that. But you're drinking too much."

"So *what*?" Brennan exploded, this time unable to keep his anger in check. He shoved against the table and out of the chair and moved away from her. "I'm a grown man! I can drink a river if I want!"

His mother did the wrong thing—she gave him a patient, motherly smile. "Brennan . . . don't you see? You're drinking too much because you're depressed."

"Don't even try," he snapped. "I'm not *depressed*. I'm tired. I'm *exhausted*," he said, sweeping his arm wide. "Do you have any idea what my life has been like?" His life had hit a wall head-on, and he couldn't seem to peel himself off of it. No one could peel him off of it.

The world knew him as Everett Alden, the lead singer and cofounder of Tuesday's End, the chart-topping band of the last decade. Brennan Everett Alden had been Brennan's name for the first twelve years of his life. But then his mother had married Noel Yates and Noel had adopted him, and Brennan had become Brennan Yates. Brennan Yates was a nobody in the music industry, but Everett Alden was about as red-hot as rock stars came. And right now, at this point in his life, for a few weeks, Brennan desperately needed to be nobody but Brennan Yates.

So what if he was a little depressed? He'd just finished a 150-city tour on the heels of a new album that had gone platinum. He'd ended a yearlong relationship with Jenna O'Neil, one of the hottest young actresses filling movie theaters, because she couldn't keep her pants up in the company of her costar—a fact that was displayed on every magazine on every newsstand, lest Brennan forget. He'd dealt with a batshit crazy forty-year-old woman who kept breaking into his house in LA and stealing his boxers. He'd had a major artistic disagreement with Chance, the guitarist of the band, and Brennan's best friend since they were two fourteen-year-old outcasts in a California middle school. They'd formed Tuesday's End in Chance's garage. And oh yeah, the big one, the topping on his cake: their other best friend, Trey—who had been there in the beginning, too, who had been their drummer until his heroin addiction got so bad they couldn't rely on him—had overdosed and died a few months ago.

Or committed suicide. Depended on who you listened to.

Brennan had tried to reach him, had tried to pull him out of his own ass, but Trey was so messed up. He'd flown out to Palm Springs to see Trey the day before he was found dead. Trey had just come out of his third stint in rehab and he swore he was clean. He'd looked gaunt and a little yellow. He'd said, "Look at all we've got, Bren," and had cast his arms around his big house.

"We've done pretty well for ourselves," Brennan had agreed.

"No, that's not what I'm saying. I'm saying *look* at what we've got. We're at the top of the world. So . . ." He'd leaned forward, peering at Brennan. "Is this all there is?"

"Buddy, I don't—"

Trey had grabbed his wrist and gripped it tightly. "No, man, I need to know. Is *this* all there *is*?"

The next day, Trey was dead.

I don't know, Trey. I don't know. Maybe it is. Maybe this exhaustion I feel is all that there is at the end of the day.

So yeah, Brennan was tapped out, and okay, he was a little depressed. He'd had enormous success, beyond his wildest dreams. But somehow the grueling road tours, the selfish beauties, the constant stream of women wanting to suck his dick, the artistic differences with someone whose opinion he highly valued, and the loss of a good friend to drugs were not exactly how he'd imagined his career unfolding.

Brennan didn't know who he was anymore. He didn't know where he was supposed to be going with all of this. He couldn't even say with any confidence what sort of music he wanted to make at this stage of his life. He needed some peace and quiet away from it all to *think*.

He needed to be here, in this little town on a peaceful lake, in his mother's house, because no one here knew Brennan Yates.

But his mother seemed determined to get deep into his business. "Think about how much you sleep," she said, apparently thinking his silence was an invitation to keep talking. "Think how much you've been drinking lately, how you have no enthusiasm for *anything*. Not music, not girls. You aren't working—when is the last time you picked up a guitar?" she stubbornly continued. "I get it, I do," she said, pressing a hand to her heart. "I was *very* depressed when you were born."

Brennan snorted. "Gee, thanks."

"And there have been other times, if you want to know the truth. But *you*, Brennan! You've never been depressed. You've always been my rock. You've had such a brilliant career and a life I could never have imagined for you and I am scared to death you're going to let it all slip away because you're depressed. Your father was like that, but he—"

"Don't bring him up," Brennan said curtly.

His mother sighed heavily. "Will we *ever* be allowed to talk about him?"

God, how could she gloss over it? He felt a painful prick every time she mentioned his dad, like an old wound that appeared to be healed over, but was easily opened with the wrong move. "I don't know, Mom. Seems like the time to talk about him was before he died."

She colored. She sniffed. "All I want to do is help," she said.

"Don't help me, Mom," Brennan said. "I came here because I thought, for once, I could have a little refuge from all the bullshit. I thought this would be the one goddamn place on earth I could be *me*. Not Everett. *Brennan*. But you've been dogging me since the day I showed up."

"That's not true. I know you must be hurting. I know you loved Jenna—"

"You have no idea what you're talking about!" he said angrily. "Mother, listen to me. I was not in love with Jenna. I may have loved her at some point, *maybe*, but I doubt it, and if I did, it was a very long time ago. I haven't felt anything but resentment for months. I knew what she was doing. I knew she was using me for publicity and sleeping with her costars. And you know what, Mom? I could have ended it last fall, but it was a hell of a lot easier just to finish the fucking tour and then dump her. I'm glad to be rid of her."

Her eyes widened with surprise. She chewed on the inside of her mouth a moment as she considered him. "Then what about your music?" she asked, her voice softer. "What about the gift God has given you and no one else? The world is waiting. Your *band* is waiting."

Brennan suddenly felt bone-weary. As if he'd been carrying a boulder on his back for a very long time. "The world and the band can go to hell," he said low. He swiped up his beer and took a long swig.

The truth was that Brennan didn't know about his music. Chance and he weren't seeing eye to eye on the artistic direction. Chance and the band's manager, Gary, were angling for more commercial music. They'd included some on the last album, against Brennan's wishes, and the album had gone platinum. Give the masses what they want, Chance said. But Brennan couldn't feel it—it wasn't in him. He truly felt heart-blocked from that sort of music. He felt truly heart-blocked in general. That style of music felt like a sellout, a moral corruption of his soul. His music—it was all he had when he got right down to it. It was the only thing in his life he could depend on, the only thing he could completely trust. Without it . . . was this all there was?

His mother reached for his hand and covered it with hers. "I know you'll figure it out, honey. But maybe you need some help."

She didn't understand the stakes for him. Brennan needed help, all right. But it wasn't the help of a doctor and antidepressants. It was more spiritual than that. He needed help finding his path. He pulled his hand free of hers and turned away. "I'm good, Mom. I'm just asking you— nicely, now—to postpone the renovations a couple of months," he said tightly. "I don't need people in my space right now."

He could see the tension in his mother's jaw as she poured a healthy serving of white wine. She was biting her tongue. "Sure, honey. If that's what you want."

"That's what I want."

She shrugged and drank from the glass. "Okay then. No renovations inside the house for a couple of months."

"Thank you." Brennan moved to the fridge and withdrew three beers. He grabbed a bag of chips from the counter and walked out. He ignored the muttering he heard under his mother's breath, and made his way upstairs to his room.

Maybe he needed to get out of here, go someplace overseas, away from his mother and the tabloids. That wasn't a bad idea, he thought as he took the stairs two at a time. Someplace remote where he could molt in peace. A tropical place, maybe. With a girl. Any girl. He could use some good, wall-banging sex about now.

Brennan walked into his slightly reeking wreck of a room and paused, looking around.

He had taken the second master suite with a stunning view of the back lawn and Lake Haven on one end, and the front drive on the other. Too bad the walls were painted lime green and the bath was done in pink tile. He threw the bag of chips on a bed that had gone unmade for two weeks now, put down his beers next to an army of empty bottles on the dresser and the nearby windowsill. He walked past his guitar and paused, looking down at it.

His mother was right. He couldn't remember when he'd last picked up an instrument of any kind. Madison Square Garden?

Brennan picked up his guitar now and took a seat on the edge of the bed, balanced it on his thigh, and struck a minor chord.

Since a time he could no longer recall, he'd had the ability to hear a chord and instantly hear a melody in his head. He could easily imagine the bare bones of a song, the chorus, the bridge. But in the last two months, he'd imagined . . . nothing.

Everett Alden, the lead singer of Tuesday's End, heard nothing.

Brennan put his guitar aside and fell onto the bed beside the bag of chips. He closed his eyes, saw himself on stage, heard the melody of one of their greatest hits, "Dream Maker," as an acoustic number in his head. He'd written every bit of that song—the melody, the lyrics. Chance had tweaked the rhythm of it, but mostly, it was Brennan's creation. It had stayed at the top of the charts for more than a year. He was the architect of that massive hit, and now, he couldn't even dredge up a few chords.

Yeah, he was going to get the fuck out of here.

He was going to find his laptop in this mess and Google the Canary Islands. He turned his head on the pillow and looked across the room. He didn't know where the laptop was, actually.

He'd do it tomorrow.

Brennan sat up and looked down at his disgusting bed. It just seemed like everything required so much *effort*. He drank more beer, brooded more. He wrote a few things in a notebook, tried to read.

He didn't know when sleep drifted over him, but it was the sound of a buzz saw that startled him awake. He sat up with a jolt; weak sunlight was drifting in through the windows. His room smelled like dirty socks and beer, and he blinked, looking at the clock next to the bed. It was seven in the morning. He shoved his hair out of his eyes and stumbled to the windows. Below him, a ground crew was fanning out around the thicket his mother was determined to cut back.

And there was Mom, pointing to things to be cut and edged and generally made loud.

Just to annoy him.

Five

Aunt Bev had called at o-dark-thirty this morning, and it had scared Mia to death. She'd assumed something had happened to Grandpa, but it turned out that it was nothing more alarming than some of the pictures Mia had taken at the old Ross house had gone missing in Aunt Bev's cluttered office.

"I know what happened," Aunt Bev said. "That goofy kid at Cranston's screwed it up. He's one pair of boxers short of a full load of laundry."

"I don't think that's a saying—"

"So here's what you do, kiddo," Aunt Bev said, pushing on. "Go ahead and stop by Cranston's and ask that goofy kid to check again."

"Okay, but Cranston's doesn't open until nine—"

"Just do it as quick as you can. I need to get this bid up to the Ross house as soon as possible. Oh, and pick up some Reese's Peanut Butter Cups while you're there."

Quite honestly, before this gig, Mia had never truly appreciated what a head case Aunt Bev was. Sure, Bev's daughter, Skylar, had always complained about her, but Skylar was one of those troubled teens who ran away and smoked dope and generally could not be trusted to be accurate about anything. Once, Skylar had breezed in unannounced to Mia's place in Brooklyn. Mia hadn't even known Skylar was in the city; the last she'd heard, her cousin had taken off in the night with some guy she'd met in Black Springs and had ended up on the West Coast. That was Skylar, always taking off for something bigger and better, preferably something that didn't require her to work. Inevitably, she had to come home when the bottom fell out of whatever scheme she was involved in and try again.

She'd shown up in Brooklyn with an overnight bag and a joint that she'd smoked at the open window. "My mom is bananas," she'd said. "She's disorganized and thinks everyone else is to blame. And I'm an easy target for her."

"Really?" Mia had asked, shaking her head to Skylar's offer of the marijuana. Mia never went near drugs after what happened to her that summer. It was one of those family stories that everyone tacitly agreed not to mention again, but Mia had never felt the same about Skylar since.

"I know, I know, Mom seems so nice," Skylar had sighed. "And she runs a very successful business, so you wouldn't think she's that disorganized. But she's a mess." Skylar had lifted her chin and blown smoke out the window. "She drives me crazy."

The next morning, Skylar was gone, off to bigger and better things.

Turned out, Skylar was right—Aunt Bev was a little nutty. For the last two days, she'd been locked in her office at the storefront, finishing up the bid for the Ross house. Mia had heard nothing but the whir of the adding machine and Aunt Bev muttering under her breath.

Mia had manned the counter. Which meant she'd been reading a lot of magazines. It was excruciatingly boring.

Anyway, Mia got herself up and made her way to Cranston's. As the kid with the bobbing Adam's apple and big brown eyes went in the back to look for the missing photos, Mia perused the magazine rack. "William Steps out behind Kate's Back!" screamed the *National Enquirer*, complete with a picture of the Duchess of Cambridge looking like she might be ill at any moment. "Why Everett Alden Disappeared from the Alternative Rock Scene," said the top of the cover of *Rolling Stone*. Mia couldn't see the picture that accompanied that headline because in the slot below it was *Us Weekly*, and Chris Pine was on the cover. "Chris Revealed," the title read.

The kid returned. "There's nothing back there," he said. "I put them all in the envelope. You were there."

"Yes, I know. Just checking."

"Need anything else?" he asked, rubbing his hand under his nose.

She grabbed the *Us Weekly* and put it down next to a pack of peanut butter cups. If she had to spend another afternoon writing the prices of decorative items in calligraphy onto thick vellum tags, she was going to need a reward, and that reward was a revealing look at Chris Pine, thank you very much.

She walked down the street with her purchases to the John Beverly storefront wearing a knit hat and oversized sunglasses. She had hardly stuck her oxford shoe in the door when Aunt Bev was rushing at her, red-faced.

"You will not believe what happened," she snapped, taking the plastic bag from Mia's hand. "That woman is certifiable! You know she loved *everything*," she said angrily, one hand swinging freely, punctuating her speech. "*Everything!* And then she tells me, well not right now."

"What? *Who?*" Mia asked, grabbing her magazine before Aunt Bev disappeared with it.

"Who! Nancy Yates, that's who! You know what she's done, don't you? She's hired *Diva Interiors*! But I have spent a *lot* of time working on this, and so have you, Mia! She said she *loved* this, she *loved* that, she wanted to do it all—but not now. Not now! What the hell does that mean, *not now?*"

"I guess it means not—"

"You don't think I'm giving in, do you?" Aunt Bev all but shouted. "No sir! First of all, I told Nancy to at least wait and see what I could propose to do and for how much. And I told her that you lost the dining room photos—"

"*I* didn't lose—"

"And that you'd be up there first thing this morning to take them again, and that by the close of business tomorrow, she would have a proposal to turn that pile of shit into a show palace! Okay, so *go*. Go get those photos! Take them on your cell phone and I'll print them here."

"I don't have a car—"

"Wallace will take you. Wallace!" she bellowed toward the back. "Take Mia to the Ross house!"

Mia heard a groan from the back. Aunt Bev tore into her package of peanut butter cups as she stalked off toward her office.

"Well come on then, toots, I don't have all day!" Wallace shouted from somewhere behind the carpet samples.

◆ ◆ ◆

Wallace Pogue, the self-proclaimed Bitch of East Beach, was an interior designer. He was also a floral designer of some repute. He made such stunning arrangements with artificial flowers that the shop's clients often ordered them to be shipped to their Manhattan lofts. Wallace had a thriving career in East Beach, and yet, he'd been very obviously perturbed that Mia had come to work for Aunt Bev. Mia had been forewarned by Aunt Bev that Wallace was in a snit about her working in the shop. She'd confided to Mia that he felt displaced by her unexpected arrival on the scene. "It's just been the two of us for so long, you know," she said. "And he can be kind of sensitive."

That was an understatement.

Mia thought Wallace was being ridiculous. He knew very well Mia had very reluctantly moved home to live with her parents and had very reluctantly accepted the offer to work in her aunt's shop until she found her footing.

To make matters worse, Wallace had been tasked with driving her up to the Ross house and picking her up when Aunt Bev couldn't. And Wallace was not one to let his emotions stew. He liked to release them to the wild the moment they popped up in him.

The motor on the shop van was already running when Mia walked outside. "Hurry *up*," he said as Mia put her messenger bag on the bench behind the passenger seat. "I have a *lot* to do today, which does not include driving *you*."

The moment she closed the door, he gunned it, sailing out of the gate and onto Juneberry Road. Why was everyone in this town determined to die on Juneberry Road?

"Honestly, I don't know why I am putting up with this," he said. "The last thing I need is to be driving Miss Mia across town." He jerked the wheel around the curves. "Why don't you have a car, anyway? If you're going to live and work in East Beach, you're just going to have to get a car. It makes absolutely no sense that you're working up here. It's not like you *know* anything," Wallace continued ranting. "But try telling that to Beverly. I swear if that woman listened to one word I said, she'd double her revenue, but no. She brings *you* in and you're completely useless."

"Hey, I'm not completely useless," Mia said breezily. In spite of all his bluster, Wallace couldn't get to her—she found him quite amusing. "I bring you coffee, don't I? And I can measure a room as well as any trained monkey."

"Oh, you're useless," Wallace reaffirmed. "I know what you think, toots. You think you're going to grind out the summer, then go back to the city," he said, fluttering his fingers at her. "And in the meantime, I have to put up with you, and then I'll probably have to clean up your messes when you're gone. The least you can do is get a fucking *car*."

This was exactly the reason why Mia didn't feel very awful for poking Wallace when she could. Like right now. "I don't believe in cars." That was not even remotely true. Mia had exactly zero emotions surrounding cars.

"What?" Wallace peered at her through his Dolce & Gabbana tortoiseshell frames. He was wearing a Ralph Lauren button-down shirt and coordinating crewneck sweater, 7 For All Mankind skinny jeans, and Rocket Dog sneakers. The man was into labels. "What do you mean you don't believe in *cars*?" he demanded irritably. "What does that even *mean*? What *do* you believe in, a horse and buggy?"

"Emissions are dangerous and destroying our environment," she said gravely.

"Oh, of course, the *emissions*!" Wallace said grandly with a roll of his eyes. "That's right, no one likes *emissions* until they need to be somewhere, and then suddenly, emissions are okay, aren't they?"

Mia looked out the passenger window and bit her lip to keep from smiling. It was almost as if he wore a big, red Alice-in-Wonderland-type button on his chest that said *Push Me*. "*Someone* has to care."

"Well, if I were you, I'd care about the clothes you have on. That is the most disturbing conglomeration of fabrics I have ever seen in my *life*. I assume you made it," he said with a sniff. "I'm sure you think it's high-concept art that none of us mere mortals can grasp, but *that* my dear, is a *disaster*."

Mia glanced down at her leather and red brocade skirt. "Yes, as a matter of fact, I did make this. And I designed the brocade. See the floral pattern?" she asked, pointing out a panel in the skirt. "If you like, I could make you some pants from this."

Wallace snorted. "Stick to painting."

Wallace knew very well that Mia wanted nothing more than to stick to painting and to "high art," but had failed miserably at it. So now, she'd have to make him some pants, if for no other reason than spite.

"In the meantime, what are you going to do about getting to work every day? Or am I to assume that this morning jaunt is going to continue into infinity?"

"I could walk," she said helpfully, but Wallace looked almost alarmed by that.

"*Walk?*" he echoed in disbelief, as if the concept was foreign to him. "What, you're going to walk three miles all uphill in your strange little frocks?"

"Why not?" Mia asked with a shrug. "At least I won't have to listen to you, and you won't have to be annoyed by my breathing the same air."

"Your breathing is *not* what annoys me," Wallace corrected her.

"Walking. Well *that's* great advertisement. John Beverly Home Interiors—walking uphill to you on a steamy summer day."

"Okay, all kidding aside," she said, twisting in her seat toward Wallace. "I don't want to work up here. Get this—turns out, Nancy Yates has a son she's been hiding."

"Really?" Wallace said, perking up, looking at her with renewed interest. "Please tell me he's hot. I swear to God, I haven't had a decent date in a year."

"He's not hot," Mia said. "And I don't think he's gay."

"That's what they all think. Is he hideous?"

"Semi-hideous," Mia said. "And obviously high and incredibly rude."

"That's the summer crowd for you," Wallace said, his interest gone with a flick of his wrist. "They think everyone else exists to serve them."

"Exactly. I don't want to be around that all summer."

"Oh no. You're not going to try and shove this job off on me now that I know there is a heathen involved. Don't worry about it, toots. He won't be here long. They *never* stay here, why would they? There is nothing *here*. And even if he did stay, you'll be walking up in your peculiar little frocks. Trust me, he won't bother you."

"Gee, thanks."

"I'm telling you this as a friend. Did you find an apartment?" he asked. "Or have you been too busy with your *job*?" he drawled.

"Not yet."

"All right, that's it. I'm taking you to see an adorable garage apartment my friend Dalton has for rent. And you better snatch it up, girl, or you'll be living with your parents for the rest of your life and painting in the utility shed."

Mia didn't need Wallace to tell her that she'd ended up a wannabe artist living with her parents, and not a celebrated artist living in New York and dining in swank restaurants and entertaining Important People. Nope, she would be doing her painting in a repurposed yard shed. And Wallace couldn't seem to stop mentioning it.

Oh yeah, this had all the markings of a *great* summer.

Six

The slam of a car door startled Brennan awake. He opened one eye. Maybe two. His vision was so blurry he couldn't be sure. As he was still slightly drunk, he had to think where he was. He winced at the dull throb behind his eyes and blinked until he could focus on the plaster medallion on the ceiling of his room.

Right. Mom's new house.

Another car door slammed.

Shit. Brennan desperately wanted to get out of bed and close the damn window—he'd opened it at three this morning, hoping the cool night air would keep him awake, keep him going. He'd been writing lyrics, and for the first time in months, they'd gushed from him with uncharacteristic ease and a flow he'd not felt in years. Were they any good? He was afraid to look. That was the thing about drunken creativity—what seemed brilliant in the moment turned out to be crap by the light of day.

He would look, he would . . . but at the moment, Brennan couldn't dredge up the will necessary to actually get out of bed.

"I'm just saying, you can't live with your parents forever. You're going to have to work enough hours to pay rent. Hello, it's called adulthood," a man's voice said, drifting up to him from somewhere down on the drive.

"Why, thank you, Wallace. I didn't know what it was called until you came along to enlighten me."

Brennan knew that voice—it was the groupie girl. No, no, not a groupie. The decorator. What was her name again? Mary?

"You're going to have to move along now, Mr. Pogue."

He knew *that* male voice. That was the dude his mother had hired for security. Some great security—people were in and out of here all day long.

"Yeah, Wallace, you're going to have to move along," said the woman, who was maybe Mary, maybe something else. He couldn't remember.

"Perfect. I have the two misfits of East Beach telling me what to do now."

She laughed, and the sound of it was lilting and sweet. It made Brennan horny, made him think of hearing that laugh when he was inside her. Now he was hard. Great—he'd been reduced to getting hard at the sound of a woman's laugh.

"Please, sir, I need you to move the van now," said the security guard.

"Whatever," the other man said. "Apparently I have to do everything, don't I? I'm calling my friend Dalton, and then I'll be back to pick you up *as usual*, Miss Mia-I-don't-drive."

Mia. That was it. Mia, Mia, with the cinnamon hair. Brennan suddenly imagined her on top of him, on his cock. He imagined pert breasts, dark areolas, and him, *pumping, pumping . . .*

A door slammed again, and Brennan winced as the force of it reverberated through his head. *"Damn,"* he muttered. There went the fantasy.

"Thanks for the ride, Wallace!" she called out. She sounded a little too singsongy. As if she were trying to provoke the man who didn't want her living with her parents. Wait . . . she lived with her parents? She'd seemed too old for that . . . but then again, he'd been a little drunk when he'd met her, so who knew how old she was.

The vehicle started up with a grind that didn't sound right. It moved away from the house, the sound of the rattling engine lessening the faster the van went.

"How are you, Drago?" she asked when the van had gone out the gate.

"Good. Did you try that spin class yet?"

"I have not," she said solemnly. "But it's definitely on my to-do list this weekend. Is Mrs. Yates here today?"

"Yep. She's inside," the security guy said.

So Mom was home. Brennan was not up for another conversation with his mother. He listened as the decorator walked across the drive and up to the front door directly beneath him. He heard the door open, the dogs attacking her feet, and the door closing.

Silence.

He rolled onto his back and pushed two empty beer bottles off of his bed. They landed with a clatter on the wood floor. He grabbed a pillow and pulled it over his head, closed his eyes, and let sleep take him again.

He next awoke to the sound of sheet music rustling and falling from his bedside table, moved about by the breeze that had come in through the open window. Brennan groaned, tossed the pillow aside, swung his legs over the bed, and sat up. He rubbed his face with his hands. His eyes felt scratchy—he'd slept fitfully, which seemed to be the norm these days. Sleep refused to come on any normal schedule, sometimes passing an entire twenty-four hours before blessing him with its presence. And when sleep did come, it rolled over him in great crashing waves, forcing him down into its depths.

He yawned, scratched his bare belly. He was hungry. And he needed to piss. He stood up and walked unsteadily into the en suite. He took care of business, washed his face and scrubbed the sleep from his eyes, brushed teeth that felt like tiny fur babies in his mouth. He wandered back into his room and glanced around dispassionately. God, it smelled in here. He went to the windows and opened them wider to air the place out, then bent down, swiped up a T-shirt and some jeans off the floor.

The T-shirt was one he'd used to work on a car he'd had in LA. It had some serious axle grease stains that his housekeeper had never been able to get out. And . . . something else. Brennan didn't know what that stain was, but it didn't look too offensive. His jeans had seen better days—or at least a washing machine at some point. He buttoned them only enough to stay up. He couldn't even be bothered to finish off a row of five buttons now. Yeah, well, whatever.

He padded downstairs in bare feet, pushing his overgrown mop of shaggy hair back from his face and scratching at his beard stubble.

Just as he reached the foyer, the front door swung open and his mother's housekeeper, Magda, stepped in with two stuffed tote bags, one over each arm. From the kitchen, the tiny demons his mother called dogs came yapping and scampering down the hall.

"*Out!*" Brennan said sternly, and pointed toward the kitchen. The dogs reversed course and ran back to the kitchen. They didn't like him any more than Magda did.

Magda dislodged one tote, then the other, and set them down before reaching around to shut the door. She straightened up and allowed her disapproving gaze to flick over Brennan.

"Hello, Magda," he said. He was used to her disdain now. "Little late for you, isn't it? I thought you preferred the five a.m. start time."

"Hello Mr. Yates."

"You know, I've been here for almost three weeks now. Just call me Brennan." He'd said the same thing almost every day since he'd arrived, but the woman refused to call him anything other than Mr. Yates. Even now, Magda responded to his request in whatever language it was that she spoke. He thought it might be Hungarian, but until she called him by his name, he was tacitly refusing to ask.

She leaned over, picked up both tote bags and walked past Brennan on her way to the kitchen.

"I guess this means no breakfast," he said drily.

"No breakfast, Mr. Yates. No lunch. It's after noon."

Was it? Brennan hadn't bothered to note the time.

She lumbered on to the kitchen, favoring her right side. He sat down on the bottom step and listened to the sound of things being moved around the kitchen, cabinet doors slamming, and water running. The water reminded him that he was hungry. Hunger won over reluctance, and Brennan went into the kitchen. But as he entered, Magda went out another door, carrying a bucket and a bottle of some type of cleaner.

"Is it me? Is it something I said?" he asked after her.

She didn't respond.

Brennan opened the fridge. He stood there, staring at the contents, his visual search turning up nothing that interested him. He looked at the coffeemaker. He wasn't interested in that, either. What he really wanted to do was get in his new car—talk about an impulse buy—and head up to one of the quaint little villages around here and find something to eat. That was actually easier said than done, as it would require some exertion on his part and he still hadn't determined if he could make even the slightest effort today.

He walked out onto the back terrace and looked around. The day was turning gray, fingers of rain clouds slowly sliding across the sky. A flock of birds glided across the southern end of the lake, ducks or geese or, hell, even ostriches for all Brennan knew.

It was peaceful here around Lake Haven. Just like he'd wanted. He'd thought that was all he needed, but now he knew there was something else lurking in the shadows of his soul that he needed. If only he knew what the hell it was. Whatever it was, it went deep. Marrow deep. It was an itch turned inward that he couldn't figure out how to scratch.

Yeah, he'd get out and drive. Have a drink somewhere. Eat something that wasn't out of a bag. He'd risk discovery, but what the hell, he didn't care. His manager said everyone was looking for him. "There's going to be a huge bidding war for whoever gets that first shot of you," Gary had said. He'd called a couple of nights ago to deliver a general diatribe about Brennan having dropped off the face of the earth and not making the decisions he needed to make. For leaving when Gary and Chance were so eager to change directions that they reeked of it.

"That means you've got a bounty on your head," Gary had said. "It's better if we control the story."

Brennan knew that was true. He'd once found a TMZ guy hiding under the table at the studio. Those guys would do anything for a scoop, and the sooner he put something out explaining his absence, the better.

But right now, he didn't care what anyone thought. Or wanted. Right now, the only thing he cared about was a burger.

Brennan walked back inside, and as he passed the kitchen table, he happened to notice a canvas messenger bag in a chair and a sketchbook on the table. He paused—that was new. The sketchbook was covered with stickers: Mellow Johnny's Bike Shop. A peace symbol. The apple that came in the box of every Apple product ever sold. Some of the pages had gotten wet at some point and paper had swelled, making the cover a little wavy.

He picked up the book and opened it. He looked with surprise at the drawings, made both in pencil and ink, and covering a wide variety of subjects: three musicians in a park. A skyline he guessed to be New York. A vase of flowers.

Brennan flipped through, only mildly interested until he reached those that obviously depicted this house. He recognized some of the empty rooms, but things had been added in the sketches. In the living room, which was currently empty, the sketch included a couch and a woman dressed in a period costume. He recognized the dining room by the strange wallpaper, but not the table around which several people sat. That sketch reminded him of an old Norman Rockwell painting—people laughing, leaning over one another.

The Palladian-style windows on the front of the house had been drawn with shutters instead of the actual thick drapes that seemed to catch dust. Azaleas lined the house where there were no shrubs. Nor were there goats foraging in the grass as the next sketch suggested, and Brennan highly doubted the security guard ever stretched out on a lawn chaise to catch some rays.

He turned the page. The next sketch was of the kitchen. The dogs were curled into little balls on their pillow next to the cheap table and chairs his mother had picked up somewhere. Atop the kitchen island was an ape. The ape was hunkered down, his arms scraping the counter top. And he had a surprisingly familiar face. Not identical, but close enough—

"Hey!"

The sound of the girl's voice startled Brennan so badly he almost dropped the book. He jerked around; she was standing in the door of the butler's pantry. And she looked furious.

"What the hell are you doing?" she demanded as she strode forward, her hand outstretched.

Brennan looked at the sketchbook. "Is this yours?" he asked dumbly.

"Give it back." Her brows had sunk into a dark vee, and her amber eyes turned stormy. She managed to get her hand on the book, jerking it out of his hands.

Brennan lifted his hands, surrendering. "Sorry."

"*Sorry?* Do you often go through people's things without their permission?"

"You're right, I shouldn't have done that," he conceded. "I saw it lying there and I . . ." Well, he'd picked it up, obviously. He shouldn't have. But he did. He shrugged. Was it really such a big deal?

Apparently so, because if looks could slay, he'd be lying in a bloody pool right now, gutted and left to die. He put a hand to his nape and rubbed it. "Who's the ape?"

"Who do you think?" She turned away from him.

Wow. Brennan had absolutely no idea what to say to that. Part of him wanted to laugh. Another part of him thought he ought to be mad about it, but he couldn't really get there. "What are the drawings for?" he asked.

"For *me*. I like to draw. What else would they be for?"

"I don't know. Maybe you mean to show them to someone."

She turned around and looked at him like he'd lost his mind. "To *who*? Who would care about your kitchen? It's a diary, obviously."

Not so obvious to him, but he believed her. "Your diary includes a drawing of me as an ape in this kitchen?"

"Well, yeah," she said, and looked down at her book. "It's not every day I run across someone like you."

"That doesn't sound like a compliment in any way," he said.

"I didn't mean it as a compliment."

"Huh," he said, because Brennan was beginning to believe that this woman really had no clue who he was. God, he could be an idiot sometimes. He ran his hands over his head. He hated always being on edge.

Worse, his body was beginning to take notice of her. He could smell her again, this woman in the wild clothing. She smelled sweet, like fresh cotton sheets. That was a female for you—so soft, so fragrant. Venus flytraps, luring men into their jaws with beauty. Only this one wasn't luring him into anything. She looked like she wanted to shoot him. With a bazooka.

As she picked up her bag and stuffed the sketchbook into it, he noticed she was wearing a skirt today, one made with a lot of different fabrics. She also wore a long-sleeved silk top that was open at the neck and revealed a glimpse of a purple bra beneath. She had on kneesocks and oxford shoes, and was wearing a knit hat over her hair. If he didn't know that she worked here with some designer, he'd wonder what the hell her story was—had her house burned down and these were all the clothes she had left? Was she a performer? Maybe blind to color and different fabrics? But at the same time, there was some conformity and cohesiveness in the different articles of clothing. It was weird, but he could see how they went together. He liked the way she looked. It was very cool in an off-the-reservation kind of way. Moreover, he liked her curves, her big, expressive eyes. The same eyes that were viewing him with not a little bit of loathing right now.

"Hey, come on, I'm not as bad as you think," he said, and unthinkingly touched her arm.

She recoiled from his touch, grabbing her bag and clutching it tightly to her.

"What?" Brennan asked, casting his arms open. "I said I was sorry."

Her gaze flicked over him. "Should I be honest?" she asked, backing away from him.

"Sure, be honest. Be totally freaking honest."

"You seem kind of crazy."

"Okay," he said, nodding. Maybe he did seem a little crazy to someone who didn't know who he was. Hell, he'd been feeling a little crazy the last few weeks. "I'm not crazy, but I will concede that I may appear a little bit strange to someone who doesn't know me."

"A *little*?"

"I'm not *that* strange," he said defensively. "Trust me, I have a good reason."

"Whatever you say." She stepped farther away from him.

"Take it easy," he said. "It's not like I have a communicable disease."

She arched a dubious brow.

"Will you lighten up? I'm not going to touch you. I'm not going to give you any reason to touch me. You don't have to back off like you're afraid of me."

"I'm not *afraid* of you," she scoffed. A little too quickly, actually.

Brennan frowned. "Why are you acting like I've got Ebola? I'm sorry I looked at your book, okay?" He held up his palms. "Truce."

She didn't speak.

Brennan sighed with exasperation. *"What?"*

"Nothing."

"It's obviously something."

She shrugged again and gripped her bag more tightly, backing up another step. "It's your T-shirt."

He glanced down. "Yeah, it's old. So it's got a couple of holes. And a couple of stains. Okay, a lot of stains." This shirt suddenly looked a lot dirtier than it had when he put it on.

"And, perhaps you don't know it, but . . . you stink."

Brennan looked up. "Excuse me?"

"You *stink*," she said again. She'd made it almost to the kitchen door.

"What are you talking about?" he asked, curious now.

"I don't know how else to say it. You smell."

Brennan looked at her blankly. In all his life, no one had ever said something like that to him. Never.

"Ohmigod, are you going to make me say it again? Let's just put it this way—if there were gas masks lying around, I'd be wearing one. Look, I'm sorry, Mr. Yates, fire me if you want, but I don't want to get any closer to you. You're rude and you stink and I really think you need to know that."

"Wow, okay," he said, nodding. "Anything else, Miss Perfect?"

"Hmm," she said thoughtfully, studying him now. "I already mentioned the crazy part. No, I think that's it. Crazy, stinky, and rude. Have a good day, Mr. Yates." With that, she turned and disappeared into the hallway. He heard her rubber-soled shoes on the tile as she hurried away from him, heard the front door open, heard it close behind her.

Brennan remained seated, staring at the space where she'd just been. He couldn't smell himself. But his hair did feel a little slick. He glanced down at his clothes, grabbed a fistful of his T-shirt, and bent over to have a sniff.

God, that was awful.

Brennan tried to remember the last time he'd showered. Day before yesterday? Three days ago? Longer? *Wow.* He used to be fairly fastidious about hygiene. But since he'd slid into this dark hole . . .

Crazy, stinky, and rude.

A smile slowly spread across Brennan's face. He could feel it cracking him open bit by bit, a screwdriver to the lid of a rusty old paint can. When was the last time someone was completely straight with him? Or someone didn't have an agenda? The woman in the knit hat had made him smile.

Yeah, he was going to go get something to eat, drive around a bit. But first, he was going to take a shower. He thought of Mia again, of how angry she'd been with him for looking at her sketches—which, admittedly, he deserved. That *was* rude.

But then he thought of the knuckle-dragging ape she'd drawn and chuckled.

Seven

Mia waited outside the gate so she wouldn't have to chat it up with Drago while she waited for Wallace. Not that she minded talking to him—but today, her head was spinning around Brennan Yates. Mia had known a lot of summer people in her life, but she had never known one who was so disgusting and rude . . . and yet, could be so *hot* if he would clean up a bit. How did *that* happen, anyway? How did a man with privileges that most people only dreamed about end up looking like a street bum?

Whatever the reason, Mia was done with the Ross house. She wasn't coming back here. She didn't feel at all comfortable with George of the Jungle hulking around in the shadows.

She could hear a car coming up Juneberry Road, and stood up, expecting it to be Wallace. But a white Range Rover appeared and slowed as it reached Mia. A dark window rolled down. "Hey girl!" Nancy called out cheerfully, as if they were chums. She was wearing tennis togs and a sun visor, although Mia could have sworn she'd left Ross house this morning in a dress and sandals. "Are you finished so soon?"

"Yes, ma'am. I just had to get a couple of pictures, that's all."

Nancy's smile faded. "What's wrong?" she asked. "Something's wrong, isn't it? You look very unhappy."

"I do?" Mia asked, surprised.

"Terribly," Nancy said, nodding. "I hope none of the workers or Drago—"

"No, no," Mia said quickly. The workers she'd encountered the last few days had all been very polite to her, and Drago had never been anything but completely respectful. "It wasn't any of them."

"Then who was it?" Nancy asked, her gaze narrowing.

Oh, Mia was so stupid. Why hadn't she just said no? "Ummm . . ." She glanced back at the house. She might as well say it. Might as well put it out there so Nancy would understand when she didn't come back. She winced a little as she turned to Nancy and said, "I hate to say it, but I had a little run-in with your son."

"Oh *Lord*," Nancy said, and suddenly dropped her head to the steering wheel. She sat up again. "You know, I should have told you he was passing through. My bad," she said, patting her chest. "I didn't think he'd be here *this* long, you know? He never stays so long. But . . . well, just between us girls . . ." She paused and looked through the gates at the house.

Mia did, too, if only to assure herself Crazypants hadn't walked up and heard her.

"He's not himself," she whispered very loudly. "He didn't say anything, did he?"

"Say anything?"

"About . . . anything," Nancy said vaguely and dramatically, as if he were hiding a body up there. Nothing would surprise Mia at this point.

He'd said a lot—but not about anything that Mia could actually recall just then.

"He doesn't like to talk about it," Nancy said quickly.

Holy shit, what did *that* mean? "About the smell?" she asked carefully.

"You noticed it, too?" his mother exclaimed. "I thought maybe there was a sewer problem. But no, not that. He won't talk about the bad breakup he went through recently."

That was it? *That* was the big hush-hush? It wasn't the least bit surprising—when someone smelled and acted like that, the bigger surprise was that he'd had a girlfriend or wife at all.

"Not to excuse him," Nancy added quickly, waving her hand at Mia, "but it was bad. She *cheated* on him," she added in another loud whisper, as if Brennan could hear them all the way back at the house. "Openly, too. For the world to see, so to speak."

Okay, well, Mia had been through a breakup or two, and she knew how it stung. But that didn't mean—

"You're probably too young to appreciate how painful it is to end a long-term love, sweetie. Sometimes people lose their way when that happens, you know?"

"I'm not that young," Mia said, but Nancy was right. She'd never had a long-term love. Somewhere along the way, Mia had learned that if she got too close to anyone, eventually, they would want her to change. "I've had relationships fail," she said defensively.

"Oh sure," Nancy said. "But this one was really deep. More painful than your run-of-the-mill thing."

Was she implying that Mia's relationships were run of the mill? Was she supposed to say it was okay that he smelled and was rude because someone had cheated on him?

"I'm just saying that it was very bad," Nancy said, almost as if she could read Mia's mind. "I'm not asking you to excuse him, but he's definitely not himself. He's usually such a nice man, a *good* man. He didn't say anything offensive, did he?"

"Not exactly *offensive*," Mia said, feeling almost guilty for being appalled by him.

"That's a relief!" Nancy smiled. "We'll have to make it up to you the next time you're back. Oh goodness, look at the time! I really have to run, sweetie. Talk soon!" she said breezily, and rolled her window up before shooting up the drive, cheerful and busy again.

These people were flat-out *nuts*.

Ten minutes later, Wallace arrived, the van sputtering as it came up the hill. "Well?" he demanded as Mia climbed into the van. "Did you get the all-important photos?"

"Of course."

"A lot of good those pictures are going to do us now. I told Beverly *she* ought to come up here, but your aunt puts bids together about as well as she does floral arrangements—she *doesn't*. Now, how was your day? Did you see the semi-hideous son?"

"Boy, did I," Mia said, and on the way back to the shop, told Wallace about her encounter with him today.

They'd pulled into the back lot behind the shop as Mia finished. Wallace said, "Don't worry about it, kid. Trust me, we'll lose the biggest job to come to East Beach in a decade because of Beverly's disorganization, and you won't have to see the cretin again. Go on in, don't wait for me. I have to get some things," he said as he dug through some papers on the console between the seats.

Mia walked in the back door of the shop and into the darkened storeroom. She sneezed at the overwhelming scent of potpourri. She was fumbling for a light when the door to the showroom suddenly flew open and florescent light from the shop flooded into the storeroom. *"Mia!"*

Startled, Mia squinted in the direction of the voice.

Her cousin Skylar materialized before her, grinning, her arms wide.

"Skylar? Where did you come from? When did you get here?"

"Last night." Skylar threw her arms around Mia and hugged her, then stepped back, her gaze traveling down Mia's clothes. "Now there's a look," she said with a giggle. "Never let it be said that my cousin has a dull imagination. I keep thinking that after all the flak you took in high school, someday you might scale it back."

"Thanks," Mia said. She would have pointed out that Skylar was one to talk, but Skylar would take issue. Her blonde hair was long and choppy, as if someone had taken scissors to it at different times. She had a nose ring and the ink of what Mia thought was a new tattoo was peeking out from beneath the long sleeves of her T-shirt.

"Where have you been, anyway?" Mia asked.

"Here. There. Everywhere." Skylar shrugged. "Along for the ride, you know?"

No, Mia really didn't know. "Aunt Bev didn't say you were coming."

"That's because I didn't tell her until I rolled into town last night. But she's so freaked out about this job with the Ross house right now, I don't think she really knows I'm even here."

"Just passing through?" Mia asked, sounding a little more hopeful than she intended.

"Yeah, of course. Always passing through. I'll probably be here for the summer unless something better comes up."

Mia's heart sank. When Skylar was around, there was always trouble, and Mia sucked at deflecting it.

"I definitely want to be here for the Lake Haven Music Festival. I'll be living with the 'rents," she said. "Just like you, right? Isn't that wild? Whoever would have thought we'd *both* end up back here in this dump of a town?"

Mia didn't like the idea that she and Skylar were anything alike. Skylar never settled anywhere for long, never held onto a job for more than a minute. She'd been running for years, running away from home the first time when she was fifteen years old. Mia loved Skylar on some level, but during the summer of her senior year, it had all ended in disaster because Mia *wasn't* like her cousin. Not even close.

Wallace walked in at that moment, and at the sight of Skylar, he stopped dead in his stride. He scowled.

"Hello, Wallace!" Skylar said brightly. "I bet you're super happy to see me. Am I right?"

"I wouldn't say that," Wallace drawled. "What cat dragged *you* in?"

"Oh, come on," Skylar said, and threw her arms around Wallace, giving him a bear hug, too. "I've actually missed you, you old meanie."

"I'm very serious—what are you doing here?" he demanded. "And I don't mean East Beach, I mean in this store."

"I'm going to answer phones," Skylar said proudly. "We've actually had a call this morning, can you believe it?"

"What do you mean?" Wallace demanded.

"I *mean*, when it rings, I pick it up and say, 'Hello, John Beverly Home Interiors and Landscape Design, how may I help you?'"

Wallace huffed impatiently. "Are you answering phones for a short while today? Or will we have the pleasure of your company longer than that?"

"Oh, *longer*," Skylar said, clearly as delighted as Mia to torment Wallace. She looped her arm through Mia's. "Don't look so pissed, Wallace! Remember how much fun we had last time I was here?"

"*No*, I do not," he said gruffly. "Well isn't this just fantastic? John Beverly's Home for Wayward Girls," he groused as he stalked past them into the shop.

Skylar laughed. "He's such a queen."

"Really, you're going to work here?" Mia asked, feeling just as stunned as Wallace. It was one thing that Skylar was in the same town, same family. It was something else entirely if she was in the same work space.

"Sure! Why not?" Skylar asked. "Geez, don't look so worried. This is going to be *loads* of fun." She reached into her pocket and pulled out a joint, holding it up so that Mia could see it, then slid the joint back in her pocket.

Mia stared at Skylar.

"Don't be a wimp, Mia!" Skylar said, and put her arm around Mia's shoulders. "Come on, let's catch up. I have *so* much to tell you."

Eight

Skylar's arrival back in East Beach put new urgency to Mia's need to get her act together. There was something about being lumped into John Beverly's Home for Wayward Girls that made Mia want to prove she'd only suffered a small setback, but nothing more.

First things first, she was *not* going to be the Lassiter kid who had no choice but to live with her parents. So Mia took Wallace up on his offer to introduce her to his friend, Dalton Blaylock.

Dalton was a plastic surgeon who summered in a house on the northern edge of East Beach. He'd bought property that had once been a farm and had built an ultramodern, lots-of-windows, spectacular lake house right out of *Architectural Digest*, which, naturally, had been decorated by Wallace.

Dalton had left the old barn standing and had renovated the second floor into an apartment.

Mia hated to say it, but Wallace was right—it was perfect.

"I'm really looking for someone who will keep an eye on the place when I'm in the city," Dalton said. "Not that you'd have to do anything, but, you know, a presence is always nice. A *quiet* presence. I don't want to hear garage bands cranking up in the middle of the night."

"Luckily, I haven't been in a garage band since I was twelve," Mia assured him.

The apartment was small, but immaculately turned out. On one end stood a kitchen with modern appliances and glass countertops. On the other end, a double bed on a raised wooden platform. In true Wallace style, the bed sported so many decorative pillows that there was hardly enough room to sit on the foot of it.

A potbellied stove was on the north wall, atop marble tile that matched the tile in the kitchen. The furniture was rustic chic—big chairs and a sofa with soft cushions and canvas coverings that frankly could have used some of Mia's fabric designs. But what caught Mia's eye were the French doors that opened onto a small balcony. The amazing view out those doors was an expensive one—through the trees, Mia could see the beach and the lake. She could imagine sitting on the balcony on Sunday mornings with a cup of coffee and a piece of toast, her easel and her paints.

"Quite nice, isn't it?" Wallace asked smugly, always happy to be right.

"It's beautiful," Mia agreed.

"Five hundred a month," Dalton said. "Eckland's Hardware and General Store is at the bottom of the drive. They'll have all the groceries you might need," Dalton said. "And of course, you know it's a quick jog into the village."

"Only a mile or so from Ross house," Wallace added, looking at her pointedly. "A much easier walk from here than from town."

Oh yes, this place exceeded Mia's wildest expectations.

"Well," Dalton said, "while Mia thinks about this, *I'm* thinking of redoing the master, did I tell you?" He touched Wallace's arm with one fingertip.

"Again?" Wallace exclaimed.

"Again," Dalton purred. "Mia, take all the time you need. Take a walk down to the store and see what the old man has in stock while I show Wally what I'm thinking."

The two men went out. Mia stood alone in the loft looking out the French doors at the view.

It *was* amazing. She'd have to search long and hard to find a place like this for the price. The thing about it was she could actually work here. There were two slight problems—one, she didn't know how she'd pay for it, especially if Aunt Bev didn't get the Ross house. And she still owed her brother Derek the cost of the van they'd rented to haul her few things home from Brooklyn.

And two—if she took it, did that mean she was staying here? Was she going to give up and live in East Beach? Was she really ready to admit defeat?

But still . . . she loved it.

Mia walked downstairs and outside to look around. Below, on a little patch of grassy green, there was a bistro table and chairs outside the door to the barn. Someone had put a tiny pot of flowers on the table. There was a slight breeze, enough to lift the ends of her hair, and it carried the scent of new pine needles with it.

Between the disaster of her senior year and having fled East Beach for the city, Mia had forgotten how truly beautiful Lake Haven could be. She had forgotten how this vista had often inspired her to want to create stunning art. She felt the draw of that desire to create now. This very minute. Give her some paper, a pencil—*something.*

This was what she needed. Wasn't it?

She decided to take Dalton's suggestion and walk down to Eckland's Hardware and see if the general store had anything even remotely organic.

She was surprised to discover that the store hadn't changed one bit in all the time she'd been gone. Mr. Eckland, who had been ancient when she was sixteen, was still here, only more ancient. His ears looked as if they might have grown another inch or two, and the shock of white hair on top of his head was noticeably thinner, but still sprung up, untended.

"Hello, Mr. Eckland," she said.

"Huh?" He looked up from his spot near a window where the spring sun was streaming in. He was seated in an old wicker lawn chair, his feet propped on a pile of boxes, reading the paper. He squinted at her from over the top of it.

"I said, *hello*," Mia said louder.

He waved at her as he turned his attention back to his paper, clearly uninterested. "Lemme know if you need anything."

There was no one else in the store, so Mia wandered around its aisles of hammers and canned goods, weed whackers and frozen pizzas. This was not a Home Depot–type hardware store—this was the hardware store of the idle wealthy. That didn't mean there weren't serious bits of machinery, but there were more colorful watering cans and hammer sets for junk drawers and old-fashioned, gasless crank lawn mowers for the environmentally conscious than one might find in a big box store.

Memories of this store and her childhood began to surface as Mia moved through the aisles. Snatches of her and her cousins riding their bikes up the beach and leaving them in tumbled piles of handlebars and banana seats at the end of the footpath to run up to this store and its candy aisle. Of buying snow shovels with her father one year when the winter was particularly bad.

And, of course, the night of her ultimate humiliation, when she and Skylar had stopped here for lighter fluid.

Images of that night suddenly overwhelmed her, coming in a flurry of memories so quickly that Mia had to grab onto a stack of cheap lawn furniture to steady herself. There had been a bonfire on the north end of the beach, just below the Ross house. It was secluded there, out of sight of the three East Beach cops that patrolled the streets.

Mia hadn't wanted to go. Her boyfriend, Aiden Bowers, had broken up with her the night before graduation, and she'd been moping around for weeks, not knowing what to do with herself. It was supposed to have been a glorious summer—she was out of high school, bound for college in Brooklyn, and those should have been her last few weeks of pure freedom. But Aiden had ruined that and Mia didn't know how to bounce back.

She hadn't had many friends to rely on because Mia had always struggled to fit in. She'd always been different. She saw the world around her in shapes and angles, in shading and light. She noticed the motion in some things, the stillness in others. She loved colors beyond reason and even claimed them as her own as girls will do—chartreuse, magenta, azure.

The world of color and light had been a wonderful one to inhabit as a girl. But then Mia had started school, and her view of the world had already been set apart from the other kids. As she'd grown up, teasing turned to mocking. In high school, she'd worn her difference like a crown, and some of the mocking had turned downright derisive.

The more some kids pushed, the more determined Mia was to be different. She sought the company of other kids on the fringe, experimented with drugs and sex. She'd had a hard time maintaining friendships when it seemed like every girl her age wanted to be a cheerleader, and she wanted blue hair.

Mia was a senior when she started dating Aiden. He was her first real boyfriend. He was an unlikely boyfriend, too, because Aiden had always been one of the cool kids. Mia had been surprised when he showed interest in her, but when they started to date, Mia had believed that her class had grown up, and maybe, at last, they were all ready to accept people for who they were. *Maybe.*

Aiden broke up with her after four months of serious dating. It was a shot out of the blue, his reasoning that he wanted to be free of commitment during his last summer at home. It had seemed so easy for him to do, and Mia had been crushed.

Skylar, a year older than Mia, had taken pity on her. She'd introduced her to her friends. Mia found some of them to be aimless and more concerned with the easy way out of life. She wasn't like that—she wanted to succeed. She wanted to be an artist, and she worked hard for it. But she also wanted to matter to someone, and that summer, she mattered to Skylar.

The night of the bonfire, Mia had been at home when Skylar had come around. "Come on, go with me," she'd said.

"Nah. I'm going to stay in," Mia had said, not impolitely.

"Jesus, don't let Aiden Bowers ruin *everything* for you," Skylar had said. "This is the last summer before college, Mia! It's just a little get together on the beach anyway."

Mia could see that Skylar was right—she couldn't let Aiden rule her summer. So she'd reluctantly put on a dress she'd made herself and gone with her cousin.

The "little get together" turned out to be more of a mob, and worse, Aiden was there with his new girlfriend, Shalene.

Someone was passing around big fruit jars of a homemade liquor concoction. There were several fat joints floating around, too. Skylar passed Mia the drink. At first, Mia shook her head.

"Just take a few sips," Skylar said. "Don't be an asshole."

Seeing Aiden with Shalene had made it easier for Mia to drink—anything to dull the pain.

"That's my girl!" Skylar had shouted over the boom box.

But either the concoction was deceivingly strong or Mia drank more than she could remember, because the night quickly got away from her. She could remember dancing, she could remember Aiden's leering grin. She could remember him asking if she missed him.

Wow, Mia hadn't thought about that night in a long time. She took a deep breath and shook it off. She'd definitely put it behind her when she'd left for New York . . . but sometimes that horrible night came creeping into her thoughts like an uninvited guest.

Like right now.

Mia took a deep breath and moved on, wandering down the aisles. *Long time ago. Doesn't matter.*

But she couldn't shake the memories of that night. Even now, she could recall how heavy and oppressive the air was, how the fire felt too hot. She could remember feeling hazy, like she didn't have full control of her body. She'd been confused and woozy, and somehow, she ended up dancing with Aiden.

A lewd and suggestive dance.

Of course Mia could remember Shalene very clearly, and how she'd taken great exception to their dancing. She'd gotten in Mia's face about it, too, her dark head bobbing around on her shoulders as she hurled insults and threats with a finger in Mia's face.

Mia had looked for Skylar, desperate for her help. Shalene had sneered when she told her that Skylar had left with a guy.

That's where Mia's memories got really hazy and weird, nothing but snatches of color and movement. Someone's hands on her. Someone's alcohol-soaked breath on her neck. The feel of dew on her back, the smell of a dead fire, the taste of ashes in her mouth.

Whatever happened, Mia woke up the next morning next to the smoldering remains of the bonfire. The ground around her was littered with bottles and cans. Dirt was in her mouth, muddy sand in her hair. She sat up and realized her dress was up around her chest, her torso and legs exposed. She looked down and had felt sick when she saw that someone had scrawled the word *freak* across her bare belly.

It was horrifying, humiliating, and Mia was filled with crushing shame for not knowing what had happened to her. She stumbled home through a path in the woods to her grandmother's house. Fortunately, no one was home, and Mia showered, scrubbed away the word, scrubbed away her humiliation before anyone saw her.

She could kill Skylar for leaving her, but she thought the whole ugly thing was over. One super bad night.

It was far from over.

Skylar found Mia later that day, and Mia knew the moment she saw her cousin's ashen face. Skylar showed her the pictures that had begun to circulate. They were of Mia passed out on the beach, the word *freak* on her belly clearly visible.

Mia begged Skylar not to say anything, but Skylar couldn't let it stand and told Mia's parents. Naturally, her parents went to the police with a list of names they'd forced Mia and Skylar to give them. A few days later, the detective came to their house and said that as Mia had not been sexually assaulted, and couldn't remember what had happened, it was basically her word against the other kids', none of whom seemed to remember anything except Mia getting wasted. No one saw anything. "Bottom line," he said, "we're lucky no real harm was done."

Oh, but so *much* harm was done. Mia was the laughingstock of East Beach. She couldn't sleep; she lost her appetite. She rarely left her house. Nevertheless, she thought it was truly over, that all she had to do was wait out the summer and go to school.

And *still* it wasn't over. One afternoon, Derek ran into Shalene and Aiden on the street and words were exchanged. Derek was arrested for disorderly conduct.

That's when Mia's family decided it was probably best if she moved to Brooklyn early, and Derek went off to law school as he planned.

Now, of course, almost nine years had passed and Mia could put some perspective around the events of that year. The only true scars were emotional—she could see her teen years for what they were and would be forever grateful that by the time she went to college, she was through experimenting. She didn't do drugs or sleep around. She actually lived fairly conservatively.

She wasn't going to let those memories keep her from the best apartment on Lake Haven.

Mia moved past the frozen foods section, the gourmet cheese and wine section, and walked outside to the garden area. Just outside the door, dozens of lanterns, made from paper, mason jars and tin cans, glass and bottles, hung overhead in a delightful array that covered the garden section. She grabbed her phone to take some pictures of the lanterns so she could paint them later.

She was startled by a crash of what sounded like plastic and leaned to her right, peering past a rack of hoes. Plastic watering cans had scattered across the brick walk, and a man was squatting down to gather them up.

That shaggy head of hair looked familiar. Mia squinted at him. *"Brennan?"*

His head came up at the sound of her voice. He gained his feet and turned toward her.

It *was* Brennan. But not the same Brennan. This was a much better Brennan . . . a *much* better Brennan. For starters, his clothes looked clean. And while she wasn't standing close enough to smell him, *he* looked clean. He was wearing snug khaki slacks that rode low on his hips, a long-sleeved chambray shirt open at the collar, and boots of soft leather. The stubble of two or three days ago when she'd last seen him had filled in, his hair had definitely been combed, and it looked as if it had been trimmed, too. Combed *and* trimmed!

"Hey," he said, looking past her, as if he expected her to be with someone. "What are you doing here?"

She looked around her. "I live in East Beach. This is a hardware store. What are *you* doing here?"

"At the moment, I'm picking up watering cans," he said, and dipped down to gather several of them.

Mia was unable to tear her gaze away from his much-improved self. His broad back strained against his shirt as he reached for the watering cans. He did not look like a slouch today. No ma'am, he looked really *hot*—

"Are you going to stand there gawking, or are you going to help me?"

Mia was startled into action and accidentally knocked a paper lantern with her head, causing it to swing around and knock against several others.

"Careful, careful," he said, and reached for her leg to steady her, his hand landing on her thigh. She looked down at his hand, then at him. Brennan's gaze moved over her, and the slightest hint of a smile . . . a knowing smile . . . appeared on his face.

Acutely aware of his hand and eyes on her body, Mia put both hands to the lantern to stop it from swinging and hitting others, then ducked down and away from his hand, and picked up three of the watering cans. "Seriously, what are you doing here?" she asked curiously as she handed the cans to him. "Besides picking up watering cans."

"Looking for flowers."

"Aha." *Aha.* Like she'd made some important discovery. But flowers, huh? For the ex who cheated on him? Or better yet, someone new? That would certainly explain the big spring cleaning of his person.

"For Magda if you're wondering."

"I wasn't."

"Yes you were," he said, giving her a look. He paused in the work of restacking the watering cans and said, "She doesn't like me, either." He smiled wryly.

Well she wasn't going to deny it, and he didn't seem to expect her to. He leaned down to pick up another can at her feet. When he stood up, he was so close that she could smell him. Or rather, she could smell his spicy cologne. He smelled good. He smelled like a man. An attractive, virile man.

He was looming above her, that dark-blue gaze peering into her. "And for the sake of full disclosure, I had to get away from my mom for a bit."

"Huh?" Mia said, momentarily distracted by his scent. God, was she leaning into him? She quickly straightened up. "Oh, I know, right?" The moment the words left her mouth, she realized how that sounded and said, "I meant *my* mom. Definitely *my* mom—not yours."

One corner of his mouth tipped up. "I wasn't offended either way. So . . . you're living with your mom."

He said it as if that explained something. Mia felt a flash of guilt— she'd judged him for living with his mother while she was sleeping in the twin bed of her childhood room. "Temporarily," she said, avoiding his gaze. "I was laid off a couple of months ago, and I . . ." She shrugged—it suddenly didn't seem like the best idea to announce why she'd come home. It sounded sort of pathetic, even though she wouldn't be the least bit surprised if he'd never held a job of any sort. "Actually, I'm here because I was looking at a garage apartment up the road from here." *Yes! Focus on the positive!*

"Oh. Great."

That sounded a bit perfunctory, as if he wasn't really listening. Or interested. "You really don't like it here, do you?" she asked curiously.

"East Beach?" He shrugged. "It's okay. Do *you* like it here?"

So many responses flitted through her mind. There was a beauty to Lake Haven and East Beach that she'd missed. But there were other, darker memories here. And none of that even touched the fact that not a whole lot happened in East Beach, unless you were up in arms about the new traffic circle in the middle of town as everyone in the coffee shop seemed to be. Still, Mia had a certain affinity for the town. "Sort of," she said, in answer to his question. "My family is here."

"Mine too. So let me ask you something, Aunt Bev's helper," he said, and having finished restacking the cans, he turned to face her, hands in his pockets. "Do you ever think about getting out of here?"

Mia snorted. "All the time."

He smiled. "So why don't you get out of here? Why rent an apartment? You're young. Get out while you can."

Mia blinked. "That's presumptuous. And nosy."

"Is it? I'm just trying to save you." He winked.

"It's not like I can just decide to jet off to Paris or Rome," she said with a laugh. "And I didn't say I was *taking* the apartment." This conversation reminded Mia of her eleven-year-old self when she'd made friends with the girl from New Haven. She used to ask Mia questions that made her feel defensive. *Why don't you have Atari? Your house is small. Do you like Chanel or Dooney & Bourke?*

"So you're not taking it," he said.

She winced a little. "I didn't say that, either."

He tilted his head to one side. "Okay, I give. What *did* you say?"

Why did she even care what this guy thought of her? But like her eleven-year-old self, she kind of did. "This is not something you can probably relate to, but right now, I don't even know if I can get enough work to afford an apartment. I definitely don't have the money to leave East Beach. It's not that simple for me."

One dark brow arched high above the other. "You think it's that simple for me?"

"Well, yeah," she said. "Of course."

"Of course," he scoffed.

"You're not from here. And you have means," she said, gesturing to him. "See? Easier."

"Huh," he said, and folded his arms across his chest as he considered her. "Do you honestly believe you know anything about me?"

No, she didn't know anything about him, other than he lived in the Ross house and from all outward appearances, didn't have a job. She rubbed her earlobe. "No," she admitted.

"Right. Look, I don't know what your situation is. But I know from experience that nothing worth having is ever simple."

Okay, well, she might have been wrong to judge him, but she wasn't going to take advice from him, either. The guy had only recently found a bar of soap. "Sounds like someone's been brushing up on their Confucius primer," she said, and glanced at her watch.

"At least give me an A for effort here," he said. "I'm trying to have a conversation. I'm not drunk. And I don't think I stink."

Something fluttered in a dusty little corner of Mia's heart. "You actually smell pretty good," she grudgingly admitted.

"Progress, baby. I'm working on the rude." He suddenly smiled, and his whole face transformed with it. He looked warm. He looked sexy. He looked like the kind of man a girl would hope to run into at the wine section of the grocery store and start a conversation about the new cabernets, and then somehow, end up at a bistro table drinking said wine. Which was a really strange thing to think about when it came to Brennan Yates. God, what was *happening*?

"By the way, in case I don't get another opportunity—I'm really sorry for looking at your work," he said, and placed his hand on his chest. "I wasn't thinking. But for what it's worth, I liked what I saw. The scenes from the house looked great, and honestly, your depiction of me was spot on."

Mia flushed with embarrassment. "I shouldn't have drawn you like that." She sheepishly pressed the toe of her Converse sneaker into a seam in the floor. "At the very least, I should never have admitted it was you."

He laughed. "I'm glad you did. I was an ass and I deserved it."

She could not suppress a small smile. "You did, a little."

He arched a brow. "You might have at least taken a breath before you agreed that I'm an asshole."

Her smile widened. "I should have given you the benefit of the doubt and realized there was probably something behind your obnoxiousness."

His other brow rose to meet the first. "Clearly, I made quite an impression."

"I just mean that generally people aren't obnoxious without good reason, and you had a good reason."

"I did?"

She'd said too much. "Maybe I should have mentioned—your mom filled me in."

His smile faded and his demeanor changed. He looked at her coolly. *God, Mia.* What did she think she was doing, talking like they were old friends? "She didn't tell me any details," she amended quickly, as if that would reassure him.

"Any details about what?"

In what universe was it okay to bring up someone's ex to a guy one hardly knew? What was the *matter* with her?"

"Details about what?" he asked again.

Mia tucked a strand of hair behind her ear. "She, ah . . . she just mentioned your breakup."

She spoke so softly that he had to lean forward. "Come again?"

Mia sighed. "Your breakup," she muttered like a guilty child.

His gaze was unwavering, boring through her. "Did my mother say any more than that? Did she lay out my entire history for you?"

"No," Mia said. She felt flush, now. Hot. That wasn't precisely true.

He glanced away.

"I mean . . . nothing other than it was pretty bad."

His gaze shifted back to her.

"But that's it," she said, and made a slashing motion with her hand.

He put his hands on his waist and turned partially from her, clearly exasperated.

Should she tell him everything? Because there was more. "And I guess she said that you're having some trouble getting past it and that's why, maybe, you weren't so friendly." *Shut up, Mia. Shut up, shut up.*

He closed his eyes with a groan. "Well, I guess that explains everything, then, doesn't it?"

"I—"

"No, don't say anything," he said, and put up a hand before she could offer any more details. "My mother is wrong. She's *very* wrong, in fact. That's not why I've been an ass. Nope, I have a whole list of reasons for being an ass, but not *that*."

"I'm sorry. I should really learn to keep my mouth shut."

He studied her a moment. Then he flicked a wrist. "Forget it. It's not important." He looked down a moment, as if gathering his thoughts, then said, "I don't know if this will make sense to you, but I look at the world in a different way than most people. I don't mean that to sound as pompous as it probably does, and I don't mean what I see is better or worse than what anyone else sees. I just mean that I tend to look at things through a different prism, and unfortunately, that has caused me some problems recently."

Mia was momentarily taken aback. He had just described *her*.

"Okay, so now you think I'm a psycho," he said with a crooked smile. "But I don't know how else to adequately describe what it feels like when your internal sea turns over on itself, and the silt and trash at the bottom rises to the top and pushes all the glittering surface to the bottom. You know?"

Mia was stunned. The last thing she expected this man to say was something that perfectly described her feelings about herself and her life right now. She was seeing a completely different person before her. Not a summer person, but someone she could actually relate to. He was flesh and bone and thoughts and feelings and he was *her*. "I get it."

"What?"

"What you said. I get that. I—"

"Mia! Are you back there?"

She jumped a little at the sound of Wallace's voice. "Coming!" She looked at Brennan, suddenly desperate to be gone before Wallace wandered back and saw her with him, because she'd never hear the end of it. "I have to run."

His gaze was locked on hers, and she could feel the heat of it shooting down to her groin.

"See you around, Brennan." She turned away and ducked under the lanterns and walked quickly to the front of the store without looking back.

Wallace was standing on the sidewalk checking his phone when she emerged outside. Her gaze landed on the black Porsche, and she felt another shiver of heat race up her spine.

Wallace did not look up from his phone when he asked, "Well? Are you going to take it?"

Mia glanced up, to the top of the hill, where she could see the corner of the stone fence that enclosed the old Ross house. "Yes. I'm going to take it."

Nine

From the garden area of Eckland's, Brennan watched a Prius pull out of the lot and disappear around the corner of Juneberry Road.

There was something about that girl, although Brennan was at a loss to say what. She *got* him? He talked about his fractured prism like a lunatic, and she understood?

Part of him called bullshit. But she was so different than anyone he'd met in so long now that he honestly wasn't sure. He generally ran across wildly creative musicians who could only think of music, sycophants, and opportunists. Moreover, he didn't know if different was a good or bad thing—Brennan would be the first to admit that his perceptions and judgments of people had been compromised by a lot of booze and the occasional joint these last couple of weeks.

One thing was certain—he liked her eyes. He could read what she was thinking in those eyes. And he liked her curves. He liked them so much that at moments during their chat beneath that crazy array of lanterns, he had to force himself to stop imagining her naked.

He was horny. And apparently a pig as well.

He'd known a slight moment of panic when Mia said she'd spoken to his mother. He'd expected the worst, that his mother would have told Mia he was a drunk, and needed rehab, or God, that he was an actual bona fide rock star who had broken up with an A-list movie star. That sort of news generally turned a person's indifferent attitude around to a desire to be his very best friend.

In fact, he was so used to people looking at him like eager puppies, waiting for some pearl of wisdom or artistry to drop from his mouth, that he didn't know how to react to this woman. She had no idea who he was, she didn't want his advice, and she thought she understood him on some level. It was strangely rejuvenating.

Battered and used, my soul badly bruised. You see me standing here, you feel my fear. Come closer, girl. Rescue my shipwrecked heart.

Come closer.

In the garden section of that funky hardware store, otherwise known as the last place Brennan ever thought he would find himself, he paused to take conscious note of his thoughts. *Come closer.* A rush of warmth swept from the top of his head to his feet, his body's acknowledgment that while the thought wasn't much, it was a true start.

This was how the good music was born—a tiny seed of thought or chord would turn into tiny shoots of leaves and limbs. As the idea grew, he'd prune some of those limbs, and nurture others into something bigger. He'd keep at it until he had a creation with its own unique beauty that could stand on its own.

Trey used to say Brennan was their Svengali, because when he got an idea, and played a few chords, they all knew their parts. They'd always been that in tune with each other. Brennan hadn't been anyone's Svengali in a long time, but for the first time in weeks, maybe months, he could hear the chord, A minor, could hear the acoustic tone of it on a single guitar.

But not Chance's guitar. *His* guitar.

Chance would never agree to it. Chance wouldn't like the minor key, he wouldn't like the lyric, he wouldn't like acoustic. He'd say the sound was too sullen, the rhythm too slow. He'd say they needed something up-tempo, a dance beat. He'd play a series of chord progressions that he liked better that would clash with the budding tune in Brennan's head.

Chance disagreeing was not a bad thing. God knew that had been the way with the two of them since the beginning—two completely different mindsets once they had the basic song in mind. Their process was the yin and yang that had created some platinum hits and had worked for them for many years.

Chance would say it was Brennan's fault it wasn't working now, and maybe it was. But Brennan didn't want to think about it. He didn't want to imagine Chance's face, or the frustration in his voice.

He turned back to the table of potted flowers.

Chance was the elephant sitting on his shoulder, and Brennan was going to have to face it sooner or later. Over the last few days, Chance had sent him a string of text messages, each of them more profane than the last. The band was essentially "broken up" because of Brennan, Chance said, because without their lead singer and songwriter, they had no band. Brennan was taking them down the path of losing everything they had worked for years to achieve. Did he think of the rest of them? Had he seen the latest issue of *Rolling Stone*? They were already making him sound like a has-been.

Brennan had drunkenly texted that he agreed they had some serious business to discuss, but first, he had to figure out what space he was in at this precise moment in his life. He was trying to convey that he needed to exist without tours and studio dates and *Rolling Stone* covers for a few weeks so he could think through his options and what direction he was going.

Chance responded in a tirade that had blurred together on the phone screen. The upshot was that Chance believed that unless they moved in more of a mainstream direction, they would become irrelevant in a fast-paced, digitalized world. They'd be competing with YouTube and Meerkat and iTunes instead of topping the charts like they had done consistently over the last fifteen years.

For what it was worth, Brennan really had tried to be logical, to take the emotion out of his thinking. But he kept coming back around to the same idea: a move to mainstream pop was not the kind of music he and Chance and Trey had ever wanted to make. He didn't care if he sank into irrelevance because of it—it was more important for Brennan to be true to himself.

He had tried to explain to Chance that he was at a major crossroads in his life, but apparently, he'd done a piss-poor job of it, because Chance had responded with a single *Fuck you*.

Brennan picked up some daisies and walked down the aisle.

His problems with Chance notwithstanding, he felt good today, especially now that he had something to work with. He'd been waiting for an idea to take root for weeks, and in the last couple of days he'd gotten so annoyed with himself and his lack of creative spark that he'd begun to pick up his room, putting things in their place. Maybe he'd cluttered his head with all that shit on the floor.

This morning, he'd cleared out trash in an effort to find the source of the sour smell that had begun to invade every corner of his suite. He'd gathered up empty beer bottles, crushed Cheetos bags, and a Chinese food container that he vaguely remembered his mother bringing to him completely full.

When he was done, he'd dragged an extra-large bag of trash and a duffel bag full of laundry downstairs.

Magda had glared at him, eyeing the two bags suspiciously.

"Where would you like me to put them?" he'd asked.

"What is it?"

"Trash. Beer bottles, food containers—"

"No food containers in the recycling," she'd said, and snatched the bag from his hand.

"And this is my laundry," he'd said, ignoring how she'd wrinkled her nose at the duffel full of dirty clothing as he let it slide off his shoulder. "I personally picked up the most offensive pieces from the floor of my room and stuffed them in here, hoping some Good Samaritan . . . or paid employee . . . would launder them for me."

Magda had frowned darkly.

"I'd do it myself, but my mother left laundry out of my basic education."

"All right, Mr. Yates."

"It's Brennan," he'd said, and had walked through the kitchen, grabbing a banana off the banana tree, walking past the kitchen table where piles of scrap materials and paint chips had been stacked for the last few days.

It was the twinge of guilt for laying all of that on cranky old Magda that had prompted him to stop at Eckland's for flowers to brighten her day—although he was fairly certain even frolicking puppies couldn't brighten that woman's day.

But it was his day that had been made brighter. Aunt Bev's helper was still dancing around his mind's eye as he paid for the flowers and chatted up the old man.

The image in his mind's eye was telling Brennan he smelled good as he walked out to his car and got in. She was smiling shyly as he headed north with no destination in mind. And her honey-colored eyes were staring up at him when his phone rang.

He punched the Bluetooth button on the steering wheel. "Hello?"

"Don't hang up."

It was Phil, his agent. Had Brennan hung up on him before? The phone calls had begun to run together into one long foggy memory. "I'm not going to hang up," he said. "Did Gary tell you to call me? Because if you're calling to make the band's case for him, you're wasting your—"

"No, no. Listen, something's come up. Something I think you're really going to dig, man."

Brennan doubted it. "What?"

"I've been in touch with a Hollywood producer, Kate Resnick. Heard of her?"

"No."

"You're kidding. Kate is *huge*," Phil said, and rattled off several movies she'd made. Not that any of them meant anything to Brennan, and to Phil, every opportunity, every celebrity, every music exec was *huge*. "She's a big fan of yours, man," he said. "I mean, if you were standing before her she'd drop to her knees and—"

"What do you want, Phil?" Brennan interrupted.

"She's doing this film about that kid who was kidnapped and taken to Mexico, right? The one who lived?"

Brennan vaguely remembered that piece of news from a couple of years back—a rich white kid from San Diego whose father was mixed up in the Mexican drug trade. The cartel kidnapped the kid, and when they got the ransom, they took him out into the desert, shot him, and left him for dead. But he survived and somehow managed to walk out. "I remember."

"Well, she wants you to write the soundtrack to the movie."

Brennan laughed. "I'm not a composer. I've never scored anything."

"Not a score, a soundtrack. She has this idea that some of the narrative will be told in original song. Isn't that great? Great exposure, great opportunity."

Brennan had to pause to think. "Did you run it by Chance?"

"No, man. She doesn't want Tuesday's End, she wants you and you alone to do the soundtrack. I mean, if you want to bring some of the guys in, that's fine. But she wants this to be *your* baby."

The news was so surprising and unexpected that Brennan pulled over onto the side of the road. "Phil—is this for real?"

"Hell yes it's for real!" Phil said, his voice buoyant. "There's a lot of money in it, too. This has the potential to launch you into a whole new category of songwriter, you know what I'm saying?"

This was exactly the sort of vehicle that Brennan needed to test the waters of his creativity. It was a challenge, a path to something new. So many questions and thoughts pinged like a barrage of bullets in his head. There was a lot he had to consider before he would ever commit to something like this, but it felt as if the universe had heard his cry and was responding by dropping this in his lap.

"It's fantastic, right?" Phil asked again, sounding a bit more uncertain.

"It's fantastic," Brennan agreed. He could hardly think, his mind was reeling with the improbability of it all. "Have you mentioned it to Gary?" he asked carefully, referring to the band's manager.

"No, of course not," Phil said. "I won't until you tell me to."

"Please don't until I give you the okay," Brennan said, and released a slow breath. He could just imagine Chance's fury when he heard about this. "I need to think about this, Phil."

"Yep, of course. I'm emailing you the script right now. Take a look, tell me what you think. But let me hear from you. Don't make me chase you down."

"No," Brennan said. "I won't. But give me a few days."

When he'd finished the call, Brennan sat a moment, staring blindly out the windshield, the possibilities racing around his head. It felt as if something had cracked inside of him. Light and sound were slowly filtering into that dark, dank space he'd been filling with booze for the last few weeks.

He finally put the car in gear and pulled out onto the road, driving slowly at first, then accelerating. He flew down the two-lane road, his speed hitting eighty-five. Phil had just cut the shackles from his body. He'd just set Brennan free.

Brennan exploded into a shout of laughter and banged a fist against the steering wheel.

Ten

Brennan read the script, "Out of the Desert," in one night. His head had been filling with ideas for days now. He'd done some reading about Mexican drug cartels and deserts. He was working, filling in sheet after sheet of music notes and tempos. Ideas were turning, growing, feeding off an internal hum. He was finding his groove again.

It was a gorgeous, crystal-clear afternoon, the sky a cobalt blue, the air crisp. He walked out onto the terrace of his suite and turned his face up to the sun while he munched on some baby carrots. It was nice here by the lake. Personally, he couldn't last an entire summer, but it was a good escape for a few weeks. He had to give his mother credit—she'd picked the perfect location for that.

He thought about going down to the lake. Maybe he'd arrange to rent a boat. When had he last been on a boat? Wasn't it off the coast of Capri, with Dave Grohl? Yes, that was it—Dave's daughters had been there, too.

Brennan turned to step back inside, but he happened to catch sight of a lavender bike with a big, wide seat and a handlebar basket leaning against the guardhouse. Through the windows of the guardhouse he could see Drago, his bulky form bent over his phone. Did the bike belong to his mother? It was hard to imagine her on a bike, but then again, it was hard to imagine a lot of what she did. He'd never known she was into karate until a couple of mornings ago.

He decided to walk down to the lake. He waved to Drago as he came outside and followed the brick path around to the back. The north wing of the house ended in a circular sitting room with windows that provided a panoramic view of the woods. The French doors were opened onto a terrace that Brennan had no doubt would be torn up and redone.

He walked in through the doors to have a look. The empty room smelled of paint; he supposed Magda had opened the doors to air out the room. Three cans of paint sat on the floor at a strangely angled brick wall, and on the wall, someone had painted four patches of blue, each one a little lighter than the last. But it wasn't the patches that interested Brennan. It was the painting on the wall beside the patches. Someone had painted a body of water nestled between some hills, all of it different shades of blue. On the surface of the water was a small white boat.

It was a placid little painting that looked a little slapdash, as if someone had been bored and was playing with the paint. Of course Brennan knew who the "someone" was—the same girl who had chronicled her life in drawings in a sketchbook.

A scrape of something behind him caused him to turn. The artist was standing at the threshold, watching him.

"I didn't expect to run into you," he said, surprised to realize how pleased he was that he had.

"I wasn't expecting you, either," she said. "I'm waiting for someone to come up and look at this room so they can give my aunt an estimate for some work. They're late."

"Ah." He looked at the wall again.

"That wall is coming down," she said. "I mean, if you're worried about the paint."

"Nope. Not worried. It is a strange wall," he said. He remembered his mother cornering him one evening when he was buzzed, talking about a wall that should come down, how a larger, open room would be ideal for summer. Brennan could remember thinking that three distinct living areas in one house seemed like at least one too many, and maybe even two.

"So you're doing a little doodling, huh?"

"Doodling," she repeated. "I don't think I've called it that since I was in the first grade, but yeah, something like that. Just seeing what I could do with blue." Mia walked to where he was standing and squatted down, picking up a paintbrush lying across an open can.

He hadn't meant anything by it; he was just making conversation, really. He felt strangely awkward, as if he'd never talked to a pretty girl before.

She glanced at him from the corner of her eye and smiled a little. "So what do you think?" she asked, gesturing to the wall.

"Umm . . ." It was obvious she had some talent, but this scene, dashed up onto a brick wall, was not talented. "Is it Lake Haven?" he asked uncertainly.

She cocked her head to one side and studied the wall, too, as if she wasn't sure. She dabbed a bit of light blue onto darker blue. "I guess it could be." She gave him another sidelong look. "So? What do you think?"

Was she really asking for his opinion? Brennan looked at the fleck of paint on her cheek. "It's nice," he said.

Her eyes suddenly danced with light and she giggled. "No, it's not."

"No?" he asked, feeling uneasy now. What was he supposed to say?

"You know what I think it looks like? A high school art project. *Lake in Blue,*" she said dramatically, as if announcing the painting at a show.

"I didn't think that—"

"Well if you didn't, you should have. It's really amateurish. Boring. But, in my defense, I only had blue." She smiled and held up the paintbrush.

"It may be amateurish, but I've never seen such a good use of one color. You obviously have talent."

"Mmm. That's debatable," she said skeptically. She dipped down again, dabbed the brush into another small can of paint, and then stood up. She leaned to one side, intending to dab more paint on the wall. But she misjudged where she was in relation to the paint cans, and tried to hop over them to keep from stumbling. She was too late; she stumbled and Brennan caught her arm to keep her from falling, and her wet paintbrush connected with his belly.

"Oh my God!" She stared with horror at the smear of paint on his T-shirt. "I am so sorry!"

"Don't be," he said, looking down. "It's just a T-shirt."

"Yes, but it's a *clean* T-shirt and I don't think you have a lot of those. Take it off. I've got a little turpentine. I can get the paint off as long as it's wet."

"That's not—"

"Take it off!"

"Okay, okay." Brennan took it off. "This shirt is nothing special . . . other than clean, apparently."

She wasn't listening. She was down on her knees with the paint cans. She'd put the brush aside and was pouring a bit of turpentine onto a rag. She looked up, her hand outstretched for the shirt . . . but her gaze landed on his torso, and she faltered. He could practically feel her gaze sliding down his chest, lingering at his waistline. Her cheeks turned red.

"Hello?" he said.

She snatched his shirt and turned her full attention to it, although the red in her cheeks just seemed to get brighter. "I'm *so* sorry," she said again, and quickly came to her feet. She bent over the shirt, dabbing at the bit of paint on his shirt with the corner of the towel. "Painting 101, don't smear it on other people. I could die."

"Don't die. You have to finish this wall."

She glanced up at him; Brennan merely smiled. Her blush deep-ened even more and she concentrated on the shirt again. "You are tal-ented, Mia," Brennan said. Hell, he didn't know how talented she was, but from what he'd seen of her drawings, it looked like talent to him.

She shrugged. "Maybe a little." She handed him his T-shirt. It stunk now.

"If Magda puts it in the wash right away, I hope the rest will come off," she said, and eyed his chest again.

Brennan could feel her gaze on the inside, tingling through his veins. He could feel it on his skin, could feel the path her eyes took. For a man who had stood on a stage without a shirt and knew that women ogled him, he was unusually shy. But then again, in all those times, he couldn't recall actually *feeling* a look quite as intimately as he was feel-ing this one.

"You know, Mia . . . if you believe you only have a little talent, that's what you'll have. You have to believe in yourself. No one else will if you don't."

Mia blinked. A smile suddenly lightened her face. "Oh *no*," she said with mock gravity as he pulled the T-shirt on over his head. "A *pep* talk. Allow me to spare you the effort, because I've had quite a lot of them from well-meaning people lately. But here's the thing—I've been at this a very long time. I know what my talent is. And you know what? I couldn't cut it."

"You won't know if you don't—"

"Try," she finished for him. "I did. Hey, it's the truth and I can say it," she said to his look of surprise. "Not everyone is cut out to be a world-class artist. My work lacks vision, among other things. Trust me on this—I have a degree in fine art and I know what I'm talking about."

She turned around and stooped down to put the lids back on the paint cans.

Putting aside, for the moment, that she wasn't buying what he was selling—another new experience for Brennan outside the tiny realm of his mother—he wasn't sure if she wanted him to argue or not. Quite unexpectedly, he understood this unusual woman, because he felt the same way about music. For every true musician he'd known in his life, he'd known ten more who worked hard at music but would never discover some innate talent for it.

On the other hand, he also knew that the song he was currently trying to find in him was nothing but a few chords right now, and it would probably sound very amateurish to Mia if he were to hum it. The difference was that he was older than she and probably more experienced. He'd been making music long enough to know that it would turn into something real. He'd learned to trust his talent. He'd learned to keep hammering away at it until it became something.

He looked again at the wall. "Tell me, what do you see in your painting?" he asked curiously.

She snorted. "I know what I don't see."

"What?"

"There's no movement to it. No story. Not that I would expect that, given that I have four cans of paint and nothing to help create the movement. But that world? It looks like it is stuck in molasses. Without movement, it lacks soul."

"Maybe your true talent is art criticism," he said solemnly.

She giggled, her gaze still on the wall.

Brennan couldn't help himself. He put his hand on her shoulder. Mia flinched, but she didn't move away. "Relax," he said, and let his hand slip away from her shoulder. It didn't belong there. "Let the work come. Don't worry over it, just relax."

"Maybe your talent is art instruction," she said with a saucy sidelong look.

"Smartass," he said with a grin. "I'm only trying to help. You always seem so keyed up when it comes to your work."

"Are you kidding? How do *you* know?" she asked with a disbelieving laugh. "What do you know about my work?"

"Only that every time I look at something you've done, you tense up. Look, I'm just offering a piece of advice from experience. If the vibe is missing, it will come to you."

"An art instructor *and* a philosopher," she said cheerfully. "Who knew?" She used the back of her hand to push her hair back, managing to smear another dash of paint across her cheek.

"Laugh if you will, but I really am both of those things. I'm a musician. So I guess I know a little something about the artistic journey."

Mia suddenly burst out laughing. "You're a *what*?" she cried, and laughed again. Her face transformed with her amusement—she was beautiful when she laughed.

"What?" he asked, unable to suppress his laugh, too. "What's so damn funny?"

"Nothing, nothing." She held up her hand as she tried to quell her laughter. "Far be it from me to—oh come on, *really*? You're a *musician*?" She tried to contain another laugh but it came out as a snort.

"Is that so hard to believe?" he asked, smiling, infected by her mirth. "Why not a musician? I write songs."

"Ooh, okay, a songwriter," she said gaily. "Now it's totally believable."

Brennan didn't know what to say.

"What kind of songs, anyway?"

He shrugged. "Love songs. Songs about people and emotions."

"*Nice.* So *that's* what you've been doing upstairs all this time. And here I thought you were watching endless loops of *Jeopardy.*"

"Give me a break," he said, grinning. Brennan sort of liked that she didn't believe him, and he didn't correct her. "I've been drinking and sleeping."

"Aha! I like a man with priorities," she said with happy skepticism. "You like music, right?"

"Sure," she said. "Mostly classical. Give me Bach over the radio any day."

Well that explained it. No wonder he didn't look even vaguely familiar to her.

"So tell me, Music Man . . . do you relax and let the vibe come to you?" She laughed again at her ribbing.

"I try."

"Maybe you can play some of your songs for me sometime. Do you play an instrument?"

"How do you think music is made?"

"I don't know," she said. "Computer?"

"I play a little guitar, a little piano."

"Good for you!"

She said it in a tone one would use to encourage a small child. He knew she believed him to be a slacker with grandiose visions of himself. He would have said as much, but Mia's sparkling gaze was locked on his, and Brennan lost his train of thought. He seemed to forget everything but those eyes shining up at him. He realized what he was doing and abruptly looked down at the wet spot of turpentine. "I better leave you to find your vibe while I find mine."

"Good luck with that," she said merrily.

"You too," he said, and pointed at the wall as he started for the door. "Because that wall is going to need it."

She laughed, the sound of it light and amused. It was the sound of happiness, which was something Brennan hadn't heard in a while now. He liked it. It made him feel warm.

He paused at the open French door to look back at her. She was staring at the wall, her head cocked to one side, a finger tapping against her bottom lip. He looked at her bare, shapely legs that ended inside a pair of Converse high tops. He looked at the snug fit of her skirt, and how the hem swung around her knees. At the flowing silk top she wore with it. His gaze moved to the skirt again, because he was a guy, and he couldn't help himself . . . and that was when he realized the fabric was familiar to him.

He walked on, remembering—he'd seen that same pattern on the kitchen table.

The girl was wearing a skirt made from an upholstery sample.

Maybe it wouldn't be so bad having her around for the renovations. It might actually be amusing. Maybe Brennan would discuss starting small with his mom. Nothing too loud and drastic. But enough to keep Mia coming up here every day.

He would like that.

Eleven

It was family tradition for Mia's entire extended family to meet every Monday night at Grandma and Grandpa's house for a potluck dinner.

This Monday night, when Mia arrived with Derek, her mother met them at the screen door dressed in dark green ankle pants with tiny yellow flowers that matched her yellow sweater set. Her golden-red bob of hair was tucked neatly behind her ears.

"Hey, Mom," Derek said, bending low to kiss her cheek. "Guess what? Mia's getting an apartment."

Mia gaped at her big brother. "Are you kidding me right now?" she demanded, and Derek snatched her hat from her head and twirled it on his finger. "I told you not to say anything!" Mia tried to snatch the hat back, but Derek held it high over her head.

"An *apartment*?" Mia's mother exclaimed. "You can't afford an apartment! What's wrong with your room?"

Mia gave her brother a sideways kick to the ankle. "I'm almost twenty-eight, Mom. I'm too old to live at home."

"Who is?" Skylar had emerged from the kitchen, eating from a bag of chips. She had that glassy look, the same one she'd get when she'd smoke pot in the school parking lot before class.

Mia's mother ignored Skylar and glared at her daughter. Her hands found her hips as Derek stuffed Mia's hat back on her head. "You have no business getting an apartment."

"You're getting an apartment? Why didn't you say so?" Skylar exclaimed. "We could have gotten one together." She held out the bag of chips to Mia.

"No, we couldn't." Mia took some chips, then pushed the bag away.

"Your father and I are more than happy to let you save up to get back on your feet," her mother said petulantly. "He even made that studio for you out back!"

Mia laughed. "He moved the riding mower out of the shed and set up an easel. It's not exactly a studio."

"You know what I mean. It's at least a place you can have some peace and quiet to work on your art."

The only problem was that Mia *wasn't* working on her art. She felt stifled in her family home, a thousand steps backward from the woman she'd been in New York.

"I'll take her place, Aunt Randa," Skylar said, shifting closer to Mia to share the bag of chips. She did indeed smell faintly of marijuana. "I'm thinking of writing a book. I could use the shed for that."

"I don't think my brother is going to agree to that," Mia's mother said, referring to Skylar's dad.

Skylar shrugged. "Maybe Grandma and Grandpa will let you have one of the cottages," she suggested to Mia.

Their grandparents owned and operated the East Beach Lake Cottages, four one-bedroom cottages just below the pine trees on the edge of the beach. Grandma and Grandpa's Victorian house with its enormous wraparound porch was nearby. This was where Mia had grown up—she'd spent summers here with her brothers and cousins in this house. She'd built snowmen with Grandpa, chased fireflies into the lake on long summer nights, had celebrated birthdays and holidays here. All of their lives were well documented by framed photos that hung on a long hallway wall, which Mia's oldest brother, Mike, called the wall of shame.

"Living in a cottage would be like living at home. Only Grandma would be watching me instead of you."

"I don't remember inviting you to live in one," Grandma said as she puttered into the living room with a crystal bowl newly refreshed with the soft, pastel-colored mints commonly found in nursing homes and octogenarian living rooms. She was a tiny thing, with a white head of hair. She was wearing red Keds—a shoe she'd been partial to for as long as Mia could remember. "Why do you need a cottage anyway?" her grandmother asked.

"Apparently, she thinks living with her father and me makes her a loser," Mia's mother snapped as she sailed off into the kitchen.

Mia sighed, then fixed a pointed look on Derek. "Happy now?"

"Totally," he said.

"You could come and live at our house," Skylar suggested.

"Well, I don't think *that's* a good idea," Grandma said. "And right now, you need to go help your aunt." She pointed toward the kitchen. "You," she said to Derek, "go and find your brother."

"What'd I do?" Derek asked, but he swiped up a half-drunk beer from the entry console and went out.

"I've got to put the rolls in," Grandma said. "Mia, you can toss a salad—What is all that racket?"

Someone was climbing up the porch steps.

"Hel-*lo*!" Aunt Amy was standing at the screen door, her forehead touching it, and one hand cupped around her eyes as she peered in. "Mia! Can you open the door? Our hands are full."

Behind Aunt Amy was her daughter Emily with her two young children, Ethan and Elijah. Ethan was about two years old, Elijah six months old. He was strapped into a stroller. Both Emily and Aunt Amy wore Lululemon running tights and jackets. Aunt Amy had swept her blonde hair into a ponytail and wore a pink ballcap. She'd probably run five miles this afternoon. Emily had styled her short dark hair and was wearing makeup. Emily had not run five miles since high school cross-country.

Mia opened the door for them. "There's Cousin Mia," Emily sang as she unstrapped Elijah from the stroller and handed him to Mia. He gave Mia a big, toothless grin.

"That's an interesting hat," Emily said to Mia. Her slender nose crinkled as she stared at Mia's repurposed fedora.

"I *like* it," Aunt Amy said a bit defensively as she stepped into the house.

"I just said it was interesting," Emily said.

"Hey, weirdo," said Skylar, having escaped the kitchen again. She wrapped Emily in a tight hug. Then said, "Let me see that baby," as Ethan darted past Mia into the kitchen. She took Elijah from Mia's arms.

"Mia, guess who is getting married?" Emily asked as Skylar covered Elijah's face with kisses. "Frederica Holland. She's marrying a *millionaire*. He has a house on Greystone Drive. She met him at the beach last summer and now they're getting married."

"Okay," Mia said. Freddie Holland had been the valedictorian of her class. Mia had hardly known her.

"*You* should totally find a millionaire," Emily said, as if one just went down to the corner store and picked one up.

"Right. Because every woman's goal should be to marry rich," Mia scoffed.

"Well if you want to be an artist, it might not hurt," her father called from the kitchen, apparently having arrived by way of the back door.

"Anyway," Emily said, "she's getting married and I need a dress for the wedding. Will you make me one?"

"You want one of *her* dresses?" Derek asked, passing by them to open the screen door for his wife, Tamra.

"Not one of *hers*," Emily said. "One that I would wear. No offense," she hastily added to Mia.

"I'll try not to take any."

"Hello, everyone," Tamra said as she stepped inside. She was several months pregnant and had one hand on her distended belly, the other firmly wrapped around the wrist of her five-year-old son, Hayden. Ethan ran out of the kitchen, his steps slowing as he took in Hayden. Hayden was oblivious to the toddler, however, as he had spotted some toys on the lower shelf of Grandma's entry console.

"Skylar, I heard you'd come back. Good to see you." Unlike the rest of the rowdy McCauley-Lassiter-Painter clan, Tamra was very reserved. What wasn't reserved was her beauty—she had pale-blue eyes and blonde hair.

"Come in, everyone!" Grandma called. "Let's eat before it gets cold!"

As the family came in from other rooms and outside, there was the usual confusion about where the children would sit, who needed to be on the ends, until everyone found a seat. Derek was dispatched to find Uncle John, and the two of them came in together, sliding into their seats just as Grandma began to say grace. She was almost through when Mia's brother Mike flew in the back door and skidded to a halt at an empty chair next to Mia, bowing his head as Grandma finished.

"Glad you could make it, Mikey," Grandma drawled, and picked up a huge bowl of mashed potatoes.

"Are you kidding? I never miss your cooking, Grandma." He looked at Mia. "Nice hat."

"Shut up," Mia said, smiling.

"Grandpa said to start without him," Mike said as he took the bowl of potatoes from Grandma and put a huge serving on his plate. He passed the bowl to Mia. "They haven't finished the work on number two cottage."

"Speaking of that," Grandma said, "do you know who is doing the work for Grandpa, Mia?"

Mia blinked. "No. Should I?"

"Jesse Fisher," Grandma said and smiled slyly. "You remember him, don't you?"

"Of course I remember him. I grew up with him," Mia said. Jesse was a jock—he'd played football and basketball, and he'd dated all the popular girls. Mia had not been in his stratosphere. She'd been the furthest thing from the kind of world Jesse lived in as a girl could get.

"*I* remember him. He was a *cutie*," Skylar said with enthusiasm.

"He owns a construction company now," Emily said.

"I mention him because I thought maybe you'd want to come by some afternoon and say hi to him," Grandma said to Mia. "He is the *nicest* young man—"

"Grandma, *no*," Mia said sternly, and put the platter of chicken down so firmly that her glass rattled.

"I'm just saying," Grandma said, unruffled. "There are a lot of nice young men in East Beach. Did you hear about Freddie Holland?"

"Yes, I heard about Freddie Holland," Mia said, trying not to let her annoyance show.

"I really like Jesse, and he's not married," Grandma blithely continued.

"No matchmaking, Mother," Mia's mom said. "I thought we'd agreed."

"What?" Mia asked, confused, but the sound of the screen door slamming shut startled them all. They heard the familiar footfall of Aunt Bev striding across the living room, and then she burst into the dining room carrying a cake pan. "Could you not wait five minutes?" she demanded of everyone. "John, I told you I was on my way!"

"Calm down, Bev. We just sat down," said Aunt Amy. She smiled and held up a plate to her sister-in-law.

"You will not believe what's happened!" Aunt Bev announced grandly, forgetting her impatience. She slapped the pan onto the long table and took the plate. "I got the bid. I *got* the *bid*!"

"You have to explain what you're talking about, Mom. No one can read your mind," Skylar said.

"The Ross house!"

"The Ross house," Emily repeated thoughtfully. "Is that the one the Saudi sheik bought?"

"Close, Emily. But it was actually a crazy bitch from Seattle."

"Beverly!" Grandma protested.

"Well, she is," Aunt Bev insisted as she shed her sweater and purse. "Anyway, that woman has been stalling me and stalling me, but I put together a *great* bid, and she called this afternoon and said we could do this in stages. The north wing first, then the south. She's sending the retainer down tomorrow and we can get started right away."

"Way to go, Bev," Uncle John said, and lifted his hand, which Aunt Bev promptly high-fived.

Aunt Bev leaned across the table and heaped some mashed potatoes onto her plate. "Even better, Mia is going to be our on-site representative."

Mia's fork froze midway to her mouth. "I am?"

"You are. All you have to do is report what's going on every day. I'll schedule everything, and if anything comes up, I'll handle it."

"Aunt Bev—"

"Now, Mia, I know the woman is a little looney, but you'll be fine."

"It's not the woman, it's her crazy son she's afraid of," Skylar said with a snort. Surprised, Mia looked at her cousin. How would Skylar know? *Wallace.* His gums had been flapping again. Mia reminded herself not to talk to Wallace about anything that mattered.

"Her son?" Mia's father asked, looking at Mia. He had that look in his eye, that worry that he'd carried for months after the summer of Mia's senior year.

"Mia discovered him up there," Skylar said. "Nancy Yates never even mentioned him!"

Wallace was thorough in his report, apparently.

"I don't always mention my children, either," Grandma said.

"What—are you worried about *him?*" Aunt Bev asked, and waved a spoon at Mia. "Oh, Mia, you wouldn't believe some of the stuff Wallace and I have seen. Not to worry, sweetie. The son is probably just passing through. None of those rich kids ever stay out here for long."

"My theory? He's a mama's boy with issues," Skylar suggested.

Mia regretted ever mentioning Brennan to anyone. She wished she'd given him the benefit of the doubt instead of jumping to conclusions about him. "That's not really true," she tried.

"I've figured it out," Skylar continued, pointing a fork at Mia. "He's an addict. Addicts are paranoid and erratic. Trust me, I've known a couple."

"An addict!" Mia's mother exclaimed. "I don't like the sound of that, Bev."

"He's not paranoid. Not in the classical sense," Mia said. Whatever that meant.

"He's harmless," Aunt Bev scoffed, even though she'd never met him. "He's probably one of those summer people who thinks his eccentricity is charming."

"I wouldn't be surprised if he's cooking meth up there," Skylar said darkly.

"God, Skylar," Mia said, and laughed. "No one is cooking meth up there. Drago Kemper is the security guard and he would never allow it."

"Just hear me out," Skylar said. "It's a huge house. And you told Wallace he looks drugged out half the time."

"I said he looked *tired,*" Mia corrected her. At least she hoped that's what she'd said. She wanted to add that he'd looked completely different in Eckland's. And again today, in that empty room, looking at her stupid wall. He'd looked . . . *sexy.* That was it. His body was so hot, and when those blue eyes locked on her . . . a tiny shiver flitted up Mia's spine and spread warmly into her cheeks.

"Maybe it's agoraphobia," Aunt Amy said. "I saw that on *Dr. Phil* once. Agoraphobes don't like to be around people."

"You're mixing up your phobias, Mom," Emily said.

"Maybe he's just a jerk," Aunt Bev said with a shrug. "It's probably nothing more complicated than that."

"He also could be recovering from something. A death in the family?" Mia's mother suggested.

"Oh, poor baby," Derek said. "It's like, if you have money, you have the luxury of wallowing in heartbreak. The rest of us have to get back to work."

"Well if *that's* it, he'll probably take off on one of those eat, pray, love things before long," Aunt Amy said. "And then you won't have to worry about it, Mia. Listen, one thing is for sure—he's not going to hang around boring East Beach. Pass the ham, please."

"Why don't you just befriend him, honey?" Mia's mother asked.

"Better yet, invite him into town so we can all get a really good look at him," Emily said brightly.

"No," Mia said flatly. "You're all making a big deal out of nothing. You know how Wallace embellishes anything said to him. The truth is I hardly see the guy. It's not that bad."

"Hey, *you're* the one who complained about how rude and smelly he was," Skylar reminded her.

Well thank you, Wallace, for leaving no word of the story untold.

"I don't care how *smelly* he is, I need you, Mia. Nancy really likes you. I am not going to lose this deal because you think her son stinks."

"She *likes* me?" Mia said, mystified by that. She'd spoken to Nancy only a handful of times.

"Yeah," Mike said. "Has she noticed what Mia wears?"

"She likes it," Aunt Bev said to Mike. "She understands that Mia marches to the beat of her own drummer."

"Hello, I'm right here," Mia said, gesturing to herself.

"I march to my own beat, too," Skylar said, unwilling to share everyone's attention with Mia. "But I am going to use *my* individuality to get a gig with the music festival."

"Good luck with that," Aunt Amy said.

"What about transportation?" Mia asked her aunt. "Wallace doesn't want to take me every day."

"Ride the bike," her brother Mike said. "It's only a mile from your new apartment, right?"

"Apartment? What apartment?" Mia's father demanded.

"Mia's moving out, Dad. Can't take the heat."

"Since when?" her dad demanded of her mother.

"We'll work it out, Mia," Aunt Bev said imperiously. "In the meantime, ride the bike."

"No one said anything to *me* about an apartment," Mia's father groused. "I don't know why I'm always the last to know anything."

"Would everyone just pipe down?" Aunt Bev demanded. "I just got a *huge* job. Can we worry about bikes and cars and who is moving where later? I think a toast is in order."

"Beverly is right," Mia's mother said. "We should always celebrate the good and cling to that when the bad comes around. Cheers, Bev!" she said, and lifted her wine glass to her sister-in-law.

"*Cheers!*" everyone chimed in.

"Cheers," Mia said, a little less enthusiastically.

Twelve

That weekend, Mia's brothers and parents helped her move into her garage apartment, which was completely unnecessary, given that she had only two suitcases, a few boxes, and her easel. She could have handled everything but the ancient sewing machine she'd bought with the money she'd earned working at the bistro in high school.

"Pretty isolated out here," Mike said, looking around after he tossed a box onto the bed.

"Yes. But it's peaceful," Mia pointed out.

"You're not very far from the north beach here, are you?" her mother asked as she stepped inside from the balcony, and exchanged a look with her husband.

Mia's face flushed with the reminder of that awful summer. "I don't think about it," she said, averting her gaze from everyone.

Her mother apparently thought about it. She hugged Mia, then patted her cheek. "I don't like you being out here by yourself, sweetheart. I wish you'd stayed at home. We loved having you and it's not the end of the world to need to lean on your parents for a little while."

Mia felt like a kid just then, a fragile little flower they were all worried about. When had that happened? When had they gone from not worrying about her while she was living in a dicey part of Brooklyn to worrying that she couldn't cut it on the north end of East Beach because of what happened nearly ten years ago?

◆ ◆ ◆

On Monday morning, Mia reported to work, riding up the hill to the Ross house on the bike Mike had found her, huffing and puffing until she reached the gate and could coast down to the house.

The first wave of demolition and tear out was to begin that morning. "You keep a close eye on those crews," Aunt Bev instructed her. "You call me the moment something doesn't go right, and trust me, something is not going to go right. I told Dave Karpinski he better not send up a bunch of day laborers who don't know what they're doing."

"I don't know what I'm doing," Mia pointed out.

"That's different." Aunt Bev waggled her bejeweled fingers at her. "*You* know when to call me. Say that you know when to call me."

"I know when to call you," Mia had said dutifully.

Shortly after noon, Aunt Bev phoned. "You haven't called me."

"Because no one has come," Mia said.

Aunt Bev responded with a string of expletives and hung up.

Not only had no one come, no one seemed to be around. Mia was a little nuts, because every sound she heard brought her head up and a flutter in her veins, thinking it would be Brennan. Unfortunately—or fortunately?—she never saw him.

No one showed up the next day, either. Nancy left bright and early with a cheery *ta-ta*. And still, no Brennan, which, surprisingly, disappointed Mia more than she cared to admit. She was intrigued by the man she'd seen at Eckland's and the one who had looked at her story-less, bland wall painting. Forget the painting, she wanted to know more about *that* guy. But if he was lurking around, he was doing a good job of hiding from her. She was certain she would have run into him at some point, especially since all she did was wander around from one room to the next. Once, she thought she heard the strings of a guitar drifting out of a window, but when she went outside to listen, she couldn't hear anything and supposed she'd imagined it.

Maybe he was camped out upstairs. Nancy had expressly asked her not to go up to the living quarters. "That will be our third phase of renovation," she'd said. "But I'd like to keep it off-limits for now."

"I can only imagine the hoops I'm going to have to jump through to get *that* redo," Aunt Bev groused when Mia told her about it later.

Mia had taken her frustration out on her lifeless wall mural. She mixed more blues and applied more paint, but that didn't fix it. So she loaded some paints in the basket of her bike and brought them up, her lungs and legs heaving the last few yards to the gate.

The new paints didn't help. It seemed like no matter what she tried, the painting looked increasingly amateurish. It began to take on that desperate look of an artist trying too hard to be relevant. Whatever that meant, really, but if Mia had to define that look, she'd say that stupid wall was it.

She abandoned the painting and took to wandering around the grounds.

On Thursday, Mia reached the gate, perspiring quite nicely in the humid air. As she rolled through the gates, she saw a truck waiting in the drive and Drago talking to the driver. She almost leapt off her bike with joy—at last, something to *do*. She rolled past Drago and hopped off her bike. Four men were crammed onto the single bench inside the truck.

The driver's gaze flicked over her, casually taking in the dress she'd made with one sleeve, a gathering on one side of her waist, and the asymmetrical hem. She was wearing a sun hat, too, which she'd festooned with flowers from Dalton's garden.

"It's the demo crew," Drago said.

"That's great!" Mia said cheerfully. "Follow me." She wheeled her bike to the guardhouse and picked up her lunch bag from the basket.

When she turned back to the truck, she saw that the men inside the truck were laughing. At her.

Mia's face turned hot. There was a time in her life, in the not-too-distant past, where that sort of laughter had hurt her. Not anymore. Mia knew who she was. *Screw them*, she told herself. *They don't appreciate an artistic view of proportion and volume in plaid.*

The men's first task was to strip the wallpaper, which the men piled on the broken-up terrace. They worked through the morning, and when they took a lunch break, settling down under a big sycamore tree, one of the men said, "You wanna sit with us?"

The other men seemed amused by that, and it made her uncomfortable.

"No thanks. I have some things I need to do," she lied. She held up her sketchbook as if it was an important item, then set off with it and her thermal lunch bag. She went around the corner of the house and took a newly cleared path down to the bluffs.

When she reached Lookout Point, she dropped her things on the bench, then walked to the edge and stood there, enjoying the feel of the breeze lifting her hair and her skirt. She idly wondered if she would ever have the guts to jump into the lake like she had when she'd been a fearless kid. Probably not. Jumping hadn't scared her then. Now, different things scared her. Like broken limbs. Broken hearts. Broken dreams.

She was hungry. Mia returned to the bench, tossed her hat onto the grass, and set her lunch bag next to her. She opened her sketchbook and began to draw.

"Mind if I join you?"

The sound of Brennan's voice startled her so badly that Mia almost fumbled her sketchbook right off her lap as she leapt to her feet. "Yes!" she said quickly.

He hesitated.

"Wait, *no*. I mean," she said, making herself take a breath, "please do." She swept her hand gregariously toward the bench.

"Are you sure? I'm not interrupting you, am I?" he asked, nodding at her sketchbook.

"What, this? Not at all. I was just doodling."

"I didn't think you used that word." He walked around to the bench, and sat down. Mia did, too. She tried not to stare at him, but she couldn't help herself. He was clean shaven today, the beard gone, and his jawline was much squarer than she had realized. He was wearing jeans and sandals, and a shirt he'd only partially tucked into the waist. He'd pulled his hair back into a little ponytail at his nape. He looked hip. Hip and *hot*. And Mia was alarmed by how ridiculously delighted she was to see him.

He tilted his head to one side, smiling with curious amusement at her study of him. "What's up? Do I have something on my face?" he asked, and touched two fingers to his cheek.

"Nope," she said, trying to sound nonchalant. "Sandwich?"

He looked startled. Well, of course he was—who offered a sandwich like that? But he glanced at her industrial-sized lunch bag and said, "So you're brown bagging it."

"This," she said, pointing at the bag, "is a time-tested money-saving technique. That, and I don't have a car, so it makes going into town for lunch difficult."

"What about the van guy?" he asked as he opened the top of her bag to peek inside.

"Who, Wallace? He has clients. And he's kind of persnickety about driving people around."

"So I've heard through an open window or two. I guess that makes you the owner of the purple bike."

"That would be me."

"I'm glad to hear it," he said with a crooked grin. "I was having a hard time picturing Drago on it."

She grinned at the image of Drago's beefy form on the bike.

"You're riding up from town?" he asked. "That's a long hill."

"Actually . . . I took that apartment," she said, avoiding his gaze as she dug in her lunch bag. "The one by Eckland's?"

"I remember."

She glanced up; his navy eyes were studying her.

"I know what you're thinking," she said.

"Yeah?" He shifted around so that he was facing her and draped one arm over the back of the bench. "What am I thinking?"

"That I should have gone back to the city. That I won't find my groove here."

"I wasn't thinking that at all," he said, and smiled in a way that waved through Mia's belly. "I was thinking how rude it would be to take your sandwich. And I know how strongly you feel about rude."

Something warm began to wrap itself around Mia's ribs and hold tightly. "It's not rude if I offered it. And besides, I have two."

His eyes widened with surprise.

"You know . . . in case I'm stuck here."

"Stuck?" His eyes shone with amusement.

"Delayed?" she amended. "Between you and me, that crew doesn't seem like they're in a very big hurry to strip all that wallpaper."

"Ah. How about I make you a deal," he said, peering into the contents of her bag. "If you get stuck, I'll make you a sandwich."

How odd that only a week ago, she would have been appalled to touch anything he'd touched, but today, his offer of a sandwich sounded like a five-star dining experience. "What kind?"

"What kind do you want?"

"Gourmet," she said. "What I'm giving you can't be replaced by just any old bologna."

"You have a deal, Aunt Bev's helper."

Mia grinned. She reached into her lunch bag and pulled out the sandwich and handed it to him.

Brennan unwrapped it and gave it a look.

"It's multigrain bread, sprouts, ham, and cheese. And the ham is uncured and local. I mean, if you're into that sort of thing."

"Are you kidding? My favorite kind of ham just happens to be pig, in all its forms." He took a bite of it and nodded. "It's good. Thank you. I hope I can live up to this. My idea of gourmet is PB and J."

"You tricked me!"

He shrugged. "I was hungry."

Mia knew she was smiling like a girl who'd just won a giant teddy bear at a county fair. She wasn't falling for this guy, was she? No, no, absolutely not—had she forgotten he'd been a royal jerk just last week? Not only that, he was summer people. Girls like her didn't fall for guys like him. Period.

"By the way, I owe you another kind of thank you, I think," he said.

Unless he turned out to be a nice guy. Then maybe. But surely this couldn't be the same man she'd met at the beginning of this job. "Another thank you? This is my lucky day."

"You woke me up. I owe you for that."

A tingle of self-consciousness slipped through her. "You heard me shouting at Wallace. I'm sorry about that. He just makes me so *mad—*"

"The van guy?" He laughed. "No, I'm speaking in more cerebral terms. You woke me up from a major funk. And if you hadn't, I don't know how far into that funk I would have gone."

"I did?" That was an amazing admission. And a little unbelievable, given how she'd tried to avoid him completely in the beginning.

"You did." He eyed her as he took another bite of sandwich. "I think it's safe to say that for the last few weeks, I haven't been myself. But I think I'm back in the land of the living, and I owe that, in part, to you."

"No way. I hardly spoke to you."

"I know." He bumped his fist against her hand. "You very plainly pointed out what I was becoming, and I didn't like it. So . . . I started to get my act together."

Mia blushed self-consciously. "You mean, you didn't smell yourself?" she asked teasingly.

A laugh burst from his lips. "No," he said. He touched the earring dangling at her lobe. "I needed someone to tell me."

Now she was feeling all fluttery and pleased with herself . . . but she was also curious as to why he'd been in such a major funk. "Of course now I'm dying to know why you were so . . ." She made a whirling gesture with her hand at him.

He flicked the little teardrop of her earring. "It wasn't any one thing. Sometimes, life gets you down."

"Right." She knew that feeling. Life had certainly gotten her down in the last few months. Life had put her on the floor the summer of her senior year.

"A couple of things happened," he added with a halfhearted shrug. "One of my best friends died of a drug overdose, for one."

Mia gasped softly.

"That definitely put things in a new perspective for me," he said. "It made me ask the age-old question: What's it all about?" He smiled sheepishly. "I came to the conclusion that even though I've had some success in life, my success hasn't matched my potential, and I needed to do something about it."

"That's heavy." Mia was riveted. Not only by the look in his eyes, but the fact he was voicing aloud the same things she had wondered from time to time.

"I was sliding into a hole, and I began to fear that if I slid too far, I wouldn't be able to find my way back. I didn't know what was ahead of me, I wasn't sure about the way back, and . . . well, it got the best of me."

That was exactly what had happened to her. What *was* happening to her? "Were you into something . . . dangerous?" she asked, her mind racing around what sort of wrong path he'd gone down. Drugs, crime—it could be any number of things.

"What? No," he said, and chuckled. "I mean in a more philosophical sense. Forget it, Mia. You must think I'm a real nut job. And if you do, not to worry—so does my mom." He smiled.

She didn't think he was a nut job. She thought he was fascinating in a way that surprised her. "Do you know what's ahead of you now?"

He laughed. "No clue. But at least there is some light. And I'm working again. It's slow going, but I'm working, and that's a huge improvement over the last several weeks." He brushed his fingers against her cheek and held her gaze for a long moment. Mia thought he was going to say something more. She thought, in a sliver of space that seemed to catch between reality and imagination, that he was going to kiss her. But Brennan shifted around and took another bite of his sandwich, and looked out over the lake.

Of course he wasn't going to kiss her. Why would he? That was ridiculous.

"Looks like you've been working, too," he said. "I checked out the mural on my way down here." He glanced at her sidelong. "You've added a few things. Am I wrong, or is some guy now hanging from a tree on the beach?"

"Oh that," Mia said with a dismissive flick of her wrist. She hated that thing now. It was true that she had painted a hanging victim both as a story prop and as a symbol of how she'd hanged herself pursuing an art career. "I was just passing time. The crews didn't show up earlier this week when they were supposed to, and I was kind of bored, so . . . I hung him."

"I noticed. The whole thing looked a little angrier to me. The lake looked angry. The sky looked angry. The woman in the chaise longue staring at me looked absolutely furious. That wasn't anyone we know, was it?"

She'd forgotten the hastily added self-portrait. His remarks were a revelation. "You know, you're *right*. I hadn't realized how pissed off that scene is."

He laughed again at her surprise. "There is something familiar about that painting. Reminds me of a similar painting I saw at a bistro in town. My mother finally managed to drag me out one night. I noticed a painting there with a similar view of Lake Haven. It's a little more cheerful, however."

That damn painting. Warmth flooded Mia's face. "The Lakeside Bistro," she said.

"Right."

"My parents own it."

"Oh yeah?" he said, smiling with surprise. "I'm no expert, but I thought there were some similarities. I have to say, I liked the happy Lake Haven. It made me want to buy a boat."

Mia had never explained to anyone what that painting meant to her, and especially not her parents. But she looked at Brennan and said, "Would you like to hear the God's honest truth about that painting?"

He blinked. "Yeah."

"It's a view of Lake Haven I absolutely love—it's the view from my grandmother's porch, which is just below the bluff here," she said, pointing to the lake. "I have always loved the lake at sunset. The water looks so pretty then, with the coral and gold of refracted sunlight turning to deep greens and browns in the shadows. And the hills in the background are always the perfect shade of blue." She'd painted hazy forms of distant houses dotting the lake's southern shore. And there was a ghostly form of a sailboat puttering back to dock.

"I agree. I thought it was beautiful."

"It's okay," she said. "It was my senior oil-on-canvas project and it took me weeks to perfect. I thought it was some of the best work I'd ever done. I can honestly say I've never been prouder of another piece."

"You should be. That's pretty cool to have your painting hang in a local restaurant," he said.

"Right." She looked down at her lap.

Brennan touched her hand. "So what's wrong?"

Mia looked at Brennan. "It's my parents' restaurant."

"Still—"

"No, you don't get it."

"Then tell me," he said. He looked interested. He was listening.

"That painting was good enough to be included in the student auction at Benjamin Autry Art Gallery during my senior year. That's a juried show, and it's a huge honor to be selected. But the best news was that it sold at auction for eight hundred dollars to an anonymous art patron. *Eight hundred dollars!*"

"That's fantastic," he agreed.

"Actually, it was unheard of. My professor was floored. And I thought, yes, I really *do* have talent. The thing is, my professors were never as effusive in their praise for my work as they were for others, and one of them had even suggested that maybe painting was not the right path for me. But when that painting sold, it said to me I could really be an artist." She suddenly laughed. "I had this image of my work showing up on the walls of all these fancy Manhattan apartments, and people would see them on some real estate show."

"If it sold, how did it end up in your parents' restaurant?" he asked.

"The anonymous art patron? Turned out, he was my dad. Only I didn't know it. It was a surprise. Dad even drove up the bidding just so that it would be a splashy sale. And I didn't know any of that until Christmas, when he surprised me with an unveiling at the bistro."

"Ah." Brennan winced. He understood.

Mia didn't tell him that she'd been so stunned to see her best work hanging in the bistro that she'd been incapable of speech, her thoughts and her tongue tangling in confusion. Or that knee-buckling realization that the buyer wasn't a curator of fine art who would set off her career at all, but *her father.*

"So what'd you say?"

She shrugged. "Nothing. I was shocked. And hurt. And bewildered," she admitted. "But Dad? He was so damn proud, so excited.

Champagne toasts were on the house," she said, sweeping her arm as she remembered him that night. "And then he took me around to introduce me to the diners as his daughter, The Artist."

Brennan smiled sympathetically.

Mia shifted her gaze to the lake. Time had dulled that particular ache, but the reality of her situation had brought the whole incident into sharp focus. That's the sort of thing that happened to wannabes.

Brennan said nothing, just quietly let her think about it. "You know, I've never told anyone that before," she said softly. "I mean, I would rather die than have my dad know how disappointing the whole thing had been. I don't think he's ever really even thought about how expensive that painting is. Way more than eight hundred dollars."

"How so?"

"It's the only thing to have come out of my pricey art degree from Pratt Institute. Oh, the irony!" She laughed ruefully, then looked at Brennan a long moment. What had possessed her to tell him? What had made her open up the vault of deep, dark secrets and give him one? "It's weird—I've never told anyone the truth, and yet I just told you. Why is that?"

"You must feel pretty confident. It's hard to top stink," he said.

Mia laughed.

Brennan grinned and casually twined his fingers with hers. His touch reverberated up her arm, tingling in its wake. *They were holding hands.* Everything in her brain screamed no, but Mia *liked* it.

"You know what you said about your success not matching your potential?" she asked. "I think mine has gone the other way. My success has surpassed my potential."

"Hey, you're only starting out. Don't be so hard on yourself."

"I don't think I am. I've been trying to break in for years, and I have a painting in my parent's bistro and a fascinating career in asking workers to pick up their trash. I didn't get here by chance."

"Come on," he said, tugging at her hand.

"No, really," she said. "You know how it is when you go out with someone for a long time, and you think you're so in love, and then you break up—sorry," she added apologetically.

He waved her off. "And?"

"And you break up, and then some time goes by, and you see that person on the street, and you're like, *how* did I ever think he was the one? I'm starting to wonder that about painting and art. I was in love with it for so long, but it hasn't worked out and now I am wondering—how did I think that was it?"

He said nothing, just quietly watched her.

"I think I'm being practical. I have a degree in fine arts and I can't find work. I can't find anyone who is interested in my work. And you know what else? August Brockway said I suck."

Brennan's expression didn't change. "Who is August Brockway?"

"Just one of the most important American artists today. I studied him in school." She laughed bitterly. "I *emulated* him. There's some irony for you."

"Art is in the eye of the beholder," Brennan offered.

"No offense, but I wish I had a buck for every time someone said that to me."

"Yeah, okay, so the only thing I have is clichés." He smiled a little. "But I hear what you're saying."

"No you don't. You're being nice to me. I'm just babbling."

"You're not babbling."

"Most people believe that if I can paint Lake Haven like I did, that I should be able to do that all the time, and people will buy my paintings. But it's nothing like that. Art has to find its audience. Probably music, too, right?"

"Right," he said quietly. He tugged on her fingers. "And August whoever is one audience. He has one opinion. You have to believe in yourself. Sometimes when no one else does, you have to believe harder than ever."

Mia appreciated his effort, she did. But she never understood why people had such a difficult time accepting the truth about themselves. She could accept it. She didn't like the truth about herself, but she could accept it. She smiled at him.

"Uh-uh," he said, and lowered his head with a dark look of exasperation. "*That* is a patronizing look."

"No it's not!" she insisted, but her cheeks were blooming with her lie. "How'd you get so wise, anyway?"

"I've had my share of hard knocks." He casually stroked her face. "Look, Mia, there will always be all kinds of critics if you're going to travel an artistic path. If you buy into their shit, you will lose yourself in it. Don't make that mistake."

He caressed her cheek again. It was surprisingly soothing. Mia's heart swelled with appreciation for his effort. Her veins swelled with a rush of blood. She wanted to lean into his caress, put her head on his shoulder and feel his arms around her.

"I have a far more serious question for you," he said gravely.

She'd already said too much. "What?"

"What else is in your lunch bag?"

Mia laughed. She leaned over the bag, stuffed her hand inside, and pulled out a little baggie full of Oreo cookies. "I thought it might be a long day," she said.

Thirteen

Funny how things worked out when he wasn't paying attention.

Brennan hadn't planned to walk down to the bluff. It wasn't that he hadn't thought about Mia since running into her at the hardware store; he had. But he'd been too caught up in developing the music for a feature film to seek her out.

The work he was doing was hard, much harder than anything he'd done in a long time. For days he'd been working to find the right rhythm, the right chord progressions, the right tone. He was growing his seed of an idea, working it around and over itself, erasing and rewriting, erasing and rewriting, for days and all night. The music was what consumed his thoughts.

But something was missing from the work he'd done this week. A spark, an illumination that Brennan couldn't figure out. This was generally the point in song creation where he and Chance would bat ideas around and try different things. Brennan even thought of calling Chance—in spite of their differences, he knew that Chance, the artist, would be more interested in the song than in being angry.

Only this work felt different. It felt solo. As much as he hated to admit it, solo was not something Brennan did very well. The process was arduous—he felt rusty and ungainly, like a colt trying to learn to run with its young body. But because the work was solo, he didn't feel comfortable calling Chance.

He didn't want to drink, either, as had become his habit of late. So Brennan decided that day he'd take a drive and listen to some music. Fill the creative well, so to speak. Maybe find some inspiration in someone else's work.

The day was perfect, the weather mild and bright . . . and as he'd walked to his car, he'd seen Mia walking down to the bluff. She was wearing a strangely angular plaid dress, and a funky hat with real flowers, and military-style boots with fishnet stockings. Brennan had paused, watching her. In the end, he couldn't resist that magnetic blend and he'd followed her down to the bluff.

And on the bluff, sitting on the rotting bench, eating sandwiches, he'd had a surprisingly insightful conversation with her. It had been the only real conversation he'd had in weeks in which someone wasn't yelling at him or demanding he do this or that.

There was something about Mia that really spoke to Brennan. She was very different from the women he generally met. He'd been famous for so long that he'd forgotten what it was like to meet a pretty, single woman who wasn't hopeful she'd get something out of knowing him.

And yet, it was more than that. For the first time in years, he felt someone was seeing the real him. Not Everett—Brennan. The guy underneath the fame. If there was anyone he knew right here, right now, who would understand why he didn't want to keep on the path Tuesday's End had started down, Brennan believed it could be Mia.

The only other person who would have understood was Trey.

God, but Brennan missed Trey. He thought about his old friend a lot. He thought about how lonely his death was with that needle in his arm. He missed talking to Trey—whereas he and Chance had always been about the music, Trey and Brennan talked. About everything. About life, about women, about music, about dreams and desires. Trey was the only one to whom Brennan had ever confided his feelings about his father. He'd told Trey about the absence he felt in his life, the confusing mix of rejection and anger. Trey got that.

In a lot of ways, Trey and Brennan's dad were a lot alike. Brennan's dad had chosen another life over his son and Trey had chosen heroin over his friend. It was a weird thing to acknowledge, but in some respects, Brennan felt just as betrayed by the heroin addiction as he had by his father's abandonment a long time ago.

Mia reminded Brennan of Trey. He liked how she talked about her art. She'd clearly thought about it, which he could relate to, because he thought about music in a very similar way.

Frankly, he could have remained all day on that bench with her, enjoying a beautiful spring day, talking about life. It was Mia who'd ended their impromptu lunch. She'd glanced at her watch and gasped, "I'm late!" She'd quickly gathered her things, stuffed the hat on her head lopsidedly, and had smiled at him. A beautiful, warm smile. Genuine.

"I have to go," she'd said. "Aunt Bev would kill me if she thought people were stripping wall paper without a chaperone." And she was off, leaving him on the bench.

After that half hour with Mia, Brennan was feeling a different kind of energy. He felt ready to try again and instead of taking that drive, he'd gone back to his guitar and his work.

♦ ♦ ♦

It was seven o'clock when Brennan heard the roar of a truck's motor and the unmistakable sound of it driving away from the house. He glanced up. The sun was sliding down behind the trees. His belly rumbled; he hadn't had anything to eat since the sandwich.

Brennan found a pair of boat shoes and slipped them on, picked up a leather jacket and a hat that he could pull low over his eyes and some aviator glasses Jenna had given him on his birthday. He opened a bedside table and rummaged around until he found a wad of hundred dollar bills. He shoved them into his pocket and went downstairs.

The dogs trotted out from the kitchen to greet Brennan, then followed him down the north hall when he went to see if Mia was there.

She was. She had her messenger bag slung over her shoulder, her lunch bag in her hand. Her back was to him as she studied the wall she'd painted. Something was different about the wall, but it took Brennan a moment to see what. The boat was gone.

Mia heard him walk into the room and glanced at him over her shoulder before returning her attention to the wall again.

"What happened to my boat?" he asked.

"I sank it."

"You *sank* it? Was it a storm?"

"Nope. That would be too easy. It was a submarine attack." She gave him a sideways smile. "That's what you get for partying on your boat and not paying attention. I submarine attacked you."

"That's impossible," he pointed out. "The lake is too small for a submarine. Not to mention the mechanics of getting it *in* the lake."

"It was a mini. I had it trucked in."

He smiled. "So now you have a story."

"Not really. The boat had to go because the proportions were all wrong."

"That's amusing coming from a woman wearing a dress with some interesting proportions."

Mia glanced down. "But that's so different! The dress is *supposed* to be asymmetrical. The sailboat is not, hello."

His smile deepened and he ceremoniously bowed his head. "I stand corrected." He looked at the mural again. "The lake still seems angry."

"You're absolutely right," she readily agreed. "I'm having trouble finding inspiration for a non-angry lake."

"What would inspire you?"

She cocked her head to one side and studied the wall. "Something happy," she said.

"Happy, huh? I might have just the thing. Wanna see?"

She laughed. "I don't know. Do I?"

"Come on, you have to see it. But we have to hurry."

"Hurry?"

He reached for her hand. "Trust me on this."

"Dude, I don't trust you at *all*." But her fingers closed around his.

"Good," he said, and pulled her closer. "Then it will be an even better surprise."

He led her outside and down the path to the bluff, ignoring her complaints about how fast he was moving. He silenced her remark about the temperature dropping by pulling her into his side and putting his arm around her shoulders.

"Where are we *going*?" she demanded when he turned in the opposite direction of the bluff and started down the rocky path to the beach.

"You'll see. Now be quiet," he said with a squeeze of her shoulders. He helped her pick her way down the path, and about halfway down, he stopped. He let go of Mia, made a leap up onto a flat rock, then leaned over and looked down.

"Are you crazy?" she said, her voice full of alarm.

"Come here," he said, and held out his hand to her.

Mia looked at his hand warily. "What is it, naked people on a boat? Trust me, I've seen plenty."

"You have?" he asked, surprised. "Nobody is naked. Come look."

Mia groaned as if he were being unreasonable, but allowed him to pull her up onto the rock with him. He stretched out on his belly. So did Mia, lying next to him. Brennan pointed.

Mia looked in the direction he pointed—and gasped with delight. Just down the bluff, nestled in a crag, was a nest with three baby owls in it. Three fluffy little heads swiveled around, their big eyes blinking up at Mia and Brennan.

"How did you *find* them?" she whispered.

"Remember the day I threw my phone in the lake?"

"Like I could ever forget."

"I went down to look for my phone. I know, I know," he said before she laughed. "I saw them from the beach. They weren't hard to spot. So what do you think?"

"I *love* them," Mia said, and watched as the baby owls swiveled between looking for their mother, and then fixing their big eyes on Brennan and Mia.

"Does it make you happy?" Brennan asked.

"Very." She beamed at him. "Thank you so much. I am feeling inspired."

That smile, full of gratitude, and ending in two dimples, made Brennan feel like he could lift this rock and hurl it into the lake. He reached for her hand, helping her to stand on the rock. He hopped down onto the path, then grabbed her waist and lifted her off the rock. Her body brushed against his as she slid down to her feet. That brief bit of contact was enough—Brennan's blood began to sizzle.

Neither of them moved; he kept his hands on her waist, and she kept her hands on his shoulders. Behind her, the sun was sinking into the lake and house lights were starting to dot the hills in the shadows. The setting was beautiful, and in this light, her eyes looked even more golden than normal. His body was stirring to life, wanting her. "Mia?"

"Yes?"

"Don't freak out . . . but I'm going to kiss you."

"Oh." Her eyes widened. "Really? Like, now?"

Brennan circled one arm around her waist and pulled her closer, so that she had to tilt her head back and stare up at him with those brilliant eyes. "Like now. Are you freaking out?"

"A little," she said, nodding. But her gaze was locked on his, and she was pressing against him.

He stroked her cheek with the back of his knuckles. "Close your eyes."

Mia didn't move. Her eyes remained fixed on his.

"Just close them."

With her face still tilted up to his, she slowly closed them. Her lashes fanned dark against her skin. A sprinkling of freckles danced across the bridge of her nose. Her lips parted slightly, full and rosy in contrast to her pale skin. Damn, but she was pretty. Very alluring to the man in him.

"What's happening—"

Brennan kissed her before she opened her eyes. Mia made a tiny sound of surprise, but then she was sinking into him, and her hand grabbed his shirt, clinging to it, as if she were afraid he would end it too soon.

Her lips were so soft, and the touch of her tongue electric. He hadn't felt a charge like this in so long, *too* long. He wanted more and caught her chin in his hand, angling her head and kissing her fully, feeling the wave of desire slink through him and curl around his organs.

Mia rose on her toes to respond to his desire, her tongue tangling with his. Jesus, if he'd known Mia could kiss like this, he would have kissed her before now. She made his pulse throb, revved him up, pushed his mind past rational thought. He pulled her into him, one hand sliding down to her breast, eager for more. When Mia made a kittenish sound of pleasure, it sent him over the edge. Fire was sliding through his veins; Brennan forgot who he was, why he was here. He forgot everything but that Mia felt and tasted so damn good, and she was exciting in a way he would never have expected and that—*that*—made her incredibly sexy.

Incredibly.

Brennan finally lifted his head before he gave into his urge to lay her down on the rock and have his way with her. Mia's eyes were still closed, and she swayed a little, smiling softly. "Can I open my eyes now?"

"Yes."

She opened her eyes and locked her gaze on his, the pleasure in her eyes glittering up at him. "I'm not sure what to think about that," she said.

"Did you like it?"

"Yes. A *lot*. Maybe too much."

"I know what you mean. Maybe we should think about it over a dinner."

Her smile deepened into dimples again. "I've taken enough of your time today."

Oh, but she hadn't taken nearly enough of him today, not nearly enough, and he wasn't ready for this to end. "It's getting dark. We can drop off your bike and grab a bite. I've got at least that much time to spare," he said with a wink. "Besides, I owe you a sandwich."

"A gourmet sandwich," she reminded him. "Not peanut butter."

"I know just the place."

"You do?" she asked skeptically.

He took her hand in his. "Don't you trust me yet?"

"Are you kidding? Not in the least."

This was a smart girl. "I promise—gourmet sandwiches and maybe a slice of pie."

Mia's eyes widened. "Pie! Why didn't you say so? I'll do circus tricks for pie."

"Then pie it is," he said, and kissed the top of her head like they were lovers and walked with her back to the house.

Fourteen

This was a bad idea, a very bad idea, Mia thought, for all the reasons it was *always* a bad idea to get mixed up with summer people. Especially if you were working for one of the golden people.

Mia hated how easily persuaded she was by one searing kiss . . . but oh, how she'd been persuaded. That kiss had jolted her, had tingled and swelled and heated her blood and she was *still* feeling it.

She was definitely intrigued by him, more than she would have thought even possible several days ago. Maybe intrigued wasn't the right word. Enthralled? For Chrissakes, how could she not be? He'd taken her down to the bluff and shown her baby owls. If that wasn't the sum of all romantic movies rolled into one act, she didn't know what was.

So Brennan Yates was very sexy, very attractive . . . but Mia wasn't completely stupid. This was dangerous territory, and she told herself that when he dropped off her bike at her apartment, she would thank him and say good night. *Been a great day, but lots of work to do*, she'd say. Or, *thanks, but so tired.*

Only she said nothing as she watched him strap her bike precariously into the front compartment of his expensive sports car for the short trip down the hill. She remained stupidly silent when he drove to her apartment and deposited her bike next to the steps going up to her apartment. She didn't even get out of that cockpit of a car. She uttered nothing but a squeal as he peeled out onto Juneberry Road.

And then she surreptitiously admired him for the rest of the drive. *Coward.*

This was pie. That was it, nothing more. Just pie. *Yeah, right.*

Brennan drove her up a county road, about twenty miles out of town, and pulled into the parking lot of EZ's Diner. That definitely was not what Mia was expecting. She leaned forward and looked up at the blinking light, then at Brennan.

"Think pie," he said, and donned a ballcap that he pulled low over his eyes. "Let's go."

Mia laughed. "What's with the hat?" she asked. "What are you, a rock star?"

"Maybe."

Summer people. They all thought they were rock stars.

Inside, Brennan asked for a booth and sat with his back to the door. As they settled in, a waitress wearing a grimy black apron walked over with her pad to take their order. "What are you folks having tonight?"

"A burger and a beer," Brennan said without looking at a menu. He grinned at Mia. "And we'll follow that up with pie."

Mia suppressed a giggle of delight. She looked up at the waitress—and was struck momentarily speechless. She knew the waitress. Becky Sorenson had been a year ahead of Mia in school.

The waitress did not seem to recognize Mia and looked at her expectantly, her little pencil poised. "Ah . . . me too," Mia said. "Burger. Fries. A beer, too."

The waitress jotted it down, then glanced at Brennan. She hesitated. And for one surreal moment, Mia thought she was going to tell Brennan that Mia was a freak, or that something happened on the beach nine years ago. But she didn't say that. She frowned and said to Brennan, "Do I know you?"

"Nah, I don't think so," Brennan said. He kept his gaze on Mia, but his smile seemed a little thinner.

"You really look *so* familiar."

"I'm not from around here," Brennan said, and turned slightly away from her and appeared to be studying the condiments. "We'll need some ketchup with the fries."

"Yeah, sure. I'll be right back with the beers."

It was a relief that Becky didn't seem to notice her over her interest in Brennan. When she left, Mia said, "I think she may have the hots for you." Of course she did. A sexy man driving an expensive sports car walked into this diner and all the girls' heads turned.

"Nah," he said, with a dismissive flick of his wrist. He settled his arms on the table between them. "So tell me more about yourself. What kind of love life do you have?"

Mia blinked. Then burst out laughing. "Talk about cutting to the chase!"

He shrugged. "Can you blame me? An attractive woman like you wandering around this village? I would think there'd be any number of guys following you around."

She blushed furiously at the compliment. "Thanks. I think."

"I'm assuming, after that moment on the bluff, that there is no boyfriend," he said easily.

Mia groaned. She pressed her hands against the table and leaned back, glancing about. "Honestly? I'm not that good at meeting guys," she said.

"No?"

"No. A lot of guys don't get my aesthetic."

"Your *what*?"

Mia giggled. "My aesthetic. My artistic outlook," she said, gesturing to her dress.

"Ah," he said, nodding. "Well, I think it's hot."

Mia smiled curiously at him. "I'm going to be honest—I'm not sure what to make of the shiny new you."

"Simple. The shiny new me likes you." He leaned back, stretched his arms across the back of the booth. "And when I like someone, I'm curious."

Men who looked like Brennan never liked girls like her, at least not in Mia's experience. That kiss had been . . . well, it had been fantastic, but it was one of those times the moment had been right. As flattered as Mia was, she was skeptical. "You don't really know me enough to like me."

"That's not true," he said. "I may not know everything, obviously, because you're clearly not cooperating with my interrogation. But what I know about you is this—you're real."

Mia laughed. "What else would I be? It's not like I catfished you."

"You might be surprised," he said, and fidgeted with the cheap utensils on the paper napkin before him. "So . . . we were talking about your last serious boyfriend or lover or whatever you artists call them."

"We were?" she asked, still grinning.

"You were about to tell me what happened."

"Gee, I wonder how I forgot that. Well okay, let's see, my last boyfriend . . ." She paused. Micah hadn't exactly been a boyfriend, had he? "Lover," she amended shyly, "got a job in Philadelphia."

Brennan waited for her to go on. "And?"

"And, that was it. We weren't that into each other, to be honest. He was in accounting and I was in art."

"So what were you doing together?" Brennan asked curiously.

Mia smiled shyly. She fidgeted with the napkin. "The, ah . . . the usual," she said with a slight shrug.

"Ah." He smiled, amused by her. "So what about around here? Surely you've dated some of the East Beach's more illustrious characters, right?"

Where to begin? Mia glanced absently out the window as a history of boys and disasters flitted through her head.

"Here are your beers."

Startled, Mia jerked her gaze around to the waitress. Becky was looking directly at her, and Mia's blood began to drain from her face. But Becky said nothing. She put the beers down and walked on.

"What's that about?" Brennan asked, gesturing to the waitress's departing back.

"Nothing. Forget it."

"It's not nothing," he said. "You looked like you were ready to crawl under a table."

Funny how something as simple as seeing a vaguely familiar face could bring so many unpleasant memories streaming back to her. "It's a long story," Mia said. "The bottom line with her and the boyfriends is that I never really fit in around here."

She expected a look of concern, maybe even some reassurance. But Brennan chuckled and picked up his beer. "No shit," he said, and touched his beer bottle to hers.

Mia was grateful for that. She smiled a little. "Okay, so it's obvious," she conceded. "But back in the day, people weren't so nice about it."

"Like her?" Brennan asked, indicating Becky with his chin.

"Not her, exactly, but people she knew." Mia shook her head, preferring not to think about it. "It's just easier to cut a wide berth around anyone I knew then."

He frowned a little as he took a swig from his beer. "Seems like there's more to it than people not liking your look."

He was a perceptive hunk, she'd have to admit. But the last thing she wanted to talk about was a drug-fueled night on the beach, of the pictures and everything that happened later. She'd had a good time today. She wanted to keep it that way. "Nope. That's all." She began to peel the label from her beer bottle.

Brennan watched her do that for a moment. He finally sighed and said, "I'm sorry for whatever happened to you."

How did he *know*? "It's water under the bridge," she said with a fleeting smile. "I told you something about me. Your turn."

He shrugged. "What do you want to know?"

"Will you tell me about the friend you lost?"

Brennan blinked. He seemed to consider it a moment. "There's not much to say, really. He could never kick the habit. Trey always did walk a different path than the rest of us. But that's what I loved about him—he was unique. He had a cool vibe." He took another drink of beer and said, "Like you."

Mia blushed again. "I'm sorry about your friend. I can't imagine it, really."

"Tends to dull one's creativity, that's for sure," he said, frowning now. "And makes me question things more than I ever have."

"Like what?" she asked, curious.

"Like . . ." He suddenly leaned forward and planted his arms on the table and looked her in the eyes. "Like I don't know what the universe wants from me. I don't know what the fuck anyone wants from me."

Mia was startled. She didn't know what he meant, really, other than whatever he'd just said seemed really important to him. He winced almost immediately, as if he regretted saying anything at all. He eased back, shifting his gaze across the room.

"What do *you* want?" she asked.

"That's easy," he said, with a wave of his hand. "To write music that fulfills me. It's that easy, and yet it's not easy at all."

"No kidding," she muttered.

Becky returned then with the burgers and set them down. She smiled at Mia this time, her gaze flicking over Mia's dress before walking away.

When she'd gone, Mia said, "I know what you mean," and tucked a fry into her mouth. "I may not be a good artist, but I'm still an artist, and I know how hard it is to stand in front of a blank canvas and wonder what professors or art critics would like. But I also know when I try to paint to those visions, the paintings never turn out right. The idea, the vision, has to come from me. And yet, I've lost all this confidence," she said, gesturing to herself.

Brennan tilted his head to one side. "You know, you're pretty smart for someone who has a career telling people to pick up their trash. That's very astute of you."

Mia smiled and picked up another fry. "Of course it's astute, Brennan," she said, pointing the fry at him. "You don't just show up and get a plum job like directing trash pickup without having learned a few things." She popped the fry into her mouth. "And we both know what I said is true. It's just that sometimes we forget."

"Yep. I feel like I've been trying to please others for so long and meet all of these unwritten expectations that somewhere along the way I forgot why or how my music evolved in the first place. It's been stifling."

She didn't know what to say to that. She looked down at her plate.

"I bet you didn't find burgers this good in the city," he said.

Mia told him about a diner down the street from her apartment with the greasiest burgers, perfect for a hangover. He asked what she did in the city, and Mia ended up telling him about her textile design job. And then about how she was laid off and looked for work.

When they finished the burgers, Becky brought around a tray with slices of pie on it.

"Pie?" Brennan asked Mia.

"I'm so *stuffed*," Mia said, putting her hand on her belly. "I really shouldn't . . . at least not without ice cream."

Brennan laughed and asked for two orders of hot apple pie à la mode.

When the pie came, Mia regaled Brennan with the story of her final search for an apartment in Brooklyn she could afford. "Everything is so insanely expensive," she said. "But I knew I had finally hit rock bottom when I answered an ad for a small room with kitchen privileges." She licked her spoon. "I mean, I knew it would be small, but at least I could afford it with the money I had in savings."

"So what happened?"

"It was a closet," she said, and put her spoon down. "I don't mean the size of a closet, I mean an actual *closet*," she said, sketching that out with her hands.

Brennan laughed.

"And I wasn't getting any interviews. Not a single one! A friend of mine told me to dress in something less colorful."

"*No,*" Brennan said, sounding shocked.

"I know, right?" Mia said laughing. "Here I was, finally feeling comfortable being who I am. I mean, hell, I'd gone to Pratt so I'd fit in. And I was very defiant with my friend," she said, without rancor. "I said, 'This is who I am, Kelsey, and I'm not backing down.'" She had to laugh at the memory of that morning now, standing in Kelsey's apartment, acting as if she were an ar-*teest*. "But Kelsey explained to me that while she totally got it, some people, like employers, might think I was expressing full-blown schizophrenia, and no one wanted to hire that." She grinned. "I saw her point," she said, holding up a finger. "Probably because I'd just come back from an interview at a bookstore, and the guy couldn't even look me in the eye. So I tried it Kelsey's way. I borrowed this suit she bought at some store—*ugh*, I still remember it," she said with a shiver of revulsion. "It was square and cheap and *gray*. Who wants to wear gray? But I put it on, and I tromped all over Brooklyn putting in applications, and guess what?"

"You got a job." Brennan was smiling, his gaze moving over her face as she told her tale, his amusement evident in his eyes.

"An interview! It was at a bath and kitchen fixtures shop, but it was an interview, and a job is a job, right?" Mia laughed again. "I had dressed for success to sell *faucets*. So I go for the interview, and the woman said, 'We can offer you part-time work,'" she said, mimicking the manager's voice.

"Well okay, then," Brennan said. "That's all you needed."

"That's all—just one really good part-time job and a room somewhere. I'd have time to paint and I could stay in Brooklyn. And then the lady said, 'I can offer you ten hours a week!'" Mia leaned across the table. "Like it was a million dollars."

Brennan laughed. Mia shook her head and scooped up a big bite of apple pie. "That's when I called it—my life in the city was no more. I couldn't make it without a real job, and I was almost out of money. I had no idea what else to do, so . . ." She shrugged. "I came home."

"You know what? I'm glad you did."

Mia's smile deepened. "At the moment, I am, too. So what about you, Brennan Yates?" she asked. "Why did you come to East Beach? And where were you before this?"

She noticed the slight hesitation. He stuck his spoon into the bowl. "LA," he said. "I hadn't seen my mom in a while, and thought now was as good a time as any."

"Did you have a job?"

He looked up at her. "Not exactly," he said.

Must be nice, she thought. She could just picture him in some very nice house, playing around with his guitar or piano. Oh, the idle rich! How freeing all that money must be. Brennan didn't have a job because he didn't need one.

Mia wanted to ask more, but Becky returned with the check and laid it down on the table. Brennan grabbed it up, reached into his pocket, and pulled out a thick roll of bills. He peeled off a one hundred dollar bill and laid it down on the ticket and stuffed the roll of cash back into his pocket. "Let's get out of here," he said with a smile.

Mia looked at the hundred dollar bill on the table, but Brennan was already standing, offering his hand. She scooted out of the booth and, with his hand on the small of her back, allowed him to lead her out of the diner. But before they made it through the glass door, Becky came hurrying toward them. *"Wait!"* she called.

Brennan opened the diner door, almost as if he hadn't heard her, and with his hand on Mia's back, ushered her out.

"I think she's calling you," Mia said.

"Excuse me! *Wait!*" Becky called again.

Brennan looked down, his jaw tightly clenched. It was such an odd reaction that for a moment, Mia thought he must really know Becky.

"Sorry," Becky said breathlessly. She smiled at Mia, and Mia's pulse fluttered. She'd remembered her. "I'm sorry, I wanted to catch you before you left."

"Me? Why?" Mia asked. *Don't say it. Don't say that you remember me from that night on the beach.*

"Because I *love* your dress! It's adorable. Where did you get it, if you don't mind me asking?"

Brennan's head came up. He looked at the waitress, then at Mia.

"My dress?" Mia looked down. "I made it."

Becky's eyes rounded. "Are you serious?"

"Yes. I made it."

"I love it. I want one," Becky said. "Do you have a shop?"

"A shop?" Mia laughed loudly. "No, it's just a hobby."

"You should open a shop," the waitress said as she eased back into the diner. "I'm not kidding. You should." She disappeared inside.

Mia turned a big grin to Brennan. "She liked my *dress*," she said proudly.

"I heard," he said and, with his hand on her back once more, steered her toward his car and opened the passenger door.

"So did you know her?" Mia asked curiously before stepping in.

"Who, the waitress? No. Never saw her before tonight."

"Are you sure?" Mia asked. "Because you looked like you were trying to run when she was calling us."

"Did I?" He smiled and tweaked her cheek. "Are you going to get in or stand here all night?"

"Oh, I get it," Mia said as she got into the passenger seat. "You're used to women chasing after you, is that it?"

She couldn't guess why Brennan looked so uncomfortable, but he sort of shrugged her remark off and shut the door.

On the drive home, Brennan tuned the radio to classical music. It was as if the talk had gone out of him, and they listened to a piece Mia recognized as Mozart. She gazed out the window, at the stars above Lake Haven, her thoughts awash in the fantastic scenarios of *what if*. What if she had one hundred dollars in her pocket?

He turned into the drive to Dalton's house, killing the lights as they coasted toward the barn. It was eleven o'clock, Mia realized. Where had the time gone? Brennan got out of his car and came around to her side as she got out. "Thanks for feeding me," she said.

"Thanks for keeping me company." He put his arm around her waist, pulling her into his chest. He kissed her softly, his lips gliding across hers, his tongue casually twirling around hers. The spark of the kiss began to grow, flaring out into her veins. He cupped her chin, lifting her face up to his, and Mia put her hands on his waist, sinking into him. When he lifted his head, he stroked his thumb across her lip. "Are you going to ask me inside?"

Mia tilted her head back and looked up at the stars glittering overhead. She thought of how many millions there must be shining down on them, and how they reminded her of the way she felt when Brennan kissed her—a million stars glittering in her veins. "No," she said, and lowered her head to meet his gaze.

One of his brows arched above the other, surprised. "No?"

She shook her head, rose up, and kissed the corner of his mouth. "Thanks for a great evening. Good night, Brennan." She stepped around him and jogged up the steps to her loft.

When she got to the top of the stairs, she turned around. He was still standing at his car, and cast his arms out in the universal symbol of *why?*

Mia smiled. She waved at him, then stepped inside her apartment.

Once inside, she leaned back against the door and closed her eyes. Her body was still thrumming with that kiss.

Kissing was one thing. Being lured into a summer fling with a handsome face and a piece of pie was quite another. No, she hadn't lost her mind completely. At least not yet. Thank God for small favors.

And she wasn't taking any bets on how long her resolve would hold.

Fifteen

Mia was in an exceptionally good mood Friday morning when Aunt Bev called and asked her to come to the shop. She sent Wallace to pick her up.

"What's that smile all about?" Wallace asked accusingly when she climbed into the shop van. "Did you come into a windfall? Find another job? Or maybe you got a bargain on discontinued furniture slips and are envisioning a whole new wardrobe?"

"I'm just so happy to spend this time with you, Wallace. I was hoping we could talk about conservation."

Wallace shot her a suspicious look.

"I was thinking we could begin a recycling program at the shop—"

"Stop *right* there," he said sternly. "And what, pray tell, shall we recycle? I'll tell you what I'd *like* to recycle—your aunt's endless fascination with beige. What is it with her and Chico's and *beige*?"

Wallace continued to catalogue all the things he found objectionable about Aunt Bev's wardrobe all the way to the shop.

They were the first to arrive, but Aunt Bev was right on their heels and instantly dispatched Mia out for coffee. When Mia returned, Skylar had managed to drag herself in, yawning loudly and settling in on a stool behind the counter with a magazine.

"I need everything dusted today," Aunt Bev said imperiously, and tossed a feather duster at her daughter. "Mia, you can busy yourself around here, too. The wall demolition won't begin until Monday, and the materials won't arrive till then, either, so there's no reason for you to be at the Ross house today."

Well, that was disappointing. Mia had tossed and turned most of the night with thoughts and images of Brennan.

"I'm going to run a few errands," Aunt Bev said, and disappeared into the back room with her long bell sleeves billowing out behind her. They were beige.

Once she'd gone, Skylar tossed the duster to Mia.

"Hey," Mia said. "That's *your* job."

"My job is to man the shop. This is manning it." She fluttered her fingers to Mia and opened her magazine.

Mia groaned with general exasperation at her cousin, but the truth was that she'd rather have something to do than to sit around and read magazines all day long.

She started with the porcelain figurines on the back wall and was still working there when she heard the little bell sound at the front door, indicating someone had come in. She didn't hear Skylar greet anyone, and when she leaned to look around a display of pillows, she saw that, not surprisingly, Skylar had left her post. "Be with you in a moment!" she said, and put down the duster. She walked out to the front of the store, her head down as she dusted off her faded jeans, and looked up at the last moment.

Mia gasped with surprise. Jesse Fisher, the unchallenged hunk of her high school years, was smiling down at her. "Hey, Mia," he said. "I heard you were back in town."

Good God, Jesse had definitely filled out. He'd always been tall, but he looked even taller. Moreover, Mia had forgotten how green his eyes were. No wonder girls used to swoon over his handsome physique and face, and time had only enhanced those good looks.

"You remember me, don't you?" he asked uncertainly.

"Yes, of course I do."

"Well, well, look what the cat dragged in," Skylar said low, appearing next to Mia.

"Hey, Sky," Jesse said, his smile not quite as bright as it had been a moment before.

Skylar elbowed Mia in the ribs. Mia ignored her, but she got Skylar's point. Jesse looked good. *Really* good. And Mia felt suddenly shy, the overlooked high school girl standing on the edge of the in-crowd. It was amazing how quickly the role a person played in her high school class came back to her. "Umm . . . did you need some help?" Mia asked curiously, wondering why a guy like Jesse Fisher would be in a home décor shop.

"Jesus, Mia, at least say a real hello," Skylar chided her, then sidled forward. "Jesse *Fisher*," she purred. "You sure grew up, didn't you?" She nodded approvingly as she blatantly checked him out.

Mia was appalled. She put her hand on Skylar's arm and stepped in front of her. "Sorry, I should have asked how you are, Jesse," she said apologetically, and nervously wiped her hands on her hips and extended one to him. "It's been a long time."

"About nine years," he said, his smile warming again. "I'm doing great. I took over my dad's construction business this year when he retired. How about you? Are you back for good?"

"Just the summer," Mia said quickly. She averted her gaze from his curious green eyes as she pretended to straighten a little bowl. "So what can we do for you?" She glanced at him again.

"Oh. Right." He wouldn't stop smiling at her with those dancing eyes, and Mia could feel heat rising up her neck. "I have a list of things we're going to need for Beverly, and I thought as long as I was here, I'd look for a gift for my mom. Her birthday is Sunday."

"Well . . . um . . . what does she like?" Mia asked. "Skylar can help you—"

"Mom's not here. I'll take the list and put it on her desk," Skylar said, and gave Mia a push, causing her to hop awkwardly forward. "*You* help him, Mia. Give him lots and lots of help."

What the hell was Skylar doing? Something clicked in Mia's head, and she suddenly looked at Jesse. "Did my *grandmother* ask you to come by?"

"What?" He laughed. "No! Your aunt gave me the demolition job at the Ross house. And I need a gift for my mom."

Mia didn't believe him.

He handed the list of items to Skylar. "I'm serious," he said, holding up his hands.

The heat in Mia had now spread into her cheeks and neck, making her look like a beacon of insecurity. "Okay. I believe you," she lied. She turned partially from him, and to her horror, she saw that not only was Skylar grinning at them like a loon, Wallace had stopped working to have a look, too. As if Mia were fifteen and a boy had come around to invite her to her first prom. She wanted to kick them both right in the ass.

"Skylar, weren't you going to go and put the list somewhere?" Mia asked low.

"Right," Skylar said.

"Well, here are some silver salt and pepper shakers," she said, pointing to a pair that was shaped like pigs.

"Hmm. Okay," Jesse said.

"What about this?" she said, quickly moving on. "It's a silk couch pillow."

"Yeah, that's nice. You know, Mia, I saw your painting at the bistro."

Well alrighty then, it was official. Mia could die at the age of twenty-seven from pure humiliation.

When she didn't say anything, he added quickly, "I thought it was fantastic. I always knew you had real talent."

Mia smiled a little at that because she was human and was touched by the compliment. But honestly, she couldn't imagine that he'd ever thought anything about her at all. She couldn't imagine that he ever knew she existed before this moment. "Thank you," she said. "What about a picture frame?" She held up one made of ivory pearl.

Jesse's expression was indulgent. He seemed to sense that she was uncomfortable with everyone watching them and took the picture frame from her and pretended to examine it. "Okay. I'll take it."

"It's seventy-five dollars," she softly warned him.

But Jesse merely shrugged. "Do you gift wrap?"

"We do." She carried the picture frame to the counter, found some tissue paper and a gift bag, and began to put the wrapping together.

Jesse watched her, standing patiently, his eyes fixed on her as she wrapped the frame and charged him for it. When she put the wrapped package in the bag and tied the cheerful pink ribbon through the handles and handed it to him, Jesse caught her fingers in his and held on a moment. "Hey, what would you think about getting a drink sometime?"

"A drink?" she repeated stupidly, her mind swirling as she tried to think of an excuse out of habit, a thought that was quickly followed by the silent question of why she would ever turn him down.

"There's a new Italian place in Black Springs. I haven't been, but my sister told me about it. She said it's pretty nice. I'd love to catch up," he added.

Catch up to what, she wondered? She and Jesse had never run in the same circles. She didn't know much about him, other than who he'd dated. And it didn't help her to think when she was acutely aware of the gazes her cousin and Wallace were boring into her right now.

Surprisingly, it wasn't Aunt Bev or Skylar who swept in to push her practically into Jesse's arms; it was Wallace. "Of course she would like to go," he said, appearing from nowhere and putting the gift bag firmly in Jesse's hand, thereby freeing Mia's. "She doesn't know anyone in town anymore but me. And she *needs* to get out. She's living in a garage apartment behind Eckland's, off Juneberry Road. You can't miss it. I tell you this because you will have to pick her up. Miss Mia doesn't drive."

"*Wallace!*" Mia cried.

"No problem," Jesse said quickly. "How about tomorrow? Seven okay?" he asked.

"Ah . . . sure," Mia said uncertainly.

"Great." Jesse grinned at her. "Tell you what." He stepped over to the counter and picked up a pen. "Here's my number. Text me later with the address." He handed her the paper, all smiles, and walked backward a step or two. "Looking forward to it." He turned and went out of the shop, carrying his little bag.

The door jingled behind him.

No one said anything for a moment, until Skylar startled Mia by throwing her arms around her from behind. "He is so *cute*!" she said. "I just want to eat him up."

"Cut it out," Mia said, shaking Skylar off her back.

"Don't be like that—I'm so glad you're going, Mia!"

"Why? Why do you care?" Mia said irritably. "Stop acting like I'm a charity case. I don't need anyone setting me up!"

"Honey, you need all the help you can get," Wallace sniffed. "It's not going to hurt you to spend some time with the opposite sex."

Mia desperately wanted to tell them all that she'd spent time with the opposite sex recently.

Aunt Bev appeared from the back room. "Is this what you three call working?" she demanded.

"Mom, Mia has a date with Jesse Fisher. We can all rest easy now!"

"Well that's great. Now everyone can get back to work," she said, and disappeared back into her office.

Aunt Bev didn't seem the slightest bit surprised. Mia whirled around and gave Skylar a look; Skylar threw her hands up and lifted her brows as if to say, *who, me?* And then she grinned and moved behind the counter, plopping herself down on a stool.

"Skylar—"

"No, I didn't do it," Skylar said. "I have no knowledge. Not much knowledge, I should say. Jesus, just take it for what it's worth, Mia and have a good time. You'd think we'd sent you off to join the Scientologists or something." She picked up her magazine.

Mia couldn't wait to get out of there. She didn't know why she was so perturbed, really—a few years ago she would have been ecstatic that Jesse Fisher wanted to take her out. And maybe she was just the slightest bit giddy at the prospect. But mostly she felt nervous. She didn't want to explore the East Beach scene. She didn't want to give anyone the impression—least of all herself—that she had given up and was settling in this little town.

Least of all, anyone who lived up on the hill at the Ross house. In case anyone up there was interested.

◆ ◆ ◆

The next morning, Emily and Skylar appeared at Mia's apartment—Emily, to try on the dress that Mia had been making for her, and Skylar . . . well, who knew why Skylar did anything.

"I *love* this place," Emily said, twirling slowly around in the middle of it. "It's secluded and pretty. All you need is a car, Mia."

"I don't need a car," Mia said. A car would imply she was staying. Not only that, she liked her bike. She could feel herself getting stronger by tackling that hill every day. She held up the dress to Emily.

Emily gasped.

"Is that a good gasp or a bad gasp?"

"Mia . . . it's *gorgeous*," Emily said.

That was good to hear. Mia was pretty pleased with it so far. It was pale green silk with a fitted bodice and short skirt. She'd put some tulle beneath the skirt to lift it, and had made tiny rose appliqués to add to the hem.

Emily snatched it out of her hand and laid it on the bed, then began to strip out of her clothes.

"So guess what?" Skylar asked as Emily put herself into the dress. "I'm meeting with one of the festival guys tomorrow."

"Again?" Mia asked.

"Yes, *again*," Skylar said. "You never know."

"What about the shop?" Emily asked as she presented her back to Mia to be pinned and fitted.

"What about the shop?" Skylar asked with a shrug. "It's not like Mia can't answer phones."

"Thanks," Mia said, and gave Skylar a withering look. "I'm working up at the Ross house, remember?"

"I know, but Mom can get someone else to do that."

Something hitched in Mia's chest. She didn't want anyone else to do it. She wanted to be at the Ross house.

"Which reminds me. You haven't mentioned Crazypants," Skylar said curiously. "Is he still there?"

"Oh, ah . . . I guess," Mia said, and squinted at the back of the dress, pretending to concentrate, even though she'd already tucked Emily in.

"I can't believe he's still in town," Emily said as she examined herself in the full-length mirror. "Maybe he's sticking around for the music festival."

That idea hadn't occurred to Mia. It made perfect sense—he was a musician and he'd come to take in the music festival. He'd be gone after that. He would have figured out what the universe wanted from him, and he'd hear some music, and he'd take off, back to Los Angeles or someplace where he had a life. She could just ignore that nauseating little curl of disappointment in her belly. It was inevitable—the summer people *always* left.

"That's what I'm sticking around for," Skylar said. "After that, I'm moving on to bigger and better things."

"Like what?" Mia asked.

"I don't know yet," Skylar said. "But trust me, I'll have a new gig before long."

"I *love* it," Emily said. "I absolutely freaking adore it, Mia."

"It is gorgeous," Skylar agreed, eyeing the dress Emily had donned. "Maybe you can make me a dress."

"For what?"

"For whatever. A maxi. Yeah, that's it! I want a really nice maxi to wear to the music festival parties. And not in plaid or leather, please."

"Which brings us to your date," Emily said, twirling one way, then the other.

"How does any of that bring us anywhere near my date?" Mia protested. "And it's not really a date. It's drinks to catch up. And you guys are way too deep in my business."

"Whatever it is, maybe you should wear something a little less . . . creative," Emily said, ignoring her protests that it was none of their business.

"Ohmigod," Mia said. "Really?"

"No one wants you to show up looking like the Bride of Frankenstein," Skylar said.

"The *Bride* of Frankenstein?" Mia echoed, insulted.

"That's not it," Emily said. "It's just that everyone is really conservative around here. And besides, I have this super cute dress you could borrow," she added. "It's pink—"

"*No.* I fundamentally disagree with pink," Mia said irritably.

"Don't look so horrified. It's not bubblegum pink. You'll look great in it."

"No," Mia said. "I am what I am."

"Sure you are. But it doesn't hurt to look sexy and mainstream sometimes, either," Emily said cheerfully.

"So, not only am I the Bride of Frankenstein, I'm not sexy?" Mia demanded.

"Please," Skylar said. "Don't act like you don't know how weird you are, kiddo." She threw a companionable arm around Mia's shoulders. "But that's why we love you."

"Being different and unique and being weird are not the same thing, Skylar."

"I'm just going to pop out and get the dress," Emily said.

Surprisingly, Mia didn't mind the pink when her cousins made her put it on. She couldn't disagree that she looked nice. What Mia didn't say was that she looked like any woman in any city in any part of this country. She felt strange, like she wasn't herself. She wasn't this kind of girl. She was not a pink girl.

But pink is what Mia had on when Jesse arrived to pick her up. His gaze skimmed over her, and he grinned broadly. "Wow," he said. "*Wow.* Nice dress, Mia."

Mia resisted the urge to squirm. She tried not to take his obvious pleasure in this dress as an indictment of what she generally wore. "Thank you." She moved stiffly in the gold heels Emily had provided, and picked up the wrap and clutch that Emily had almost tearfully insisted she carry, because Mia's leather jacket, she maintained, would ruin everything.

Jesse cupped her elbow to help her down the stairs. "Relax," he said. "You're not going to fall."

Mia shook her head and took a breath. "I'm sorry. I'm not the best at heels. Or dates. I mean, if this is a date. If it's not, it would be great if you would say so now so I can let my guard down."

He laughed. "Well you better keep your guard up then, because I'm counting it as a first date."

Great. Emily and Skylar were right. Mia had had second thoughts about "catching up" with Jesse after spending the day and evening with Brennan. Brennan was the one on her mind . . . but Mia had lived in this town long enough to know that there would never be anything more than that day, or maybe a handful of them. And she'd be a fool to dismiss a guy like Jesse out of hand.

"Okay, then," she said. "Then I'll do my best." She flashed him a smile. She was aware that she hadn't felt so awkward with Brennan as she did with Jesse. It was a completely different vibe. Maybe it was because with Brennan, she'd been wearing her own dress. And her own shoes.

Jesse drove them to Black Springs to a standard Italian restaurant with standard Italian décor and standard Italian fare. She discovered that he was easier to talk to than she would have believed ten years ago. He reported on people that had been in school with them. Hillary Davis, who had been every guy's dream, had turned out to be gay and had married the high school volleyball coach last year. Danny Richards was killed in a car wreck five years ago, hit by a drunk driver. The girl he'd dated their senior year, Deanna, had moved to Arizona.

He ran through an entire list of names that sounded only vaguely familiar to Mia now. People who meant nothing to her, other than a memory of a snub, or someone who'd sat near her in a class. Jesse remembered them all, had kept up with them. It was as if time had stood still for Jesse, but for Mia? It was all a distant memory. It wasn't a past she belonged to anymore.

Jesse told her about his business and the many renovation projects he had underway. About how thrilled he was to get the Ross house job. Maybe, Mia thought, as she watched the way his eyes sparkled and how his grin remained irrepressible, being in East Beach wouldn't be as bad as she feared. Maybe someone like Jesse would surprise her, and actually be the right person for her. Maybe she'd been so sure of what people saw in her that she lost sight of her good qualities. Maybe people really did grow up.

Maybe all that was true, but Mia was also aware that there was nothing about Jesse that touched her in the same way Brennan had touched her. It was almost as if he was speaking another language entirely. An un-artistic language. But was that fair? Did normal people really speak like artists?

Jesse took her home after dinner and walked her up the stairs to the little landing outside her door. They stood awkwardly on the landing—Jesse with his hands shoved into his pockets, Mia with her hands behind her back.

"This was great," Jesse said at last. "I really enjoyed it."

"Me too," Mia said. All she wanted was to get out of these shoes and take Emily's dress off. She fit her key into the lock, and when she turned back to say good night, Jesse had closed the tiny bit of distance between them. His lips landed on hers. His hand landed on her arm. His kiss was soft and undemanding. It was nice.

He lifted his head. "So I guess I'll see you at work on Monday."

Mia blinked. "Umm . . . yes." She nodded. "Thanks for tonight. I had a good time."

"Me too." He touched her hand before he jogged down the steps, and at the bottom he paused and waved up at her.

Mia opened the door of her apartment and walked in. She kicked the shoes off, dropped the clutch, and stood just inside the door as she wiggled out of the dress and left it on the floor and stood in the middle of the room in her bra and panties, her hands on her hips.

Jesse's kiss was sweet. A perfectly acceptable, perfectly reasonable first-date kiss.

But there were no stars in that kiss. There was nothing tingling inside her. Not like when Brennan had kissed her.

She suddenly had the urge to paint, a habit she'd developed years ago when she was unsettled or anxious. She went to the easel she'd put up and began to paint the lanterns hanging in Eckland's Hardware.

Sixteen

Brennan's work was progressing and getting stronger every day. He'd thought a lot about the script, had put some notes together for the producer and sent it back through his agent. "So let's present this to her together," Phil said.

"Next month," Brennan said. "Give me another month."

Phil groused about it, but Brennan wasn't ready to return to his life just yet. He liked that he was slowly rebuilding his work muscle and his creative strength. He liked the feeling of finally being in a groove. He was making progress—albeit slow progress, but progress nonetheless—to the extent that he didn't even feel guilty when Chance texted him. *Can we talk?* Brennan texted back: *Give me a couple of weeks, bro, and I'm yours.*

He heard nothing after that.

His spirit was renewing, sloughing off the outer layers of his depression and the self-doubts. Brennan was feeling more like himself every day. And yet there was something nagging at him, something that kept dancing around the edges of his thoughts, wanting attention.

It didn't take a psychologist to ferret it out—he knew it was Mia who kept teasing his thoughts. Brennan couldn't be entirely sure if his growing obsession with her had more to do with not getting past her apartment door than genuine attraction—he was used to getting what he wanted from women with very little effort. Not that all women fell at the feet of a rock star, but women who tended to put themselves in the path of a rock star were generally up for anything. It was the selling point of this life, wasn't it? Drugs, sex, rock and roll.

It had been so long since a woman had refused him that Brennan hadn't known how to respond, other than with disbelief.

And yet it was more than that. He'd had conversations with Mia that he had never had with anyone besides Trey, really. He honestly couldn't recall ever having a conversation with Jenna about anything important. Sure, she talked about scripts she'd received and things her agent said, and he supposed he'd mentioned songs he was writing or tour problems. But he could honestly say he had no idea what her political or religious beliefs were. He had no clue who she admired or what was on her bucket list, if she'd known her grandparents, had ever kissed a girl. And he'd been with her for more than a year.

To be fair, Jenna's interest in him had been just as shallow. She wanted the bad boy of the stage. She had been happy to be the arm candy, to appear at his concerts and soak up applause when he pointed her out. She was happy to amuse him in the bedroom, to smoke a little pot with him. She never asked him much about himself, either. She never asked him what had happened to his real father, or how he got into music, or where he was going.

And that had been okay. Brennan preferred an emotional arm's length distance with most people. It was easier that way. There was no hurt that way. He'd never really bothered to think too deeply about why that was. It just was.

But Mia didn't see the rock star. She was genuine, had let some of her own emotions show. She had let him in, if only a little, and still, Brennan couldn't help but wonder if this epiphany about his feelings for her would have happened if she'd let him in her apartment that night. Would it have been another one-night stand? Probably.

Brennan didn't like what that said about him.

Come closer, girl. Rescue my shipwrecked heart. Come closer. Don't let me fall apart.

By Saturday evening, Brennan had the bare bones skeleton of a song.

"Brennan?"

He hadn't noticed his mother at the threshold of his suite until she spoke. "Come in, Mom."

She was dressed in yoga clothes, her long graying hair tied up in a towering knot atop her head. She stuck her head in and looked around with some trepidation, as if she expected the mayhem of trash and beer bottles and music. *"Hey!"* she said brightly, nodding approvingly at his more hygienic state. "Not bad!"

"What's up?"

"I'm flying to LA tomorrow," she said, stepping over his guitar case. "I'm going to be gone for a couple of weeks. I'm feeling the need for a new summer wardrobe befitting my status as mistress of this house," she said, and struck a funny pose.

He smiled at her. That pose sparked a flash of memory in him— he was four or five, his mother was playing dress-up with him, walking with exaggerated swagger, wrapping him in silk scarves and pulling him up, making him dance with her.

"But you'll be in good hands," she said, and he noticed that her smile was especially bright as she bounced down on the bed beside him.

"What's that mean?"

She tweaked his cheek. "Rough as sandpaper. You might want to think about shaving—"

"Whose hands, Mom? I know you're not talking about Magda— she wouldn't care if I starved to death up here, you know."

"I know she's a little crotchety, but she does keep this house sparkling," his mother said. "Most of it, anyway. But I meant that Mia seems to have everything under control."

"Okay," he said warily. He knew his mother too well and knew when she was up to something.

And as if to prove he was right, his mother said, far too casually, "She's a good girl, don't you think?"

Brennan leveled a look of warning on his mother. "Don't even try it, Mom."

"I'm not trying anything!" she protested, and airily waved her hand at him. "Good Lord, I learned *years* ago that you won't listen to a thing I say, so why would I try anything? But I do think she is very sweet, and she's interesting, and it just so happens that she'll be around to oversee the renovations while I'm gone. That's all I'm saying."

"Great," he said. He leaned back against the cushioned headboard as he studied his mother's face.

She picked at the bedspread. "I happen to like Mia."

And there it was. She was matchmaking. Brennan stifled a groan. "So you've said. Over and over." He picked up his guitar. "I know what you're doing, but I think you should turn down your enthusiasm a notch or two, Mom. She's not exactly the kind of woman that fits into my world."

His mother made a sound of surprise.

Even Brennan was a little surprised he'd said those dickhead words aloud. Worse, he couldn't believe he'd actually *thought* them, but there they had come, flowing like a fountain out of him. As if he was living such an exalted life. Wasn't that the kind of elitist thinking he and Chance had written about with their music?

But wasn't it also true to some extent? Wasn't that part of what had been bugging him the last couple of days? He was too emotionally distant, he had a different life than most—

"She certainly won't fit in with *that* attitude," his mother huffed. "I don't know what happened to you, Brennan. You were always such a kind little boy."

"Here we go," he muttered.

His mother clenched her jaw, and he had a funny feeling she was trying to keep from slapping him. "Sometimes, I really don't get you," she said curtly.

Join the club. "I'm not going to hook up with a woman you picked out for me," he said, trying to make a joke of it.

"Because you've done so well on your own, huh? Well I know one thing, you've certainly taken arrogant prick to a new level." She stood up, hopped over the guitar case, and glared at him over her shoulder before disappearing through his door.

"Have a good trip," he called after her.

She did not respond.

On that note, Brennan needed a drink to wash down the niggling feeling that he *was* an arrogant prick. Unfortunately, he discovered the liquor cabinet was bare, thanks to his mother's concern that he was becoming an alcoholic. He grabbed his keys and drove into East Beach and to the little package store there to pick up a few items.

On his way back, he saw Eckland's Hardware on the right. It was closed, but Brennan pulled into the parking lot, debating whether he should turn up the road here and pay an unexpected call on Mia.

He turned up the road.

The lights in the main house were blazing, but there was no sign of life at the barn. He got out and looked up at the apartment windows. They were dark. Brennan glanced at his watch. It was a quarter to nine and she wasn't home. But he'd come this far, so Brennan walked around to the stairs and jogged up to the door and knocked.

No answer.

Okay, she wasn't home. Not surprising, really—it was Saturday night. Of course she'd be out with friends. It was just that he had this idea that Mia was the girl who stayed in on weekends to paint.

He drove home, and once there, with a vodka in hand, he tried to resume his work. But he found it difficult to concentrate. He kept seeing Mia in one of her funky outfits hanging out in some bar. He could see guys walking up to her, could imagine their thoughts—none of them good. Jesus, he was fretting like a teenage boy about where she was.

He managed to put her out of his mind the next day and concentrate on his work.

Monday morning, Brennan was startled awake by the sound of some pretty aggressive hammering. *Shit.*

Eventually, he made his way downstairs to the kitchen for coffee. His mother had failed to take her little beasts with her, he grimly noted as they attacked his feet. Magda emerged from the laundry room with a basket of folded towels as he studied the contents of the fridge. "Hi, Magda," he said.

"Mr. Yates."

"There's no food. Are you going to the grocery store, by any chance?"

"Not my job," she said, walking past him and out of the kitchen.

"What about lunch?" he called after her.

He heard nothing but the sound of a door being slammed. Magda had to be the toughest crowd Brennan had ever played to, and early in his career he had played in some very rough joints.

Okay, so he would have to make a run for food. He fired up the coffeemaker, and as he waited for a cup to brew, he heard laughter. He walked to the doors that led to the back terrace and looked out. A man wheeled a barrow full of debris past the door. Brennan heard the laughter again—male laughter, but not the guy with the wheelbarrow. He craned his neck to look to the edge of the terrace and caught sight of Mia. She was wearing paint-spattered overalls with a cropped top beneath. And she was smiling up a man who could only be described as an Adonis.

Brennan's heartbeat quickened slightly—the guy was handsome and muscular. Mia was smiling as she spoke to him, her hands fluttering in the air as she animated whatever she was saying. Brennan was rooted to the floor, watching her and the man through the panes of the French doors like a jealous lover.

Adonis casually tucked Mia's hair behind her ears, then lifted a long necklace she was wearing to have a look. And then the two of them strolled out of sight and around to the back of the house where he could no longer see them.

Brennan turned back to the kitchen, and stared blindly around him, trying to absorb this new knowledge of Mia. He didn't know who that guy was, but his intuition told him that's where she'd been Saturday night when he'd driven by her apartment like a pimply teen boy. Was she *seeing* Adonis? If she was, why hadn't she told him? Why did he think she would? And did he really have the right to care? It was Mia's life; he should be happy that she had someone. He should be happy that he didn't have to answer the questions he'd had about her the last few days.

But Brennan didn't feel happy; he felt pissed. He felt hot and unpleasant, and wronged. He liked Mia, and in that moment, he didn't give a shit that he had no right to interfere in her life.

So that's exactly what he did.

He abandoned his coffee and went upstairs to dress to go out. He came back down and walked through the house to the work going on at the end of the north wing.

He was surprised that the room had been completely stripped since the last time he was here, and, even more astonishing, her mural was half gone. That's what the hammering had been, he realized—they were knocking down that brick wall, a chunk at a time, and Mia's painting, the view of Lake Haven was just . . . *gone.*

"Hey!"

Brennan turned around. Mia had come in through the French door. She smiled at him. "How are you?"

"Hello," he said.

"I see you're doing the rock star thing again."

"What?" he asked, startled by the remark.

She gestured to his hat and his shades. "The rock star thing."

"Oh. Right." He glanced back at the wall. "Your mural is gone."

"Yep." She moved to where he stood and looked at what was left of the wall with him. "It wasn't any good anyway."

"Yes, it was," he said curtly. He stooped down to pick up a chunk of brick and mortar.

"You don't have to say that on my account. It was angry, remember?"

"I happen to like angry lakes and people hanging from trees on the beach." He looked at the chunk of wall he held. It had been part of one of the hills around the lake with hazy forms of houses on it. Looking at it now, Brennan could see details he hadn't noticed before—like the dark and tiny strokes of trees around the houses. The shadowy form of a dog romping on the lawn of one house. "I liked it."

"Did you?" She sounded surprised. "I warned you the wall was coming down. I never would have painted it otherwise."

He wished she'd warned him that other walls were coming down, inside and outside of him.

"Is there a problem?"

Brennan's head snapped up at the sound of a man's voice.

"He's just looking. I think." Mia shoved her hands into her pockets, and with eyes twinkling with light, she said to Brennan, "This is Jesse Fisher. He's doing the construction work. And this," she said to Jesse Fisher, "is Nancy Yates's son, Brennan."

"Hey," Jesse said. He grinned and extended his hand. Brennan shook it. Yep, Jesse Fisher was a good-looking guy. He was big and fit—put a fig leaf on him, and he was Adonis. Standing next to him, Brennan couldn't help but feel a little run-down by the years he'd spent on tour.

"Man," Jesse said, squinting at him. "You sure look familiar."

"He *does*?" Mia said and peered closely at Brennan.

"Are you from around here?" Jesse asked.

"Me? No," Brennan said.

"I could swear we've met," Jesse said.

"Why does everyone say that about you?" Mia asked laughingly.

"I must have one of those faces," Brennan said. Whatever that meant. He turned away from the two of them back to the wall so that Adonis couldn't study him too closely.

"You know how it is, Mimi. Everyone looks like someone we went to school with, right?"

Mimi? She was Mimi to this guy?

"Remember David Green?"

"Umm . . ." Mia squinted into the distance, apparently trying to conjure up David Green. "I think?"

"I swear I see him about every three months," Jesse said. "Only he lives in Europe now, so I'm pretty sure it's not him. But so many guys look just *like* him. It's weird."

The two of them laughed together about the weirdness of David Green's doppelganger.

Jesse turned his big, friendly smile back at Brennan. "So what do you do, Brennan?"

"Not much, really," Brennan said vaguely.

"That's not true," Mia said. "You're a musician."

In this context, *musician* sounded so lame. For the first time in his life, Brennan wished he were a Navy Seal or a spy, especially when he glanced at Jesse and could tell he thought *musician* sounded lame, too.

"What kind of music?" Jesse asked.

"All kinds," Brennan said.

"Love songs," Mia said.

Something flickered in Jesse's eye. "Cool," he said, although it was clear to Brennan that Adonis didn't think it was cool at all. Yeah, well he'd bet the bastard had probably sung a few of his songs driving around town.

"Do you teach?" Jesse asked.

Did he *teach*? This guy thought he was a school teacher? "No."

"Hey, that's a *great* idea," Mia said. "You could get a job with the East Beach schools and teach guitar lessons. We never had a music teacher at school. Did we?" she asked Jesse curiously.

"I don't think so. I don't know—I was always into sports."

Naturally. "Speaking of work," Brennan said, "I should get back to it."

"He's writing music," Mia said to Jesse.

"Oh yeah?" Jesse's gaze flicked over him. "A song?"

Brennan adjusted his sunglasses. "Actually, a soundtrack for a film."

Jesse's smile was full of undisguised amusement. "Good for you! You know, I should get to work, too. Mia, I want to show you something . . . that is, if you're all through here," he said, gesturing between her and Brennan.

"I think we are," she said and looked questioningly at Brennan. He didn't say or do anything. "Okay. See you later?" she said, and with a smile, she walked away with Jesse.

There was a swing to her hip Brennan hadn't noticed before. *Damn it.*

He reminded himself he wasn't in competition with Adonis. There really was no good reason for Brennan to take off his sunglasses and tell him the truth as he so badly wanted to do. *Yeah, fuckwad, you know me. I am Everett Alden from Tuesday's End. Think I ought to teach guitar lessons now?*

The moment he did something like that, word would get out, and Chance would find him—not to mention the press—and Gary, too, and Brennan couldn't face that. Not yet. He needed more time. He just needed more time. And since when was he so jealous, anyway? He hadn't mustered up this much energy when the grainy photos of Jenna kissing her costar had cropped up on all the tabloids.

Brennan dragged himself back to his work, feeling dejected that Mia was interested in some other man. He told himself to forget it. He was determined to hammer out some of the rougher transitions in the song and improve the bridge. Forget about East Beach and honey eyes and conversations he never got to have with anyone else. He looked at the sheets of music he'd written.

Was this all there was?

His work that afternoon was a mess. Around five, he heard laughter drifting in through the open windows of his room. He got up to look out and saw Mia walking with Jesse. He stood in the shadows and watched Jesse put her bike in the back of his pickup truck, then watched Jesse walk her around to the passenger side of his truck, his hand on her shoulder. And then on her neck.

What was that tightening in the muscles of Brennan's neck and jaw as the pickup moved out of the gate? Ah, yes, that would be your standard full-blown male ego feeling a jealous rage.

He brooded about it all night.

The next morning, Brennan was waiting for Mia when she stuck her foot in through the front door. "Get back!" she shouted at the dogs who rushed to attack, and she pushed the door wider, nudging them away from her as Brennan strolled out of the kitchen with coffee in hand. He whistled; the dogs turned and raced back to the kitchen.

She inched her way in, saw him standing there, and smiled so brightly that the dimples appeared in her cheeks. "Oh, hey! You're up early. Was there a fire?" She laughed at her joke.

His gaze skimmed over her. She was wearing a dress that looked as if it had been made from maps. Actual road maps, with the creases of the folds still visible.

"What's the matter?" she asked, and glanced down at herself. "I didn't get paint on it, did I?"

"No. I like it." Jesus, he felt nervous. He had a plan, but he feared he was standing on the precipice of utter rejection, and frankly, he feared how he would handle it if that happened.

"Well *that's* a ringing endorsement," she said sunnily. "I don't suppose you know how hard it is to glue maps to muslin."

"I don't. But it's cool."

"Really? Maybe I'll make you a matching shirt. Well, not matching. I ran out of New York maps. You would have to be Connecticut. Or California. Name your state."

He didn't name his state.

Mia smiled, but she looked confused. She hoisted the bag on her shoulder and took a step toward the north hall. "Okay, well . . ."

"Wait," he said quickly.

She waited.

"Ah . . ."

Mia shifted. Brennan swallowed, madly debating what he was about to do. She peered closely at him. "Have you been drinking?"

"What? No!" he said, and held out his coffee cup as proof.

"Sorry," she said, throwing up a hand. "But you're acting kind of weird."

"Right. I wanted to ask . . . I was thinking about . . ." For God's sake, he couldn't even talk. He dragged his fingers through his hair and blurted, "Have you ever heard of Stratford Corners?"

"In the Adirondacks? Sure."

"They have a juried art festival there this weekend."

"Yep, I know all about it," she said, nodding. "Actually, I've entered twice."

"You have?"

She giggled. "Don't look so shocked. It was a long time ago. And I didn't win, thank you very much." She bowed. "Now you should look shocked," she teased him. "One entry was a painting. The other entry was this really bizarre idea I had for tin cans." She shook her head and laughed. "Let's just say it didn't work out. Tin cans are definitely not one of my better mediums."

"Do you want to go?" he asked, inwardly wincing at his lack of finesse.

Mia's smile faded. "Huh?"

"Do you want to go? To Stratford Corners and the art festival? Because . . . because I do."

"Are you asking me to go to the art festival with you?" she asked, her voice full of disbelief.

"Yes, but—"

"Mr. Yates, do you have laundry?"

Magda's timing could not be worse. Brennan whipped around. "I don't—"

"I do laundry now," she announced loudly, as if he should know that.

"Okay, Magda. Would you like me to trot upstairs and get it for you?" he asked, gritting his teeth.

Magda shrugged. "I do laundry now," she said, and disappeared into the kitchen. Brennan sighed and turned back to Mia. She looked worried, and he assumed it was because she was going to turn him down.

How much worse could this get? He couldn't even ask a girl out anymore. He felt like an idiot and he shrugged sheepishly. "I'm doing this very badly," he said. "But I would like to take you to Stratford Corners' art festival this weekend. If . . . if you're free."

Mia let the bag slide from her shoulder and caught it in her hand. It dangled next to her shin. She looked at the wall a minute, then at him. "You want me to go to Stratford Corners with you," she repeated.

"Well. Not to put too technical a point on it, I want you to go to an art festival with me."

"It's hours from here," she pointed out.

"Okay," he said, wondering what the distance had to do with anything. He could not recall another time in his life that he'd had so much trouble asking a girl to go out with him. Not even when he was fifteen and told Brenda Wesley to meet him somewhere. He didn't ask, he instructed, and she told him she would *never* go *anywhere* with him. "It's not a trip you can make in a day."

"I know."

Her cheeks began to turn pink. "It's also a big fancy resort area. Did you know that?"

"No," he said uncertainly. "Does that mean something? Is it not the kind of art festival I think it is?"

"What it means is that the toilets up there have two flush buttons and heated seats."

He shook his head.

"It's not cheap."

"Is that . . ." He shifted uncomfortably. God he sucked at this. Everything he said made it worse. "Is that a problem?" He heard the sound of a pickup in the drive, and suddenly, Brennan was desperate for her answer. "Mia . . . do I look like I care about money?" he asked her honestly.

She shook her head, her gaze skirting over him. "Most of the time you don't look like you care about anything, really. Not money, not puppy mills, not the rain forest—"

"Then I guess my look is working, although I have to draw the line at puppy mills. I'd really like to take you to this art festival. That's it. Yes, it's an overnight trip. Would you like to go?" he asked, and tried not to flinch at the sound of the truck doors slamming outside, of men walking to the north wing.

She stared at him, debating. "That depends," she said, as if she hadn't heard the workers' arrival, as if she had all the time in the world to torture him with her answer. "Are you willing to walk around and look at a lot of paintings and sculptures and things made out of wood and tin cans and glass?"

"Yes," he said with an adamant nod.

"Are you willing to listen to me talk about them? And explain things? And critique things? Because I am pretty ruthless when it comes to art shows. I figure if you're going to enter, you'd better be good."

"I . . . I'm totally down with that," he assured her.

"And you're not going to sigh or look bored or act like you would rather be anywhere else than some little town in the Adirondacks looking at art?"

He heard the men in the salon, their voices carrying down the hall. "I'm not going to sigh or look bored. I'd really like to spend some time with you, Mia. If those are the conditions, you have my word. I will not look bored."

"Are we going to stay in the same room?" she asked.

He blinked. Was there a good answer to that? "Whatever you want."

She tilted her head to one side, mulling that over. But then she smiled. "Then yes, Brennan Yates, I would like to go with you."

He felt such a wave of relief that he almost swayed with it. "Great," he said. He was grinning. He was grinning like the day his mom bought him his first bike, like the day he'd signed his first contract, like the day Tuesday's End had their first real hit.

"Great," she said. She was grinning, too.

"Good morning!" Adonis strolled into the foyer. The dogs raced toward him, yapping, and Adonis dipped down onto his haunches to pet them. "How is everyone today?" he asked cheerfully, scratching both dogs behind their ears.

"I can't speak for everyone, but I'm fabulous," Mia chirped.

Jesse's gaze was on Brennan. "Hey, buddy," he said to Brennan.

Buddy was the last thing Brennan was to Jesse Fisher. "Good morning."

"Hope I'm not interrupting," he said, rising up to his full height, which, regrettably, was about an inch taller than Brennan.

"Not at all," Mia said.

"Good. I hate to interrupt—again," he said with a laugh, "but Mia, I'm not sure where the door is going to go in the new wall. Can you show me? And then the crew and I will get out of your hair." He smiled so charmingly that Brennan almost smiled back.

"Sure." She looked at Brennan. "Did we cover everything?"

"I think we did," he said, and sipped his coffee.

"Okay. Talk to you later." She turned around to Jesse.

"Hey, did you check out the spin class Drago was talking about?" Jesse asked as they began to walk down the corridor.

"Not yet. But I'm going to. Really, I am."

Mia's voice floated back to Brennan, who was still standing in the foyer. Still gripping his coffee cup so tightly it was a wonder it didn't shatter in his hands.

"Mr. Yates, I do laundry now," Magda called out to him.

That was the moment Brennan decided he was going to get a plane.

Seventeen

Mia was excited about Stratford Corners.

She wasn't naive; she knew what she'd signed up for. She knew that she'd be in the same room with him. It was a little soon for that, maybe, but Mia was a healthy woman with healthy desires. She couldn't stop thinking about Brennan, she couldn't stop thinking about sex with Brennan, either, and the more she thought about it, the more she wanted to give it a whirl.

Mia was ready to explore this budding relationship. Even if he was a summer person and it went against every rule she'd ever made for herself.

At the end of the day Friday, she was picking things up, packing it in for the weekend. As she went outside to put her lunch bag in her basket, she heard the faint strains of a guitar from an open window upstairs. It was a haunting melody, a sad melody. Mia liked the bits and pieces she heard and wondered what Brennan intended to do with a song like that.

But then the music stopped, and Mia walked on.

She found Jesse sweeping up in the "north salon." They'd taken to calling it the north salon this week in an affected British accent, and giggled like children when they did. The wall was down, and Jesse's crew had braced the hole with some two-by-fours. Next week, Jesse explained to her, they would build some columns to secure the floor above.

Actually, Jesse had explained quite a lot to Mia about what they would do next week, but her attention had drifted. Jesse liked to talk about his work.

"It's Miller time," he said cheerfully when she walked into the room. "At last!"

"Got any plans this weekend?" he asked as he dumped debris into a big plastic bag.

"Actually, yes," she said. "I'm going to an art festival."

"Oh yeah?" He picked up an extension cord and began to wrap it end over end in a circle. "I was hoping maybe we could get together."

She smiled apologetically. She'd never in her life had two guys ask her out at the same time. She wasn't the most experienced girl when it came to dating, much less more than one man. "Maybe next weekend?"

"Maybe." He didn't seem to like that, either, and in fact, he stared at the floor a moment. "Actually, I've been invited to a wedding in a couple of weeks. I've got a plus one if you're interested."

If she was interested? As if she would go to the wedding of people she didn't know because she was interested? It seemed an odd thing to say, but Mia let it go. "That might be fun," she said. "Anyone I know?"

"Nah. He's a guy I used to work with." Jesse leaned down and picked up his things. "Can I give you a ride home?"

"Sure."

Jesse loaded Mia's bike into the back of his truck, then helped her into the cab as he had done every day this week. He chatted about his work on the way down to her apartment—he never asked about hers, Mia noticed—and once they arrived, he lifted her bike with one hand and leaned it up against the barn. "So," he said, shoving his hands in his pockets and looking shyly at her. "May I ask you something?"

"Sure."

"It's the wedding," he said, sounding almost apologetic. "I'd love for you to come. I thought about inviting you before today, but I'll be honest, Mimi—I had cold feet."

"Oh." Mia was not offended by that. Frankly, she completely understood it—the universal rule of weddings was if you took a date, you could expect that the whole world would want to make you the next couple to head to the altar. "I totally get it," she said. She felt magnanimous. The kind of girl who understood things, who would not make trouble for a guy like Jesse Fisher.

"You get it?" he asked, looking hopeful and sounding surprised. And then he suddenly laughed with relief. "Thank God, because I was really sweating it."

She couldn't imagine why he'd be sweating anything. She didn't think she'd come across as high strung or needy in any way. "You didn't really think I'd make a thing of it, did you? We've only been on one date."

Jesse looked confused. "Are we talking about the same thing?"

"I think so," she said. "You don't want everyone to think we're a couple."

Jesse's smile faded. "No," he said, "that's not what—I was talking about what you wear, Mia. I can't—I was just hoping you could wear something normal."

The bottom fell out of Mia's stomach. A swirl of emotions rose up in her, carrying some old hurts. Hurts she thought she'd grown past. "Normal," she repeated. It was amazing how words like that still carried the same punch they had when she was a teen.

"Oh hey, I'm sorry." He quickly grabbed both of her hands. "I didn't mean that like it sounded. I *like* the way you dress. But these people are just really conservative, and I—"

"No, I get it," she said, pulling her hands free of his grip. "Really, I get it. It's okay—you don't have to explain. I can wear something . . ." She tried to think of the right word. *Bland. Cookie cutter. Pink.* "I'll borrow a dress from my cousin."

Jesse smiled again, clearly relieved. "Thank you," he said. "I didn't mean to upset you." He leaned down, kissed her lightly on the lips. He lifted his head and laughed a little. "I can't be the first person to ask you that, right?"

No, he wasn't the first, but that was beside the point. The point was that Mia wanted to be with someone who didn't ask her at all. "It's fine," she said.

"Great," he said, grinning boyishly again. "I'll see you Monday. Have a good weekend at your art festival."

"Yep." She stood rooted to the drive as he put himself back in his truck and backed it up. She waved when he waved, and watched as he drove down the road. Even when he'd turned onto Juneberry Road, she didn't move.

Were her clothes really so offensive? They were unusual, yes. But they weren't indecent. They were interesting, they had substance to them, and thought behind them. What was wrong with that? Why were people always so surprised by it? Why did people want to look the same as everyone else in the world?

"Whatever," she muttered. It had taken a long time, but Mia had come to terms with her style. She didn't care who got it, because *she* got it.

She went into her apartment and looked around. It was funny how her view of the world had invaded this small space so quickly. There was the painting of the lanterns she'd started, waiting for her return to the easel. Emily's dress was on a form, and the fabric for Skylar's maxi neatly folded on the kitchen bar. She'd left the maps she'd used to make her dress on a chair near her bed, and beneath that, the fabric she'd designed with which she intended to make pants.

Normal.

Mia couldn't be normal if she tried. She'd known that for ages, and she thought Jesse knew that, too. It wasn't that she couldn't put on a simple dress for the wedding; she could definitely do that. It was that his asking her, and her bending to his wishes, went against who she was, who she had worked hard to become.

Mia used to think that all she wanted was a career in art. But it was much more fundamental than that. What she wanted was for someone to come along and accept her just as she was. Someone who wouldn't ask her to look "normal." Someone who understood how her clothes, her art, her desires were all bits and pieces of what was on the inside of her, and to appear "normal" was to reduce and hide who she really was.

♦ ♦ ♦

Mia was still brooding about being normal when Brennan arrived, and in private defiance of Jesse's request, she'd dressed in the capri pants she'd made the night before, the knee-length sleeveless vest she'd made last week from some remnants she'd kept from her old job, a silky T-shirt underneath, two long strands of necklace, and around her head, a silk bandeau she'd made from her father's repurposed ties.

She walked down the stairs before Brennan could come up. He had a first-day beard, and was wearing a knit hat and aviator shades this morning, a T-shirt beneath a denim jacket, and some pants that fit him snugly in all the right places. Mia's pulse quickened just looking at him. The man was hot as hell. How had she ever thought otherwise?

"Wow," he said, nodding as she walked down the stairs in her ankle boots. "You look fantastic. Like you stepped off a new designer's runway. That's the perfect thing to wear to an art festival, if you ask me."

She smiled. She relaxed. "Thank you."

He took her overnight bag without comment. Mia got in the car and pulled out her phone. "I was looking at the map," she said as he climbed in and started the ignition. "It's going to take several hours to get there, so I found us the quickest route."

"It may not take that long," he said as he pulled out onto June-berry Road.

"Because you're going to drive like an escaped convict?"

He smiled and covered her hand with his. "You'll see," he said.

She liked his hand on hers. "Just don't kill me, that's all I ask."

"I'll do my best." He pulled her hand across the center console and held it against his thigh as he drove up Juneberry Road. Like he didn't want to let go.

When they reached the road that would lead to the freeway, Brennan turned toward Black Springs.

"This isn't the way," Mia said.

He squeezed her hand. "Can you just relax and let this date go as I've planned?"

It was impossible for her to deny him that request when he made it with such a winsome smile. "It totally goes against my nature to relax, but because you've made some progress from the first time we met, I'll give it the old college try."

He chuckled. "Thank you. You won't be disappointed."

True to her word, Mia didn't say another word until they pulled off that road and entered the gates of the tri-county executive airport.

"You're not a pilot, are you?" Brennan asked as he coasted to a stop.

"Are *you*?"

"No."

"Then what are we doing here? You do realize that you've gone in the wrong direction, don't you?"

"Breathe," he said, as a man emerged from the hangar, walking crookedly in their direction. His face was craggy and his wiry hair stuck out from beneath his cap.

Brennan stepped out of the car.

Mia did, too.

"You Yates?" the man asked, peering intently at Brennan.

"I am. You must be Willie." He extended his hand.

The man shook it. "I'm ready if you are," the man said, and turned around, heading for a small plane sitting on the tarmac.

Mia looked at the plane, then at Brennan. Her mouth dropped open with shock. "Are you kidding? We're *flying* to Stratford Corners?"

"You were the one who said we haven't got a lot of time." He reached into the back of his car and pulled out their bags, then held out his hand to her.

Mia laughed with delight. "This is crazy!"

"You seem the sort to appreciate a little crazy," he said, and tugged her along with him.

A quarter hour later, they were airborne, and Mia was giddy with delight. Pressed into Brennan's side, she kept pointing out things below, unable to believe that she was here, in this plane, with this handsome man, flying up to an art festival like they were rich and famous.

They landed at an airstrip outside of Stratford Corners where a red minivan was waiting for them. Brennan told the pilot where he'd put him up for the night, and handed him two crisp one hundred dollar bills and sent him off to have a nice evening.

The minivan driver put their bags in the back. "I'll take the bags on to the Crosswater Inn after I let you folks off," he said.

Mia gasped—she knew about the Crosswater Inn. It was just outside of Stratford Corners, a picturesque resort with five-star dining and a PGA golf course. It was one of the preferred mountain getaways for the old money of the East Coast, famed for its seclusion and breathtaking scenery. She couldn't imagine how much it would cost to stay there and she didn't want to guess.

"It's too much," she said softly, shaking her head as the man drove them into town. "The plane, the Crosswater Inn—"

"It's a date," Brennan said. "I'm supposed to impress you, remember?"

"You already impressed me just by knowing about the festival," she said. "You didn't have to do all this."

"I *wanted* to do this. And I can." He kissed her temple. "Just enjoy it, will you?"

How could she not? She had never done anything as exciting as this. Mia sat up, cupped his chin and turned his face toward her, and kissed him on the lips.

When she lifted her head, Brennan's eyes were twinkling with pleasure. "It would appear my stock has risen," he murmured. "One room?"

"One room."

When they reached the festival, Mia was bouncing with delight. He held her hands as they strolled through the streets and stopped at various booths to admire the work. She loved that he held true to his promise and never complained. He stayed in the background when she talked with different artists and seemed genuinely interested in the things she showed him, the things she admired. She pointed out the depth of color of some works. The motions and emotions of others. She talked about the intricate craftsmanship in the wood- and metalwork, the difficulty in putting some pieces together.

In the booth of a renowned artist, they stood side by side examining a small oil painting of a red door in a blue building. To Mia, that painting was magical. The artist had employed light so brilliantly that it looked as if the sun were shining in over their shoulders on a real door. "This is how I want to paint," she said.

"You should do it," Brennan said.

Mia nodded. "I know how to do these things, but it's the execution that sets the best apart."

"That's true in music, too," he said. "Anyone can play a few chords. But it's knowing how to put emotions into those chords that separates the best from the rest of the pack."

She looked at him from the corner of her eye. "And where do you fall on that spectrum?"

Brennan laughed. "Better than some and worse than others."

She nodded, understanding that place completely. "Me too. Somewhere in the middle. Not the best, not the worst."

At the end of the day, the driver returned for them in his red minivan and drove them up to the Crosswater Inn.

It was as beautiful as Mia had always heard; azaleas lined the drive to the hotel, and trees formed a canopy overhead with the fresh greens of spring. In the portico of the inn, a fire blazed in an open hearth and liveried doormen took their bags and opened the doors for them.

Still wearing his knit hat and shades, Brennan chatted with the desk clerk, then accepted the thick brass key to their room. He slipped his arm around Mia's waist and escorted her up to the third floor.

Their room had a gorgeous view of the mountains and the valley below, where the lights of Stratford Corners were just beginning to twinkle up at them in the dusk. Their balcony, complete with a bistro table and chairs, was lined with gerbera daisies. A bottle of wine had been opened before their arrival and left to breathe.

Mia walked around the spacious room and took in every detail, emerging from the bathroom with a grin. "There is a two-button toilet in there with a heated seat!"

Brennan laughed.

"I can't believe it," she said, and slipped up behind him where he was pouring wine for them, put her arms around his waist, and pressed her cheek against his back. "I can't believe you did this for me."

"That's not all," he said. "The chef has made us something special." He turned around in her embrace and handed her a glass of wine. "It will be served in our room at seven thirty."

Mia took the wine he offered, but her eyes were on him. "You're amazing, Brennan Yates. I never would have guessed it."

He laughed. "Me either, if you want to know the truth." He clinked his glass against hers before leading her to a couch.

"I've never been on a date like this. Ever," she said as she settled in next to him. "But I bet you do things like this all the time."

"Not really," he said. "I haven't felt inspired to do things like this." He looked at her, held her gaze. "But I'm starting to figure out that I haven't always been looking for the right things in a companion."

"Oh yeah? What should you have been looking for?"

"I'm still not sure," he said thoughtfully. He picked up a strand of her hair and rubbed it between two fingers.

Who was sure? It had always seemed to her that you could never know if someone was right for you until you'd spent a lot of time figuring them out. She didn't know what she should be looking for, either. She wondered about him and the upbringing he'd had. "Is it just you and your mom? No siblings?"

"No siblings."

She traced a line over his brow. "What happened to your dad?"

Brennan's smile instantly disappeared.

"Sorry." Mia took his hand before he could drift away. "I didn't know it was a sore subject."

"I didn't say it was a sore subject."

"You didn't have to. Your look says it all. You don't have to talk about it."

He sighed again and sagged back against the couch. "It doesn't really matter anyway."

"How can you say that? It matters to me," she said. Brennan gave her a dubious look. "What? I'm curious, too," she said. "I'm starting to come around to you, Brennan Yates. I want to know what makes you tick. Or doesn't make you tick. In my case, I literally wear what makes me tick on my sleeve." She smiled. "You're a little harder to figure out."

"Really?" he asked curiously.

"Really. And I would like to know more about you. I mean, I'm here, right?"

"Okay," he said, sounding a bit reluctant. "Here it is—my dad left before I could walk. Dan Yates was my stepfather."

"Okay." That wasn't a unique story; half the people she knew had divorced parents. "Is that all?"

"No, it's not all. Danny Yates was a good man. He adopted me and raised me like I was his son. He was a good father to me. Unfortunately, he died of cancer a few years ago."

"I'm sorry."

He sighed and rubbed his face with his hands. "Thank you. As for my real dad? All that time, I thought he was dead. My mother always told me he just left one day and never came back. No explanation, no contact. When I was a little kid, I couldn't figure out where he would have gone. I made up these great stories about him. Just ask Chance—" He winced. Then he stood up and walked to the bar.

"Who is Chance?" Mia asked.

"An old friend," he said. "I told my friends that my dad died in the war, or he died in a skydiving accident. I invented all kinds of tales about him because I just knew he *had* to be dead or he would have come to see me, right? Who doesn't want to see his own kid?" He turned around to face her. "But when I was fourteen, I found out he'd been living a couple of miles from me all along."

Mia's heart twinged; she gasped. "No way! Why? I mean, *how*? That must have been devastating."

"It was," he agreed, and looked down again, his jaw clenched.

"Did you ask him why?"

"No. I couldn't. The only reason I found out about him at all was because he'd died."

Mia stared at him. "Oh my God," she whispered. The story felt earth-shattering to her; she couldn't imagine being without her father, her biggest champion. She couldn't imagine losing him at an early age, either, and wondered how Brennan had survived it. The questions he must have had, the shock he must have felt. "But your mother—"

"Yeah, my mother," Brennan said flatly. "I don't know, she was a good mom. She's had her own colorful life, and she's quirky, and God knows she can spend a dollar—but she loved me and she did the best she could for me. Except that," he said wearily, and moved back to the couch to sit beside her once more. "For some reason, she allowed me to think my dad was dead, even when she knew otherwise."

"But why?" Mia asked. "What could she possibly—"

"I don't know," he said, interrupting her before she could bury him in questions. He took her hand into his, stroked her palm. "It's not worth the aggravation now. I can't change it—it is what it is."

Mia gaped at him. "You must have been so angry with her. With *him.*"

Brennan shook his head. "I got over being mad at Mom. For the most part, anyway." He picked up his wine glass and drank, then stared out the window for a very long moment. "I guess I never really got over the fact that my father knew where I was and stayed away. And I never got to ask him why."

It was amazing to Mia how much suffering there was in the world. She was blessed, truly blessed. If the only thing she had to worry about was one horrible summer, she should be ecstatic.

"So there you have it," Brennan said and glanced away. "It's complicated. I'd rather not dwell on it."

The mood had definitely changed, and Mia was suddenly desperate to right the listing ship. She didn't know what to say to him about his tragedy, and it *was* a tragedy. "Well . . . I guess this just goes to show that money can't buy happiness, huh?"

That brought Brennan's attention back to her. He arched a brow with amusement. "I tell you *that* sad tale, and that's all you've got? A cliché?"

She smiled. "You don't like it? How about time heals all wounds?"

Brennan laughed. He took the wine glass from her hand and put it aside.

"Wait . . . is there anything else about you I should know?" she asked as he slipped his hand behind her nape.

"Like what?" he asked, his gaze on her mouth.

"I don't know. Maybe you have a secret desire to be a gardener," she said, and pulled the cap off his head, tossing it aside. "Or wait, maybe that soundtrack you're writing is the story of your life." She pushed her fingers through his shaggy hair.

He shifted, pressing her onto her back on the couch. "That's not a bad idea. I'll write the music for the story of my life, and you do the set design. I know it would be very colorful and off kilter."

Mia laughed as he kissed her neck. "I can see it already. Very futuristic with lots of neon lights and spandex."

"That sounds perfect," he muttered, and kissed her languidly. He lifted his head.

His eyes were deep pools of blue. Two tiny oceans staring back at her. How had she ever thought him repulsive? Right now, he was the sexiest man she'd ever known.

"What are you thinking?" he asked, narrowing his eyes.

"That I like you, Brennan Yates."

"I like you, too, Mia Lassiter. More than I want to."

"So, would you agree that opposites attract?"

He groaned and kissed her again to silence her clichés. He kissed her much more passionately, tightening his embrace and crushing her to him as if he were afraid she would flutter away.

Desire quickly enveloped Mia and pushed any other thoughts about him and his screwed-up parents from her mind. His touch was pleasurably tormenting, leaving her panting for more. There was something about his reverence of her that jolted her into hyperawareness; her skin sizzled when he touched her, her body shivered where he kissed her. She clung to him, pressing against his body, her desire for him now as deep and fervent as her dislike of him had been only days ago. He groaned with want as he kissed her, his pleasure apparently as stark as her own, and Mia frantically needed to have every inch of him on every inch of her.

He nipped at her lips and swirled his tongue around hers, and Mia eagerly met his kisses as she explored the hard planes and stiff curves of him. Her fingers tangled in his hair. She stroked his bristled cheek and slid her hand down to his hips.

Brennan suddenly lifted off of her and stood up. Before Mia could move, he swept her up and twirled her around, depositing her on the bed, and bracing his arms on either side of her, he dipped down to kiss the hollow of her throat.

She pressed her hand against his chest, could feel the strength of his body and the heat in his skin, the rhythm of his heart. But that tingling she felt was her melting, giving into the craving for sex with this man. Her heart was hammering in her chest, her thoughts racing around the sensations of being touched and desired, and Mia took his head between her hands and opened her eyes.

He was gazing directly at her, his eyes dark and blue. He brushed the back of his hand across her cheek. "This is how it should always be," he said.

She knew exactly what he meant—every encounter should be this intense, this full of need.

He nipped at her earlobe. "What do you want me to do to you?" he whispered into her ear.

"*Everything.*"

Brennan groaned again. He moved his hand down her body and between her legs. Mia sighed with contentment and lifted up to kiss him; her hands slid over the corded muscles of his back and shoulders, and all she could think was that she wanted him to make love to her *now*. She couldn't remember ever feeling this desirable. She couldn't remember ever feeling this intense lust. She wanted to feel him inside her, that white-hot, searing feeling of unity.

Brennan was a master at exploring her body with his hands and his mouth. She was still kissing him, yet somehow, her clothes came off, as did his. She slid her hands over his body, but his kisses were blistering, making it impossible to think. She was still desperately wanting him, but he took his time to enter her, moving so languidly, so unhurriedly, that she thought she would cry out with the torment of anticipation.

Her desire was urgent and imperative, and Mia wrapped her arms around him, pressed against him, urging him to move faster. Brennan understood it; he continued his gentle assault on all her senses, his hands and his mouth arousing her every place they touched, as he rocked inside her, pushing her along a building wave of pleasure. His fingers danced about the hardened core of her, his body deep in hers, until she couldn't bear it another moment and cried out with release.

Brennan thrust into her with his own soft roar of completion, then collapsed alongside of her on the bed, his breath fast and furious.

Mia was speechless. She couldn't even open her eyes; her heart was still lingering where they'd just been.

Brennan brought her back to the land of the living with a soft kiss, then touched his fingers to her lips.

She opened her eyes. "That was incredible," she said.

"You're beautiful," he said, and kissed her again.

"I think you ought to write a song about this," she said, and brushed his hair from his face.

"I'll start right now." He hummed, the sound of his voice low and deep. Mia could feel the reverberation in her skin, and it sent another little shiver of delicious sparkle up her spine.

"Promise me you'll never hum that to anyone else," she said solemnly when he stopped. "That's my song."

Brennan grinned. "Come here, come closer," he said, and gathered her into his embrace and rested his chin against her head.

They lay that way, contented to be together like this . . . until the phone rang.

Brennan rolled over and picked up the receiver. "Hello," he said, and rubbed his face with his hands. "Great. Thanks." He hung up the receiver and rolled back into her. "Hungry?"

"Ravenous."

He chuckled and stood up, his body magnificent in the low light of sunset that filtered in through the windows of their room. He walked into the bathroom, and a moment later, Mia heard water running.

She sat up, pushed both hands through her hair. Brennan was right. *This is how it should always be.*

Eighteen

Brennan awoke to the sound of birds chirping. He saw the French doors were opened onto the balcony, and ominous-looking clouds had rolled in. He rolled over onto his back and looked around. Mia was sitting in a chair, her feet tucked up under her, her sketchbook in her lap. She was wearing his shirt but nothing else, her hair a glorious mess of tangles. She smiled.

"What are you doing?" he said, and threw the covers back. "Come back to bed."

She turned the sketchbook around to show him a pencil drawing of him in bed, one arm over his face, the sheets bunched up around him. She'd even sketched in the French doors and balcony, and the hills beyond. She'd sketched the painting that hung above the bed. But instead of a painting of an Italian villa, Mia had sketched in the mural she'd done at his mother's house.

He came up on one elbow. "A souvenir?"

"Sort of." She stood up, walked over to the bed, and flopped down onto her belly with her sketchbook in hand. He caressed her back and her bare hip. Three times they'd made love last night. He felt like a fucking stallion.

He looked at her sketch, laughing at the small details he found in it—a guitar on the couch. An easel on the balcony. She had sketched in a perfect life for the two of them after a perfect night.

They had just ordered breakfast when his phone rang. He looked at the display; it was Phil. "I'm going to take this, if you don't mind," he said.

"Sure. I'm going to grab a shower." She disappeared into the bathroom, stretching her arms high above her.

"Hey, glad I caught you," Phil said when Brennan answered. "So Kate Resnick took a look at your notes," he said, jumping right into it. "She wants to meet. She loves the ideas, loves the direction you're going, but she wants to talk about some storyboarding around it. When can you get to LA?"

Brennan looked at the closed door of the bathroom, then stood up and put his back to it. "I told you—not now."

"Listen, Everett. This thing is on a fast track. We don't have weeks to wait for you to get your shit together. Just fly out this week, let's have a sit down, then you can fly back to wherever you are and contemplate your navel some more, okay?"

"If I fly out to LA, everyone is going to know it, and then it's game on," Brennan said. "I need until the end of the month."

"What if it's someplace else? What if I can convince her to meet up in someplace like Topeka? Will you come?"

Brennan considered it. This was something he really wanted to do and didn't want to lose the opportunity because he was enjoying being anonymous for a time. "Yeah," he said. "If you can get her to meet somewhere no one is going to see me, I'll make it happen."

"Great. Fantastic. I'll be in touch," Phil said, and clicked off.

So did Brennan. He turned back to the room, but almost jumped with alarm when he saw Mia standing there, wrapped in a towel, drying her hair with another towel. She smiled. "You look guilty."

"I'm always up to something."

Mia laughed and turned back to the bathroom.

He was guilty, all right. He hadn't told her who he was. He'd thought about it—last night, during the night, they'd talked about everything.

She'd told him about her longing to be an artist and how painful it was to know that she might never realize her dream. "I always thought it would be easy," she said. "Just get up and paint, right? But it's not easy at all." She'd told him about high school, and how, after years of being teased, she went to the extreme and tried to be as different as she could. "It worked, too. No one liked me by the time I was done."

He'd laughed with her, sympathized with her. He'd liked listening to her talk, and the stories she told. He hadn't said much in return, and she didn't ask probing questions. He guessed that the truth about his father had been enough for her for now.

But not for him. Brennan was increasingly aware that while he hadn't actually lied to her, he'd left out some significant details. He puzzled over why he was holding back. He'd found a comfort level with Mia that he hadn't felt with another person in years. He was at ease with her. He loved her sense of humor, and he loved the way she felt in his arms. But he was deathly afraid of how the truth would affect her, how it had the potential to change her somehow.

Even more frightening was how it would change him, make him revert to the way he'd lived the last fifteen years.

He didn't tell her.

◆ ◆ ◆

They returned to East Beach like a pair of lovers. Brennan saw Mia every day as the work week started. They'd walk down to the bluff and have lunch, or she'd join him in the kitchen at the end of the workday for a drink.

But in between those moments, he would hear her laughing or talking with Adonis.

In the middle of the week, she invited him to her apartment.

Brennan looked up from the salad he was making. "Tonight?"

"Tonight," she said.

"You're going to let me in, right?"

"Maybe, if you play your cards right," she said, her honey eyes twinkling with mirth. She was wearing the paint-spattered overalls, the bib of which looked as if she'd embroidered it, and high-top sneakers. She'd wrapped her hair in some sort of turban thing, and she was covered with a layer of dust. "But first, I have to know. Are you okay with tiny apartments? And a handle flush on the toilet?"

"Heated seat?" he asked.

She shook her head.

"Lucky for you that I love tiny apartments with cold toilet seats. In fact, that's the only kind of apartment I will visit."

She laughed. "I'm going to cook for you, too," she said.

"Now I'm excited."

"Don't be. I'm not a very good cook. But I can bake chicken and toss a salad as well as the next guy."

"I can't wait," he said. He meant it.

"Can't wait for what?"

Brennan was startled by the appearance of his mother walking into the kitchen, bags of purchases in her hand. "You're home early," he said, and tried to convey a warning to his mother in his gaze. "I thought you'd be gone another week."

"I didn't find the shopping to my liking," she said, and smiled at Mia. "Can't wait for what?" she repeated.

"Mia is going to feed me tonight since my own mother won't."

His mother snorted and put down her purchases. "You're a grown man, Brennan Everett," she said. "I would hope you could feed yourself by now." She smiled broadly at Mia. "Is it just my son who is so disabled and unable to feed himself, or did you invite Jesse, too?" she asked as she headed for the wine cooler.

Mia's face flushed. "No, just . . . just Brennan."

"Fantastic!" his mother trilled, and opened the cooler.

"I better run," Mia said quickly, her gaze darting between Brennan and his mother. "I'll see you tonight," she said, and grabbed up her messenger bag and bolted from the room.

Brennan waited until he heard the front door close before he turned around to his mother. "Was that necessary?" he asked, gesturing vaguely in Mia's direction.

"That young man is besotted," his mother said airily. "You should have seen him when he came to work before I left. He couldn't take his eyes from her. I would hate to see that ruined because of you."

"*Thanks*, Mom," Brennan said.

"You know what I mean. You yourself said she wasn't your type."

"I didn't say that," he argued.

She clucked her tongue at him. "Have you told her?"

He felt himself flush under the collar, a sure sign of guilt.

"Oh God," his mother said, reading the answer in his expression. "How long are you going to let her go without knowing who you are?"

"I will tell her when the time is right," he said. *Maybe tonight.*

"The time was right when you first met her," she said.

"So she can tell all her friends and then have them tweet about it, and then have the press look into it and start nosing around? Is *that* how I'm supposed to recover? What's wrong with a little anonymity? I haven't lied to her. I've answered every question honestly."

His mother didn't look as if she believed him.

"Stay out of it," he warned her. "I'll be gone in a few weeks, and then you can resume passing your judgments about me from afar."

"That's exactly what I'm afraid of," she snapped. "That you'll just up and leave that poor girl."

"Then why the hell did you insist on putting her in my face?" he asked angrily. "*You* made this happen. *You* wanted her here. Don't blame me for the consequences." He stalked off then, unwilling to argue with his mother another moment.

But he couldn't deny what she said was true.

The problem was that Brennan didn't know what he wanted. He didn't know where he wanted this to go. He didn't know what the hell he was doing right now.

♦ ♦ ♦

When he arrived at Mia's some time later, she opened the door wearing a long, backless dress that tied around her neck. The material was soft and looked almost hand painted, and Mia looked sexy as hell in it. "Nice dress," he said, nodding approvingly.

"Thank you. I made it for Skylar, but she said it looked too much like Grandma's couch. So I'm going to make her another one." She stepped back and cast her arm wide. "Welcome to my tiny little piece of quiet."

Brennan stepped inside and took it all in. The apartment was small, but stylish. He noted the trendy features, like the glass countertops and the raised platform bed, but what he really noticed was the evidence of Mia. She had filled the space of this studio with her essence. There was an easel with the half-finished canvas painting of the lanterns at Eckland's. There were two dress forms, one with a stunning green dress on it, and the other that looked as if she was working out a pattern. Her sketchbook was open on a small dining table, and stacks of materials— cloth, metal, things he couldn't identify—took up one entire corner. And tacked along the walls were her attempts at fine art. Small paintings and big drawings, leather and cloth hangings, metal sculptures.

"Wow," he said, walking inside. "It's a studio." His gaze settled on the green dress. "You're really good with clothes, Mia."

"Tell that to my brothers. They think I'm weird. Wine?"

She held up a bottle of wine that could be bought in any grocery store and poured two glasses. On the bar that separated the kitchen from the main living area was a plate with crackers and spreads. "This is my date presentation," she said, teasing him. "Don't mess it up."

He accepted the wine from her with one hand, reached for her with the other, and kissed her, his lips lingering on hers. It was strange how he felt the weight of this relationship in his heart after such a short time of knowing her. Like his heart had been nothing more than a whisper until she began to fill it up. There was definitely some substance here between them, and Brennan believed now was the right time to tell her. "Listen, Mia—"

"Please don't apologize for your mom," she said, interrupting him. "I had it coming. She saw me and Jesse together a few times before she went out of town, and I'm sure she thinks there is more to us than there is."

Brennan stilled. He lost his train of thought and put the wine down. "What is between the two of you?"

"Nothing." She said it so quickly that even she groaned a little. "That sounds suspicious, doesn't it? Okay, there is some . . . flirtation," she said, clearly searching for the right word. "We've been out on a date . . ." She peeked up at Brennan. "And I sort of said I'd go to a wedding with him." She waited for his reaction.

Brennan's belly roiled. He felt a surge of jealousy. Ownership. Things he had no right to feel. "You don't owe me an explanation. You should see who you want to see."

"Well, *thank* you, I don't disagree with that," she said with a funny little laugh. "But as it turns out, I suck at playing the field. All these years, I thought it would be so cool to, you know, date around," she said, making invisible quotes in the air. "But it's not cool. It's hard."

Brennan put his hands on her waist. "Am I holding you back?" he asked bluntly.

"No," she said with an adamant shake of her head. She peeled his hand from her waist and held it in hers, squeezing it. "I *really* like you, Brennan. I mean, I didn't think I would *ever* like you, much less, you know, *be* with you. But I do, I really like you."

"That's great," he said.

"No, it's not. Look, I've lived in East Beach all my life. I know how it is."

"How what is?" he asked, confused.

She groaned to the ceiling and sighed. "Summer people."

"Who is that?"

"That is *you*," she said. "Summer people is what we year-rounders"—she gestured to herself—"call people like you. People who come up to Lake Haven for the summer and live in big fancy homes that are much nicer than anything we live in. They—*you*—are generally rich, and generally just passing through."

"Wow," he said, sinking down onto a barstool.

"Please don't be offended," she pleaded. "I mean, I'm right, aren't I? It's not like you're moving to East Beach. Maybe I'm wrong, but I can't help thinking that this," she said, gesturing between the two of them, "is a temporary thing. You're going to leave eventually. And without a miracle, I may never leave."

Brennan wanted desperately to argue. But how could he? She was looking at him so hopefully, so clearly wanting him to say that it wasn't so, that he wouldn't leave, or that he'd take her with him, and Brennan knew he had to tell her.

He was going to tell her then and there, but her phone rang.

"Oh. Sorry," she said, and held up a finger as she picked up the phone and answered, turning her back to him. "I can't talk right now," she said into the phone, and smiled furtively over her shoulder at him. "Because I'm *busy*," she said, and grabbed up her wine and moved into the kitchen. As if that helped—the apartment was so small there was no place she could go for a private conversation. "I can't come to the bistro tonight, Skylar, I don't care who is there. I have plans tonight . . . none of your business!"

She paused, drank wine. Then put the glass down.

"I don't know what he meant because I wasn't there, obviously. Seriously, don't you have better things to do than keep tabs on my social life? No, that's not what I am doing . . . ohmigod, I have to go. Bye. Tell Mom I'll call her later."

Mia hung up the phone with a snort of exasperation and threw the phone onto a chair. She looked sheepishly at Brennan. "That was my cousin. She's very nosy."

"I gathered."

"The whole world wants to live my life for me," she said, and put her hands on her hips, obviously frustrated.

That statement resonated with Brennan and opened his eyes to just how improbably connected to her he was. They shared so many of the same experiences, just on different scales. And knowing that gave him a surge of desire so strong that he abruptly put down his wine, crossed the room to her, and took her in his arms, cupping her face with his hand, kissing her long and hard and with all the doubts and desires that were brewing violently inside of him. When he lifted his head, she blinked with surprise. "What was *that* for?"

"Because I've missed you," he said. "Because I want—"

Screw that. He suddenly hoisted Mia up onto the table. She made a little cry of alarm and grabbed the wine before it toppled, but Brennan didn't care if it did. He grabbed her skirt and lifted it up, then pushed in between her legs as he kissed her, his tongue seeking hers, his hands seeking her flesh.

Mia responded quickly; she was suddenly fumbling with the belt of his pants. They worked feverishly together, kissing and caressing, clearing the barriers of clothing between them, desperate for the connection of flesh. In a moment he was freed, and he slipped his hand between her legs. Good God, the woman wasn't wearing panties, and she was slick. Mia wrapped her legs around his waist, her arms around his neck, and then bit his lower lip.

Brennan lost all reason—he plunged into her, sighing with contentment as he sank into her body, the sensation of it so electrifying and satisfying. He pumped into her as she clawed madly at his shoulders, trying to draw him closer, trying to press as much of her body to his as she could. And just as quickly, her head fell back with the bliss of her release.

His release happened just after hers.

He dropped his head to her shoulder, dragging air into his lungs, his mind flitting around all the things he was in this moment. Elated. Spent. Emotional.

"Wow," she said breathlessly, and with her hand, pushed his head from her shoulder. She stared into his eyes, caressed his cheek, brushed his hair from his face. She kissed his lips softly. Mia didn't say anything, but she didn't have to—she was a master at reading his expression. Or maybe it was the artist in her that could sense a man's vulnerability. If she could read his conflicting emotions, if she could see that he was torn between her and the world beyond East Beach, she didn't say. If she could see that his feelings for her had gone well beyond sex, beyond general curiosity, and were drifting into uncharted waters of love, she didn't give any hint. She suddenly smiled and said, "Are you trying to avoid my chicken? Because that's definitely the way to do it."

"Not your chicken. *Never* your chicken," he promised her, and ignored the voice in his head that roared at him to admit the truth.

Nineteen

Mia was in a fabulous mood. After months of watching everything she thought she'd worked hard to achieve crumble around her, things were finally happening for her.

Her creative juices were flowing at last, but interestingly, not in the usual direction. Lately, she'd been making so many clothes that she hadn't had time to paint. What surprised her was that she really enjoyed it. She'd found a creative outlet that had piqued her interest.

And, for the first time in her life, she was having above-average sex. Way above average. Knock-your-socks-off sex. And, bonus, there were *two* men flirting with her on a daily basis. She'd had lunch with Jesse yesterday while Brennan was out and had let him flirt with her. It was fun! This had never happened in her life, and Mia had to admit, she liked it. She liked it a lot. She walked around giddy and giggly and so damn happy to be alive it was amazing she didn't float to work every morning on a balloon of her happiness.

Last, but not least, while Aunt Bev could be a pain in the neck to work for, she paid well, and Mia was actually earning a little bit of money for once in her life.

Mia annoyed Wallace with her bubbly demeanor when she asked to borrow the shop van the next night. She wanted to drive over to Grandma's house to meet Emily and Skylar and deliver the dresses she'd made.

Grandma met her at the door and swung it open. "There she is! Skylar informs me you're dating Jesse Fisher. Is that true?"

"Ohmi*god*," Mia said cheerfully. "Hello, Nosey Parker." She dipped down to kiss her grandmother's cheek. "And no, I'm not *dating* him. I'm going to a wedding with him. That's not a date, that's a favor."

"Sounds like a date to me," Grandma said, eyeing her shrewdly.

"Nope. Not a date. Skylar needs to stay out of my business. Where is the big blabbermouth, anyway?"

"She and Emily are out on the porch with the boys," Grandma said. "Hope you like cabbage soup. We're having it for dinner."

"Are you on a diet?"

"Diet! Why would I need to diet at my age? I happen to *like* cabbage soup, and so does your Grandpa."

Mia wrinkled her nose.

"Go out there with your cousins. They don't have any sense, either. I'll call you when it's ready." Grandma retreated to the kitchen.

Mia walked out onto the back porch and was met with shrieks of joy from her cousins, which, for a brief moment, she was foolish enough to believe were for her. But the shrieks were for the dresses, which they snatched out of her hands. Little Ethan joined them in the screeching, and Elijah slept through the ruckus.

"I can't *wait*," Emily said, holding her dress up to peer at it. "It's gorgeous, Mia. Remember that picture I took of it? I put it on Pinterest and now one of my friends is dying to meet you," she said excitedly.

"Emily," Mia groaned. "Why did you do that?"

"Well? Think about it, you could make a little money on the side."

Mia hesitated. "I could?"

"Of course you could, silly," Skylar said, holding her dress up to admire it. "I *love* it," she said. "*So* much better than the first one."

"According to you. I like the first one better."

"Then you can wear it on your date with Jesse this weekend," Skylar said, and waggled her eyebrows at Mia.

"Skylar, butt out of my life," Mia said cheerfully, and fell into a wicker chair.

"How can I?" Skylar asked. She hung her dress from a hook for a potted plant. "I work at Mom's shop where there is nothing to do but gossip. Wallace has a lot of gossip, by the way. About everyone." She looked slyly at Mia. "A *lot*, if you know what I'm saying."

"I don't."

"And then Jesse came in to get a check and totally volunteered the wedding this weekend. Which, frankly, surprised me. Because according to Dalton, you've got all kinds of stuff going on."

Mia sat up and pinned her cousin with a look. "Wallace, too? Seriously, butt *out*," Mia warned her. "I'm having a good time, okay? I don't need anyone messing things up for me."

Skylar giggled, clearly unperturbed.

"Wait, what's going on at your apartment? Aren't you dating Jesse?" Emily asked as she lifted her dress high out of Ethan's reach.

"No! We went out for drinks, and I'm his plus one at a wedding. That's it."

"He's a great guy," Emily pointed out.

"I know, I know, Jesse is a great guy. But I'm not looking for a relationship—"

"Of course not," Skylar said. "You're playing the field!" she added grandly. "But here's what I don't get. Why would you play the field with that odious summer guy from Ross house?"

"What?" Emily cried so loudly that she awakened Elijah.

"It's true! She's blushing!" Skylar cried, pointing at Mia. "Wallace was right. Mia, for God's sake, not a *summer* guy. Especially not one living with his mother."

"Okay, all right," Mia said, waving her hand at her cousin. "You're reading way too much into it. I'm not sixteen, you know. I know what I'm doing and I'm just having fun." That was so not true, but Mia wasn't about to tell Skylar the truth. "You of all people should get that."

"Oh, I get it," Skylar said as she dipped down to pick up the baby, "but when I have fun, it's with *fun people*. Not summer people with psychological problems."

"He doesn't have psychological problems," Mia sighed.

"Skylar, leave her alone," Emily said. "You are the last person to give relationship advice. Mia can see who she wants to see, and if Little Lord Fauntleroy is as weird as she said he is, it won't last." She smiled at Mia. "Just don't blow it with Jesse. We love him."

"Oh, great, you too?"

"So *anyway*," Emily said, holding up a hand to silence Mia's protests, "you could get three hundred bucks for one of these dresses, easy. You should really think about it."

Mia forgot her irritation with Skylar for a moment. "Really?" she asked doubtfully.

"Yes, really," Emily said, and began to extol the benefits of making clothes for other people as a side job. Mia was interested, and she listened. She didn't think more about Skylar's meddling, because Grandma called them to a dinner of tasteless cabbage soup, and the talk turned to other things in East Beach.

When Mia left that night, she had agreed to let Emily bring her friend up to her apartment to talk about another dress. She was nervous and excited about it. It was one thing to make clothes for herself or her cousins, but it was another thing entirely to make something for a stranger. It was a challenge she was looking forward to.

♦ ♦ ♦

The next day, Mia was so busy with work and the dress she was making to wear to the wedding, she could scarcely carve out the time to meet Emily's friend. So naturally Emily showed up with not one friend, but three, all of them wanting dresses. It was amazing to Mia how she saw colors and shapes when she looked at these women. It was as if each of them presented a different canvas upon which she could create something beautiful and special. She was creating art for them. Up until now, she'd never thought of creating anything other than paintings for others. It was a new and stimulating way to look at her art.

The day quickly bumped into evening, and Mia made herself stop sewing to get ready for Brennan. He never let a day pass without coming down to see her and chat about her day, but it had been two days since they'd had any quality alone time.

He arrived at her apartment after Emily and her friends had left and made love to her like she was the last person on earth.

Jesus, the sex was fantastic. But that's not what drew Mia to him—what drew her was their conversations. He admired the fabrics she was creating, the sketches of dresses she was going to sew for extra cash. He talked about how creating music was such a fickle thing, how it always started with a chord, but grew from there.

"I'd love to hear your music sometime," she said.

"You will," he promised. "When I finish this song, I'll play it for you."

They also talked about things that Mia never really discussed with other people, topics that didn't really come up in casual settings. Gender equality. The plight of the hungry in Africa. The drought in the West. Mia loved it; she loved expressing her thoughts and opinions and not having them shot down. Brennan never shot her down. He listened to everything she said and just *discussed* it.

Her life was beginning to feel very full.

But there was a part of Mia that knew she was feeling things for Brennan that were going to hurt in the end. She didn't really care at present—the inevitable end seemed very far away, something she could worry about when the time came. It was too early to broach the subject of where it was going between them, to assume anything. The only thing Mia knew with all certainty was that her heart swelled with happiness when she saw Brennan. She told herself it was okay for the moment. She told herself she could handle what would come. She told herself she was being cosmopolitan and experiencing life. What could be wrong with that?

And then there was Jesse.

Jesse made her laugh. Jesse spoke her language. When the gold-plated fixtures were delivered to the Ross house, Mia and Jesse stood side by side, wide-eyed and aghast that someone would spend *that* kind of money on a light fixture for a closet that no one was going to see. They had grown up in the same town, had experienced the same sort of life. They were surprisingly compatible.

Mia liked Jesse well enough . . . but he didn't make her heart pitter-patter. Thoughts of Jesse didn't wake her up at night. He was handsome and he was fun . . .

But there was that niggling memory in the back of her mind when she thought of him. He'd asked her to tone down. She could imagine, if she were to seriously date him, how many times that would happen. She could imagine, if their relationship progressed, that it would become an issue. Maybe she wasn't being fair. Maybe she ought to give him the benefit of the doubt. Maybe.

Brennan had never been anything but complimentary of her look.

Oh God, who was she kidding? Was it really so wrong to daydream about a relationship with Brennan? Was it foolish to walk around Ross house and imagine them together at Thanksgiving or Christmas? Or to envision a shared apartment in the city? He would work on his music, and she would work on her art, and they would go for coffee, arm in arm, and talk about the world.

It was just a fantasy; Mia knew in her heart that it was only that. Brennan had never mentioned the possibility of staying. She just wished her hope wasn't so large.

Late Friday afternoon, Mia was packing up to go home. She heard Brennan walking down the hall to the kitchen as he normally did, but was surprised to see him with his guitar case and a duffel bag, dressed in jeans, boots, and a leather bomber jacket. "Hey, handsome," she said.

He glanced around as he set the items down. "Where's Mom?" he asked.

"Tennis, I think."

"Good. I might need to ravage you here on the kitchen island." Mia laughed as he gathered her in his arms and kissed her. He lifted his head and said, "Listen, I'm taking off for a few days."

"Oh." She tried not to appear as surprised as she felt. He'd been at her apartment last night and hadn't mentioned anything. "Where?"

"California. There are some people I need to talk to."

"What people? About what? About your music?"

"Hopefully." He glanced at his watch. "You're going to a wedding this weekend, right?"

She colored. It felt odd to mention that now. It felt odd to think of Jesse now. "That's the plan."

He glanced up from his watch and his gaze flicked over her. He smiled and averted his gaze again. "You should go and have fun."

"Are you . . . you're okay with that?"

"Yeah," Brennan said, and drew a breath. "More than okay. You should go."

Why should she go? Mia pressed her lips together. She wanted him to tell her not to go, to take her in his arms and ask her not to go out with Jesse. Just a few days ago he was asking what was between her and Jesse. Now he was telling her to go out with Jesse and have fun. "I mean, if you'd rather I not," she said uncertainly.

Brennan didn't take her in his arms or ask her not to go. In fact, he did the opposite. "I can't tell you what to do. I don't have any claim to you."

Mia was stunned into silence. Of course he had no claim to her . . . but was he not even going to try? Didn't he *want* to claim her? Jesus, just claim her already! Claim her caveman style, say she was his, and that was that!

He frowned. "What?"

"I don't know," she said. Her stomach was suddenly churning. "I just thought you might—"

"Hello! Mia?" The sound of Skylar's voice startled her. The dogs leapt from their pillows and, barking with their miniature ferociousness, raced down the entry hall. "Oh no," Mia said.

"What?" Brennan asked, glancing over his shoulder.

"That's my cousin." Mia hurried out of the kitchen.

"Can you make them stop?" Skylar cried, trying to nudge the dogs away from nipping at her feet.

"Come!" Brennan said sternly, and the dogs reversed course, racing back to the kitchen.

Skylar's head came up at once, and she looked past Mia to Brennan. Mia looked at him, too. He'd picked up his bags, was ready to walk out the door. Skylar's timing could not be worse. Mia looked back at Skylar— she was going to ask her to wait outside, but something was wrong. Skylar's gaze was fixed on Brennan. She was gaping at him. And Mia was sure Skylar knew him. *How* she knew him, Mia was afraid to find out.

"What are you doing here, Skylar?" Mia asked.

"What?" Skylar spared Mia a glance. "Jesse had to go get something, so I talked Wallace into letting me bring up the tile that came in today. I thought I'd give you a ride home." She shifted her gaze to Brennan again, her eyes moving over him, her expression one of pure delight. "Aren't you going to introduce us?"

Mia wanted to kill her. It had always been this way with Skylar, poking her nose in where it didn't belong. "This is Brennan Yates," she said stiffly. She glanced at Brennan, who was regarding Skylar warily. "And this is my cousin, Skylar McCauley."

"It's *really* nice to meet you," Skylar said. "*Brennan*, did you say?"

"Yes, *Brennan*," Mia said curtly. "Come on, I'll show you where to put the tile," she said, and touched Skylar's arm.

But Skylar shrugged her off. "So what is it you do, Brennan?" she asked.

"Skylar," Mia said low. She put her hand on her cousin's arm and turned her around. Skylar's body came, but her gaze would not leave Brennan. "The renovations are down there. Go ask one of the guys where we can stack the tile."

"I haven't seen you around the village," Skylar continued, ignoring Mia. Behind her, through the open door, a Lincoln Town Car rolled onto the drive and stopped when Drago appeared.

"I've been tied up," Brennan said coolly.

"I bet you have, *Brennan,*" Skylar said, and laughed.

Drago walked in the front door. "Mr. Yates? Your car is here."

Mia looked frantically to Brennan. She wanted to say good-bye. She wanted to talk to him. "I'm so sorry," she said.

"Sorry for what?" Skylar asked.

He gave her a fleeting smile, but Mia could feel that something had shifted between them. Mia didn't know what, but something had changed, and it didn't feel good. It felt dangerous. It felt like a heart was going to break somewhere in this foyer.

Brennan walked forward. He took Mia's hand and squeezed it. "We need to talk," he said. "I'll call you as soon as I can." He let go of her hand and started out the door.

Mia stared at him, unable to think clearly. He was going to *call* her and tell her he wasn't coming back? "Brennan, wait." She started after him.

"Mia—" Skylar tried, but Mia swept her arm against Skylar, pushing her back. "Will you please just go ask where to put the tile?"

"But you—"

Mia hurried out onto the drive as Brennan handed his things to the driver. When he glanced up at her, she blurted, "Are you coming back?"

"What? Yes, of course." The words came out of his mouth, but they didn't sound terribly convincing. He touched her shoulder and leaned down to give her a kiss on the cheek. "Of course I'll be back," he said again.

"Is something wrong?" she asked, sounding a little desperate.

The driver looked at her sidelong as he opened the back door.

"Nothing is wrong," Brennan said. "I'll call you and explain when we can have a little privacy and some time to talk." He smiled. "But I have to go."

Mia stared at him, her thoughts racing around a million questions.

"Mia," he said, and cupped her face. "I swear I will call you just as soon as I can. I wish I could stay and talk to you now, but I *have* to catch this plane." And with that, he got in the car.

Dumbfounded, Mia stood rooted as the car pulled away from the house. She couldn't see him through the darkened windows, but she could feel his gaze on her. As the car pulled around and drove down the drive, Mia's stomach sank to her toes. She knew. She didn't know how or why, but she knew that very moment that her glorious love affair had ended, just as she'd always known it would.

Her heart was twisting, the blood roaring in her ears. She didn't notice Skylar at her side until she spoke.

"Is he gone?"

Mia slowly turned her head to Skylar. "Yes," she said coolly. "He's gone."

"What the fuck, Mia?"

Mia's mouth dropped open. "*Excuse* me?"

"Are you kidding me right now?" Skylar demanded. "You look like you're mad at *me*."

"I don't even understand why you're here, Skylar!" Mia snapped. "Other than to meddle."

"Why didn't you *tell* me?" Skylar shot back.

"Tell you *what*?"

Skylar glared at her. But then her eyes widened. She gasped softly, then abruptly grabbed Mia's arms. "Oh my God, you don't *know*," she said, her voice full of disbelief.

Mia pushed Skylar's hands off her arms. "Know what?" she demanded angrily.

"I can't believe it. Mia, you *really* don't know? *That man* is Everett Alden! Does Drago know? Does Jesse?"

Mia knew that name, Everett Alden, but for the life of her, she didn't know why. She just stared at Skylar, her mind racing through all the people Everett Alden could possibly be.

"Ohmigod, I can't *believe* this!" Skylar laughed, and turned a full circle with her palms pressed to her cheeks. "This is crazy, Mia. He's on the cover of every magazine right now, and the whole time, you've been sitting on him. Everett Alden is the lead singer of Tuesday's End. *Please* tell me you've heard of Tuesday's End, because if you haven't, you must be an alien."

Mia felt something seismic shift in her. She was furious with Skylar for saying anything like that. For ruining everything. "No he's not," she said, unable to believe it.

"Yes," Skylar said, nodding adamantly, "he is. He's like one of the biggest rock stars on the planet. How could you not know that? You really do live under some pretty painted rock, don't you?" Skylar said, gesturing at Mia. "This is so typical of you, Mia! It's like you take pride in being oblivious. I can't believe my *cousin* has been fucking Everett Alden!" She laughed hysterically.

Mia was shattered. She was confused, disbelieving—and her chest felt as if there were a vice around it, squeezing the air from her. How could it be possible? It couldn't be! His name was Brennan, not Everett. This couldn't be some joke and she the only person who didn't get it.

But then a moment wafted back to her. His mother had called him Brennan Everett.

"Are you okay?" Skylar said.

"Why is he on the cover of all the magazines?" Mia asked.

Skylar's eyes widened. "Oh, Mia—because he fell off the face of the earth. He walked away from one of the most successful tours in years and no one knows where he is."

The tightness in her chest was choking Mia, making her feel sick.

A million thoughts and questions pinged in her brain. Why hadn't he *told* her? Why did he have two names? She thought of all the times she'd teased him for being a rock star for wearing hats and sunglasses outside. And his music! She wanted to die, thinking of how she'd dismissed his music as a hobby of the idle rich. But he'd let her do that. He'd let her tease him and assume things and he'd never said a word. He knew what a fool she was, and he'd let her believe that there was something between them. Why? Just so he could fuck her?

Everything in her felt upside down. She'd just spent three amazing weeks with this man, only to find out he was toying with her. *Using* her.

"Oh my God, I can't believe I found Everett Alden," Skylar said, her voice full of wonder.

Mia's world cracked and opened beneath her feet.

Twenty

Disaster.

This was an unmitigated, irreparable disaster.

Brennan tried calling and texting Mia on his way to California, and then again on his arrival. Goddammit, he should have told her, but he'd let his emotions and his twisted thoughts get in the way. He could strangle himself for it.

He knew the moment her cousin looked at him that he'd been outed. And then the car service had come, and he hadn't known how to drag her off to the side and tell her, then leave. He had decided that it would be better to call her.

That was a horrible mistake. He should have told her long before today. He should have called Phil and told him to hold off. But he hadn't. He'd kept those feelings for her at arm's length.

To make matters worse, he had only had a moment here and there to try and reach her. The moment his chartered plane touched down at the Van Nuys Airport outside of Los Angeles, Phil whisked him away in a plain Suburban with tinted windows like he was moving a jewelry heist to Kate Resnick's palatial home in the Pacific Palisades. "The label is getting antsy," Phil complained on the way there. "So's Gary. I can't fend them off forever."

Brennan leveled a look on his longtime agent. "Why not, Phil? That's what you're here to do—fend people off so I can have a little space."

"Dude, we all have to make a living," Phil had said testily, and had turned his attention to the window again.

Brennan marveled at it. He'd been out of pocket for what, six or seven weeks? Everyone around him acted like he'd been stranded for years on a desert island.

Kate Resnick and two of her assistants invited Brennan onto the back terrace with a view of the ocean. She served freshly made lemonade and gourmet canapés. "I love the direction you've outlined," she said to Brennan. "The narrative looks really good. Could we hear something?"

"Sure," Brennan said. "It's rough yet, but I'm close." He played "Come Closer" on his guitar. He still wasn't completely satisfied with the song, but when he finished, he looked up at the small group assembled. He was expecting smiles of approval. No one was smiling. They were staring at him, expressionless. A clammy feeling of uncertainty overcame him in that moment. Could he have been so wrong about the music? Was this what happened when he went solo?

"My God," Kate said at last. "That was . . . *masterful.*"

"Did I tell you?" Phil all but shouted. "I *told* you!"

Sweet relief swept over Brennan. "So it's good?" he asked sheepishly.

"Good? I want that on my iPhone right *now,*" Kate said, stabbing her finger against the table.

From there, discussions began about Brennan's involvement with the film. They used the script as an outline, and went through it line by line, talking about the music both Kate and Brennan envisioned.

They talked most of the afternoon and broke for dinner around seven. It was late on the East Coast, but Brennan excused himself. His text to Mia—*How are you*—went unanswered. Another hour passed and Brennan stepped outside to call her. It rolled to voice mail. So he texted her again. *Please call me when you can. I'll explain everything.*

Nothing.

The next day, as Brennan gathered up his things to leave, a maid knocked on the door of his room and said someone had come to see him. For one heart-stopping moment, Brennan thought it was Mia, that she'd somehow found out where he was.

"He's downstairs," the maid said.

Not Mia. Brennan groaned. That would be just like Phil to get someone else up here to see him while he was in town. Probably someone from the label who Brennan would have to reassure that all was well.

He walked into the main living area. It was empty. He passed through the room and the doors that were open to the ocean breeze. Outside, near the pool, he saw a man in striped pants, a vest with fringe. His hair was tied up in a loose knot at his nape.

"Chance," Brennan said.

Chance whirled around at the sound of his voice. His gaze flicked over Brennan. "Hey."

"Phil told you I was here?" Brennan asked.

"No. But he told Gary, and Gary told me."

Figured. "Okay, well . . ." Brennan cast his arms out. "You've got me. Here's your opportunity to lay into me."

"Dude, I don't want to lay into you," Chance said. He reached for a backpack on the ground and sat down on a concrete bench. He withdrew two beers and held one out to Brennan. Brennan hesitated. "Come on, don't be a pussy," Chance said. "We've always resolved our differences over a couple of beers."

Brennan couldn't help but smile. Chance was right. He took a beer from his old friend. "Are we going to rehash the same old stuff?" Brennan asked. "Because if we are, I don't have anything to add to what I've already told you."

"Okay," Chance said. "I'm willing to start from scratch if you are."

Brennan didn't have much confidence that this would be anything but another heated and protracted discussion that went in circles.

But Chance knew him well. "Dude, we've been friends for more than twenty years," he said.

"Best friends," Brennan conceded.

Chance tilted his head to one side and considered Brennan. He twisted the top of his beer and took a long swig, then said, "Let me ask you something. Do you ever think of Trey?"

The question was a fist to Brennan's gut. He swallowed hard against the swell of emotions. In true guy form, he and Chance rarely talked about Trey now. For Brennan, and he suspected for Chance, talking about Trey was too painful. "All the time," he said hoarsely.

"Me too," Chance said. "I wonder what Trey would say to us now."

Brennan didn't even have to think about it. He smiled wryly. "He would have been completely useless, Chance. You know that."

Chance chuckled. "You're right. He was never good for anything but drums."

Brennan sat down on the bench beside his best friend. "I miss the shit out of him. I miss talking to him." He swallowed again, this time to hold back a burn of tears in his eyes. He looked to the ocean and squinted. "This won't make any sense, but sometimes, I think he bailed on us. Chose the easier path."

Chance didn't say anything for a moment. "Me too," he admitted.

"You know, the last time I saw him in Palm Springs, he asked me if this was all there is." Brennan made himself look at Chance. "If what we'd accomplished with Tuesday's End was all there was to life. And you know what? I didn't have an answer for him."

"What would be the answer to that?" Chance asked. "No one can fault us for pursuing a dream. A lot of people don't get that opportunity, a lot of people are stuck in boring jobs and yeah, that's all there is. But if you ask me, it's what you make of it."

Brennan couldn't disagree. Maybe that's where he'd gone wrong. He hadn't made the best of a good thing. The two of them sat silently, staring out over the ocean, sipping from the beers. After a few minutes, Chance asked, "Are we really going to pull Tuesday's End apart?"

"I don't know," Brennan said honestly. "That's not what I want. But I can't keep up the touring, and I can't do pop. It's not in me."

"We make good money on tour," Chance reminded him. "That's the gig now for bands like us. You know as well as I do that record sales aren't what they used to be."

"We don't need money. We're rich as shit," Brennan countered.

"Yeah, well I'm trying to keep us relevant while we figure things out. The commercial market moves too fast these days, and I still want to make a living."

"I know, I know," Brennan said, sighing. "I'm trying, Chance, I swear to you that I am. But I'm tired of not having a life. I can't write on the road. I need time and space to think. I need to listen to music and read books and sit here and look at the ocean for a few days before I can write. I need to think about Trey, and I can't do it from one sound check to the next. Do you realize in the last month of our tour, we had four days off?"

"It was a sonofabitch," Chance agreed.

They drank some more. Memories of them as young men, finding their fame, came floating back to Brennan. Every day had been a new discovery. Every gig a high. "Remember how simple things used to be?" he asked.

Chance snorted. "When we were writing songs in your room?"

"Yeah," Brennan said and smiled at Chance. "And when we began to get some play. We've had an incredible journey, haven't we?" It was true that the three boys who had started Tuesday's End were determined. They'd studied, they'd listened, they'd experimented. They'd go to school during the day, then play dive joints for no money at night. A few times, they even scraped together money to pay clubs to let them play. They played to empty houses. They were booed, they were cheated. But the desire to make music was in them, and they kept going back for more, because they shared that burning desire to be heard.

Brennan and Chance had talked about it before, but neither of them could really pinpoint when things had begun to change, when they'd begun to play to packed houses instead of a few old barflies. Then they were playing small theaters. Then arenas and stadiums. They'd blown up. They'd become a huge name, selling millions of records. They'd won Grammys, they'd been on the covers of magazines.

How had it all happened?

"We did it all, Bren," Chance said. "And we're still doing it. What's the alternative? Soundtracks?"

"So I guess Gary told you everything," Brennan sighed. "Is that so bad?"

"It ain't us, man," Chance said, holding his gaze. "It's not what Tuesday's End does."

"Not before now. But why shouldn't we?"

"It's not commercial," Chance said emphatically. "That's the lane we have to be in. Commercial."

"But it could be commercial. And even if there was no possibility of it, you really have no idea what we are capable of until we try."

Chance clenched his jaw. He stood up and walked several feet forward to the edge of the pool. "You're just like Trey," he said.

"Meaning?"

Chance turned around to him. "Do I even get a say?" he asked stiffly, jabbing himself in the chest. "Do you have any respect for *my* career? For my life? Neither did Trey, man. He didn't care about either one of us. All he cared about was that fucking needle."

Brennan pushed his hands through his hair and closed his eyes. Chance was the one solid relationship he'd had in his life and it hurt him to have this discussion. It was like the crumbling of a marriage. He couldn't keep Chance at arm's length—they'd been through too much together. "I care, Chance. But you have to see where I'm at, man. I can't keep doing shit that makes me so unhappy just for you."

"But I should do what makes *me* unhappy for you?"

"I didn't say that."

Chance clenched his fist and banged it against his thigh. "You know as well as I do that if I left, Tuesday's End could find another lead guitar. But without you, we're not Tuesday's End. It's not that easy for the rest of us."

"I know," Brennan quietly admitted. He'd always known that. Tuesday's End without Everett Alden was just a good band. It wasn't fair, but it was reality.

Chance looked like he wanted to punch a wall. He looked out to the ocean once more and shook his head. "So where are we?"

"Right now we are sitting at Kate Resnick's house. Think about it, Chance. It could be a very cool collaboration."

"And the band?"

Brennan didn't say anything; he held Chance's gaze.

Chance's face mottled with anger. "You know what, Bren? Fuck you," he said, and strode away from him. But he paused at the door and turned back. "Here's something else for you to chew on. Trey was a coward. That's all he ever was—a coward. He asked questions to cover up for the fact that he didn't have the balls to get clean. Don't turn him into some fucking saint." He turned around and disappeared inside.

Brennan closed his eyes and buried his face in his hands. His eyes burned with unshed tears; his throat felt thick. He swallowed again, this time against a swell of nausea. This was ridiculously hard. After twenty years, this was the most painful thing he'd ever experienced, the closest he'd ever come to a true broken heart. He loved Chance like a brother. Chance and Trey had been there for him when his world imploded when he was a boy, and he'd come to love Chance more than he'd loved anyone else. Brennan didn't want to hurt him; he'd rather cut his own throat than hurt Chance. He owed Chance the truth. He owed himself the truth.

Was this all there was? Did we all learn to love someone only so we could hurt them?

And then Mia's face flashed in his mind's eye. The bottle fell from Brennan's hand and broke on the concrete at his feet. He folded his arms and bent over, feeling physically ill.

Trey wasn't the coward. He was.

Twenty-one

Jesse loved Mia's dress. He kept grinning, eyeing her up and down, practically salivating. "It's beautiful," he said. "Did you make it?"

"Yes." It was sky blue with a fuchsia underskirt. It was simple but prim with a sweet Peter Pan collar and cap sleeves. She'd made the dress from satin and double gauze, and it flowed around her. When she walked, hints of fuchsia flashed around the hem. It was a tea-length dress, because Mia assumed that was the length one wore to a fancy wedding. She wouldn't know. She'd never been to a fancy wedding.

She'd even put her hair up in a chignon and stuck some crystal pins in it, borrowed some heels from Emily, and donned a necklace with a heart charm that dangled at her throat, a gift from her grandmother when she turned sixteen. She was trying to be what she thought Jesse wanted her to be.

But she hated it. Loathed it.

This was something Emily would wear, but not Mia Lassiter, and Mia felt like a fraud. An empty ghost of the woman she'd been just a week ago. The woman who had naively believed a summer person.

"Are you ready?" Jesse asked eagerly. He was dressed in a dark-blue suit. His tie was a little crooked, and his shoes had rubber soles, but he looked quite handsome. Any woman would be thrilled to be his date. But Mia was numb to him. She was numb to everything. She was so heartbroken, so disillusioned, that it took everything she had to muster a smile.

"I'm ready," she said. She left her phone on the counter in the same spot it had been sitting for hours now. The calls and texts from Brennan kept piling up. She wanted to talk to him. She wanted to give him a piece of her mind. She was furious with him. She was *stunned* by him. Mia still couldn't wrap her mind around it—she'd been sleeping with a famous rock star and hadn't had a fucking clue. But *he'd* known it, and he'd allowed her to be so completely clueless. Honestly, Mia didn't know what to make of it. Why would he do it? She thought—hoped—that she meant something to him. She thought she was at least someone who deserved to know that truth. Frankly, Mia was afraid to talk to him, afraid of the things that would come tumbling out of her mouth that she couldn't take back. But at the moment, she feared she would only burst into tears when she heard his voice, and she was not going to give him that.

Jesse didn't seem to notice that Mia was in another world on the way to the wedding. He chatted as if everything were fine, as if the world hadn't just imploded under Mia's feet.

They arrived at the church just in time to be seated. The wedding was okay, Mia supposed, but she didn't know the couple and couldn't connect with the vows they were making. She felt like she was watching the ceremony from afar. As if it were on television. There were bows on the pews of the church, sprays of flowers at the altar. The bridesmaids—an astounding eight of them—wore long satin dresses with wraps that made Mia inwardly cringe. It was a perfectly lovely wedding all in all, but so . . . ordinary. So lacking in artistry.

Or was that her bitterness talking?

At the wedding reception, Jesse was more animated than usual, helped along by a few glasses of champagne. He was jovial as he introduced her to a group of his friends.

"Mia Lassiter," said his friend Kevin. "Hey . . . you're that girl from high school," he said.

Mia swallowed down a lump of trepidation and forced a smile.

"Kevin Bowman, remember me?" he said. He was round, with a receding hairline. Mia had to look very closely to see anything familiar. "Oh yeah, Kevin," she said. Her palms were turning damp. Had he been on the beach that night?

"You look *great*," he said, his gaze sliding down her body.

"Thank you." She wondered if he was remembering the word *freak* painted across her body.

"So get this," Jesse said, leaning in, his arm going around Mia. "You know who bought the Ross house, right?"

Kevin shook his head.

"Everett Alden from Tuesday's End."

Mia was stunned. She looked at Jesse. How long had he known?

But Jesse had an audience and didn't notice her. "Dude, can you believe it? I've been working up there and I didn't know who he was. I mean, he looked familiar, but I couldn't place him, you know?"

Skylar. Of course Skylar had told him. She'd probably run up and down Main Street, from coffee shop to bistro, telling everyone she knew that Everett Alden was at Ross house.

"Man, that is *awesome*." Kevin said. "You should get an autograph or something. That band is *hot*. I love that song "Soldier Black.""

Jesse grinned down at Mia. "Did *you* know?"

She was certain she heard a twinge of accusation in his voice, as if he believed she'd been holding out on him. "No," she said. "I had no idea. I generally listen to classical music, so I'm not really up on the popular bands."

"Yeah, I'm a country guy myself. I bet he's here for that damn music festival," Jesse said. "There was a lot of talk in the beginning about drawing a big headliner."

"They got that new band, Whittaker," Kevin said. "But Everett Alden would be bigger. So what's he like?"

Jesse looked at Mia.

"Oh, ah . . . well." She furrowed her brow. *He's sexy. He listens to me. He understands what I mean when I talk about art. He's a liar. He's a user. He used me.* She shrugged. "He's arrogant."

"He doesn't seem so arrogant to me," Jesse said. "Seems really down with things."

Mia was surprised by that—she had the very distinct impression that Jesse didn't like Brennan.

"You know who was here last summer?" Kevin asked. "That actress. You know the one . . ."

Jesse and Kevin began to chat about the celebrities who had appeared around East Beach while Mia privately stewed. She was angry with Skylar for telling everyone. Angry with Brennan—or Everett, whoever the hell he was—for lying to her. She had to see his eyes, his face when she confronted him about the lies. She wanted to see that moment of shock just before she punched him hard in the jaw.

The dancing started and Jesse grabbed her hand and pulled her onto the dance floor, shaking his head when she tried to protest. "It's a wedding for Chrissakes. Of *course* you have to dance."

They didn't really dance, just sort of swayed from side to side. Jesse wrapped his arms around her and kissed her. Mia smiled self-consciously. She felt nothing. Not a single spark. Not a shiver, not a swell. Nothing. She thought of the way Brennan kissed her, and how she felt like an inferno the moment his lips touched hers.

In fact, all she could think about as she danced with Jesse was the way Brennan touched her, and how he moved with her, and the sounds of pleasure he made in bed with her. The memory made her shiver, and when she did, Jesse pulled her closer.

It was awful to be with one man and think of another. It was the worst sort of purgatory.

After the dance, Mia met more of Jesse's friends and acquaintances, including the bride and groom. They had more champagne, and Mia began to feel warm and fluid. She was attracted to the paper birds hanging from the ceiling of the ballroom, amused by them.

One of the bridesmaids commented on Mia's dress. "It's really pretty. Where'd you get it?"

"I made it," Mia said.

"You're kidding! You *made* that? I always wished I could sew," the girl said. "It's really beautiful."

"Thank you," Mia said.

When the bridesmaid wandered away, Jesse grinned at her. He bent his head, his mouth next to her ear. "See?"

"See what?"

"Normal. It wins every time." He winked.

Horrified, Mia stared back at him.

"What? I'm just saying, you look so hot and sexy tonight."

"Because I look normal?" she asked evenly.

Jesse's smile faded. "I'm just talking about tonight, Mia."

There it was, her problem with Jesse. He was a great guy, a handsome guy. Everyone loved Jesse! But Jesse didn't get her. He didn't understand her at all. He was attracted to her, yes. But he wanted her to fit into the mold of the woman that inhabited his head, and Mia knew, unequivocally, that if she dated him, this idea of *normal* would become a bigger and bigger issue between them.

"I have to go to the bathroom," she said, and thrust her empty champagne flute into his hand.

"Don't be mad," Jesse said, then muttered something under his breath.

Mia walked away in her tea-length dress and her Peter Pan collar. She had every intention of going into the ladies room and splashing water on her face to sober up, but she happened to see the wedding planner and veered in her direction.

"Excuse me, do you have scissors I could borrow? There is a tag in my dress that is driving me nuts."

"I think I do," the woman said, and squatted down by a large tote box and rummaged around. She stood up, holding a small pair of scissors. "Just put them in here when you're done."

"Thanks!" Mia went into the bathroom. In the handicap stall, she removed her dress. She hung it on the purse hook and stood, swaying a little, clicking the scissors open and shut. "You're crazy, Mia," she muttered, then leaned down and cut the dress off above the knee. Next, she cut out the demure little collar and gave it a more daring décolletage. And with the fabric she'd removed, she wove a belt. When she donned the dress, it came to mid thigh, and she'd cut the neck so low that the top of her lacy black bra was visible.

When she emerged from the stall, two bridesmaids reapplying lipstick eyed her in the mirror's reflection, then exchanged a look.

Mia smiled at them and walked out of the bathroom in her new dress, returning the scissors to the tote bucket before going in search of Jesse.

He was where she'd left him, laughing it up with Kevin and, now, another man. His friends looked at Mia with some interest, their gazes taking her in. But Jesse's face fell as she walked toward him. "What the hell?" he asked, clearly appalled. "What the hell did you do, Mia?"

"I didn't like the dress," she said.

"But . . . but what did you *do*?" he said angrily. "You went in the bathroom and cut it off? That's crazy!"

"Is it crazy?" she asked curiously. "I think it's artistic."

"It's not *artistic*," he said, sounding furious. "It's weird. Come on, it's time to go."

"The happy couple hasn't left yet."

His angry gaze burned through her. "Let's go." He put his hand on her elbow and wheeled her around, marching her through the crowd like a disobedient child. "Great. Fantastic. You've made your point."

"Are you sure? Because I do this kind of thing. I wear funky clothes. I *make* funky clothes. I paint things, I cut up tin cans and make hats from them. And for me, that's normal."

"Okay." He stopped walking. He held up both hands as if he was surrendering and said, "Okay, I *get* it." He was so angry, and he looked so wounded, and now, in the hazy glow of champagne, Mia regretted it. She felt like a jerk.

"Can we just go now?" he asked.

"Yes," she murmured.

Jesse escorted her to his truck and helped her in before taking the driver's seat. They drove in silence. Jesse stared straight ahead, his jaw clenched. Mia was shivering now that she'd gotten rid of most of her dress.

He turned at Eckland's and gave the truck some gas down the road to her apartment. He parked—but left the truck running, Mia noticed. She sighed. She turned to face him in the cab. "I'm sorry," she said. "I'm really sorry, Jesse. I was a little drunk, and I shouldn't have done that. You don't deserve that."

"Nope," he curtly agreed, his gaze on the path the truck lights illuminated.

"Please don't be mad," she said again, and she meant it. "Think of the stories you can tell your friends. Your crazy date to a wedding."

He suddenly sighed and looked out his window, shaking his head. "It's a joke to you, but it's not to me."

"It's not a joke, but I . . ." *I'm different. I'm a freak!* "Jesse, you're a really nice guy and you deserve a girl who looks like all those bridesmaids. But I—"

He suddenly grabbed her hand and squeezed it. "You don't have to explain. I like you, Mia, you know that I do. But I'm not blind. I know you're not into me. You're into the rock star, and I may not like it, but you don't have to apologize for that. You don't have to cut off your dress to make a point."

Mia blinked. She was set to deny it, to proclaim once more that Brennan Yates was an asshole, that she wasn't into guys like him, that she'd known from the beginning it was a summer infatuation. She wanted to say all those things, but the words stuck in her throat. They congealed into a hard lump that she could neither swallow nor spit out, because what Jesse said was true. *That* was the thing that had been stabbing at her all day. It wasn't just that Brennan had been less than honest with her. It was that she cared, and a whole lot more than she wanted to admit to herself.

Mia glanced down at her chopped dress. "You're right," she said, giving in. "I do like him. But you want to know what the sad thing is? It's such a dead-end street. Nothing will ever come of it. I know that, but I . . . I can't stop the feelings I have for him."

"The heart wants what it wants, I guess," Jesse said coolly. "I'm going to bow out. I won't ask you out. And I won't say the word normal." He smiled a little.

She did, too. "Oh, Jesse, I'm so—"

"God, don't apologize," he said, withdrawing his hand from hers. "It's bad enough that I am losing out to a rock god, but don't make me feel completely pathetic by apologizing." He cupped her face with his hand. "It's okay, Mia. It is. I'm not kidding—the heart wants what it wants, and you should never feel bad about it. Thanks for going to the wedding with me. I had a good time."

"You did?"

"Up until the dress incident." He smiled, then leaned across her and pushed her door open. "Good luck with the rock star."

Mia slid out of his truck and shut the door. She watched him drive off. Jesse had been so kind to her. That, she thought morosely, might have been the dumbest thing she'd ever done. She wished, with everything she had, that she had managed to summon the feelings she had for Brennan for Jesse instead. *The heart wants what it wants.* Well, her heart was apparently an idiot.

Mia sighed when his taillights disappeared onto Juneberry Road, and she looked down at her dress. "For God's sake, who *does* that in the middle of a wedding reception?" With a shake of her head, she went inside, annoyed with herself.

Twenty-two

Sitting on the floor of her apartment in her butchered dress, Mia made the mistake of Googling Everett Alden. She saw Brennan's face looking back at her in hundreds of photos. The list of entries about him was endless—he'd won Grammys, he'd been interviewed by various magazines and news shows, all of which she read or watched with keen interest. She found a list of Tuesday's End albums and listened to the music. His voice, husky and deep, made her shiver with familiarity. He had such a soulful quality to his voice.

She clicked on a song with a familiar title and felt another wave of disbelief wash over. "Dream Maker." She hadn't remembered the title, but she knew the song so well—it had been the only song on the radio a few years ago. God in heaven, that was *him*.

In addition to the music he'd made, he talked a lot about causes that were important to him. Music education. Child poverty. He appeared to be the greatest, kindest rock star on the planet.

But how could the greatest and kindest rock star keep the truth from someone he supposedly cared about? Mia had been so certain he cared about her, that they were developing a thing. And yet, as she perused the images of him taken over the years—with this model, with that singer, and holy hell, *Jenna O'Neil*, who had to be the most famous actress in the world right now—she wondered if Brennan *did* care for her. How could he be with women like that, then be with her? She really was the fling he'd had while he lay low. The joke was definitely on her—she'd felt so connected to him.

Mia eventually made herself shut down her laptop. She couldn't see all those pictures without everything in her grinding to a halt as she tried to sort out her feelings. She was hurt. She was confused. She was an idiot, so oblivious to fame and pop culture. However, there was a part of Mia that wasn't all that surprised. She'd been reminding herself all along that it never worked out with summer people, hadn't she? They all came and went. She'd known from the beginning it was a matter of time.

Her foolishness was in believing she'd be okay. She'd never expected it to hurt so badly.

When Brennan's call came in on Sunday, Mia let the call roll to her voice mail.

She spent the afternoon working on the dress she'd ruined, hemming it, smoothing out the décolletage, and adding some elements of the fuchsia satin on the outside of the dress. She regretted having butchered the dress at the wedding, but she loved the final outcome. She'd hung it on a clothes rack she'd bought at a bargain store. It hung next to four other pieces she'd made herself.

After that, Mia went to the spin class Drago had been urging her to try. She hadn't exercised in ages, and had to dig through a box to find sneakers. Unfortunately, the spin class didn't solve any problems for her, and, in fact, created new ones. Her legs were burning, and it felt as if her lungs had disintegrated.

And then night fell, and there was nothing to distract her, and sleep wouldn't come. She tossed and turned most of the night, unable to answer any questions and feeling brokenhearted and used. She was miserable. Tortured, bruised, and miserable.

The next morning, Mia got on her bike and went to work as usual, dreading it with the force of a thousand burning suns. The fun she'd had flirting with two men now made her life doubly miserable.

As she neared the Ross house, she saw two cars parked outside the gates. Drago was parked just inside the gate in his Jeep, and for the first time since she'd started working here, the gates were closed.

Mia got off her bike and wheeled it up to the gates, waving at Drago. He got out of his Jeep to open the gate for her. "Hi, Mia."

"What's going on?" she said as she wheeled her bike through, looking over her shoulder at the cars.

"Somebody famous lives here," he said gravely. "Mrs. Yates told me not to let them in."

Mia rode up to the house. She made her way through the attack dogs and into the kitchen. Nancy was there, dressed in yoga clothes with a mat slung over her shoulder. "Mia, darling, good morning!" she trilled.

"Good morning, Mrs. Yates." Mia put down her bag.

"Did you have any trouble getting in? I hope you weren't bothered by those people outside the gates. They scared the daylights out of me last night, banging on the door." She glanced nervously at Mia. "They're press, you know."

"I gathered," Mia said.

Nancy played with an earring as she studied Mia. "He didn't tell you?"

Mia shook her head.

"Oh my *God*," Nancy groaned. "I honestly don't understand that man. I don't. I know he was afraid of something like this happening," she said, gesturing in the direction of the front gates. "But I thought he'd surely tell *you*."

"Me too," Mia muttered.

"Oh dear," Nancy said, smiling sympathetically. "Don't let it get to you. He means well, but, well, he's a man," she said dramatically, as if his gender should somehow excuse him. "By the way, he should be back sometime today."

Mia didn't know what she was supposed to say to any of that. Don't let it get to her? Hooray, he was coming back? "I should get to work."

"Sure, sure," Nancy said nervously. "I sincerely hope this doesn't impede progress on the renovations." She dug in her purse for her keys. "Well, I'm off." She moved toward the hallway door, but paused next to Mia and put her hand on her arm. She didn't say anything, but smiled sympathetically and gave Mia a little pat before walking on with the dogs trotting along behind her all the way to the front door.

What was there to do but work?

Jesse's crew was already busy, cutting beams for the ceiling and a door in the wall. Jesse was helping one of his men mark something on the floor with a tape measure. Mia wanted to disappear, but Jesse looked up, saw her there, and lifted his chin in acknowledgment before turning his back to her.

This had all the markings of being the worst day of Mia's life thus far.

She spent most of it on pins and needles. Every sound was Brennan coming through the door. Every voice was his. Deliveries of materials arrived, and Mia sorted through the invoices, waiting.

But he didn't come back.

Maybe he knew about the press and photographers camped outside the gates, waiting for him. She'd read an old news story about his run-in with a Japanese photographer in Tokyo. He didn't like the press.

Maybe he'd left and had never intended to come back. Maybe he'd just said that so he wouldn't have to face her. Maybe Mr. Rock Star and Music Education Advocate was a big, fat coward. As the day wore on, Mia began to regret her decision not to respond to his texts or his calls. That might have been her only chance to tell him . . .

To tell him what? What did she say to this betrayal?

At the end of the day, she got on her bike and rolled past the cars parked outside. One of the drivers called out to her, "Is Everett Alden in there?"

She kept peddling.

Safe in her apartment once more, she opened a bottle of wine, picked up her sketchbook, and went out to the little patio below her balcony. The evening was cool; a slight breeze ruffled her hair. Mia opened her sketchbook and tried to capture the shadows on the lake, but it was pointless. She couldn't concentrate. She couldn't think of anything but Brennan. She put her sketchbook down and propped her head on her fist, staring wistfully at the lake.

"Mia."

His voice startled her so badly that Mia whirled around and stood in one movement, knocking her wine onto her sketchbook in the process. It was Brennan; finally, it was him, and he looked every inch the rock star. He had on a sleeveless leather jacket over a T-shirt, tight red pants. His hair was tucked into a knit cap, and his aviator sunglasses dangled from his fingers.

Mia pressed one palm against her abdomen. She was both sick and hopeful, and as he tentatively moved toward her, she felt paralyzed with grief for what might have been and regret for having allowed herself the fantasy. He moved forward, as if he intended to take her in his arms, but Mia stopped him by putting up her hand. "Don't," she said. "Don't come near me."

He winced painfully. "I'm sorry if I surprised you. But I need to talk to you and I've gotten nothing but radio silence."

"That's because I wasn't going to have this conversation over the phone," she said coolly. "This is one that needs to happen in person."

"I agree." He put one hand on his waist and looked out at the lake a moment. "So now you know," he said. "Are you familiar with Tuesday's End?"

"Of course. The whole world knows who you are." The magnitude of that statement shook Mia. The whole world knew him, but he hadn't had the decency to tell her. She suddenly lurched forward and shoved hard against his chest, knocking him back a step. "Why didn't you tell me?" She shoved again, and he held his ground, but lifted his arms in surrender. "Did you think it was funny to make a fool out of me?"

"I didn't make a fool of you."

"Oh, *right*," she said angrily. "Lying to me, letting me think you were a hobbyist, not telling me that you really *are* a rock star—"

"I know, but we—"

"*We* is not the right word! *You* did it, Brennan. *You* lied."

"Will you let me talk?" he asked calmly.

"No! Who is Brennan? Why does your mother call you Brennan?"

"I'm Brennan," he said. "It's my real name. Brennan Everett Alden Yates."

She couldn't quite grasp it. The name was so long. "No it's not," she scoffed.

"It is. Yates is the name of the man who adopted me," he reminded her. "Alden is my biological father's name, the name I was given when I was born. When I got started in the business there was already a guy named Yates playing with a band we'd compete with for gigs. So one night, Chance and I came up with Everett Alden. It seemed different and sexy to us then. I don't know, Mia, I was a teenager, I took a stage name and went with it. But Brennan Yates is my true name. It's who I am."

"Who you are is a liar," she snapped.

Brennan shoved his hands in his pocket. "Mia—I'm sorry. I am so desperately sorry. I made a huge fucking mistake. But will you at least talk about it? Or do you only want to yell at me?"

"I want to yell at you. Actually, I'd like to punch you in the mouth." She swiped up the wine bottle and her sketchbook, and marched for the stairs to the studio without looking back.

Of course the bastard followed her, crowding in behind her on the landing, then reaching around her, his chest to her back, to open the door when she fumbled with it.

Mia was shaking as she deposited the wine in her kitchen. She didn't know what she was doing—was she going to let him in here to tell her more bullshit? Was she going to *believe* him? She flicked her gaze over him. He stood on the other side of the bar, his head down, his hands braced against it, watching her closely, his expression earnest.

"I Googled you, you know." She cringed a little at how accusatory she sounded.

"Okay." He waited as if he expected more. He didn't seem surprised.

"I know everything about you. I even know your net worth."

"You'll have to tell me, because I don't know."

"You know what I couldn't find out? Why you didn't tell me. Why you let me go on thinking you were someone you're not."

"I know it must seem that way, but here's the ironic thing—the person you know is the person I am. The rest of that is for stage. You've seen more of me than most anyone."

"Bullshit," she scoffed.

"It's true. And what else is true is that this isn't so easy to explain."

"What's so hard, Brennan? All you had to say is, I'm a huge fucking rock star, Mia. See how easy that is?"

"I don't expect you to understand—"

"Good. Because I won't."

He shook his head and pushed away from the island. He slid his hand over the top of his head, thinking. "I don't know how to tell you everything. I came here because I desperately needed anonymity. When I first met you, I thought you were a groupie—"

"A *what?*"

"It wouldn't be the first time a groupie had managed to get onto one of my properties. I didn't know you, and I didn't care what you thought of me. But then . . . then I realized you really had no clue who I was. It was so freeing, Mia," he said, tapping his fist to his chest. "I was just a guy to you. A guy you didn't like too much, either. You didn't look at me like I could do something for you. You didn't hang on every word I said and wonder how you could parlay it into fame and fortune."

Mia made a sound of disbelief. "Did you also like the fact that I wasn't a model or movie star?" she asked skeptically.

"Yeah, actually, I did."

"So when were you going to tell me, Brennan? When were you going to let me in on your big secret?"

"I don't know," he answered truthfully. "I should have told you in Stratford Corners. I should have told you when I met you in my mother's kitchen. I should have done a lot of things. But I didn't, and I am so profoundly sorry for it, you can't begin to know."

Her pulse was racing. She was so damn angry with him for having deceived her. But she was also confused—she wanted so badly to believe him. She wanted to believe that she really was different to him in some way. That she'd mattered.

Her anger was squeezing the breath from her. She couldn't catch it. "Shut up. You were just using me, Brennan. I was an easy piece for you, that's all."

He smiled ruefully. "Except that if you think about it, you know you weren't the slightest bit easy, Mia. Do you honestly believe that I couldn't have invited a model or actress up here if I'd wanted one? I wanted to be with *you*. And I loved every single moment of it."

"But . . ." she said, gesturing for him to continue.

"But?"

"But it was all temporary. Say it."

Now he looked slightly exasperated. As if he was annoyed she might have expected more. "Wasn't it *always* temporary? You said so yourself. You said I'd go and you'd be here. You've worried more about how to find your artistic voice than this relationship."

Mia hated him for being right. "That was true in the beginning," she said. She could feel tears beginning to build. "But after Stratford Corners, I thought . . ." She turned away from him. "Fuck it. I don't know what I thought."

"Mia," he said softly. "You didn't think—"

"No, of course I didn't think so, asshole," she said. "But I *hoped* it, okay? I hoped it," she said again, softer. She dug her fists into her belly to stop the roiling. The only thing that could make this moment worse would be to vomit, and she felt dangerously close to that. "Can you blame me, Brennan? These last few weeks with you have been so . . . *right*. I feel so right," she said. It was the first time she'd put that nebulous and raw feeling into words. "You don't understand—for the first time in my life there was someone in this world who could look at me and not be annoyed or mystified by the way I look. You're the first guy I've known who really gets my need to express myself."

"I do understand you," he agreed from somewhere behind her.

She turned around and looked at him over her shoulder. "When I had to come back to East Beach, I was scared that meant I didn't really belong anywhere. Not in art, not here, not in Brooklyn . . ." She paused, wincing a little. She had never voiced her fears out loud, and it scared her now to say them, as if giving voice to them would make them come true somehow. "I was scared that I didn't matter," she said, her voice hoarse. "But Brennan, *you* made me feel like I mattered and that I belonged. And I believed it," she said, swallowing back tears. "I honestly, truly *believed* it. And now I discover that you weren't being honest with me at all. How can I believe you were being honest with me about anything? How do I know you're not here right now because you are avoiding the photographers camped out at your house?"

"The photographers," he repeated, then groaned. *"Great,"* he muttered, dragging his fingers through his hair. "Never mind that—I never lied to you, Mia," he said earnestly. "Maybe I am guilty of the sin of omission, but I never lied. I told you I was a musician. I told you my name. I told you I was writing a soundtrack. *You* didn't believe me. You could have asked about the soundtrack, but you didn't. You pigeonholed me from the beginning, lumping me in with the summer people you usually dislike, and assumed I was the idle rich. I shouldn't have let you believe it, you're right, you're absolutely right. But everything else has been one hundred percent real. What we've shared is real. But I think we both knew from the beginning that this was . . ." He looked wildly about, as if searching for the right word. "Improbable."

"Improbable," she slowly repeated.

"Isn't it?"

"Maybe. But if that's true, it only makes this much worse. I felt something real for you, Brennan. And I thought that just once . . ."

God, no, don't say it. Don't beg. Mia stopped and hung her head. She sounded like a pathetic wreck. Everything was falling down in her, collapsing under her own expectations. She was so stupid.

Brennan moved cautiously around the bar to her. He slid his arms around her. Mia made a feeble attempt to push free, but he silenced her with a *"Shhh"* and a kiss to her temple.

That tenderness was more than Mia could bear—she closed her eyes and sagged against his body, dropped her forehead to his shoulder and squeezed her eyes shut. Her heart felt painfully tight, as if the life was being wrung from it.

"I feel something for you, too," he said into her hair. "God, I have feelings for you that I don't know I've ever had for another woman. You think I understand who you are? That goes both ways—you understand me, too."

He put his hands beneath her chin and forced her to look up at him. "I didn't expect any of this, any more than you did," he said. "I never expected this," he muttered, and kissed her cheek. "Or this." He kissed her mouth.

Against her better judgment, Mia slid her hands up his chest to his shoulders. She began to move without conscious thought, just moving, wanting him to erase the pain, needing him to hold her. She was an idiot to want him, but part of her wanted once more with him, wanted to feel the magic between them one last time before it was over. She pushed Brennan back, pushed him again, until he bumped against the armchair. Then she pushed him down onto the chair and climbed on top of him.

"I definitely didn't expect this," he said, gazing up at her. He put his hands on her hips; she could feel him hardening beneath her and leaned down to kiss his cheek and his ear.

"What are you doing?"

"Don't talk," she whispered. "Don't be a super rock star just yet. Please just be Brennan."

He caught her head between his hands and made her look at him. "I *am* Brennan."

No, he wasn't. He was Everett Alden, and before he went into the world as Everett again, Mia desperately needed him. She kissed him before she could say it was too late, that he could never be Brennan again. She kissed him because she didn't know what would happen, but he was here and she was clinging to the short time they'd had and she wasn't ready for it to end.

Brennan gave in to her desire; he slipped his hands under her skirt, moving his fingers over her skin, then in between her legs, guiding her to sink down onto his body.

This, she thought, was what she wanted. *It should always be like this.*

She let him lead her into sexual oblivion on that chair, thrusting into her with all the heartache and desire and hope that she felt, and all Mia could think was that she loved him. She truly loved him.

At some point, they moved to her bed and lay in each other's arms. Brennan told her about his reasons for going to LA, about the discussion with Kate Resnick, and the view from her terrace. He told her about talking to Chance, and how he wasn't sure where they stood, but how the whole world seemed to be listening in on their personal struggle.

Mia told him about the wedding, and how she'd gone into the bathroom and inexplicably cut off the dress. Brennan laughed roundly at that, holding his abdomen as if he was trying to keep the laugh from exploding out of him. They made love again, their rhythm slow, caressing each other, whispering to each other.

Mia would think of that night often in the weeks to come and how they had lain in that bed and talked like lovers. How they managed to keep reality from seeping in through the windows and the cracks in the door. She would remember how that had felt in her breast and her veins, how her heart had beat so strongly and quickly for another person. She would remember how it felt to realize what falling in love felt like, and how it filled her up as much as a beautiful piece of art.

And she would think of how he never answered the question of whether or not he had ever intended to tell her who he was.

Twenty-three

Brennan woke Mia before dawn, whispered that he was heading up to Ross house before the paparazzi spotted him, and kissed her fervently until she groaned and buried herself in a mound of pillows.

Brennan drove home, sliding in through the gate. There were no photographers around this early. He parked in the garage and walked around the back of the house, entering through the kitchen.

He could avoid paparazzi—but he could not avoid his mother.

"You will not believe how many people are trying to get in here!" she complained. She was already up, making coffee, dressed in what he thought were sailing clothes.

"Hello to you, too, Mom," he said with a yawn as he nudged her dogs off his feet. "I told you this would happen."

"*I* didn't tell anyone you were here, so how on earth did they find out?" she demanded, hands on hips. "Don't say Mia, because she said she didn't know." She punctuated that statement with a glare in his direction.

Brennan didn't need his mother's disdain—he hated himself enough for not telling Mia, especially after last night.

"I *told* you to tell her," his mother grumbled.

There was nothing worse than an *I-told-you-so* delivered by one's mother. "I know," he said, giving in.

"She looked absolutely shell-shocked, by the way. That's on you, Brennan."

Because he'd effectively tossed a bomb in her life. "I get it, Mom," he said, feeling his exhaustion take hold of him again.

"How was your trip?" she asked, a little calmer now.

"It was fine. I'm going to grab a shower." He moved past her on his way out of the kitchen.

"Just so I know, how long is this going to go on?" his mother asked, gesturing toward the front of the house.

Jesus, it felt like the pressure to *do* something was coming at him from all sides. He glanced at her over his shoulder. "I'm doing the best I can right now, Mom. I don't know the answer to your question, but it won't be long." He walked out before she pressed him for details.

In his room, he pulled out his phone and glanced at the notification of more than a dozen calls, texts, and messages.

He hadn't answered his mother about who had alerted the world to where he was, but it was obvious Mia's cousin had been the one. Everything had been fine until she'd shown up, and then suddenly his phone was blowing up, his email was flooded, people were camped outside his gate, and everyone wanted an answer.

His phone messages were from Phil and Gary; those, he expected. There was another call from Tyanna, the woman who handled the band's publicity. She said her message was urgent, so Brennan called her back. "Hello, Everett," she said crisply when her secretary put him through. "Gary told me to leave you alone, but we've had a bazillion requests for interviews this week. Please tell me it's not true that you've been living like a mountain man in a cabin in the woods."

"A cabin." He laughed. "Where'd that come from? I've been doing a little R and R at my mother's house."

"The idea came from *OK!* magazine. Apparently they photoshopped a picture of you outside a run-down cabin in a place that looks like the Blue Ridge Mountains to me. The article says you have no running water."

"What the hell? No, Tyanna. I am at my mother's house at Lake Haven."

"So she's sick?" she asked, all business.

"No, she's not sick, she's fine. I told you—I came here to decompress."

"Decompress? That sounds like a drug problem. We'll say you've been taking care of your mother," she said. "Are you up for some interviews?"

"*No.* I don't have anything to promote. I don't owe anyone an explanation. There's nothing I have to say to the media, and I'm damn sure not going to pretend my mother is sick."

"We're not going to be able to hold them off for long," Tyanna said. "We're going to have to say *something.* People think you're living in the mountains without toilets, Everett."

"Figure it out, Tyanna," he said. He hung up before she could talk him into any interviews.

Brennan then listened to Gary's messages—and all of them were the same. *Where are you? We're getting heat. Band wants to know what's up.*

Phil's messages said that there were several calls into his office about the possibility of Brennan appearing at the Lake Haven Music Festival. It was happening next week, and Whittaker, a band that had opened for Tuesday's End, was the headliner. Brennan would have dismissed those messages out of hand, but he had another message from the drummer who had taken over for Trey in Tuesday's End. Justin hadn't tried to get in touch with Brennan since the end of the tour. His message said that he'd gotten a call from Whittaker's drummer. "They heard you were up there somewhere and wondered if they could talk you into sitting in. Anyway, here's his number," Justin said, and rattled it off. "In the meantime, man, you ought to get in touch once in a while. Later."

Brennan called the number Justin had left him. Ben Whittaker, the lead singer and founder of the band, answered. "What's up, man?" he said happily when Brennan phoned him. "Dude, you're on the cover of *everything.*"

"Slow news cycle," Brennan said.

"So look, man, we're playing the Lake Haven event," he said. "It's the first year, supposed to be a small crowd. I heard you were up there somewhere, so why don't you come out and sit in on our set? Piano, guitar, whatever you want to do. We can cover a Tuesday's End song."

"What would you think about letting me test a new song?"

"Sure," Ben said.

"It's acoustic."

There was a pause. Then, *"Sweet."*

The offer was tempting. The opportunity to play "Come Closer" before a test audience would tell Brennan a lot. And the thought of jamming with Whittaker excited him. Brennan hadn't realized how much he missed playing with a band. "Count me in," he said.

By the time Brennan hung up, he was feeling more optimistic about his return to music than he had in several months. He'd found his groove, he was back in the game. He was weeding all the noise out of his head and his path was slowly becoming clear.

But in the midst of that burgeoning euphoria—a natural high after his unnatural depression, two shadows still lurked: Chance and Mia.

Mia, Mia. That quirky young woman with a peculiar taste in clothes. Brennan's feelings for her didn't fit into his new groove. He didn't know where to put his feelings, but they couldn't be tucked away or forgotten. He felt utterly incapable of focusing on music and the show ahead of him, of putting that before everything else. He'd always managed to keep his eye on his music without letting unnecessary emotions get in the way. But when he was at his lowest point, Mia had come traipsing into his life in combat boots. And since that moment, his emotions felt entirely necessary and messy and had rooted into him like a stubborn vine.

A fast-growing, gargantuan vine that he didn't know how to cut back or train.

His growing affection for her had kept him awake last night. His heart had swelled, and he'd felt new and awkwardly tender things for her as he'd lain beside her. It was a flow of warm desire that had scared him a little, coming so hard and heavy to him on the heels of his trip to LA. He didn't know what the emotions meant in his life or how to mesh them into everything that was happening.

He glanced at the time: a quarter till noon. He looked out his window and saw the purple bike propped against the guardhouse. He called Mia. "Good morning," he said, aware of the smile that instantly lit his face when she answered.

"Hey," she said softly.

He waited for her to say more. She didn't. He heard hammering in the background that matched the rhythm of his hammering heart. "So you're working, huh?"

"I am," she said. "Life goes on."

"Can I see you?"

There was a pause. A very long pause, he noticed. "I'd like that," she said at last. "I'm taking a lunch break in an hour. Lookout Point?"

"Perfect. I'll see you then."

But Brennan didn't see her. He had a conference call crop up over the lunch hour with his label. The management there had been unnerved by reports that he'd been holed up without plumbing or running water in a cabin in the woods. They thought he was flaming out, or worse, doing drugs. This, according to Phil, who had been texting messages that were increasingly frantic. So Brennan gave in. He texted Mia, told her he'd be late. He thought the call would take five minutes.

"I'm with my mom," he said to the label head, Blake Rendon. "It's a ten-thousand-square-foot house for God's sake. There are more bathrooms than there are people. I am not living in a cabin without water; that's crazy."

"Good. Great. We need you in the studio," Blake said, apparently satisfied that Brennan had not turned into some antigovernment nut.

"Have you talked to Chance?" Brennan asked Blake. After their conversation in LA, he wondered what Chance might have said to the label.

"Yes, I've talked to Chance because he is the only one who will return my calls," Blake said. "He says it's up to you. You need to give me some idea of when the band will be back in the studio. We have a contract, you know."

That prompted a drawn-out argument about when the band would be back in the studio, with Brennan holding firm that he wouldn't agree to a date at this point. They could threaten him all they wanted—they knew as well as he did that the label needed Tuesday's End more than the band needed the label.

By the time the call ended, he realized Mia's hour was nearly over. He rushed downstairs, hoping to catch her and explain, but Mia had gone back to work. He could see her down the north hall, taking fixtures out of boxes and cleaning them off for installation.

He didn't interrupt her. He texted her an apology, then went back to work. He was so engrossed in it that he didn't look up until six o'clock. The afternoon had slipped by in a blink of an eye. Brennan went downstairs and strode out onto the drive, looking about. Everyone had packed up; all the vehicles but one were gone. Drago stepped out of the gate and waved at Brennan.

"Have you seen Mia?" he asked.

"Yes, sir. She's gone for the day."

Brennan shoved his fingers into his hair and groaned skyward. The world was closing in on his oasis here, pushing him out and back into the spotlight. The demands for his attention were increasing. This was the kind of thing that used to make Jenna crazy—he could never turn off his world.

Brennan sighed and turned to go back inside—but he met Jesse Fisher striding out of the house carrying a lunch bag that looked just like the one Mia brought up every day. Jesse gave Brennan a once over and nodded at him. He did not speak. Brennan watched him walk to his truck. Okay, so now he was aware that Jesse knew all about him now, too.

He went back inside and called Mia. "I'm sorry," he said instantly when she picked up.

"Don't worry about it."

"I do worry about it. I want to see you. Come up," he said.

"I can't. It's getting dark and I only have the bike."

That damn bike. "Then I'm coming to you. Okay?"

He heard the clink of glass. "Okay," she said, sounding less than enthused. "But I'm making a vegetarian dinner. Can you deal with vegetarian?"

"Baby, I can deal with whatever you throw at me. I'll be there in a few minutes."

◆ ◆ ◆

To Mia, vegetarian apparently meant a monster salad. Brennan had brought a bottle of decent wine and uncorked it as she chopped tomatoes. "I'm really sorry about today," he said after he poured two glasses. "The phone call was important and it got away from me."

"That's okay," she said, her gaze down.

He couldn't read her precisely—but she didn't seem particularly annoyed.

She paused and held up her knife. "I, on the other hand, had so many fixtures to unwrap and clean off that if I never see a chandelier again, I'll be happy."

He smiled. "Long day?"

"Long, *boring* day." She brought the knife down hard on the tomato and it spattered. "Oops."

"One of the calls I had today was about the Lake Haven music festival," Brennan said. "Seems like the whole world knows I'm here now."

"Yes, that would be my cousin Skylar," Mia said as she chopped more tomato. "She's appointed herself the town crier. She was so excited when she discovered you," she said, and glanced up. "I'm sorry."

Brennan shook his head. "It's not your fault. And what the hell, it would have come out sooner or later."

"Hmm," she said thoughtfully. She picked up two plates and walked around to the side of the kitchen island where he was sitting and put them down. "So are you going to go to the music festival?"

"Now that the cat is out of the bag, I think so. Whittaker asked me to come sit in on their set."

Mia stilled. She turned a wide-eyed look to him. "*What* did you just say?"

Brennan had no idea what he'd just said. "Whittaker?" he asked uncertainly.

"I *love* them!" she cried, and punched him in the arm.

"Ouch," he said. "I hope your reaction was this strong when you found out about me."

"I had a very different reaction," she said, her brows dipping. "And it was a lot stronger."

He wrapped his arms around her waist and nuzzled her neck. "You should definitely come to hear Whittaker. You can come backstage with me and watch from there."

Mia blinked. She leaned back, staring up at him.

"It's a good view," he assured her.

"Umm . . ."

"What?"

"I don't think that's a good idea."

"Backstage isn't a good idea? That's a first. Why not?"

"I mean, it would be *amazing*," she said. "But people would see us, and then everyone would wonder." She shrugged out of his embrace.

"I don't give a damn what the press says, if that's what you think."

"The press! I was talking about my family and friends."

It took Brennan a moment to understand what she meant. "Wait, what . . . are you *ashamed* of me?"

"No, of course not!" she said, but her cheeks were turning pink. "It's just that no one really knows about us, not even Skylar, no matter what she *thinks* she knows. And that would be so public, and then there would be all these questions and expectations and *can we meet him*," she said with a roll of her eyes. "It's not a good idea."

"Wow," Brennan said, nodding with amazement. "No one has ever turned down backstage before."

"I can see better from the front anyway," she said, and turned back to her salad, as if it was nothing to turn down backstage passes with one of the most popular bands currently on tour. Passes that would be scalped for fifteen hundred dollars in some parts of the United States. It was not what Brennan expected. He supposed he expected her to assume the role of every other woman he'd ever been interested in— wanting the glitz that came with his career. And that she didn't made him feel strangely clumsy. "But I . . . can I at least see you after the show? There's an after-show party. Your family won't be there to see you with the dregs of humanity," he said drily.

Mia tilted her head to one side and appeared to think about it.

"I'll get you some tickets, whatever you want. Just come. *Please.*"

One of her brows rose with surprise. "Are you begging?"

"Apparently," he admitted.

"Okay," she said. "Since you're begging, I'll come to that."

"Thanks," Brennan said grudgingly.

"But only as a favor to you. Which means you owe me. Again." She smiled pertly at him.

A surge of emotion rattled Brennan. He abruptly grabbed her up, took the knife from her hand and put it aside. "God, I love you." The words fell from his lips without thought, as if they were naturally part of him. That he'd said it so easily shook Brennan.

Mia gasped. *"What?"*

"I . . ." He faltered, unsure what he was doing. Did he love her? That word carried so much weight, meant so many things to him. Happiness. Pain. Death and rejection. A thousand self-protective protests rose up in him, some of them based in reality, some of them based in fear. But there was another thought, struggling to rise above the others, clawing free of the baggage he'd carried around with him all these years. He *did* love her. At least that's what it felt like—and it was both electric and terrifying.

Worse, Mia's shrewd gaze unnerved him. Brennan had the uneasy feeling that she was reading each and every one of those protests. "You're just so damn different from anyone I've ever known," he said, fumbling the moment badly.

Her gaze narrowed. Then she relaxed and even managed a small smile. "Well don't make it sound like I'm weird."

"Not weird. Priceless," he murmured, and kissed her to silence his conflicting thoughts.

Twenty-four

When Mia arrived at the family's weekly dinner with her mother, Skylar was holding court in Grandma's living room, regaling Emily and her husband Garret, Mike, Derek, and Tamra with her "discovery" of Everett Alden.

"You should have heard Misty Garner when I called her and told her he was *here*, in *East Beach*."

"Who is Misty Garner?" Tamra asked.

"She's the one from the mayor's office working with the concert promoters," Skylar said. "They've been trying to get more big names in, and she about wet her pants." She spotted Mia then and threw her arms wide. "Hey, *there* you are!"

"Here I am," Mia said and walked in with her arms full of clothes she'd made for Emily's friends.

"Move, move," her mother said from behind her. "This dish is *hot*." She hurried past Mia and into the kitchen.

"So Mia, this Everett Alden is the same guy who was so rude to you, huh?" Mike asked.

"Apparently," Mia said vaguely.

"Can you believe it?" Skylar went on effervescently, waving her hand at Mia. "She had *no idea* until I told her. It's like you live in another world, Mia."

"I don't live in another world. I just didn't recognize him. And I wasn't the only one—honestly, Skylar, no one knew about him until you started flapping your gums all over town," Mia said, her voice betraying her irritation.

Skylar blinked. "Okay, so? Is it a big secret or something? By the way, have you talked to him? I heard he was back in town. Is he going to stay here for a while or is he going back to LA?"

"I don't know," Mia said sharply.

"What's the matter with you?" Derek asked.

"Nothing." Why oh why had she even opened her mouth? She felt uncomfortably exposed, as if they could read her thoughts. Why didn't she just confess she'd been sleeping with a rock star? It's what Skylar would do. Just get it out on the table and go on. But Mia wasn't Skylar. And everyone was looking at her, surprised by her anger.

Mia shrugged. "It's just been crazy at work because Skylar told everyone, and now there are all these people coming and going and it's making my life miserable." She held out the clothes she'd made. "Here are the clothes for your friends, Emily. I'm going to go and help Mom."

"These are fantastic!" Emily said. "Tamra has some friends who want dresses, too."

"That's right," Tamra said. "They saw Emily's dress and are dying to meet you. Is that okay?"

"Sure," Mia said.

"She's going to need a shop!" Emily said proudly.

"Four or five dresses isn't a shop. But it is fun," Mia said, grateful to have something to talk about other than Brennan. "Give me a call, Tamra." She walked on to the kitchen.

Unfortunately, Skylar wasn't going to let her escape. She caught up to Mia and grabbed her hand in hers, tugging her back before Mia could make it to the kitchen. "So really, you haven't talked to him?"

"Not about anything but work."

"Oh, come on, Mia. Surely he's said something. Like, hey, I'm Everett

Alden of Tuesday's End, and not this Yates guy like you thought I was. *Something*."

"Actually, Skylar, I've been really busy with the renovations and making clothes for everyone. It's not like we're having long, drawn-out conversations." She pulled her hand free of Skylar's and stepped into the kitchen.

"You should ask him about it!" Skylar insisted.

"Ask who about what?" Aunt Amy asked as Skylar followed her in.

"It's nothing," Mia said.

"She always says that," Skylar complained to Aunt Amy. "Mia, he could get you tickets to the music festival."

"I could get my own ticket," Mia said.

"Who can get tickets?" Aunt Amy asked.

"Everett Alden of Tuesday's End," Skylar said.

"Never heard of him," Aunt Amy said, and turned back to her pot on the stove.

"He could get us *great* tickets," Skylar pressed.

"Us?" Mia said, and jerked around. "Skylar, I don't *want* tickets from him," she snapped. "If you want them, *you* ask him."

"Whoa," Skylar said, and backed up a couple of steps. "Okay, already. I was just asking."

Mia's mother and Aunt Amy exchanged a look. "Skylar, will you set the table?" Aunt Amy asked.

"Fine," Skylar said. She picked up a stack of plates from the counter, but she paused and looked at Mia. "If you don't want to get tickets from him, then let's go to the festival together!" she suggested brightly, and sailed out of the kitchen and into the dining room.

Mia wanted to kill her. Just put her hands around Skylar's throat and squeeze until she couldn't talk any more. She turned around and almost collided with her mother, who was standing very close, watching her. "What?" Mia asked curtly.

"You're going to go to the music festival, aren't you?" her mother asked.

Mia shrugged. "Maybe. I don't know." She shrugged again. "Probably."

"Then why not go with Skylar?"

"Are you kidding, Mom? Every time I go somewhere with Skylar, there is trouble."

"Oh honey, that was a long time ago," her mother said patiently. "Skylar means well."

"And who else are you going to go with?" Aunt Amy asked.

Maybe Aunt Amy had a point. Skylar was family and she was a companion. A bad companion, but still.

No matter what Mia thought about it, Skylar was not content to let it go. Once Mia agreed to go with Skylar, her cousin started in on backstage passes. "You know you could get passes," she said to Mia when everyone sat down to dinner. "It's a blast to be backstage."

"But I don't want to go backstage," Mia said.

"*Everyone* wants to go backstage!" Skylar exclaimed.

"I guess I'm not everyone."

"No, Mia, you're not everyone. You must seriously dig being an outsider," Skylar snapped.

"Hey, that's enough of that," Grandpa said loudly.

Skylar shut up then. But she continued to sulk about it.

◆ ◆ ◆

But Skylar had recovered the day the music festival opened. Probably because Mia had reluctantly phoned the day before to tell her she'd gotten tickets from Brennan.

She hadn't seen much of Brennan since they'd had dinner at her apartment—between his preparations for the festival and her desire to finish dresses for Tamra's friends, they'd both been quite busy that week. But he'd delivered the tickets to her personally, told her how much he'd missed her those few days, and they'd fallen onto her bed, giggling at something silly.

Brennan hadn't blurted out any other declarations of love, but Mia could feel it. She knew what it was—she was feeling the same thing for him.

She was excited about the festival, especially when the day dawned bright and filled with warm sun, a sure sign that summer was around the corner. Skylar arrived to pick her up in Aunt Bev's Cadillac SUV. She was wearing a beaded vest, linen pants, and a leather tie around her head. "It's not Woodstock," Mia said with a laugh. "It's Lake Haven."

"*Funny,*" Skylar said, laughing too. "You're the last person who should be critiquing outfits."

That was true—Mia had on her favorite distressed jeans and a halter top she'd made from one of Emily's old prom dresses. She'd also made a floppy sun hat and had festooned it with tiny gold Christmas ornaments. "And may I say you look especially creative today," Skylar added cheerfully. "That's my cousin," she said, throwing her arm around Mia's shoulders. "Always determined to stand out in a crowd."

Once they arrived at the grounds of the festival, they wandered around, taking it all in. There were food trailers and photo booths, water stations and rows and rows of portable toilets. The two of them walked by the merchandising tents where Skylar shopped the jewelry. Mia didn't have money for anything, so she roamed up and down the rows of T-shirts, purses, sun hats. She stumbled upon the Tuesday's End T-shirts quite by accident. Next to the tables set up to sell the merchandise of the bands on the official lineup, a smaller table had been dragged over and the T-shirts dumped directly out of the boxes. The front of the T-shirt had the neck of a guitar with the words *Tuesday's End World Tour.* On the back was a list of cities and the dates they'd played. Mia guessed there were at least forty cities listed.

It was staggering to see that list, visual proof of the sort of life Brennan actually lived.

Mia bought a T-shirt and tucked it into the shoulder bag she'd made from raffia ribbon.

Skylar bought a leather and silver bracelet, and the two cousins headed to the beer tent. They spent the rest of the afternoon in a mellow haze of sunlight, listening to bands that came on stage one after the other. Some of them were familiar to Mia. Some of them were not. All of them were good.

By nightfall, she was feeling the effects of having spent the afternoon drinking beer in the sun. She was relaxed and happy as she and Skylar shared a plate of nachos. After they finished them, Skylar said she was going to the portable toilet. It seemed like an hour or more had passed when Mia started to worry. Her calls to Skylar's cell phone rolled to voice mail. Mia felt a little sick—she was uncomfortably reminded of the night on the beach. Skylar had disappeared then, too, and as darkness fell, Mia's anxiety was ratcheting up.

When Whittaker, the headline act, was introduced, Mia was certain something had happened to Skylar. She had decided she would find a police officer and ask for assistance, but as the band began to play, Mia was grabbed from behind, and then pushed forward. She cried out, twisting violently around to see Skylar behind her, grinning wildly. Her headband was gone and she reeked of marijuana. She grinned at Mia with the all-too-familiar glassy gaze.

"Where the hell have you been?" Mia shouted over the din.

"Don't look at me like that!" Skylar shouted back. She swiped Mia's hat from her head. "Take it off so people can see. Come on, Mia, it's a *music* festival!" She continued to push, knocking Mia into other people who angrily turned and yelled at them. Skylar laughed at all of them and kept pushing forward until they had squeezed in at the ropes.

Whittaker came on stage to thunderous applause, lights, and smoke, and began to play.

That's when Skylar began to dance. Not just moving from side to side, but hopping and flinging her arms, oblivious to everyone else around her. Mia missed the first fifteen minutes of the concert trying to rein her cousin in. She was furious, absolutely furious. She wanted to leave, to get out of that roaring crowd and away from an impaired Skylar.

But they were hemmed in, and there was no escape. Mia could do nothing but wait for the concert to be over.

Then the lead singer from Whittaker said, "We've got a special surprise for you tonight!"

"This is him!" Skylar screeched, and fell onto Mia's back, her hands on Mia's shoulders.

"Are you ready?" the singer shouted, and the crowd roared. The band began to play a tune Mia recognized. Smoke filled the stage once more, and as the lead singer shouted, "Put your hands together for the one, the only, *Everett Alden* of *Tuesday's End!*"

Brennan appeared on stage, walking out of the smoke with a guitar, his fingers flying over the neck.

Mia was stunned. She was mesmerized. She didn't know what she expected, but it wasn't this. With his legs braced apart, Brennan played the guitar, knowing just when to crescendo, to pull back, then rush forward again so that the crowd was shrieking and whistling for him. Then the full band entered the song, the drum pounding a hard beat, and Brennan began to sing "Dream Maker."

The crowd went absolutely wild. They pushed and shoved forward, cell phones in the air, filming his performance. Mia pushed around a man in front of her, unwilling to lose sight of Brennan.

His was a truly masterful performance. She loved the deep and gritty quality of his voice. She loved the way he moved, his body swaying and bouncing along with the music. The song ended to a deafening roar of the crowd.

Whittaker then performed two of their songs, with Brennan playing along. He was clearly enjoying himself; he seemed to have gone somewhere else entirely, into a world she wondered if she could ever understand. Sweat dripped from the tips of his shaggy hair. His T-shirt—one with a dinosaur, she thought—was drenched.

The band played an encore, and still the crowd wasn't satisfied. The lead singer of Whittaker walked out one more time. "You want more?" he shouted at the crowd, who screeched back in response. "Man, we've got a special treat for you tonight." He wiped his face with a towel. "Everett Alden has been working on some new music."

The crowd roared.

"It's never been heard before."

The roar grew louder.

"He wants to play it for you tonight."

Mia had to cover her ears, the whistles and screams were so loud.

The lead singer lifted his hands and signaled the crowd to settle down. Brennan appeared again, carrying a stool and his guitar. He set the stool down, covered the mic with his hand and said something to the singer from Whittaker, and then sat on the stool and settled his guitar on his leg. "I've been working on this piece for a few weeks," he said as he adjusted the mic. He strummed a few chords on the guitar. "I hope you like it."

He began to sing, his voice raspy. *I see her on the desert's edge, auburn hair, skin so fair. She sees me standing in the sun, my head bare, no one to care.*

The melody was haunting and slow, and it washed over Mia. People whistled with approval.

She doesn't know I've come so far. I've lost my way, another day. Come closer, girl. Battered and used, my soul badly bruised. You see me standing here. You feel my fear. Come closer, girl, and rescue my shipwrecked heart. Come closer, girl. Don't watch me fall apart . . .

Mia couldn't tear her eyes from him—she didn't know if it was because his performance was so spellbinding, which it was, or because she felt as if he was singing to her. And when he finished the song, the tremendous thunder of applause and whistles seemed to surprise Brennan. He put his hand over his heart and bowed.

Mia didn't see him walk off the stage because of the tears in her eyes. That song had moved her. His artistry, his musicality, the heart and soul of a man who produced the song—all of it overwhelmed her.

Of course he had to go back to his life. To the world. He belonged to the world.

Of *course* he had to go back.

♦ ♦ ♦

The after-show party, as Brennan had called it, was as crowded as the concert itself. Skylar was practically floating on air as they stood outside the big party tent, peering in. Mia nervously clutched the credential Brennan had given her. This was not the sort of scene she liked—she always felt conspicuous and on edge.

"Why didn't you ask for two?" Skylar had asked, annoyed, when Mia had told her about the party.

"Really, Skylar?"

"*Really,*" Skylar had said. "That's how you do it. You always ask for a plus one."

Tonight, however, Skylar seemed too happy or too high to care that she didn't have a pass. "Wow, there is some star wattage in there," she said, peering into the party tent. "You won't even know how to act, Mia."

"I'm not staying," Mia said. "I'm just going to tell him nice job and then go. Will you wait here for me?"

"Sure!" Skylar said. "I'll even walk you up to the entrance." She slipped her arm through Mia's, attaching herself to her like Velcro as they moved to the roped entrance. Two burly men eyed them as they approached. Mia held up her credential. One of the men glanced at her, then at Skylar, and lifted the rope. Mia turned to Skylar to thank her, but Skylar gave her a push and hopped in beside her, jumping over the threshold with a laugh. "I'm in!" she cried. "Come on, let's get a drink." She tugged on Mia's hand, forcing her to come along before Mia could protest.

At the bar, Skylar ordered the drinks while Mia surveyed the crowd. She felt so self-conscious in this tent with her funky hat. She obviously didn't belong in here—most of the women were wearing next to nothing. They were tall and thin and had sleek, shiny hair. Mia had on jeans, and she was curvy, and she'd made her top from an old prom dress.

Then she spotted Brennan, and her heart sank a little. She didn't know what she'd expected—that he would be standing alone, a wallflower, waiting for her? No, no—Everett Alden was surrounded by people as he should be, the star of the show. He was laughing at something and a beer dangled from his fingers. He'd changed his shirt, combed back his hair, and looked as if he'd just run a race and won the whole damn thing.

She was startled by a tap to her shoulder. Before she could turn, Skylar shoved a highball glass into her hand. "I'm going to mingle," she said, and walked away, sipping from a glass that was filled with a pink drink.

Mia glanced back at Brennan, debating what to do. She didn't know how to get to him. She didn't know how to walk through this crowd of rock gods and beautiful women and interrupt his circle. She'd never felt so out of place in her life.

She'd text him, she decided. She'd text him and tell him that she'd come as she promised, but that he was busy. She'd suggest they see each other tomorrow. She dug in her purse for her phone, but before she could find it, Brennan saw her. He immediately broke away from his group, even peeling one woman's fingers off his arm. Mia glanced around looking for an escape, someone to hide behind—but she was alone in that crowd. She was standing in the desert with her head bare and no one to care.

No one but Brennan.

"Hey," he said when he reached her. He dipped down, kissed her cheek, and Mia blushed madly, glancing furtively about, almost as if she feared someone was going to accuse her of trying to accost him. "You came. I thought maybe you'd bail on me."

"No, I—I thought . . . it was wonderful, Brennan," she gushed. "Masterful," she blurted. "My God, I didn't know how good you are—I mean, I knew, of course I knew, but to see you perform was just . . ." She was fumbling all over herself like a rabid fan. She took a breath. "You were really great."

He smiled at her fluster. "Thank you. I'm glad you liked it."

"I didn't like it, I loved it. I was so moved. I wish I had the words to tell you how moved I was."

He smiled. "I guess you know the song is about you."

Tears filled her eyes again, and she nodded. "I sort of guessed, anyway. It felt like you were singing to me."

"What's the matter?" he asked, dipping down to see in her eyes.

"Nothing. I was just . . ." There were no words to describe what she'd felt listening to him sing about her. His voice and the lyrics had sunk down so deep that they were permanently embedded in her. "Such artistry," she said, fumbling for the right thing to say.

He chuckled softly and touched her face. "You slay me, baby," he said. "Listen, I—"

"Everett! Dude, that was fucking *sick*." It was the lead singer of Whittaker. He smiled at Mia, but she was too starstruck to do anything but stare back at him.

"You *killed* it, man," he said to Brennan. "Did you see who came in with your agent?"

"Who?" Brennan asked.

"Chance."

Brennan froze. He turned around. "Holy shit," he said softly. He took Mia's hand and squeezed it. "Give me a minute, will you? Do you need a drink?"

"No, I'm fine. Do whatever you need to do."

He brought her hand to his lips and kissed it. "I'll be right back. I promise."

He let go of her hand and, with Whittaker's singer, moved across the party tent, leaving Mia standing alone in the middle of the crowd.

She watched him put his hand on the shoulder of a guy with long hair. That man said something and the two of them moved farther away so that she couldn't see them any longer.

"Hey, you want a hit?"

A joint appeared before her; Mia glanced up at the man standing next to her. "You look like you could use something to take the edge off. This is some good shit."

"No, thank you."

"Mia!" Skylar popped in around the man. "Hey, I'll take some of that," she said. The man shrugged and handed the joint to Skylar. She drew long, then tilted her head back and released the smoke to the air before giving it back to him. "You won't believe who I met," she said, and took Mia's drink and sipped from it. "The drummer for Whittaker," she exclaimed, and pushed the drink back at Mia. "He is so *cute*. And I think he likes me. You should have Everett put in a good word for me."

"A good word?" Mia asked, confused.

"You know, tell him I'm cool."

It was astounding how self-centered Skylar McCauley could be. "He doesn't even *know* you."

"Yeah, but he knows you."

That was it. Mia couldn't bear another moment in this tent with these dope-smoking hangers-on. "His name is Brennan."

Skylar frowned. "Don't be a dipshit, Mia. His name is Everett. I don't know what fairy tales he was telling you, but that guy is Everett Alden, *obviously*," she said with a roll of her eyes.

She couldn't deny that was true. Tears were beginning to burn her eyes again. She had to realize he *was* Everett Alden, and she . . . well, she was not in his league. "I'm leaving," she said.

Skylar's mouth dropped open. Then closed. "Go ahead." She reached into her purse and dug out the keys, pressed them into Mia's hand. "Tell Mom I spent the night with you, okay?" And with that, Skylar was gone.

Mia put her head down and started for the exit. She was intercepted by Brennan. "Where are you going?" he asked. "I'm sorry, I didn't mean to desert you—"

A big man appeared between them holding a highball glass that looked like a toy in his enormous hand. "Everett, is it true?" he asked jovially.

"Hello, Dinkleman," Brennan said.

"I heard you're going to work with Kate Resnick."

"We're talking," he said, his hand finding the small of Mia's back. "I'll catch up with you," he said, edging away.

"I should go," Mia said as he tried to guide her to the bar.

"Please stay," he said.

"Brennan!" She grabbed his wrist, made him stop, made him *look* at her. "I need to go. This isn't . . ." She glanced around. "I feel so out of place here. Everyone wants to talk to you, everyone wants you. You don't have time to babysit me."

"I'm not babysitting you," he said, sounding exasperated.

But Mia was practical. She didn't belong here, and he knew it as well as she did. Maybe he didn't want to admit it, but babysitting was exactly what he was doing. She put her hand on his chest and pushed. "Just go and enjoy your night. You deserve this attention, every last bit of it. That song was incredible, and I'm in your way."

"That's not true." He covered her hand with his. "Come on, Mia. I'm asking you to stay."

They stood there staring at each other. She wanted to stay. God, how she wanted to stay. But she couldn't. As much as she felt for him, probably even loved him, Mia could not be this person or move in this world. It was too much. It was all too *much*. "Stay for what?" she asked him.

"For a drink—"

"No, Brennan. What am I staying for?" she asked again.

He knew what she meant; she could see it in the pained look around his eyes. He winced, then shoved a hand through his hair. "I don't know," he answered truthfully.

Those three words were perhaps the most heartbreaking words Mia had ever heard in her life. It wasn't as if she'd expected a miracle—or maybe she had. A tear slid from the corner of her eye and down her cheek. Brennan groaned, then bent his head and kissed her lips. "If you want to go, go. I understand. I'll call later."

Mia nodded. She couldn't speak; if she did, a torrent of grief would come pouring out of her.

She left. She walked out of the tent, her head down, and practically ran to the parking lot.

She drove to the other end of Lake Haven in something of a daze. Had they just ended it? Had they just mutually agreed that it was impossible? Or had she read that into what he'd said?

Whatever had just happened, Mia couldn't keep doing this to herself. She had to end it for the sake of her sanity and her woefully fragile heart.

She half expected Brennan to show up at her apartment in the middle of the night. He didn't. She thought he would call her the next day. There was no call. She texted him and asked how he was. He didn't respond.

Mia puttered around her little apartment, trying to work on a new dress. But she couldn't think. She couldn't think of anything but Brennan Yates. She tried to imagine herself making a life with him. She tried to imagine him making a life with her. She imagined how the end would come, then debated if it had already come.

Sunday night, with no word from him, Mia was a wreck. When her phone rang, she pounced on it. "Hello?"

"Well, it's official," Aunt Bev said. "We're delaying work on the Ross house until Nancy's celebrity son gets the hell out of the way."

Mia's heart plummeted. "For how long?"

"She said he should be gone by the end of next week. Can you believe it, one of his fans actually came in with one of the demolition crews and was walking around the house! There are some crazy people out there, Mia! Just come to the shop tomorrow, sweetie. We'll find something for you to do."

"Sure," Mia said. She hung up, then hurled the phone across the room. She fell forward onto her bed, face down. And she sobbed.

Twenty-five

Chance's appearance was a great surprise to Brennan. "Gary flew me out," he said. "Congratulations, Bren. The song was amazing. I get it now," he said. "I get what it is you want."

Brennan invited Chance up to his mother's house, where poor Drago was doing his best to keep fans and photographers out. The two old friends talked all night, airing their differences, working out a way to forge a path forward. In the end, they'd come to an agreement: Chance would come in with Brennan on the soundtrack, and after that, Brennan would go back into the studio with Chance. They would write a mixture of pop and alternative rock. It didn't resolve all of their differences about where the band was going, but it filled in the gaps for the near term. It was a start.

On Sunday afternoon, Brennan drove Chance into the city to catch a flight.

He returned to East Beach after dark. His mother was sitting on the terrace with a glass of wine when he strolled up from the garage. "There you are. My son, the talk of the town."

"I am?" he asked, and took a seat on a chaise next to her.

"Everyone is talking about your performance. Is that the song I've heard you tinkering with?"

"Yeah, I guess," he said.

"I'm proud of you, Bren. I was so worried about you, you know? But you pushed through it. I should have listened to you."

He smiled. "Thanks, Mom." It was not the first time, and it probably would not be the last time, that his mother admitted she was wrong. But he liked the sound of it.

"But . . . now that all the attention is on you again," she said, frowning, "I don't think you can hide out here much longer."

"No," he agreed. "I'll probably head home at the end of the week. Chance and I have agreed on what we're going to do, and now I need to get to work."

"I've postponed work on the house," she said. "It's just too much commotion. And then that woman was walking around . . . well, it's unbearable. I honestly don't know how you do it."

He smiled a little. "It's usually not this bad."

She sat up and grabbed his head, pulled him forward, and kissed his forehead. "I love you, Brennan. But I'm ready for you to go back to your life."

"I love you, too, Mom."

He continued on inside and grabbed a beer on his way up to his room. It was quarter till nine. He wanted to talk to Mia, but he wasn't sure what he was going to say. Things were falling into place, but she was the piece of his life that was the true outlier. She knew it, too. She'd asked him at the after-show party—what was she staying for?

Brennan had mulled it over, turning that question over in his head, looking at it from all angles. He couldn't stay here; he had to go back to work. He *wanted* to go back to work. Brennan debated his thoughts about Mia, groaned with exasperation at his old scars and fears. He tried to look inward, to see down to the river of desires and emotions that flowed somewhere in him, in a clumsy effort to understand. Brennan was feeling things, thinking things he'd never allowed himself to contemplate. He was wanting things he never thought he could have, much like one wanted priceless jewels behind glass walls they weren't allowed to touch. But the walls were shattering now, and the jewels his for the taking . . . and yet he was still afraid to touch them.

Finally, somewhere near midnight, he texted Mia and asked her to meet him at Lookout Point the next day.

He didn't hear back until almost ten the next morning. *When?*

Noon. I won't be late.

◆ ◆ ◆

True to his word, Brennan was pacing in front of the old bench at noon, thinking, his hands locked behind his head. Mia appeared on the path, walking up from the beach. She was wearing knee-length shorts, a flowing blouse over a tank. She had her hair tied back with a bandana. She looked like she should be painting. "The baby owls are gone," she said when she reached him. "I saw them last week, hopping around, but now they're gone, just like that. It's like we imagined them."

She moved closer.

"We didn't imagine them. My God you look so good," he said, surprised by the emotion in his voice.

She smiled. "You look pretty good yourself." She touched his face, her honey eyes skating over his features. She frowned slightly. "Are you okay?"

He grabbed her hand and kissed the palm of it. He didn't want to let go. Ever. "Yeah, I'm okay. I have some news."

"Right." She pulled her hand free. "You're like the baby owls, you know? Hopping around before you leave. And then poof—you'll be gone."

He wished he knew some way to soften this news, to let her know how he'd agonized. But what was the point? "That's what I wanted to talk to you about. I have to go, Mia. My mother's life has been disrupted, and I've got people all over me, wanting things. I have a lot of work ahead of me that I can't do here."

Mia nodded.

"Chance and I had the opportunity to talk, and we've come to an agreement of sorts."

"Oh yeah?" she asked, looking interested.

"He's going to work with me on the film, and then we're going back to the studio."

"That's *great*," she said. But her voice and expression did not match her words. She looked devastated. "Well, that certainly makes things easier."

He didn't understand her. "What?"

"I'm breaking up with you, Brennan. Well, wait—I'm not sure I have anything to break because it was never really official," she said, making air quotes around the word *official.* "But whatever it was, it's run its course. I need to move on."

"Wait, Mia," he said, and grabbed her hand. "You don't understand—I want you to come with me."

"You *what?*" she said loudly, her eyes widening.

"I've thought a lot about it, and I don't know how it will work. I mean, I've tried to figure it out—I guess what I am trying to say is that it's going to be hard, and I might not be around much at times, and part of me thinks that I am being unfair, that I will ask you to come along on the ride, but a lot of the ride you might be taking alone." Good Lord, could he make this any more of a mess? For someone who was renowned for heartfelt lyrics, he couldn't seem to muster the poet when he needed to most. "But I . . . I love you," he said, his voice catching on the word. "I *love* you, Mia, and I don't want to be without you." He roughly stroked her hair, frantically thinking. "I thought this would be so easy, this thing between us. What I'm trying to say is that *you* are easy, but life may not be easy. But it's worth it, right? It's so worth it."

She was biting her lip now. There was still hope in her, he could see it in her expression. His gut twisted—with alarm and joy at once, because he *did* love her, and he wanted her, and although he was scared by how much he wanted her, his panic and fears about what would happen if he uprooted her seemed to fade into the background when he looked at her. Everything but the beat of his imperfect heart and Mia faded away.

He smiled.

Mia pulled her hand free. "That's . . . that's very sweet to hear," she said haltingly, and Brennan's imperfect heart lurched and shuddered. "But I don't want to come with you, Brennan. This was just a . . ." Her voice trailed off and she shrugged.

"A what? What are you saying?"

"I'm saying n-no," she said, stumbling on the word a little. "Jesus, this is hard," she said, and pressed her palm to her forehead a moment. "It's time to move on. Everyone go back to their corners. You go on with your life and I go on with mine."

He stared at her, disbelieving. He had just seen the hope in her eyes. Why was she saying this? "I just told you I love you," he said, dumbfounded.

"I know."

"Doesn't that mean something?" he demanded.

"Well, yeah. I mean I am humbled by it, but I—"

Brennan jerked around. He couldn't look at her if she was going to say she didn't love him. The old wound of rejection his father had left him suddenly opened, and she had poured fire into it. He looked blindly out at the lake, his heart racing, his thoughts alternating between anger and hurt. This wasn't how it was supposed to go. The glass walls were coming up, encasing the priceless jewels. He had to get out of there.

How he managed to collect himself from that punch to the gut, Brennan didn't know. He turned partially toward her and took her in once more, biting his tongue. "I have something for you," he said at last. He walked to the bench and picked up the plain brown bag. "This is for you."

She didn't move; it was as if her feet were glued to the place she stood. So Brennan brought the bag to her. Mia reluctantly took it and looked inside. She withdrew the painting of the red door she'd admired at the art festival and held it up. "You bought this?" Her voice was full of wonder that made the wound hurt more.

"I did. I contacted the artist. I wanted you to have it. For inspiration. I was hoping that when you look at this painting, you'll see all the things you pointed out to me, and I hope that it inspires you."

Mia folded her arms around the painting. "God, Brennan . . . I will always love this painting. I will always admire it." She looked up at him. "But admiration and inspiration are not the same thing. You know that inspiration doesn't come from looking at someone else's work. It comes from living. From being out in the world and experiencing pain and heartache and joy. *You* have inspired me."

He couldn't possibly have inspired her in the way she had inspired him these last few weeks. She'd changed him—look at him, professing his love!

"Thank you for this," she said.

"Is that it, then? You're going to tell me I've inspired you, then walk away? You're going to turn my world around when no one else could and then end it?" Maybe that's why this was so excruciatingly painful to him—she had seen through his bullshit and called him on it. She had seen inside him, had pulled the man he was out of the ashes of his fame. She had picked up where Trey had left off, and he was going to miss her as much as he missed Trey.

Brennan felt at sea, riding roughly over tsunami waves of emotion he'd not felt quite like this.

"I wish it were that simple," she said. She put her hand on his arm. "It's not like I'm dead. We can still talk, can't we? When you come back, we can have a drink or something."

"A *drink?*"

Mia smiled sadly. "Brennan," she said softly.

It was his fault. He should have told her. He should have given her the chance to bail out in the beginning with the truth, but he hadn't. He'd been too selfish, too stupid.

"I'm so sorry," she whispered. "We're better off as friends, aren't we?"

Brennan relented then. He couldn't bear it, and gathered her in his arms with a choke of emotion, kissed the top of her head. "I'm so sorry, Mia," he murmured into her hair. Sorry for being who he was, sorry for having omitted the truth. Sorry for ever having fallen in love with her. It was an unbearable pressure, this suffocation of his heart.

It hurt like hell.

Twenty-six

Mia was so dumb—why had she ever said they'd be friends? She should have cut it off at the head, ending it once and for all, but she'd been too heartsick to let go completely. And now, in spite of her best efforts to put Brennan behind her, he was making it difficult. He insisted on keeping in touch, and Mia was too weak to stop it.

She wished he'd go back to his fame and stardom and leave her alone. And yet, she couldn't stop picking up the phone. She hated that she wanted to hear his voice. She hated that she longed to know what he was doing. She wanted to get on with her life and stop living the fantasy of Brennan Yates.

He sent text messages and called. Sometimes, he talked about his work, and how hard it was to produce a soundtrack that hit all the emotional beats of the movie. Mia was interested, but when he asked her opinion, she responded sparingly. She'd say things like, "I always try and find the natural rhythm," and then cringe at how absurd she sounded. Who was she to advise Everett Alden?

"Like, how do you mean?" he would ask curiously.

"It's hard to explain," she'd say, and change the subject. Because the last thing, the very *last* thing she wanted was for him to perceive her as a clingy girl. As someone who made up shit just to stay on the phone.

The last time Brennan called, she heard women in the background.

"Where are you?" she asked.

"A restaurant," he said. "I'm meeting my agent in about ten minutes."

She didn't want to be suspicious, but she wondered if he and some actress or model was meeting his agent. But she said cheerily, "That's about ten minutes more than I have!"

"Oh." He sounded surprised. Of course he was—he was used to beating off admirers with his imaginary stick. Hell, he probably had someone assigned to do that for him. He knew better than anyone that her life was not exactly a hotbed of activity. "How is work?" he asked.

"We're almost finished with the north wing."

"I meant your art," he said.

Outside of her mother, and occasionally one of her brothers or her father, Brennan was the only one to ever ask. The question made her feel heavy. How was her art? It was dormant. She'd lost more than him, she'd lost the desire to paint. It seemed to have withered along with her heart when Brennan left. "The painting of the lanterns is almost done," she said. That much was true. She didn't say it had taken her two weeks to go back to the painting. She didn't tell him that the red door painting hung on her wall, and that she looked at it every morning, every night, and thought of him. That she was trying, unsuccessfully, to replicate the use of light with her lanterns.

"I've made a lot of clothes," she said, changing the subject. "I made an extra twenty-five hundred dollars this month."

"Hey, that's fantastic!"

She pictured him trying very hard not to laugh right now. That must seem so ridiculous to him, to crow about making an extra twenty-five hundred dollars.

"What would you think about flying out to LA later this week?" he asked.

"Why?"

"Why?" he repeated, sounding annoyed. "I'd like to see you, Mia."

As if that were an easy thing to do, to pay for a ticket at a moment's notice and leave a job where she got paid an hourly wage and fly to the West Coast. "I'm kind of busy."

She heard nothing but the clink of glasses and the sound of the woman talking. "Yeah, I'm sure you are," he said, sounding defeated. "I just remembered I have to be in San Francisco."

"Maybe some other time," she said with a breeziness she didn't feel.

"Definitely. I'll call you. Listen, baby, I've got to go. Phil is here."

Mia knew how this would all end, the phone calls, the endearments. She knew, she *knew*, and yet, she couldn't erase that horrible feeling of anticipation, or the hope that every time he called there was going to be some huge surprise announcement. *I can't take it here, I'm coming back to East Beach!* There was the undying hope that he would figure it out and he would come back for her, and they would have this wonderful life together. He would write music for big feature films, and she would paint and make clothes, and somehow, *somehow*, they would make it work.

Like that was ever going to happen. Mia had to pull on her big-girl panties and get over it. This was how it was with summer people. They flitted through your life and that was it—it was over.

It was over! Get on with it! Stop pining, stop wishing, stop believing you love him!

Over the next two weeks, Brennan's calls grew fewer and farther apart. Mia found herself scouring magazine racks looking for stories about him. There were still a few articles about him living in a rustic cabin, but *People* finally ran a story based somewhat on truth—that he'd been here, at Lake Haven . . . caring for a sick mother. She couldn't help but laugh at that.

Work at the Ross house eventually moved into the south wing. Jesse started dating someone from Black Springs, and for reasons that escaped Mia, he was very keen to share the details with her.

As for herself, Mia just put one foot in front of the other and kept moving through her days, hoping that distance and time from Brennan would somehow make it easier. She had more people wanting dresses, which kept her busy. She was experimenting with different fabrics that she found interesting. The thought occurred that perhaps fashion design was her true calling. She still had a strong desire to paint . . . but she'd always struggled to be really good at it. She didn't struggle to make wearable art, and the fans of her work were increasing. The appeal of making the clothes was getting stronger every day. "You know what they say," Grandma said one afternoon as she examined a dress Mia had made for her—a shift, with the big pockets that Grandma had requested. "When one door closes, another one opens."

That seemed true for her art. But Mia didn't know what the door closing behind Brennan meant. She wanted to ease the ache in her, but the more she tried, the angrier she became. Not with Brennan. Not with herself. But with Skylar.

Naturally, Skylar seemed completely oblivious to Mia's hurt. She talked endlessly about her new friendships with the music festival organizers, thanks to finding Everett Alden right under their noses. She'd also kept up communication with the drummer for Whittaker. Damien, Daniel, something like that; Mia could hardly listen to Skylar talk about him. Unlike Mia, who would rather die than be a hanger-on, Skylar was more than happy to constantly text and call the man to keep her tenuous hold on him.

Mia realized she was irrationally angry with her cousin, and yet the anger was boiling, hotter and hotter every time she saw Skylar's smiling face. Her anger exploded in the shop one afternoon.

It didn't help that Skylar came in woefully late. She'd taken to coming in when she wanted, because Skylar never took any job seriously, and Aunt Bev didn't insist that she take this one seriously. That day, Skylar excitedly reported to Mia that she was going to Seattle to a music event. "Damien's going to be there," she said, and leaned across the counter to whisper, "and we are going to hook up in a major way. The dude is *hot*."

"Good for you," Mia muttered.

"Sourpuss," Skylar said cheerfully. "Hey, you should come with me!"

Why Skylar thought Mia would want to go anywhere with her was amazing in and of itself. But that Skylar couldn't see how angry Mia was, or how she'd ruined Mia's life, finally detonated something in Mia. "Yeah right. Even if I wanted to, I don't have the money to do that," she said coldly. "And I'm not about to ask my parents for it."

Skylar blinked, clearly stung by the dig. "Then call your boyfriend."

"He's *not* my boyfriend!" Mia shouted. "And if I ever had any hope of him *being* a boyfriend, it was blown the minute *you* ran your damn mouth!"

"Ladies, ladies!" Wallace said, appearing from somewhere in the back, his hands up. "This is a place of business, not a beer hall." He put his hand on Mia's arm, tried to force her around to face him. "It's not worth it, Mia."

"What the hell is *that* supposed to mean?" Skylar demanded.

"I know," Mia conceded. "But I can't take it. She's been doing this to me since we were kids."

"Doing *what*?" Skylar exclaimed.

"Creating bad situations and then leaving me behind, that's what."

Skylar gaped at her, clearly stunned. "I don't do that!" She sounded appalled and indignant and surprised. How could she be surprised?

"Oh no? You left me on the beach that night and you *knew* how drunk I was. You *knew* how Shalene felt about me."

Skylar gasped. "You're blaming *me*?"

"You left me, Skylar! You dragged me to that fucking party, you talked me into drinking that shit, remember? Just *try* it, you said, don't be an asshole, you said," Mia shouted, her arms flailing. "And then you *left* me. You create situations and leave me behind."

"Oh dear," Wallace said.

"*I* didn't drag you to the Ross house. That was all you, Mia," Skylar shot back. "I can't help it that you fell in love with some guy who was doing a number on you."

Mia's heart began to pound with hurt. Skylar had hurt her feelings, but it was more than that—what Skylar said was true. She'd fallen in love with a guy, the wrong guy, and it had done a number on her. "No," she said, her voice shaking. "But you dragged the world up there, didn't you." It was not a question.

"All right, that's enough!" Wallace said sternly, stepping in between them. "If you're going to fight, take it to the alley!"

Skylar was furious—Mia could see it in her gaze. But slowly the anger and indignation faded away into an expression of disbelief. "*Jesus*, Mia," she said, her voice softer. "You didn't think Everett Alden was actually going to stick around for *you*, did you?"

Mia couldn't speak. She was so angry, so hurt, and on the verge of tears. Of course she didn't. If she'd believed that, she wouldn't have broken it off, would she?

"Oh my God, you *did*," Skylar said, her voice full of amazement.

"For heaven's sake, Skylar, do you *ever* know when to stop?" Wallace snapped. He put his arm around Mia's shoulders.

"I have to go," Mia said shakily.

"Of course you do," Wallace said. "Here," he said, and dug in his pocket. "Take the shop van." He handed her the keys. "Go and . . . paint something," he said, and fluttered his fingers toward the back.

Mia grabbed the keys from him and hurried out of the shop before they saw her collapse under the weight of her grief.

Twenty-seven

The work was progressing, but not in the way Brennan had hoped after the success of "Come Closer." That song had been written in a fog of alcohol and depression and a discovery of emotions he didn't know he actually had in him. That song had its own musical juju.

But the rest of the track, even with Chance's help, was dragging. Brennan and Chance were spending long hours at the studio, working through it, but something was missing, something vital. It was a dull ache, the feeling of missing something. And it felt old and all too familiar to Brennan. He'd first felt it as the son of a single mother. Music was the thing he'd escaped to then, but music couldn't seem to fill that void any longer.

The hole in him, which he had diligently shored up throughout his life, had somehow gotten bigger. He felt as lost as he had when he'd arrived on his mother's doorstep.

It didn't help that in LA, everyone told him how great he was. The label, the fans, the press—they all said he was an American icon, a musical genius. Brennan knew that's what people said because they thought they were supposed to. To make matters worse, there was no one around him who would be completely straight with him about the music. Except for Chance—but Chance could be as blind to what was missing as Brennan.

What Brennan knew about himself was that he was a good musician, a creative one—but he needed to be pushed. He needed life to push him to greatness. A long time ago, his father's rejection had pushed him. Trey's downward spiral had pushed him. And still, he hadn't reached his potential. He didn't feel potential in him. If Brennan were honest, completely honest, he'd admit to himself that he couldn't feel much of anything but loss. That loss was eating at him, and the music wasn't happening.

He needed Mia. He *wanted* Mia. But she'd told him to get lost. He'd tried to give her space. He'd tried to keep the bond between them, hoping that she would think about what he'd said and realize that she loved him, too. But Brennan felt the gulf between them widening, and it seemed to him that she was steadily chiseling away at it, making it wider and wider. Like he wasn't worth the effort to stay in touch.

And still, he couldn't let it go. She meant too much to him.

He texted her one day and told her he was having trouble getting into the music, of finding the right space in it. That sounded like some voodoo talk, and he instantly regretted the text. But about fifteen minutes later, she texted back: *Listen to your music.*

He texted with a simple ?.

Listen to something you wrote a long time ago. Put headphones on and just listen.

Brennan had nothing to lose by trying. He did what she said, choosing the band's sophomore album, most of which he'd written. At first, he hummed along, so familiar with the music. He'd performed it a thousand times, hadn't he? But then he stopped and *listened*. His mind wasn't working to enhance or change it. He settled back, closed his eyes, and heard the music he'd created. He heard his talent, the sort of sound he was capable of creating. And he was inspired.

He texted her again, another day, but her reply was terse. He was bothering her. She was the only person he knew who wanted distance from him, and it was clear she did. So Brennan texted and called her less.

He just missed her. He felt the heartache of missing her every day.

Ben Whittaker called one day and told him the band was playing a private party for their label and handlers in Seattle and invited Tuesday's End to the event. Brennan and the band flew up on the label's jet.

The moment they walked into the venue, Brennan was surrounded by women and the inevitable posse of band friends. There was a time in his life he'd loved these parties and being the center of attention. He wasn't interested in parties like this anymore. He'd even go so far as to say he was bored.

He was nursing a beer, answering vaguely about what he was working on, and lazily debating whether or not he ought to take a blonde up on her offer to check out and go to her place. As he lifted his bottle to take a drink, he noticed a woman looking at him. He recognized her—it took him a moment to remember why, but then he squinted, disbelieving. That was Mia's cousin. What was her name—Sky?

She was wearing a short gold skirt and heels so high that Brennan couldn't imagine how she stayed upright. She had long blonde hair with pink tips and a diaphanous top through which he could see a red bra.

He watched her strut toward him. "Hey," she said when she reached him. "Remember me?"

"Sky, right?"

"Skylar. But who's taking notes?" she asked cheerfully.

Not him. "How did you . . ." He gestured to the room.

"Oh. Whittaker's drummer, Damien. Do you know him? We kind of hooked up after the Lake Haven Music Festival."

So she was a first-class groupie, the kind who followed a band anywhere. He wasn't really surprised. "Congratulations."

She laughed and tossed her hair. "You don't bother me," she said. "I know what I'm doing."

"Well, then congratulations again. A lot of people have no idea what they're doing. They just move through life blindly." He lifted his beer bottle and moved to turn away.

"I know, right? Like my cousin."

Brennan's pulse ticked up. He looked at her. "Pardon?"

"My cousin, Mia?" she said, as if he could possibly have forgotten. "Can I say something to you? I mean, for real."

Now his heart began to race. He couldn't imagine what this woman would have to say to him about Mia, and he was sure he didn't want to know.

She read his reluctance. "It's important."

He didn't trust this woman. He abruptly took Skylar's elbow and wheeled her around, leading her out of the crowded room and into a hall. "Okay," he said, gesturing for her to talk. "What about Mia?"

"First of all, it's all my fault," she said, pressing her hands on top of each other, over her heart. "If I hadn't said anything, you'd still be up there. No one would know, and you and Mia would still be together."

That was not true, but he might have stayed a little longer. "Okay, it's your fault," he agreed. "But I thought this was about Mia."

Skylar frowned. "So you're not going to accept my apology."

"Was that an apology?"

"You know what, smartass? Mia is really hurting, and that is *not* my fault. It's *yours*."

Those words knifed his heart. "What are you talking about?" he demanded angrily. "She told me to take a hike."

"God, are you that dumb? Mia has always lived in her own little world. She's always been an outsider. No one ever understood the kind of person she was when we were kids, but *I* did. *I* got her," she said, poking herself in the chest. "She let you into her world and she had this crazy belief that you would actually want to be with someone like her. Why did you do that to her?"

Brennan swallowed down bitterness. "I asked her to come with me," he said tightly. "Did she tell you that?"

"No, of course not. Mia never tells anyone anything. But trust me, I know her. I don't know what you said to her, but Mia isn't the kind to give up everything and go off on a whim."

"It wasn't a whim," Brennan said angrily, even as he played back that moment at Lookout Point in his mind. He hadn't actually made it sound very enticing. He'd been so intent on making sure she knew what it would be like that he hadn't really thought of how unappealing it might have come across to her. He'd been so nervous about telling her how he felt, he didn't really think about how she might have felt. "She doesn't want anything to do with me," he said defensively. And he damn sure wasn't going to explain himself to Skylar.

"Well, she does. You have to be able to read between the lines." Skylar folded her arms and glared at him.

Brennan cast his arms wide. "What do you want from me?"

"To make it right, *Everett Alden*. You could, you know." She turned and walked away. "You could if you wanted to!" she shouted over her shoulder at him.

Brennan had never been able to abide or trust groupies, but something Skylar said was clanging loud in his head. It was a thought that had been floating around in the ether since he'd left East Beach.

Mia did love him, and maybe he could make it right. He'd go back, try again, perhaps tell her he loved her and wanted to be with her in a better way.

The question was, did she want him to come back and make it right? And did he really want to face the pain of her rejection all over again?

Twenty-eight

Mia was thinking of getting a television. She'd made enough money now that she could afford things like that, and she really wanted to see *Project Runway.*

"Are you kidding?" Wallace demanded one day when she mentioned it. "You would put money toward a television before a car? Do you think I *like* driving you hither and yon?" he asked, waving his hand about.

"Yes. I do." She smiled.

Wallace had groaned and stalked to the back room of the shop. But she noticed he hadn't denied it.

"I'm getting a TV, Wallace!" she shouted after him.

Another reason she wanted TV was because she wanted a little company. She loved her apartment, she loved the serenity of the lake. But sometimes she hated the silence and the emptiness. The silence filled her brain with thoughts and what-ifs, and the emptiness seemed to sink deeper, turning into a bottomless pit. The truth was no matter how busy she made herself, she couldn't stop thinking about what had been.

She was looking at different TV brands on her laptop, wondering when they'd all become so much smarter than her, when she heard music. Mia paused, cocked her head to one side, listening. She didn't hear it again, and turned her attention back to the computer. "Dalton and his get-togethers," she muttered. Since summer had officially arrived, people came and went all week to the main house, and on weekends, she typically saw a slew of young, handsome, and incredibly fit men wandering about in tiny Speedos.

Samsung, RCA, Sony, Toshiba. The list was long and confusing—

There it was again. Music was drifting up through her open French doors. A guitar by the sound of it. Mia's heart leapt; her hand was shaking when she shut her laptop and looked warily at the open French doors, listening. *She knew that song.* She'd heard it played once before, and she would recognize that song anywhere. Now her heart was pounding so hard she could hardly stand up.

He couldn't be here. But that would be just like him to show up, uninvited, unannounced. Still, it couldn't be him—she would have heard about his arrival in town. She moved cautiously toward the open door, her heart racing so hard now she feared there was a strong possibility of heart failure before she found the nerve to look outside.

At the open door, Mia could hear the music so plainly. She slid one foot out on the balcony and leaned forward. She still couldn't see. So she stepped out with the other foot, to the railing, and looked down. *"Ohmigod,"* she whispered.

On the lawn below her, Brennan stood with a guitar in hand, playing "Come Closer." Behind him, near Dalton's pool, several young men were congregating near the diving board so that they could see who was playing. Brennan didn't notice them—he was looking at Mia as he reached the chorus. He sang through it once, then paused and lowered his guitar. "Hey," he said.

"What are you doing?" she asked frantically. She was shaking as she gripped the railing.

"I was hoping it would be obvious," he said. "Serenading you. It doesn't work like it does in the movies, by the way. It took you forever. I was starting to get hives."

"Why are you serenading me?"

"Why?" He muttered something under his breath and pushed his hand over his hair. "See, here again, I thought it would be obvious. But okay, it's not. I am serenading you because I love you."

"Brennan—"

"And I screwed that up the first time I told you. I was an idiot, Mia."

"What?"

"Great—should I not have said that?" he asked, peering up at her. "It's true. I made it sound like it would be so hard, and that's not . . . I didn't mean that. I meant . . ." He paused, ran a hand over his head. Someone behind him said, "Is that Everett *Alden*?"

Yes. Yes, it was Everett Alden telling Mia that he loved her. He *still* loved her.

Brennan glanced back at the group of buff young men gathered at the deep end of the pool now. He looked back to Mia, his expression pleading. "I really wasn't expecting an audience. Can I come up?"

She hesitated, biting her lip. What did it mean if she let him in? Was she opening the door to something more? Was she giving in to her feelings for him, no matter how hard the fall would be if it didn't work out?

"Please, Mia. Let me say it one more time and if you want me to go, I'll go. I'll never bother you again. Deal?"

She couldn't *think*! She wanted to slide down onto her bottom and process this. But she didn't do that. She said, "Okay." And somehow, she managed to turn around and dip back into her apartment like she was accustomed to famous rock stars showing up to serenade her.

Mia glanced around and whimpered. The place was a mess, and she was wearing a jumper made from aprons. Her hair was tied back, she wore no makeup—

She let out a little cry of alarm when he knocked on the door. She hurried the few steps to the door and flung it open so hard that it hit the wall and rattled the windows. Below her, a cheer went up. But Mia didn't move—she stared at Brennan, taking in every single thing about him. Nope, she hadn't forgotten a thing. But other than that single thought, she had no words—her mind was a complete blank. All of her reasoning about why she had broken up with Brennan Yates began to break apart, floating away like leaves from a pile.

"Could I please come all the way in?" he pleaded.

"I don't . . . I'm not—"

"Mia, just let me say something. And then you can kick me out if you want. Okay?"

Okay, okay, say anything.

"I messed up," he said. "I really, seriously, messed up. More than once. I don't have any excuse for it other than to say I wasn't expecting you, and then when you were there, and you were in here," he said, tapping his chest, "I should have told you the truth from the beginning."

True, but that wound had healed.

"And then I wanted you to come with me. But I haven't had to ask, you know? I'm rusty. Hell, I'm more than rusty, I'm awful. I said it all wrong. I told you that it would be hard and lonely instead of telling you how amazing it would be."

Oh God, yes, it would be so amazing if she could trust her own feelings about it. "Stop," she said. She didn't want to hear more, she was afraid of what more would do to her resolve.

"No, I want you to—"

She put her hand to his mouth in a desperate attempt to guard her heart. "*Stop.* You're forgetting the most important thing. We come from two different worlds. And I don't want your world, Brennan. I would be miserable alone or with you."

He looked stunned. "You don't even know," he said. "You have no idea what it would be like. You're making an assumption it won't work, Mia, and maybe you're saying that because of what I said to you that day, but you're making the *wrong* assumption."

"I don't think—"

He suddenly sank down onto his knees and cast his arms wide. "What I am trying to say, and very badly for a man who makes his living with love songs, is that I can't stop thinking about you. I can't keep you out of my mind for even a day. I don't want to be without you, Mia Lassiter. I don't want to be without you so bad that I am here on my knees, begging you to reconsider."

The pile of leaves that were her excuses was almost gone. "Brennan—"

"I know, I know—you don't want my life, I get that, but there has to be a way, because I *love* you, Mia. I *love* you," he said, reaching for her. "And I can't stop loving you. Believe me, I have tried. But you won't go away."

Mia stared at him. She was waiting for him to say *but*. She was waiting for a bolt of lightning to hit her, because that would be her luck if a man like Brennan made this declaration to her.

He dropped his arms and stood up. "Okay, well, here is the part where you say, thanks for stopping by, and I slink off to my mom's—"

No. It was time to let go of old hurts and focus on the promise he was making her. How could she ever live with herself if she let a man like him walk out of her life for good? How could she create beautiful things if she didn't allow herself to experience the love he was offering her? She could no more let him go out that door than she could stop sewing.

Mia couldn't say all those things—they were a mishmash of desperate emotions—but she definitely couldn't let him go. She launched herself at him, her arms around his neck, her lips on his face. She hit him so hard that they fell back against the door before Brennan managed to stop their fall by grabbing her waist. Mia kissed him. She covered him with kisses and grabbed fistfuls of his shirt, clinging to him, her grip as strong as steel.

"I'm going to take that as a 'you'll think about it,'" he said breathlessly.

"I love you, too," Mia said as he started walking her backward to her bed. "I was afraid to say it—"

"Me too. God, me too," he said, nipping at her lips.

"I think this is crazy," she said, kissing him as she spoke. "I don't think it can work. You're a summer person, and I'm a year-rounder, and that never works. Especially with *you*. And I'm not moving to LA and I'm not going to any more tent parties—"

"Remind me not to come to you for preshow pep talks," he said, and kissed her lips. "Are you going to let me stay? Tell me now before I lose my mind, Mia. Don't let me kiss you if you won't let me stay—"

"I want you to stay," she said. "God, Brennan—I care that you're here, and you said you loved me, and I love you, and you're *here*."

He groaned, pressed his forehead to hers. "I've missed you so damn much."

"I've missed you, too. Brennan, listen," she said, and grabbed his face between her hands. "I can't do something like this halfway. I can't go into something thinking it's going to end."

"Do you think I can?" he asked. "I have spent my entire life avoiding this very thing because of my fear of what would happen if I allowed myself to love someone. *Really* love someone. But I found out I don't get to decide that—my heart wants you, and it's a risk I'll gladly take. Even if it kills me."

This was surreal. Mia's heart slammed against her chest and left her almost breathless. She couldn't believe that this man, this beautiful, soulful, talented man, was saying these things to her. It was almost too good to be true. She held his face between her hands, studying it, feeling the image of him imprint on her. "I love you," she said again. This was the first time she'd said the words aloud to anyone who wasn't family. "I love you, Brennan Yates. So much. So very much."

The relief in his expression and the happiness that sparked in his eyes shook her to her core. No one had ever looked at her like that. He *did* love her. She could see it and she could feel it and all she wanted to do was make sure he felt the same thing from her.

"Those boy toys aren't having drinks here, are they?" he asked as he pulled his shirt over his head. "Because I'm not through telling you things." He tossed her down on the bed, then jumped on top of her, straddling her, grinning down at her. "Like how much I enjoy the way you kiss," he said, and kissed her. His hand slid down her body, to her leg. "And I like the way you feel," he said, and slipped his hand in between her legs. "And I really love the way you f—"

"You're talking too much," she said, and silenced him with a kiss.

Some day, she thought, as Brennan's hands moved on her body, and her clothes flew across the room, she would paint this moment in vivid colors and with lots of light, the shadowy shapes of two lovers on a bed. But first, she was going to float around on a little cloud of happiness and let the man she loved ravage her.

And tomorrow, she was going to make them matching pajamas.

Epilogue

One year later

Tuesday's End went on tour the following summer, debuting an album that had been proclaimed "The Album of the Decade" by Rolling Stone. It was a new departure, reviews said. A welcome change, others said. The film accompanying the music would be released in the fall, just in time for Oscar season. There was speculation in the music world that Everett Alden would be nominated for his work on the album in the category of Best Original Song for "Come Closer."

The Ross house renovations were finally completed, but not before a fallout between Wallace and Nancy Yates. Wallace had different ideas for how to improve that awful interior, which, after a lot of shouting and threatening to hire Diva Interiors, Nancy came around to seeing.

Wallace had taken over for Mia when she decided to rent a little storefront in Black Springs and make clothes for summer people. She and Emily had discovered that summer people were willing to pay a whole lot more for her dresses than the year-rounders in East Beach.

Mia loved what she did. She loved dressing women in colors and shapes that made them happy, and she wondered why she'd never thought of this before. The painting door had closed for her, other than for her own edification, and the world of fashion had opened up to her.

Brennan was there for the opening, as proud as he could be of his fiancée. He even wore a pair of pants she'd made him . . . although he confided to Chance that he couldn't wait to get them off, as they were a little too far out there, even for him. "Give them to me, man," Chance said. "They're *sick*."

The shop was sparsely decorated, but there was an eclectic collection of art on the wall: The Eckland lanterns painting hung in a place of prominence. The red door from the art festival was near the cash register. And a chunk of brick mortared together, painted blue, with shadowy houses and a dog and pine trees was fastened to the wall near the dress racks.

Brennan had kept it all this time.

There was one more piece of art on the wall in Mia's apartment— she still rented it from Dalton because she loved it—and that was the drawing of Brennan in bed she'd made at the resort in Stratford Corners. That was for her and her alone, and in those long stretches of time when she didn't see him, it was the drawing she turned to for comfort.

At the grand opening, all of Mia's family came to toast her. "Does this mean you're giving up painting?" Derek asked. "Because this looks like it could actually pay something."

"Derek, that is none of your business," Mia's mother said.

"But aren't you going with Brennan?" Emily asked as Elijah tried to reach the clothes hanging on the rack and Ethan pushed a truck around the floor.

"Eventually," Mia said, and smiled up at her rock star. He put his arm around her and kissed the top of her head. "We're still working things out. But we're cool for now."

They *were* cool. They had not yet made any immediate plans for a wedding because they were still too happy to explore what they had. It would come when the time was right, but for now, what they had was perfect—Mia was happier than she'd ever been in her life. Brennan said she was the thing that completed his life, the thing that had been missing all along. He truly seemed to mean that—even when he was away, not a day went by that he didn't call her. He sang love songs to her, told her how much he needed her. He asked for her opinion and he asked about her design work, how she came up with ideas, how she constructed things.

The truth was that Mia needed him more than she would ever have believed was possible. Brennan had become her rock, always there for her, even when he was on the other side of the world.

After the opening, she and Brennan returned to her little apartment. They made monster salads and drank wine and talked about the recent earthquake in China. Brennan wanted to gather his friends and do a charity event to aid the victims.

"I really admire that about you," Mia said. "Always willing to help others."

"Oh yeah?" he asked. "Are you still going to say that when it keeps me from East Beach for a couple of months?" He kissed her bare shoulder.

"You know what? There is something I want to show you."

"Not now," he begged.

"Yes, now." She grabbed his hand and tugged him along with her. She led him down to the beach, then headed for the north end. Sunlight was waning and the shadows on the beach looked foreboding.

"Where the hell are we going?" he asked.

Mia didn't answer, she just pulled him along, made him follow her up the path from the parking lot of the boat slip toward Lookout Point. But halfway there, she stopped. She dropped his hand, then crawled out over a rock and lay down on her belly.

"No way," Brennan said. He crawled out and lay down beside her. In the warm, pink light of the end of the day, they gazed down at a nest of eggs. Mia reached for Brennan's hand and squeezed it. "You know what's cool about those owls? They mate for life. And they always come back to the same place."

Brennan turned his head to look at her. "I mate for life, too," he said somberly. "And I will always come back. No matter how far I fly, I will always come back here. To you. Because you know what, Mia? What we have is really all there is in this life. The rest of the world can go to hell as long as I have you."

He made it sound so simple, as if there was nothing more than loving someone to cause two people to alter their very different lives and make them intersect. Regularly. Always. But she believed him, truly and deeply. "That's what I love about you, you know that?" she said.

He smiled. "I know. I'm a catch."

Mia giggled and pushed herself up to her feet. "So you keep saying."

"When I forget it, I only have to look at this," he said, and standing up, reached for his wallet. He withdrew a folded piece of paper and opened it, showing it to Mia.

She burst into laughter. It was the drawing she'd sketched of Brennan as a knuckle-dragging ape.

"It's not *that* funny," he said, but he was laughing when he swept her up in his arms and kissed her with the energy of a thousand lights held up in a darkened arena.

If you enjoyed this book,
connect with Julia London online!

Read all about Julia and her books: http://julialondon.com/
Like Julia on Facebook: https://www.facebook.com/JuliaLondon
Sign up for the newsletter: https://www.julialondon.com/newsletter
Follow Julia on Twitter: https://twitter.com/JuliaFLondon
Read about Julia on Goodreads: http://www.goodreads.com/
JuliaLondon

About the Author

Photo © 2010 Carrie D'anna

Julia London is the *New York Times*, *USA Today*, and *Publishers Weekly* bestselling author of more than thirty romantic fiction novels. Her historical romance titles include the popular Secrets of Hadley Green series and the Cabot Sisters series. She has also penned several contemporary women's fiction novels with strong romantic elements, including the Cedar Springs series and the Homecoming Ranch trilogy. She has won the RT Bookclub Award for Best Historical Romance and has been a six-time finalist for the prestigious RITA Award for excellence in romantic fiction. She lives in Austin, Texas.